embolden

PRAISE FOR *FORBIDDEN*

by Syrie James and Ryan M. James

"A YA novel that hits all the right notes ... The plot and storyline are great, and the characters strong ... If you enjoy angels, 'forbidden' romance and dashing heroes, then this should be added to your TBR."

—USA TODAY

"This new entry into the angelic fiction genre is written in both Claire and Alec's voices. Both main characters are well-drawn, with believable motivations and reactions to their situations. The ending leaves enough room for a sequel, and fans of the genre will definitely demand one."

—School Library Journal

"Quite effective paranormal suspense and intense-but-quixotic high-school romance ... Genre addicts will enjoy it."

—Kirkus Reviews

"An addictive read. It isn't like the other angel paranormal books out there. This will make you want more more more."

—Beneath the Cover

"A must read. My top 24 of all time favorite books. The characters were very unique and will grow on you ... By the way it ended, it only promised that the following book would contain more action and the move to be more intense. Highly recommended."

—*Jean Book Nerd*

"Hands down the most fascinating book I have read in quite a while. It has wit, humor, action, mystery, and is filled with just the right amount of tension. As the characters develop and the story unfolds you will find yourself wrapped up in their world, indulging in every kiss and holding your breath with every twist. Simply magic!"

—*Luxury Reading*

"Forbidden has the best trio since Harry Potter! I loved it! It had plenty of humor, romance, action, mystery, and suspense. The villain was totally badass. What truly drives this story is its amazing characters. Oh! and the cliffhanger – SO cruel. But in that I can't flippin' wait to read book two kind of way. 5 stars!"

—*The Book Slayer*

"Like angels meet X-Men … The characters had a lot of depth and they were easy to like. The next novel in the series has a lot of potential."

—*Books: A True Story*

ALSO BY SYRIE JAMES &
RYAN M. JAMES:

Forbidden

OTHER TITLES BY SYRIE JAMES:

Summer of Scandal
Runaway Heiress
Jane Austen's First Love
The Missing Manuscript of Jane Austen
Nocturne
Dracula, My Love
The Secret Diaries of Charlotte Brontë
The Lost Memoirs of Jane Austen
Propositions
Songbird

embolden

SYRIE JAMES & RYAN M. JAMES

*For fans of YA and paranormal
romance everywhere.*

*And for the many, many readers who
asked us to please continue Claire and
Alec's story ... this is for you.*

one

The December morning air made Claire Brennan shiver but did nothing to dampen her excitement. She stared up at the redbrick town house, just one in a row of similar buildings on the residential Brooklyn street. It was a sight Claire had been longing to see for months.

"This is it," her mother, Lynn, said.

"We cannot find out anything by just standing here," commented Claire's grandmother, Helena, in her cultured British accent.

If only Erica and Brian were here, Claire thought. *They'd be as excited as I am to see this place.* Claire missed her best friends big-time. But it was the holiday season, and they were home with their families. And this *was* a family mission. If she was ever going to find her father, Claire needed her mom's memories and her grandma's psychic mojo.

And her boyfriend.

Alec MacKenzie gave Claire's gloved hand a brief, affectionate squeeze. "Let's do this." He ran up the stone steps and rang the buzzer to the third-floor apartment. Glancing at the name tag beside the buzzer, he called down to them, "Someone named Arrividera lives here now." Alec's charming Scottish burr, and the way he rolled his R's, was just one of the many things Claire loved about him.

Claire, Lynn, and Helena followed more carefully, holding on to the black wrought-iron railing and avoiding the snow and ice that had accumulated along the stair edges. On the landing, Claire wrapped her arms around herself, cold despite the parka and wool hat she was wearing. Helena and Alec, of course, looked comfortable in just leather jackets. "It's so not fair that you guys aren't freezing."

"Grigori constitutions," Lynn noted with a shrug.

"If we were in the *Arctic*, my dear," Helena stated matter-of-factly, "I might be wearing an outfit similar to yours. But in a far more stylish design, and a milder shade of blue."

A smile tugged at Claire's lips. Although she'd only met her grandmother a few months ago, she'd come to appreciate Helena's sense of humor.

Alec sighed, running a hand through his dirty-blond hair. "Looks like nobody's home."

Great, Claire thought, disappointment spearing through her. Ever since she'd learned about her true nature as a Halfblood Grigori (translation: *half angel*) she'd been dying to learn how and why her father had disappeared sixteen years ago.

She tried to peer in through the leaded-glass window in one of the mahogany doors, but it was too cloudy to see inside. "Should we come back tomorrow?"

"Why wait?" Alec pulled on a pair of gloves and rested his hand on the doorknob, staring at it intently until it made a soft, clicking sound. "Got it."

"Alec!" Claire whispered insistently. "We can't just break into somebody's apartment!" His Jedi-grade telekinesis might be handy to unlock doors, but it wasn't exactly legal.

"I thought you wanted to get a reading off the place?" Alec looked to her and Helena.

"We do," Claire replied, "but what if there's an alarm?"

"If you were about to step into danger, I would know, remember?" Helena's hazel eyes were reassuring, but Claire knew that her grandmother's psychic ability wasn't foolproof.

"And if you're wrong? A breaking-and-entering charge will look great on all of Claire's college applications," Lynn warned.

"I spent two years keeping the Grigori off Tom's trail when he left to marry you, Lynn," Helena hissed. "He vanished because I could not protect him—because I was locked up for obstructing the investigation. I haven't been able to sense his essence or call up a vision of him since. This is the last place he lived before disappearing, and there is no way I am going to walk away just because the Arrivideras are not home."

Lynn threw up her hands in defeat.

"Don't worry, we'll be in and out before anybody knows a thing," Alec insisted. "I've done this a million times."

Claire winced at his words. She hated to think about Alec's former life, before he went AWOL from his celestial duties policing those members of the Fallen (the hundreds of thousands of descendants of the Nephilim, offspring of Grigori-human relationships) who used their various talents for immoral purposes instead of good.

Before he found her and helped protect her.

He was everything to Claire now; she couldn't imagine her life without him.

"Third floor," Lynn reminded them, as Alec pushed the door open.

"Are you sure this is going to work?" Claire asked Helena under her breath, as they all entered and headed up the stairs.

"No, but it is a good place to start."

The apartment's front door looked freshly painted. Alec knocked firmly.

There was no answer.

Alec glanced at Lynn, as if waiting for her permission to proceed. The suspense was killing Claire.

Lynn sighed. "No guts, no glory. Go ahead."

Claire's stomach tensed nervously as she watched Alec unlock the door and dead bolt as easily as he had downstairs, using only his mind. He motioned for them to stay put. "I'll check if it's clear."

Alec slipped inside. Claire had seen him do this type of routine plenty of times, sweeping his own apartment for potential intruders. He returned a moment later and silently gestured for them to enter.

The apartment was about a fourth the size of Claire's old apartment in L.A., with one bedroom, a small kitchen, a narrow living room, and a balcony overlooking a tiny yard.

"Wow," Lynn said softly, taking it all in. "The furniture is different, of course, and the walls are a different color. But otherwise, it's exactly the same."

I can't believe my mom and dad actually lived here when I was a baby, Claire thought. Pulling off her gloves, she touched a wall, hoping to access some memory of her father. She waited for the familiar sensation of heat that usually preceded a vision, thankful that she'd outgrown the nausea that used to accompany them.

Nothing happened. Claire gripped the bedroom doorknob, something her dad's hands must have touched. Her spirits sank. "I'm not getting anything."

"Try the kitchen," Lynn suggested. "Your father and I used to love cooking together."

Claire crossed the room and placed a hand on the handle of a kitchen cabinet. She frowned. "Why isn't it working? When I touched Dad's old jacket back home, it triggered a flashback."

"That's because the jacket belonged to your dad," Alec pointed out. "He'd worn it enough times that it retained a strong memory of him. These are just walls and doors, and they look like they were just painted. I suspect too many people have lived here since your parents did for your tactile ability to work."

"He's right. This flat's history is quite crowded," murmured Helena.

Claire's grandmother was sitting on the living-room rug in the lotus position, a peculiar expression on her face.

"Now she, on the other hand," Alec said with a smile, "might have better luck. She's a psychic antenna with legs."

Helena tilted her head. "If only that were true, young man."

"What about now, Grandma?" Claire joined her in the living room. "Are you picking up anything?"

Helena sounded distant, distracted. "I am working on it. Would you like to see? You are all welcome to join in if you like."

Claire exchanged a look with Alec and Lynn, who nodded eagerly. They all sat down on the floor beside Helena, forming a circle.

"Where are you taking us?" Lynn held her hands out expectantly.

"Not where, when," Helen replied in the same, preoccupied tone. "I have been scouring this precise location, searching for Tom's aura sixteen years ago, and … Ah! Aha!" Her eyes twinkled, and a hint of a smile spread across her lovely face. "Take my hands, now."

Claire's heart drummed to a new beat as they all clasped hands in a closed circle. Claire instantly felt the jolt of energy that connected her to Helena's consciousness. Suddenly, the room changed around her. The apartment walls were white instead of blue, the furniture was more modern, and the sky outside the window was dark.

But that wasn't the biggest change. Prickles of awe traveled up and down Claire's spine as she stared at the couch in front of them.

Sitting on the couch, reading the paper, was the same handsome man she'd seen in previous visions. He looked to be in his early twenties although Claire knew he was more than a century older. He had olive skin and dark brown wavy hair, just like hers.

It was her father. Tom.

A pretty blond woman was asleep beside him, her head nestled cozily on Tom's lap, her feet curled up on the couch. Claire's mother.

Claire gasped. This was incredible. She was actually seeing a moment in the past, when her parents lived in this place! Her mom gasped, too—her mom in the present, that is. It was so strange.

"Is that him?" Alec asked.

"It is indeed," Helena answered.

"Oh …" Tears gathered at the edges of Lynn's eyes as she whispered, "He's so beautiful … and I look so young."

"You need not whisper, my dear," Helena said. "They cannot see, hear, or feel us. We have no corporeal presence."

The sound of a crying infant erupted from the next room. Tom glanced up from his newspaper. The Lynn on the couch yawned sleepily. "Your turn."

Tom leaned over and kissed her affectionately on the forehead. "On it." He stood and headed toward the bedroom.

Helena shook her head. "This is totally useless." The moment froze, then a blur of images flew past and around them, as if they were watching it all on fast-forward.

"Wait, wait!" Claire cried. "Wasn't that me crying?"

"We only had the one daughter." Lynn smiled.

"We do not have time to look at everything that transpired here," Helena replied. "Our focus is to find the day Tom disappeared and hope he returned home, however briefly, so we can find a clue as to where he went."

Claire wanted to see more of that sweet moment with her parents. But it was gone.

Outside the window, time zoomed by, shifting between day and night, through all types of weather and seasons. A potted tree on the balcony began twig-like and bare, then burst into leaf and bloom. Claire watched wistfully as her mom and dad zipped around the apartment on fast-forward, entering and leaving, cooking and cleaning, dining and relaxing, often walking right through her and the others as if they were ghosts.

"I've been inside your head before, but I had no idea you could do this." Alec sounded impressed.

"I can attain a more accurate and detailed history when I am in the actual, physical place I need to explore," Helena explained over the various sights, sounds, and aromas.

Claire was thrilled to catch glimpses of herself as she grew from a helpless newborn to a pudgy baby. It was also kind of spooky—especially when her parents in the past stopped and stood in the exact same spot where she and her group were sitting in the present, or parked a stroller or something there.

"I'm starting to get dizzy." Lynn's face was pale.

"Try closing one eye for a moment," Helena instructed. "It will shut off the images of the past."

Lynn followed this advice and sighed in relief. "Better. Thanks."

Claire tried the technique herself. Sure enough, when she closed one eye, the whir of sights and sounds in the past disappeared, and all she saw was her mom, Helena, and Alec sitting on the rug in the peace and quiet of the present. By opening and shutting that eye, she could toggle back and forth between the two scenes. "This is amazing! I wish I could do this."

"With a quarter of my genes, you may find that you can," Helena answered, "but it would take greater concentration than you are used to. And in your case, I believe you are limited to what you touch."

"Can you do this for the future, too?" asked Claire.

"Only to a certain point. As I told you before, the future is malleable. Each moment branches into the next depending on the choices people make."

The wall behind the couch suddenly changed from white to a deep burgundy. "Oh!" Lynn took an excited breath. "We're getting close. We painted that wall a couple of months before Tom disappeared."

As Helena nodded, the visual show began to slow down, enough to register the images of Tom, Lynn, and baby Claire going about their daily routines. A light dusting of snow now covered the balcony outside. They reached a nighttime moment where Lynn walked in through the front door, carrying the baby, when Claire's mother (in the present) cried, "Stop! Stop. This might be it. A few days before Tom left—you were six months old, Claire—he bought you that pink jacket. For months afterward, every time I saw it, it made me cry."

While Lynn spoke, the time-lapse memories slowed even more, halting abruptly on the image of her younger self slumped on the couch, baby asleep in her arms, staring at the phone with a worried expression.

"You found it." Lynn's voice trembled. "The night Tom didn't come home. The next morning, he called me at work. He said he couldn't come back, that I should change my name again and leave town, that all our lives were in danger. I packed up the next day, and Claire and I left for Chicago." Her voice broke as she added tearfully, "He promised he'd find us. But he never did."

Claire felt a stab of pain in her chest at the devastated look on her mom's face, both in the present and the past. It had been hard enough to hear about this awful moment, but to actually see it was heartbreaking.

"Well then, let's go back." Helena's eyes looked distant with concentration as her hand gripped Claire's more tightly. The action around them began to rewind as night reversed into day, no sign of Tom until they saw the inverse of the family rushing out of the apartment that morning.

Time reeled slightly farther back, then froze on Tom, wearing a gray suit and a red tie. He was sitting next to Claire's high chair, feeding her oatmeal, while Lynn tossed dishes into the sink.

"Shite," Alec observed. "He never came back home that day at all."

"No." Suddenly, Helena's eyes widened, startled. She released their hands, instantly transporting them back to the present. "But the current tenants of this lovely abode will—they are on their way home as we speak. We have five minutes."

Lynn leapt to her feet in alarm. "Why didn't you warn us sooner?"

"I was a bit busy," sniped Helena as she rose. "Young man, I hope you can lock those doors as easily as you opened them."

two

The foursome hurried out of the building and started down the sidewalk.

"Saints alive!" came a surprised voice, making them all pause.

An elderly woman, who'd just deposited a trash bag into a can in front of the house next door, turned to stare at them. She wore a dark coat and paisley scarf over dyed red hair. "Lynn? Lynn Garrett? Is that you?" Her labored breaths were visible in the cold air as she studied Lynn.

Garrett? Claire's chest tightened. She knew her mom had changed her last name to Brennan when they fled New York, but Claire had never asked what her mom's real name was. She prayed the woman hadn't noticed them leaving the other building.

"Mrs. Beniov. How nice to see you." Lynn forced a smile. "How are you?"

"Getting old—but it's better than the alternative." Her cheerful tone implied she hadn't noticed anything fishy. "How are *you?* How many years has it been? I used to get such pleasure babysitting your little angel every day." Mrs. Beniov's glance took in Claire, and she added, "My goodness, is this Claire? Oh, it has to be—I'd recognize those beautiful hazel eyes anywhere!"

"She's all grown-up." Lynn gestured toward the group awkwardly. "This is Claire's boyfriend, Alec, and my mother-in-law, Helena."

As the two voiced a greeting, Mrs. Beniov said to Helena:

"Oh, you're Tom's mother? Such a delight, that young man." To Lynn, she went on: "Did that new job he took in St. Louis work out? You left in such a hurry, I never got a forwarding address. I always wondered what happened to you."

"We're fine," Lynn replied, lying so efficiently that Claire was impressed. "We didn't stay in St. Louis long. We're in Houston now. Tom travels a lot with his job."

"Well, that explains it. I swore I saw him five or six years ago, standing right there at the bottom of those steps, staring up at your old place in the pouring rain. But when I came out to say hello and bring him an umbrella, he was gone."

Claire's heart leapt. "Really? You saw him?" It took every ounce of self-control to temper her excitement, and one glance at her companions told her they were feeling the same way.

"He must have been taking a trip down memory lane. I remember how happy you three were in this neighborhood."

"That's right," Lynn lied. "I remember, Tom had a meeting in New York around that time … it was spring, I think?"

"Might have been," added Mrs. Beniov. "So what brings you to Brooklyn again? Would you all like to come in for a cup of coffee? I just made a nice strudel."

Helena smiled. "Thank you, but we are on our way to the Met. It is Claire's first time back in New York, and we have a lot of sightseeing to do."

"Of course, of course. Go get yourselves somewhere warm. It was so nice to see you again, Lynn."

After they all murmured their good-byes, and the old woman retreated back inside her building, Claire embraced her mother tightly. "He's alive, Mom."

Lynn breathed a deep sigh, her eyes watering. "At least he was, five or six years ago. I wonder if he was looking for us?"

Helena stared at the front steps, deeply focused.

"Can you see him?" Alec asked.

Helena snapped herself back to the present, visibly displeased. "No. Whatever that woman saw that day, I cannot get a read on him. Something changed after he disappeared, and I wish I knew what."

"Mom," Claire said, thinking, "when Dad called you the day after he left, he said he'd been attacked on his way home from work, didn't he?"

Lynn nodded. "Yes. He said it was in the Wall Street station. He'd just gone down the stairs to the subway platform when a Watcher appeared. They had a conversation, it went badly, and Tom ran."

"I was hoping we would not have to go there," Helena grumbled. "It will be difficult for me to find traces of him in a place so impersonal. But now it looks like that is our only option."

At the Wall Street station, the foursome exited the train and crossed over to the track that headed back to Brooklyn.

Helena rested her hand on the tiled sidewall, as if trying to orient herself. "Give me a moment. I hope I can locate the energy I felt on his last day in the apartment."

Please let this work, Claire prayed silently.

Helena stood still for a long moment, deep in concentration. Suddenly, her expression changed, to the same eerie kind of awareness she'd displayed in the apartment. She slowly turned and stared intently toward the stairs from the street, where a man in a green coat was descending. Her lips twitched in a half smile.

"Well?" The words burst from Claire's mouth, louder than she'd intended. The man in the green coat glanced at her curiously as he passed by. Embarrassed, Claire waited until the man was out of earshot, then lowered her voice to a fierce whisper as she repeated, "Well?"

"*I see him*," Helena declared. "He is walking down the stairs."

"Oh!" Claire and Lynn cried in unison, excited.

"Can you show us, Helena, if we all hold hands?" Alec asked.

"That would look odd, and will not be necessary. I will project what I see into your minds. But please refrain from speaking. This will take extraordinary concentration."

Claire knew exactly how much concentration the act of projection required, having managed to perform it once after Homecoming. It had given her a splitting headache, left her physically drained, and even made her levitate slightly—but then, she was still new at it. Helena had had almost nine centuries to perfect her abilities.

Claire looked in the direction Helena was staring, opening herself up to whatever images Helena was sending.

A gentle flickering began at the edges of Claire's vision, like an old television screen going wonky. Claire blinked. All at once, the station was filled with a crush of people hurrying down the stairs to the platform. Instinctively, Claire leapt out of the way as the sea of subway riders pushed straight toward her. But when they passed *through* her, she remembered that she wasn't physically in anyone's way.

"There's Tom!" her mother cried with delight.

Claire followed her mom's eyes, her heart lurching as she, too, recognized his face among the crowd. He wore a tan suit and was carrying a briefcase. Claire reached out as he approached, wishing she could touch him, a pang of disappointment reverberating to her core when he walked right through her arm.

He stopped a few yards away and waited for the train. Claire moved to stand beside him, her heart pounding.

"Hi, Dad," she whispered wistfully, knowing he couldn't see or hear her. "It's me—Claire."

There was something about him—his posture, the curve of his mouth, the light in his dark eyes—that suggested a deep inner happiness. She could have stood there watching him forever, but Helena's abrupt voice reminded her why they were here.

"This is not the day. His clothing is different, and everyone is dressed for summer. I am moving on."

To Claire's disappointment, Tom instantly vanished, and the scene around her fast-forwarded at lightning speed. Days, weeks, and months passed, bursts of activity in the subway station alternating with periods of stark emptiness, the action slowing every now and then when Tom came into view.

"Why doesn't Dad show up more often, if this was his regular train to commute home?" Claire asked.

"He changed his route all the time," Lynn explained. "He used different stations, sometimes took the bus or a cab. He was always worried that someone was following him."

As the rush of humanity continued around and through Claire, her head began to spin. It was too much to take in. She leaned against the wall and closed one eye, grounding herself for a moment in the present, relieved to see Alec, her mom, and Helena standing quietly a few yards away, staring into the past with intense fascination. Just then, a train arrived in the present, depositing a dozen or so people who moved for the exit.

Taking a deep breath to prepare herself, Claire opened both eyes, and was thrust again into the past Helena was projecting. When it came upon Tom again, Alec said, "Hey, check out his scarf. Freeze that, Helena."

"I am afraid I cannot freeze it, young man. There is far too much activity going on. I can only slow it down."

As the action around them continued at a normal pace, Claire caught sight of her father entering the station, wearing the same red tie, winter coat, and knitted scarf he'd been wearing that last morning when they saw him leave the apartment.

"I'd just crocheted him that scarf." Lynn's voice was heavy with heartache. "It was the only time I ever saw him wear it."

"Well, then, we have the right day," Helena said tersely. "Let us stay close to him."

Tom emerged onto the platform. Claire's heart began to pound with worry as she and her companions moved after him. *Something was about to happen to her dad.*

Suddenly, Claire felt the sharp impact of colliding with someone, even though there was nobody in front of her. She stumbled back, briefly closing one eye to observe the present. A tall man in a blue ski cap, eyes glued to his cell phone, was shoving past her, muttering, "Watch it."

"Sorry." Claire glanced around to make sure nobody else was in their path. Only three other people were waiting for a train now, on the opposite side of the tracks. Still, she couldn't help wondering, *Does this look weird, the four of us walking around staring into space?*

Toggling back to the past, Claire caught up to Alec, her mom, and Helena as they followed her dad along the crowded platform to his usual spot. Alec had an odd look on his face.

"What's wrong?" Claire asked.

"Every time Tom has shown up here, I've noticed a few people that look … *off* to me," Alec muttered under his breath.

"*Off* in what way?"

Before Alec could answer, a police officer appeared at Tom's side.

"Excuse me, sir." The officer was over six feet tall, a broad-shouldered African-American man who looked to be in his mid-forties. His expression was polite, his smile friendly. "May I speak with you a moment?"

"Um, where did this cop come from?" Lynn asked.

"He wasn't in the station a minute ago." Alec sounded tense.

Tom warily allowed the policeman to escort him to a quiet spot at the end of the station, with Claire and her companions on their heels. They halted a few steps from the edge of the platform.

"How can I help you, Officer?" Tom asked.

"Let's dispense with formalities and get right to the point—shall we, *Tom*?"

Tom's eyes widened in surprise.

Claire sucked in a startled breath. The cop's face was now *flickering* back and forth between the smiling cop and an entirely different, deadly serious man. A man Claire recognized. "Oh my God. It's *Vincent*."

Vincent: the Watcher with the power of illusions. The man who'd betrayed Alec, called Claire an abomination, and wanted her and her father dead.

"I'm not exactly surprised," Alec commented, scowling.

The two Grigori stood still in front of them, in a standoff. "We both know the penalty of going AWOL." Vincent's dark eyes flashed.

"Vincent—" Tom began.

The other Watcher gestured for silence. "I'm not the type to rat on a fellow Grigori for such an offense. If you wanted to leave the fold to spend the next few centuries in solitary contemplation, I could live with that. I could look the other way. But it's not that simple, is it? You're guilty of something far worse."

Tom's eyes narrowed, and he glanced around, as if contemplating his next move. Cautiously, he said, "I don't know what you mean."

Claire held her breath. She could hardly believe they were actually witnessing this crucial conversation.

"Let's not play games, Tom. We've known each other too long. I've been looking for you for *eighteen months*. I just got wind of where you've been working. And I'm fairly certain what you've been up to. You're involved with a human female, aren't you? I strongly suspect there's a child as well."

"That's not true," Tom replied.

"There's no point in lying. If I'd wanted, I could have found out everything for myself by following you home tonight. I could have been a fly or a bird or a homeless man on the street, and you never would have noticed. I could have turned you over to the Elders and *cleaned up* the rest, just like that." He snapped his fingers. "But that's not the sportsmanlike thing to do. That's not what a *friend* would do."

"Okay." Tom was still wary. "Then why are you here?"

"I'm here to help *you* do the right thing. If you come in now, I'll try to pave the way with the Elders so that you can return to your calling. Otherwise, I'll have no choice but to turn you in and make certain you, not to mention your wife and *spawn*, face the consequences."

Claire knew what the consequence was: death. Vincent had held it over her head before, how her entire existence was forbidden. She ground her teeth. "I hate it when he calls me *spawn*."

"It is an accurate term, my dear," Helena commented.

"There is no woman," Tom insisted, "and no *spawn*."

"Last chance, Tom. Vacation's over. Your choice how it ends. Do you want my help or not?"

Tom paused. Then his expression softened. There was a new, dreamlike quality to his voice as he said gently: "Vincent, you're confused. You're letting your imagination run away with you. I haven't done anything wrong."

Inexplicably, Vincent's eyes seemed to lose focus. "Haven't you?"

"No. You need to take a moment to think about what you're doing," Tom continued in the same, soft voice. "I'm not the criminal here. You are." Tom leaned in and said something else, his words drowned out by the sound of an approaching train.

Vincent nodded, then turned and—to Claire's astonishment—walked off the edge of the platform, directly into the path of the speeding train.

three

A lec froze in surprise. At the moment that the oncoming train would have made impact, Vincent's entire body flickered—and then vanished.

"Bastard," Alec said, realizing what had just happened. He grabbed Claire's hand, her own gasp melding with the screams of the people in the subway station in the past.

"What the hell?" Claire cried. "Why did Vincent just fling himself onto the tracks?"

"I don't know. But obviously he wasn't even there in the first place." It was just another trick of the twisted Grigori's mind. Like the time he'd projected an image of himself in Alec's apartment. Alec pulled Claire along with him, following Tom, who was pushing his way through the alarmed bystanders toward the exit.

"His illusions really piss me off," Claire cried fiercely.

"Where *was* Vincent, really?" Lynn asked, as she and Helena closed in behind them.

"Let's hope we find out," Alec replied.

As they all dashed after Tom, passing through the crowds of shouting people, Alec intermittently closed one eye to confirm that the path ahead of them in the present was free of obstacles.

Everyone in the past was heading toward the scene of the supposed "accident," except for the three people Alec had deemed suspicious earlier: an old lady who looked homeless, a bruiser of a man in an orange parka, and a skinny tweaker with glasses. Tom noticed them, too—they were heading toward him. *Busted*, Alec thought, realizing who, and what, they were. But none were Vincent, so they didn't matter right now.

That's when Alec spotted his former mentor.

Vincent, his ebony head shaved as usual, was hiding behind a pillar near the stairs leading up to the street. He wasn't dressed like the image of the police officer he'd been projecting, but instead wore a long gray coat over a dark suit, and a smug look on his face, as if everything was playing out exactly as planned.

"There he is," Claire muttered grimly.

As they approached, Alec thought he saw plugs in Vincent's ears. Strange.

Tom, a few yards ahead of them, didn't spot Vincent. But he couldn't miss Tweaker and Bag Lady, who were barreling toward him. Tom ducked out of the way, and the other two collided. Bruiser came next. Tom grabbed the guy, swung him violently into a wall, and leaped up the stairs two at a time.

Racing after Tom, Alec noted that in the present, the stairs were now filled with people exiting a newly arrived train. *Shite!* Holding tight to Claire's hand, Alec was obliged to slow his pace and file out with the throngs. Helena and Lynn got caught behind a woman bumping a stroller up the stairs, and fell even farther behind. Vincent appeared from the shadows and raced right by them, up the stairs to the street above.

At last, Alec and his companions emerged onto a street which, in the past, was busy with traffic and pedestrians at the height of rush hour. Across the street, a wrought-iron fence enclosed a small graveyard next to Trinity Church, a Gothic gem that stood proudly among the more modern buildings surrounding it. A brief check of the present nearly blinded

Alec with midday sunlight, but thankfully the streets were less congested than the subway station.

"There's Tom!" Lynn cried.

The Grigori had already crossed the busy intersection and was running down the narrow street beside the churchyard, which was closed to traffic because of roadwork. In the present, that same street was open and empty except for a few parked cars. Vincent was following discreetly, as if trying to avoid notice.

"Hurry," shouted Helena, charging into the crosswalk.

To Alec's horror, Helena was so focused on the past, she didn't see a car coming straight at her in the present.

"Watch out!" Lynn and Claire cried.

Alec raised one hand instinctively toward the oncoming vehicle, telekinetically slowing it down. The car squealed to a halt within inches of Helena, who didn't seem to notice or even break her stride. Lynn, catching up to them, breathed a sigh of relief.

"Nice reflexes," whispered Claire, as she and Alec hurried across the street, dodging another car in the present, while running straight through the ones in the past.

Tom's and Vincent's progress was visibly slowed by bull-dozers and other construction equipment. Concrete barriers outlining a trench in the road forced them to find another way around. In the present day, the construction site and trench didn't exist, allowing Alec and company to close in on Tom, leaving Vincent in their wake.

"This is so weird," Lynn said breathlessly, as they ran over an open trench in one reality, which was now concrete beneath their feet.

Alec glanced back to see a furious Vincent arguing with a construction worker, who was trying to prevent him from continuing. As they reached the corner, Alec caught sight of Tom running for the green metal fence and pillars marking an entrance to another subway station.

Suddenly, a UPS truck pulled up to the curb a few feet from Tom. The truck's rear door flew open. Four men clad in UPS brown jumped out and charged into Tom's path.

"Dad!" Claire screamed, then grimaced in realization that her father couldn't hear her.

They watched as three of the UPS workers tackled Tom to the pavement, while the fourth jammed a large syringe into his neck.

"Oh my God." Helena touched her forehead and winced.

The scene around them began to fill with static.

The UPS guys shoved Tom into the truck, climbed in, slammed the door, and sped off. Moments later, Vincent rounded the corner, glancing around in confusion. He saw the subway entrance and ran toward it.

The static worsened. Suddenly, they were thrust back into the jarring sunlight of the present. A mom with two kids walked by, staring at them strangely. And no wonder. The four of them were breathing hard, and probably looked like they'd just seen a ghost.

"Who *were* those men who took him?" Tears welled in Lynn's eyes.

"My guess? They were Fallen," responded Alec between gulps of air. "Ditto for the three in the station. They must have all been part of the same stakeout."

"So they alerted the asshats in the truck?" Claire unzipped her jacket to cool down.

"It looks that way." Helena leaned against the nearby stone wall, exhausted. "I am sorry, but when they injected Tom, something changed about my connection to him."

"Don't apologize, Grandma. What you just did, that was *incredible*." Claire hugged Helena, who returned the embrace with a weary pat on the back.

"Did anyone see the truck's license plate?" Lynn asked.

"It didn't have one," Alec answered. "I'd have memorized it already if it had."

"Damn it!" Lynn, frustrated, sank down onto the sidewalk, her back against the wall. "I don't understand. What did they want my husband for?"

Alec pushed damp hair out of his face. "He's a valuable asset. He can predict the future, remember? Just like Helena."

"I'm still confused about what happened in the subway," Claire said. "I get that Vincent wanted to turn my dad in and that he projected an image of himself when they were talking. But why did he make the fake Vincent jump in front of a train?"

"I think," Alec answered slowly, "once he realized Tom was never going to give himself up, Vincent wanted Tom to *think* he was getting away clean. So Vincent could follow Tom home."

"Oh." A horrible realization hit Claire like a stab to the gut. "So if the Fallen hadn't nabbed my dad that day, Vincent would have found me and Mom! And captured—or murdered—us."

"Very likely," Alec agreed.

Lynn shivered in dismay. "*That* is terrifying."

"One thing still doesn't make sense," Claire commented. "Dad didn't know he was talking to an illusion. He deliberately told pseudo-Vincent to commit suicide, almost like he *expected* him to do it."

"Aye," Alec said, glancing at Helena. "An interesting point." They knew Tom had the same psychic ability as his mother, but Tom also had a second Grigori talent that Helena had never disclosed. Is that what had been involved here?

But Helena's lips merely tightened. "I need rest," was her only response. "And lunch."

four

❝**I** can't feel my ears." Claire pulled her woolly hat down lower. She could barely hear her own voice over the roar of the crowd. It was New Year's Eve. She and Alec were standing in Times Square, wedged in with a bajillion other people, where they'd been waiting for the past six hours. In ten minutes, the famous ball would drop. A band played on the stage a few dozen feet away, and around them huge video screens displayed live coverage of the event.

Her mom and Helena, who was still nursing a headache from the strain of her time-traveling-vision-projection extravaganza earlier that week, were watching the festivities from the overpriced quiet and comfort of their hotel room, thirty-five floors above.

Alec put an arm around Claire and drew her even closer. "If you're cold, we can always join your family upstairs. Helena paid through the nose to get a great view."

They both had to shout to be heard over the throng. "After all the time we've been standing here?" She shook her head. "No way. Seeing that ball drop is on my bucket list."

"You're too young to have a bucket list."

Claire leaned in closer so she could lower her voice a fraction. Alec once told her he was actually about 113 years old, but his kind aged slowly, so he looked closer to Claire's seventeen. "*You're* not too young."

"Aye."

"So after more than a century," Claire said curiously, "what *is* on your list?"

He smiled. "Living like this, like you do, is all I've ever wanted."

"Cheeseball." She returned his smile. He'd had such an unhappy and stressful existence before they met. Claire was relieved that Alec had found what he wanted and that what he wanted was *her*.

Grigori law be damned.

A relationship between Grigori and humans (worse yet, with Halfbloods like her) was illegal. Alec had left the fold, a violation punishable by death. But so far, the only Grigori who was aware of Alec's whereabouts was Vincent. And they hadn't heard from him in months. Vincent was on the run from the Grigori himself, but if caught, he might reveal what he knew about Alec.

Claire shoved the worry from her mind, praying that she and Alec would be safe. "You know, you look really good for your age," she teased.

"As do you." Alec reached into his jacket pocket and pulled out a small box. "Speaking of, Happy Belated."

"Wait, you already gave me a present." Claire tugged on the winter scarf and hat she'd gotten at her family birthday dinner back home two weeks prior. "And they've been keeping me nice and warm all week."

"That was the practical gift. This is the fun one, to remember tonight by."

Claire struggled to open the box with her gloved fingers. Inside was a silver-and-lapis-lazuli bracelet, glinting in the neon glow of the billboards around them.

"Oh! Alec. It's beautiful." Claire pulled back the cuff of her parka while Alec nimbly fastened the bracelet around her wrist, his bare fingers seemingly immune to the frigid night air. She couldn't stop smiling as she admired it, then threw her arms around Alec's neck and hugged him. "Thank you. I love it," she breathed against his ear. "And I love *you*."

Alec held her tight. "I love you, too."

However cold she was before, the feel of his embrace and the affection in his voice warmed her straight through. She pressed her lips against his, concentrating in the way she'd taught herself, to prevent the contact from triggering a vision. He returned the kiss with fervor, then pulled back, their eyes meeting as he grinned.

"I thought the whole point was to kiss at midnight."

"Then, too." She laughed. "Tonight is perfect, and everything has been so awesome this week. I love New York. I can't believe how many things we've seen and done."

He nodded, his eyes narrowing. "Are you disappointed, though, that we didn't find out more about your dad?"

"Well. Seeing what happened the day he left was gut-wrenching. But at least we *saw* him. Plus, we found out he came back years later. Which is kind of comforting."

"It is indeed."

Around them, the mood of the crowd suddenly became electric. Everyone was staring up at the ball and digital timer atop the tower.

The final countdown began. Claire and Alec chanted with their fellow revelers, the air echoing with hundreds of thousands of voices shouting out the numbers from ten to zero. At midnight, an earth-shattering roar erupted. They joined in, cheering as fireworks exploded on the monitors, music played, and confetti showered down on them from above.

"Happy New Year!" Claire and Alec cried at the same moment, wrapping their arms around each other for a long kiss.

"Happy?" Alec asked as he looked down at her.

Claire was so filled with joy, she couldn't speak. All she could do was nod.

five

"The Fallen *kidnapped* your father?" Erica's fork froze in midair above her chicken enchiladas.

"Looks that way," Claire sighed.

"I've spent a century tracking the Fallen," Alec added. "I should be able to pick them out of a crowd."

It was their first day back at school after the holiday break, and Alec was sitting with Claire, Erica, and Brian at their usual lunch table at Emerson Academy in sunny Los Angeles. Erica Fisher and Brian Yao had accepted him into their group on his first day at school last fall, and eventually had learned everything about him. It had made him a little nervous at first to have all his secrets out, but now he would trust these three people with his life.

"Wait up." Brian was short in stature but had a giant intellect. His spiky black hair stuck up at weird angles as he studied Claire over his carton of chocolate milk. "CB, didn't you say your dad called your mom the next morning, to warn her to leave town?"

"Yeah," Claire replied. "I can't figure out how he managed that."

Erica shrugged as she tucked a lock of sleek red hair behind one ear. "Maybe they gave him his one phone call?"

Brian laughed. "That's jail, dumb-ass."

"He must have escaped," Alec told them. "He got away, called your mom, and told her about the bank account he'd set up. Then he vanished."

Claire nodded grimly. "But he was spotted by our old apartment like ten years ago. Where has he been all this time? Why has he been avoiding us?"

"No idea," Alec said. "Hopefully, Helena can find a way to revisit the moment he was kidnapped and figure out why she hasn't been able to track his aura since."

"Maybe it has something to do with whatever they injected him with," Brian suggested.

Alec looked at him. "What do you mean?"

"At Homecoming, didn't—" Brian began.

"Oh! That's right!" Erica placed her hand on Brian's forearm, an action that made his stocky shoulders visibly stiffen. "Vincent injected *you* with something at Homecoming that messed with your powers, didn't he, Alec?"

"Aye. Tranquilizers. But why would that break the signal Helena was honing in on?"

"I think what Brian means," Erica said excitedly, "is that since depressants tone down your powers …"

"… they might affect your Grigori aura, too," Brian finished.

Claire's eyes widened as she completed the thought. "And Helena finds whomever she's looking for through their aura's unique frequency."

Alec nodded. "It's a thought." He turned to Claire. "You should mention that to Helena."

"She'll be so pissed that three kids thought of it first," Brian said, freeing his arm so he could continue eating.

"I think her ego can handle it, Brian." Claire smiled.

Alec noted that Erica looked stung when Brian pulled away from her. It was yet another moment of discord he'd witnessed between these two over the past couple of months.

Erica lit up with another idea. "You should call that Fallen chick with the tattoos." Erica had been present both times Claire had been accosted by Celeste, along with the two meatheads who always accompanied her. "Maybe she can tell you what's up with your dad. I think her number's still in your phone."

"Yeah," Claire scoffed. "Like Celeste would ever tell me anything."

Then it was Claire's turn to stiffen. Alec watched as Neil Mitchum—the tall, dark-haired golden boy Claire had crushed on for two years, and whose heart she'd broken at Homecoming—walked by their table. Beautiful, popular Gabrielle Miller was practically glued to his side, gracing Alec and crew with a wave of her manicured fingers. To Alec's surprise, Gabrielle threw a genuine smile at Erica. Less surprisingly, Neil ignored all of them.

Once the door to the nearby library shut behind Neil and Gabrielle, an air of normalcy returned to the table.

Brian turned to Erica, his face scrunched in confusion. "Did Gabby Miller just wink at you?"

Erica seemed to deliberately avoid looking at any of them. "No, she just smiled. She smiles sometimes."

"Only at the popular kids," Brian insisted.

"Could we not make this a big deal, please?" Erica rubbed her temples. "We kinda bonded during some late nights on the Winter Formal committee, and one night she invited us all to hang in her Jacuzzi. That's all."

"It's nothing to feel *bad* about," Claire reassured her friend. "At least she's being nice. Meanwhile, Neil's pretending we don't exist."

Given Neil's complex history with Claire, Alec didn't mind that in the slightest. Trying not to seem insensitive, he asked, "How long do you think he'll keep that up?"

"How long 'til we graduate?" Claire responded with a sigh.

"You two have it easy," Brian said with his last bite. "At least you're across the room from him in Concert Singers. I have to stand next to him. The whole bass section used to be chatty. Now it's a graveyard."

The bell rang, signaling five minutes left of lunch period.

"It's still better than telling him the truth," Claire insisted, glancing at Erica and Brian. "I wasn't supposed to tell *anyone*, remember? Helena keeps saying that knowing puts you both in danger."

"Well, I'm still glad *I* know," Brian said, taking his leave. "Later, amigos."

Claire kissed Alec and gave him a look he'd learned meant: *Girl talk time.* "Don't wait for me, I'll see you in bio."

"Aye." Alec got up and strolled away.

As they gathered their stuff to leave, Claire studied her willowy friend, who had an odd look on her face.

"What?" Erica squirmed a bit under Claire's gaze.

Claire lowered her voice. "What's up with you guys?"

"Who?"

"You and Brian. You've been friends since seventh grade. But there was a minute of, I don't know, weirdness between you just now."

Erica blushed as she picked at the edge of her cardboard tray. "Can't fool a psychic, huh?"

"I just used my eyes. He moved his arm away, and you looked hurt."

Erica sighed. "Okay. Fine. I wasn't going to say any-thing, but—"

"But you're into Brian," Claire finished for her. "I've noticed. Since Homecoming, right?"

"Yeah," Erica admitted. "We went out a couple of times after that."

"You did? Why didn't you tell me?"

"We were keeping it low-key, just in case it didn't work out. It already got a little awkward when you and Alec started dating, and we didn't want to make it worse."

"Things are awkward?" Claire was taken aback.

"Aye," Erica replied, mimicking Alec's accent. "When two of your friends are suddenly madly in love and spending all their time together, holding hands and making lovey-dovey faces, you feel like third and fourth wheels."

"Oh. I. Well. That's embarrassing. Sorry."

Erica waved her hand. "It's fine, we've gotten over it. But for us … we weren't even sure if it was a good idea, we didn't want to ruin our friendship, and now it looks like that's exactly what's happening." Erica sighed again. "It was only two dates. They meant a lot to *me*, and I was hoping for more. But Brian wasn't feeling it. He said he only sees me as a friend."

"That sucks. I'm so sorry."

"Yeah, me too."

"You'll find the right guy, Erica, one who'll appreciate you. I promise." Claire searched for some way to brighten Erica's mood. "In the meantime, you have something to look forward to."

"Like what?"

"The musical!" The winter production was *Camelot*. Ever since eighth grade, Erica had dreamed of getting a lead in a school play. "Auditions are in two days, aren't they?"

That brought a smile to Erica's face. "Yeah." She paused, then glanced at Claire. "Are you trying out?"

"I don't know. Should I?"

Erica's smile faltered for half a second. Then she said, "Totally."

"I've never been in a play. Don't rehearsals take up, like, every second of your spare time?"

"Yeah," Erica acknowledged. "But it's so worth it. You should audition, Claire. It'll be more fun if we're in the play together."

Before she'd awakened and discovered her new singing abilities, Claire would never have dreamed of trying out for a school musical. Now, she had to admit, the idea of being in a play *did* kind of sound like fun.

"I'll think about it," she said.

six

"I wish Brian would get his head out of his ass." Claire was standing with Alec by his vintage car in the junior parking lot, his arms around her.

"Is that what you really want? The two of them together?"

"She's my best friend. I want her to have what she wants."

"If it's right, it'll happen."

"Since when did you become Dr. Phil?"

Alec smiled into her eyes. "I'm not. But I'm learning. Slowly." He kissed her. Also slowly.

It was a lovely kiss. As always, Claire's heart fluttered. When the kiss ended, she gallantly opened the door to his Mustang and waited until he was seated inside. "Drive safe."

"You too. We'll talk tonight."

As Alec drove off, Claire crossed the lot to where her own car was parked, unable to hold back her smile. Having Helena in their lives had certainly come with some great benefits. Besides having her long-lost Grigori grandmother around all the time, which Claire loved, money was no longer a problem. Claire's tuition was paid in full (no more stressing about her grades to keep a scholarship), and they'd moved into a luxury condo in Brentwood, just a five-minute drive from school. That meant a little extra sleep every morning, which Claire really appreciated after her late-night video chats with Alec.

And with Helena's seemingly limitless bank account, Claire could at last have a car of her own, like everybody else at Emerson. But not just *any* car. It was a brand-new Acura hybrid with a garnet metallic finish, a top-notch sound system, and all the bells and whistles a girl could want.

Claire unlocked the door, heaved her backpack into the rear, and settled on the smooth leather seat behind the wheel. The space was so snug and the instrument panel so cool, it felt like she was in the cockpit of her own private airplane. The car—*her car*—made her feel grown-up, which was both exciting and intimidating.

As she stuck her key in the ignition, the sound of a man clearing his throat beside her was so startling, she shrieked. She turned her head to find a man sitting in the passenger seat. A man who had definitely not been there a second before.

"Holy shit!" Claire's stomach jumped in fear as her hand moved to the door handle. "Get out of my car!"

"I'm sorry if I frightened you, Miss Brennan. I'm not going to hurt you. There's no need for a fuss."

Claire hesitated, some instinct making her think he was telling the truth. Maybe it was the man's eyes: they weren't menacing, but rather appraising, reassuring, and very, very tired.

She struggled to control the beating of her heart as she studied him. He was slender, with a long, smooth face augmented by a hint of a goatee, and everything about him was pale, from his white skin, to his blond hair, to those eyes, which were the gray of an overcast sky. He wore a white turtleneck with a beige blazer and washed-out jeans. His legs were so long that they looked cramped in her car.

"Damn right, there's a need," Claire said. "Who are you? What do you want? How did you get in here?"

"Locks aren't a problem for me."

That wasn't exactly an answer to her questions. "You weren't here when I got in the car."

"Oh, but I was. I've been waiting for you for the past half hour."

"That's impossible."

He gave her a small smile. Suddenly, all the color drained from his body, until it looked like he was made of ice, at which point he faded entirely from view.

Claire gasped, staring at the empty space where the man had been. He had totally, utterly *vanished*. Yet she sensed that he was still there. Definitely some Fallen witchcraft. "You're one of *them*! Did Celeste send you?"

He reappeared. "No, child. I fight for the *other* side. I am the Watcher for this city."

Claire nodded slowly. She remembered hearing Alec talk about the Grigori who watched over Los Angeles, policing its Fallen, and initiating newly awakened Nephilim. The one Vincent had temporarily replaced during the horrible events of last fall, when *she* had awakened. The authority figure Helena had to constantly check in with to confirm that Claire was walking the straight and narrow.

But far worse: the person most likely to discover Alec and ship him back to their Grigori brethren. When Claire spoke again, her voice was no more than a whisper. "You're Zachariah."

"So, you've heard of me."

Claire's heart pounded, but she just shrugged her shoulders, hoping to appear casual as she carefully chose her words. "Helena may have mentioned you once or twice."

"I see." Something buzzed in Zachariah's pocket. He pulled out his cell phone and began texting as he spoke. "Please forgive my dramatic greeting, Miss Brennan, but as Emerson is a closed campus, I had little alternative."

Claire studied him, aware that she had to keep this man on her side. "Am I in trouble?"

"Not at all. I've had you on my mind ever since I resumed my post, but this is the first time I've been able to fit you into my schedule. I've been meeting with Helena telepathically with regard to your progress, which is all positive. Well done." He glanced at her. "But I thought it important that I meet you for myself, face-to-face."

"Why? So you can see if my grandmother's been telling the truth about me the past three months?"

Zachariah silently resumed texting, his expression betraying nothing.

I guess that answers that. Claire sighed. Clearly, he'd cornered her in her car so he could give her the third degree without Helena there to influence or protect her. "Okay. Great. We've met. Now what?"

He put his phone away and rubbed his eyes wearily. "Let's take a little ride. I hope you don't mind if I accompany you home?"

Claire's jaw clenched. This was the last thing she wanted. A cold fear gripped her as she thought of all the times Alec had come over since Zachariah had returned to L.A. Thank God Zachariah had been too busy to worry about her until now. Otherwise, he could have been lurking (invisibly!) at school, in her old apartment, or the new condo. He would have recognized Alec on the spot and busted him. Good thing Alec hadn't made plans to come over today. Aloud, she said, "Do I have a choice?"

"Not really." Zachariah pinched the bridge of his nose and let out a long, exhausted breath, reminding Claire of the way her mom looked after working back-to-back open houses and carting clients around all weekend, hunting for homes they didn't buy.

"All righty then." Claire drove out of the parking lot, up the hill, and onto the busy Brentwood street, her palms sweaty as she gripped the wheel. Stealing a sideways glance at Zachariah, she sensed his confidence, which made her even more tense.

His pleasant manner could just be a mask. After all, Vincent had seemed this polite the first time they met, and look what *he* turned out to be.

Both men had a lot of power. And people with power could never be trusted. She'd have to watch her words around Zachariah.

"So," she commented after an awkward silence, struggling to keep things light, "how's the Watcher thing going?"

The question seemed to amuse him. "Fine."

"How does L.A. fit into the grand scheme? Is it one of the biggest hives of scum and villainy?"

"It ranks well behind Caracas and San Salvador, but it's still a challenge." His tone was straightforward, without a hint of irony. "The cell of Fallen in Los Angeles has a very powerful leader with a strong following. They keep me on my toes."

"Yeah, I've met three of them," Claire shot back. "They're not my favorite people."

Zachariah's eyebrows lifted. "Oh really? Helena neglected to mention that. When did this happen?"

Damn, Claire thought. *I never should have said that.* "Um. Well. That's because I never mentioned it to *her*," Claire lied. "A few months ago, at the Homecoming dance, these three kids showed up who didn't go to our school. They promised me protection and stuff from the Grigori, who they said wanted me dead. I told them to back off, but it really freaked me out that they knew I'm a—" Her cheeks flushed as her voice trailed off.

"You can say Halfblood, child. There's no shame in it."

"Tell that to your predecessor."

"Vincent was … misguided. He should never have attacked you and your mother. His duty was to steer you toward the right path. A Watcher is only allowed to take drastic measures if there is no way to sway you from the Fallen's influence."

"You call it drastic measures, I call it attempted murder." Claire would never forget that terrifying night, right after the

Homecoming dance. "Vincent turned my living room into a Biblical wasteland, then tried to kill us."

"So I heard. I'm still unclear as to how you were able to fight off someone as powerful as Vincent."

Claire felt his eyes on her as she drove and wondered if he was fishing. Did he suspect that Alec had been there and saved her life? No, she decided. Zachariah had no reason to think Alec was in Los Angeles or that he even knew her.

"I have these psychic abilities," Claire replied, hoping she sounded more nonchalant than she felt. "Or haven't you heard?"

"Is your psychic power the only talent you used on him?"

Claire's brow knotted. "Well. Yeah. Since it's the only one I have."

Zachariah nodded as if satisfied and said nothing further, just stared out the window as they entered the parking garage beneath her building. She led the way to the elevator, which whisked them to the third floor, her anxiety mounting in the awkward silence.

Claire unlocked her front door, but before pushing it all the way open, she called out, "Grandma! We have a visitor!"

The entryway opened onto a high-ceilinged, open living area with gleaming hardwood floors and fresh white walls hung with an eclectic assortment of delicate watercolor paintings. A sliding glass door, leading to a balcony, infused the room with light. A leather sofa and two overstuffed chairs were flanked by antique end tables topped with knickknacks that Helena had had shipped from her flat in London. The kitchen, immediately adjacent, was divided by a granite counter fronted by comfy stools, and a hallway led to three bedrooms beyond.

As Claire and her visitor walked in, she noticed a teapot and two teacups on the coffee table. Helena, sipping from her own cup by the fireplace, flashed a Martha Stewart smile. "Hello, Zachariah. I've been expecting you."

"Benefits of a grandma who's a psychic," Claire said in an attempt at humor.

Zachariah bowed, then glanced about the room appreciatively. "It's nice to see you again. In person, for a change. You have a lovely home."

"Thank you." Helena eyed Zachariah warily. The air was thick with tension.

Claire wasn't sure how much her grandmother knew. Was Helena able to perceive everything that had just happened? It wasn't like Claire could ask her, with Zachariah standing there. Claire worried she'd say the wrong thing and screw everything up.

Suddenly, she heard her grandmother's voice inside her head: *Don't worry, dear. I have this.* Claire felt a tickle at the back of her mind and guessed that Helena was reviewing Claire's memories from the past hour or so to find out the answers for herself. Claire blushed, recalling what might be included in that recap: not just the Watcher's appearance and the car ride, but images of Claire kissing Alec good-bye.

Zachariah broke the silence. "How extraordinary." His eyes had fallen upon an old, intricately carved wooden clock on the mantel. "What a beautiful timepiece. I seem to recall Thomas Jefferson had one just like that."

"He did." Helena set her teacup down with a smile. "Thomas gave it to me after I suggested the phrase: 'all men *and women* are created equal.'"

Claire laughed out loud. "Nice one, Grandma. Too bad *Thomas* never used it."

"It is indeed a shame." Helena sighed. "Men tend to be so pompous and misguided. It is astonishing, really, how long it took for the lesser sex to see reason. But I have always treasured the clock even though it stopped working 120 years ago."

Claire choked a little, sensing now that her grandma wasn't joking. How did you follow up a comment like that? Thankfully, her grandmother spared her the need.

"Would either of you care for some tea?"

Claire shook her head, but Zachariah gratefully accepted the cup Helena offered as he sat down on the sofa opposite.

He took a long sip, then said, "Let me get straight to the point. I have some news that I believe will help you both sleep better."

"Oh?" Helena replied.

"We have Vincent in custody."

"You do?" The words escaped Claire's lips before she could stop them. Her heart began a rapid dance. She'd wanted to hear this for months, but at the same time, had been worried that it would happen.

"We tracked him down three weeks ago," Zachariah announced. "He's currently awaiting trial."

Helena nodded. "Good. But is he secure? I should think his particular talents would make it difficult to hold him."

"I assure you, ma'am, we are taking the proper precautions. Based on your statements concerning the events last fall, we looked into Vincent's old case files. A council of Elders is prosecuting him for seventy-three potential violations of procedure concerning the newly awakened."

"*Potential* violations?" Claire blew out a disgusted breath. "The man's a murderer."

"If that's true, he will be dealt with accordingly."

"You do not sound convinced he is guilty," Helena commented.

Zachariah's expression remained neutral. "My opinion doesn't matter, only the council's."

"Can I testify against him?" Claire asked.

"No. Only a Grigori may testify against another."

That was disappointing, but Claire decided it was for the best. The farther away she stayed from Vincent and the Grigori, the better. Even so, she was terrified. It was great that the Elders had captured Vincent, but if he ratted out Alec, it would destroy everything.

Helena lowered her teacup. "It does not surprise me that Vincent's crossed the line so many times. I have long sensed a dark side to him." Casually, she added, "He probably killed that rogue Grigori he was originally sent after, as well."

"You aren't talking about your *son*, are you?" asked Zachariah in surprise.

"Heavens, no. Dear me, it seems that going AWOL has become all the rage. No, I meant the *recent* defector."

Claire struggled to keep all expression from her face. Helena was steering the conversation toward Alec in a clever way, hoping to find out what the Grigori knew (or didn't know) about him.

Zachariah shrugged as he took another sip of tea. "We have no leads yet in that particular case, and Vincent hasn't admitted any progress on that investigation."

The surge of relief that washed over Claire was short-lived. Zachariah pulled out his phone and searched for something on it. "Speaking of which, one of my many tasks is to keep an eye out for the missing Watcher. This is the last known photograph we have. Do either of you recognize him?" He held out his phone.

Claire's stomach seized. The young man in the photo was definitely Alec. But he looked different, with shoulder-length hair and a rough goatee, a contrast to his current, clean-shaven, short-haired look. Claire shook her head. "Nope."

Zachariah swiveled in his seat and showed the phone to Helena. She studied it briefly. "The council sent me that ages ago. Sorry, I do not know him."

"Well, if you do ever happen to encounter him, I trust you will let me know."

"Of course," Helena replied.

Claire just nodded.

After putting away his phone, Zachariah folded his hands in his lap and regarded Claire for a long moment. Finally, he said, "One last thing, Claire. I like you. And I hold your grandmother in the highest esteem. She's told me many good things about you. She insists that although your gifts are not inconsequential, you're being carefully watched and will not become a problem. I respect her judgment and am inclined to leave you be. That said, just in case Vincent didn't already make it clear, the bottom line is this: far too many Nephilim have been corrupted by their talents. Please don't become one of them. Because if you do, I will have no choice but to act according to Grigori policy. I'm sure you know what that means."

Claire swallowed hard as fear and fury warred within her. Meeting his eyes full on, she said calmly, "I understand. *Sir.*"

He stood with a smile. "Please give my regards to your mother. I regret that I didn't get a chance to meet her." To Helena he added, "Thank you for the tea."

"My pleasure. Allow me to show you out." Helena rose, then strode to the sliding glass doors at the back of the room.

Claire followed them uncertainly. If he was leaving, why weren't they heading to the front door?

Helena led the way out onto the rear balcony. To Claire's utter shock, Zachariah bent his knees slightly, then leapt upward, rocketing into the air above. A heartbeat later, he faded completely from view.

Claire stared, mouth agape. "Holy shit."

"Language, dear." Helena looked far less impressed. "He is such a show-off." With what looked like a smidge of envy, she added, "It must be nice, however, never to require a driver's license."

"Or a pilot's license," Claire added.

seven

"He showed you *that* picture?" Alec made a face. "There are plenty of other photos in the Grigori archives, from decades of false passports for hundreds of countries. Why did Zachariah have to pick that one?"

They were lying inches apart on a pair of lounge chairs they'd shoved together on the roof of Claire's condo. A sparsely decorated garden consisting of a few potted plants and a picnic/barbecue area, this place had served as their private meeting spot for the past few months. It was cold by Southern California standards, but not windy, and a few stars and constellations dotted the inky sky.

Claire turned on her side and stared at him. "Are you kidding? I just told you all about my afternoon from hell, and you're complaining about the picture?"

"I look like a zombie hippie in that photo."

"You do not. I think you looked hot. Sort of a cross between a grunge rocker and Shakespeare."

"Well, I guess it's a good thing I'm keeping my hair short for now."

"Let's hope if he spots you, he doesn't recognize you."

"Aye."

Claire lay back down and looked skyward, heaving a sigh. "I've always felt safe until now, meeting you up here, where we can really *talk* without my mom or grandma or anyone else listening in. But *are* we safe?"

"What? You mean, because of Zachariah?"

"Alec, he's a *Watcher*. Who can turn invisible! And can freaking fly! He could be hiding in plain sight anytime, anywhere, and suddenly appear and slap handcuffs on you! How do we know he's not here, right this very minute?"

"We know because, to remain invisible, he'd have to use his powers."

Her eyebrows lifted. "Oh! Right. And if he's using his powers, you can see his aura."

"Like a bright yellow beacon. You can see his aura, too," Alec reminded her. "It's been awhile since you practiced. Do you remember how?"

She nodded. "I think so."

"Good. We can both keep a lookout for him, then, at school or wherever."

She blew out a long, worried breath. "Great. Now we have to be on our guard every minute. How are you not freaking out about this, Alec? A 'good guy' Watcher is on the hunt for you, while the psycho Watcher is in angel jail, and might tell everyone where you are."

"Welcome to my every day. Since the moment I left the fold last year, I've been looking over my shoulder. But I can't just stay locked inside all the time. Only difference now is that I'm also looking out for *you*."

"Join the crowd. I have a brand-new, invisible friend who's watching and just *waiting* for me to screw up so he can kill me."

"Don't screw up, then." He smiled. "Which I suppose is easier said than done. I'm sure you'll at least be tempted. There's a lot the Fallen can offer you."

"Nothing I want."

"They could probably tell you why they kidnapped your father. And where he is right now," Alec countered.

"So? We'll figure that out without the Fallen's help. Helena's already meditating on Brian's aura theory. Literally."

"Good to know."

"Speaking of Vincent," Claire said. "It worries me that he's in custody. What if he rats you out?"

"I don't think he will. At least not yet."

"Why not?"

"Because I'm his Get-Out-of-Jail-Free card. If his trial goes south, he can always tell the Elders where I am in exchange for a full pardon."

"Oh." Claire nodded and briefly looked relieved. Then she said, "Wait. Would they do that? Set him free just for throwing you to the wolves?"

"Dunno. They don't have a history of being forgiving. But it's possible, and an angle he's likely to try." Alec rolled onto his back and stared up at the dark sky. "To truly guarantee Vincent's punishment, I'd have to turn myself in to Zachariah now and hope he'll go easy on me."

"Like hell!" Claire was horrified by the very thought.

He looked at her again. "If I explained everything I did to help you and Helena, he might show mercy. If Zachariah argued for my safe return, Vincent would go away for sure, and maybe the Elders would be pardoning *me*."

Alec saw Claire holding her breath. "But even if you were miraculously pardoned," she managed, "that means you'd be a Watcher again. They'd take you away. You'd go back to murdering—"

"*Neutralizing.*"

"—the Fallen bad apples. And we'd never see each other again." Her voice broke on the last few words.

Alec squeezed her hand, trying to ignore the pain that suddenly seared through his chest. "Aye. But then you'd be safe. And so would all the innocents out there who those bad apples might hurt."

Claire looked at him. "Oh my God. You're actually serious about this? About going back?"

Do I tell her? Now's as good a time as any. Alec struggled to find the right words. "I admit, it's something I've been thinking about. I can't help wondering, is it selfish of me to be hiding out here?"

He saw tears leak from the corners of Claire's eyes but resisted the impulse to take her in his arms. He felt bad that he'd made her cry, but having done so, didn't think he had the right to comfort her.

It took her a long time to respond. Finally, drying her cheeks, she said, "I get it, Alec. You're a Watcher. Born and bred to help people. And I'm just one person. But you did your job for so long, and went to so much trouble to leave it, you've earned the right to a break. I don't think it's selfish to do what's best for yourself once in a while."

"You don't?"

"No, I don't." Claire slid close to Alec on his adjoining lounge chair and laid her head on his chest, wrapping her free arm around him. His arm instantly tightened around her in response.

"Besides," she went on, "if you hadn't been what you call 'selfish,' I would've been squished by scaffolding, murdered by Vincent, or ground into were-cougar chow."

Alec relished the warmth of Claire's body against his. "I suppose so."

With a tremor in her voice, she added, "Although if I'm totally honest, I guess it *is* kind of selfish to keep you all to myself. But I don't care! I love you. I want you to be safe, and to stay here with me. Forever."

"So do I. I love you, too. And I don't want to leave you. Ever." He meant every word. He just hoped his tone didn't betray the sense of guilt that still gnawed at him. He bent his head to hers, and their lips met.

"I've been thinking," Claire murmured when they parted. "You can't come here anymore. It's not safe. Zachariah could check on me anytime, and if he recognizes you, you're toast."

"I know. I was going to say the same thing. We need a new rendezvous spot. Maybe my place?"

Her eyes rolled. "Sure. Mom will totally be cool with that."

"Where, then?"

Claire paused, then looked at him tentatively. "I have an idea. You know about the school musical, right? *Camelot*?"

"I know Erica won't shut up about it."

"Yeah, well, auditions are tomorrow, and she said I should try out. But if I do, and *if* I get in, I'll hardly ever get to see you. I mean, she said rehearsals eat up all your free time for months. So I was thinking, if you and I both try out and get into the play, it'd be a way to spend time together after school that's totally sanctioned by Mom and away from Zachariah's prying eyes."

"A school play?" Alec mulled that over. "I dunno. I've never acted before."

"Are you kidding me? All those roles you played as a Watcher? You've done nothing *but* act for over a hundred years!"

"Hmmph," Alec replied.

"With your voice, you are a slam dunk to get one of the leads."

"You're not such a bad singer yourself," he shot back at her, teasing.

"So, should we do it? I mean, I'm only trying out if you do."

"Let me sleep on it."

"Okay."

Alec leaned in and kissed her good-bye. "Good night."

"You're not leaving already?" Claire protested.

"Don't want to start World War III with your mom." He smiled affectionately into her hazel eyes. "Hey. Before I leave, want to go for a spin?"

A grin spread across Claire's face. "Um. Yes?"

Alec stood, helped Claire to her feet, and they tightened their arms around each other. "Ready? Here we go."

With deep concentration, he wrapped his mind around their bodies and lifted them a few feet into the air, spinning slowly as they hovered above the rooftop.

After that, the only thing that enveloped his mind was the feel of her lips against his.

Auras. Claire knew they weren't hard to spot if you'd learned how (and if you had some Grigori blood in you). Alec had once told Claire it was like looking at a 3-D picture. You just focused really hard, looking slightly past the thing, until you could see the image hidden within.

Assuming there *was* something hidden.

School had just ended. Claire was standing on the landing halfway up the hill where the four stairways met. That morning, Alec had agreed to the whole *Camelot* idea, and auditions started in ten minutes.

Which gave her a few minutes to study the people hurrying by. Every time she passed this spot, the hair on the back of her neck stood up with memories of the attack last fall. Now Zachariah had given her another reason to be nervous.

Gathering all her mental energy, Claire focused on the parking lot below, staring at the cars and the people, trying to see evidence of a hidden aura.

Nothing there. Claire was about to turn her attention to another area when a hand suddenly clapped on her shoulder. She nearly jumped out of her skin.

"Hey." It was Erica's voice. "Thanks for waiting for me. Where's Alec?"

Claire whirled, gathering her thoughts. "His physics class was last track today and right above the theater, so I asked him to save us seats."

"You look nervous," Erica pointed out. "Why?"

"Zachariah." Claire had told Erica about her unexpected visitor. "What if he secretly crashes the audition and sees Alec?"

"I'm sure your new invisible stalker has better things to do than hang around our high school all day, or listen to us belt show tunes for two hours."

"You're probably right."

"Of course I'm right. So why do you still look nervous?"

"Because. This play thing is new and kind of scary."

"Oh, please. You have singing superpowers, remember?" Claire noticed a flicker of something in Erica's eyes that looked like—what, anxiety? But the look was gone in a blink, replaced by a smile. "So grow a pair, Claire Bear. Theatrics await!"

Claire wondered if Erica was as nervous as she was. To bolster her friend's confidence in return, Claire replied, "After you, Your Highness."

Erica's face lit up, but she gave Claire a pointed look. "I'm not Guinevere yet."

The auditions went decently. Or seemed to. Claire, Erica, and Alec sat with about forty other students in the first seven rows of velveteen theater seats, watching each other mount the stage one by one to sing the short solos they'd prepared. Claire tried to send Neil an encouraging smile, but he never looked her way.

When her turn came, Claire handed her sheet music for Guinevere's first lament, "The Simple Joys of Maidenhood," to the accompanist at the piano, then took her place center stage. Her heart hammering, she tried to ignore the sea of faces staring back at her from below. But her eyes caught Alec's.

You've got this, Alec seemed to be saying with his silent smile.

Since they'd only agreed to try out at the last minute, Claire hadn't had any time to rehearse. With no previous theater experience, she didn't have any hopes beyond getting a part in the chorus. Still, she didn't want to totally embarrass herself. She'd heard the song plenty of times and knew the words. But even though she'd inherited the Grigori ability to (supposedly) sing any song off the cuff, on cue, and in perfect key, she didn't quite trust it.

"Whenever you're ready," declared a strong female voice from a seat at the center of the audience. Ms. Donnelly, the theater teacher, was a wiry, attractive woman in her early fifties, with a shock of auburn hair that matched her vibrant personality. The music teacher, Mr. Lang, and dance teacher, Mrs. Frank, sat beside her taking notes.

The music began. Claire took a deep breath and began to sing. At first, it was like she was on autopilot, tensely going through the motions. But as the song progressed, she felt her nerves melting away and soon realized she was enjoying herself as much as she did in every Concert Singers performance. This time, though, there was no choir to hide behind. When she'd finished, everyone applauded. She dashed back to her seat, where Alec squeezed her hand, and Erica gave her a thumbs-up, and whispered her favorite quote from *American Beauty*, "Honey, I'm so proud of you. You didn't screw up once!"

The handful of students who followed gave respectable but unmemorable auditions. Then Erica's name was called.

"Break a leg," Alec and Claire whispered.

Erica exchanged a few words with the pianist and took the stage with a confident air. The song she'd chosen, "I Loved You Once in Silence," was one of Guinevere's most heartbreaking and melodious. Erica delivered it beautifully and with a regal flair.

"You nailed it!" Claire said when Erica returned to her seat, her face shining with satisfaction and relief.

Neil was up next. He gave a stunning rendition of King Arthur's song, "How to Handle a Woman," a performance filled with emotion and nuance that perfectly showcased both his voice and his acting abilities. He left the stage with a smile to generous applause.

Claire knew, though, that the best was yet to come. She waited breathlessly until, at last, it was Alec's turn. As he sang Lancelot's "If Ever I Would Leave You," the theater filled with a kind of energy and excitement that hadn't existed before. Alec had the most beautiful voice Claire had ever heard. *A voice like an angel*, she'd thought the first time she'd heard him sing, all those months ago in the theater stairwell (unaware at the time that it was true in more ways than one). His green eyes found Claire's and rested there with a look that nearly made her heart stop, as he sang the final line:

No, never could I leave you at all!

Claire couldn't help but be overwhelmed by the deeper meaning the lyrics held, after their conversation on the roof the other night. *You're damn right you're not leaving me*, Claire thought, joining in the enthusiastic whistles and applause that followed.

As they headed for the junior parking lot after auditions were over, Erica said, "Alec, you totally blew us away! You're Lancelot for sure."

"Let's not count chickens," he shrugged as he opened his car door. "Neil has a great voice, and there were a couple of other guys who could do it."

"The part's yours," Erica told him. "I can feel it."

"And you're a slam dunk for Guinevere," Claire insisted.

Erica's smile was genuinely nervous as she fished out her car keys. "Shhhhh. Don't jinx it!"

"Did Ms. Donnelly say when she's posting the cast list?" Claire asked.

"Honey, she'll have callbacks for the leads before she casts it."

"Callbacks?" Claire repeated in surprise.

"Of course. This was just the first round to weed out the tone-deaf," Erica explained. "At callbacks, she has people *read* as well as sing."

Claire looked from Erica to Alec. "You mean, you guys have to do this all over again?"

Erica let out a short laugh. "What do you mean, *you guys?* Claire, you have a shot at Guinevere, too."

"What? No way!" Claire protested. "I've never been in a play before, ever."

Erica stopped beside her car with a shrug. "We'll see. The callback list goes up Wednesday morning."

Alec fired up the engine of his Mustang with a smile. "Well, until then, good luck. Both of you."

Claire kissed Alec good-bye through his open car window. "See you tomorrow."

"Ditto." He smiled as he backed out and took off.

Claire drove home, her mind a mixture of worry and excitement. She'd suggested the play as a way to spend more time with Alec after school. But what if it backfired? It was obvious to her that he'd get a leading role in the show. But what if *she* didn't get in?

On the other hand, the fact that he'd committed to the play was a good sign. It meant, despite his earlier anxiety, that he was comfortable enough with his human life to stick around. At least for the next three months. The lyrics of his audition song wafted through her memory, comforting her: *No, never could I leave you at all!*

As she turned onto her street, her thoughts veered in a different direction. She spotted her grandmother a half block ahead, jogging, clad in black spandex leggings and a sports bra. Claire had to admit, Helena looked amazing for being 875 years old (or thereabouts).

Slowing the car to a crawl beside her, Claire lowered the passenger window, and called out, "Hey, foxy lady."

"Hey yourself." Glancing in Claire's direction, she added, "Bless you."

"What do you mean—" Claire began. Suddenly, she sneezed. "Show-off! Your visions used to be so much more exciting."

"Prepare to be excited, then. Meet me upstairs. I have news."

"About what?" Claire's curiosity was piqued.

Helena shot her a meaningful look as she sped ahead. "I have just seen your father."

eight

Claire burst into the condo to find Helena in the kitchen, swigging a tall glass of cucumber water.

"You *saw* my father?" Claire cried eagerly. "When? Where?"

Helena set her glass on the counter and dabbed at the perspiration on her chest with a small towel. "The *where* has yet to be determined. The *when* was this morning, while I was meditating."

Claire's spirits deflated. "Oh. You didn't see him in person. It was a vision."

"Do not sound so disappointed. I managed to revisit the moment when Tom was kidnapped and confirmed that your friend was right. Whatever substance those men injected Tom with, it changed the frequency of his aura to a new wavelength. Probably to hide him from the Grigori's watching eyes. It explains why I could not detect a presence of him all these years. I was looking for the wrong aura."

"Do you think the Fallen still have him?"

"I have no idea. But the good news is, I know what to look for now. And if you and I meditate together, we'll be casting an even wider net."

"Really?" Claire was excited. She'd communed with Helena psychically before, but it was the first time her grandmother had ever proposed that they *meditate* together. "I'm in! When should we do it?"

"There is no time like the present. Just let me have a quick shower. Grab your father's blazer and meet me in my bedroom in ten minutes."

Putting her cell phone on silent, Claire scampered into her mom's bedroom and retrieved the brown corduroy sport coat they'd carried with them every time they moved. The coat meant almost as much to her as it did to her mom since communing with it had given Claire her first vision of her father.

"How are we going to do this?" Claire asked a few minutes later, entering Helena's antiques-laden room to find her clad in a cobalt satin robe. "Do we sit on the floor in a circle of candles or something?"

"Pointless theatrics." Helena lay back on her queen-sized bed, patting the space next to her. "Put the jacket on and lie down next to me."

"You want me to wear it?"

"The more bodily contact you have with it, the better."

Claire slipped into the jacket and stretched out on the bed beside her grandmother, filled with anticipation. The coat was way too big for her, but as she wrapped her arms around herself to hold it closed, she felt a slight tingle where the fabric touched her bare fingers.

"Close your eyes and take my hand."

Claire did as instructed. The moment she gripped Helena's hand, Claire felt a sensation similar to what she'd experienced months ago when Helena was in a coma. All sound vanished, and her vision filled with bright light. Then she seemed to be in an empty, white space, holding Helena's hand and standing beside her.

"Welcome back to the Grigori Nexus," Helena greeted her.

Claire glanced around the blank expanse. "Not very stylish for a telepathic hub."

"On the contrary. A clean slate makes it easy to pick out incongruent signals across the network." Helena released

Claire's hand. "For this to work, you need to know how your father's aura has changed. Take a look."

The whiteness around them slowly filled with the sights and sounds of a busy New York City street. They were back at the moment when they'd last glimpsed her father. Claire tensed anxiously as she watched the three men hold down her father on the sidewalk, while another came at him with a syringe. Then the action paused.

"Can you see his aura?" Helena asked.

Claire concentrated hard, until she could see the soft, golden glow that shimmered all around her father. "Yeah."

"Keep watching."

In slow motion, the needle jammed into her dad's neck. As the plunger was depressed, Tom's aura withered to a dingy brown. The sight sparked a sick feeling in the pit of Claire's stomach, and at the same time reverberated inside her mind, like a mild electric shock accompanied by the sounds of a discordant drum.

Claire cringed as she raised a hand to her forehead. "Oh God. Okay. I don't just see it. I can *feel* it."

"So can I. I am sorry it is so unpleasant. But it shows how strong the Fallen's hold is over Tom. And now you know what we are seeking. Keep that sight and feeling in your mind as we look outward."

The sights and sounds around them faded, taking away Claire's physical discomfort and leaving her and Helena in blessed white emptiness.

"Concentrate with me," Helena said.

Claire focused with all her might to maintain a mental impression of her father's new aura. The air around them gradually filled with glowing dots. Claire squinted at them, realizing they were fuzzy images of people moving to and fro surrounded by glowing auras, gold for the Grigori, blue for Nephilim.

"It's like we're in *Cerebro*," Claire mused.

"Focus," Helena replied curtly. "Look for an aura that is murky brown, with the signal you experienced."

A few minutes ticked by. Then Claire saw it. A dim brown orb that flickered on and off like a dying lightbulb, and sparked the same sick feeling in her stomach. "There!"

"Yes. Yes!" Helena enthused. "I see it, too."

Claire stared hard at the brown dot, the discordant sounds in her mind increasing as they zoomed in on it, and the other dots faded away.

An image of a man began to come into focus until they were in the same space as him. He lay in bed in a dimly lit room, his eyes closed, the muddy aura surrounding him. Claire swallowed hard, her head and heart pounding. Could this be her dad? His dark brown hair brushed his shoulders, and he had a mustache and beard. But on a second look, she knew it was him.

"We did it. We found him!" Claire cried. "But where are we?"

"It looks like a hotel room."

Heavy drapes covered the windows, masking whatever lay outside and casting the room in deep shadow. The bed, headboard, nightstands, and lamps all looked like the modern, mass-produced furniture typical of high-end hotel suites. Tom's head rested against a pillow, his face contorted as if in concentration.

"He's trying to use his power, isn't he?" Claire asked. "Is that why we can see an aura?"

"Yes."

Her father spoke. "What time is it?"

Another voice came out of the darkness, a deep male voice that sounded weary yet professional. "It's nine o'clock, Mr. Boulanger."

Boulanger? Claire thought.

"I'm thirsty." Tom's tone was sharp, yet polite. "May I have a glass of water, please?"

A light laugh met this request. A bald, broad-shouldered man in a dark suit appeared beside the bed. Claire didn't recognize him. "I know what you're trying to do. And it's not going to work."

Tom's eyes blinked open, his face an expressionless mask. "I don't know what you mean."

"Give it up. You're wasting your time." The man tapped his right ear, as if that meant something. "But it looks like your next pick-me-up will have to be a little earlier than scheduled."

Tom tried to sit up, glaring angrily, only to be restrained by a long cord that seemed to be anchored somewhere below the bed. Struggling fiercely against the bonds, he cried out between clenched teeth, "Damn you! Why are you doing this? I need to see my wife and daughter!"

The man withdrew a hypodermic syringe from his blazer and prepped it. "There, there, Mr. Boulanger. We've already been over this many times. You need to calm down." He grabbed Tom and injected him. As the contents of the syringe emptied into Tom's arm, his struggling eased, and, finally, he went limp.

"Get some rest, you have a big day tomorrow." The guy smirked and disappeared back into the shadows. Tom's eyes fluttered closed, his aura fading away, as the entire scene around them began to flicker and fragment.

"We're losing him!" Tears pooled in Claire's eyes.

A heartbeat later, they were surrounded by white nothingness again. "Stars above." Helena sounded strained. "That was far more exhausting than it should have been."

"Claire? Helena? Are you home?" It was Lynn's voice coming at them from far away.

Claire felt herself being ripped out of the white void and back into her grandmother's bedroom, as if she'd just awakened from a dream. Sitting up on the bed, she blinked to get her bearings. "We're in here, Mom."

Lynn entered and paused. She looked like she'd come straight from her self-defense class, a gym bag slung over her sweaty shoulder. "Oh. I'm sorry. Were you taking a nap?"

"I do not *nap*," Helena replied tartly.

Claire dabbed at her eyes. "We were doing psychic stuff, Mom. Grandma found Dad's new aura. It's different now because he's being poisoned by drugs. He was chained up in a hotel room. It was *horrible*."

"Dear God." Lynn, visibly stricken, set down her bag. "Where was this? And when? In the past, or is it happening now?"

"No clue," Helena replied. "It was a generic hotel room. It could have been anywhere—today, or years ago. But it definitely was not the day we saw him taken. His hair was longer, and he had a beard."

"So they *did* recapture him after he called me that morning. They might still have him now."

Claire's lip trembled. "We have to go back and look for him again, Grandma."

"I am as anxious to find him as you are," Helena answered, "but we cannot try anything again just yet. It is too dangerous."

"Dangerous? Why?"

"If we tap into the Nexus for too long, the Fallen, or worse yet, the Grigori, might catch wind of what we are doing. If the Grigori find Tom through us, and we have not reported his whereabouts—"

"They might put us all on trial for treason," Lynn finished glumly.

"Oh." Claire felt as if the wind had been knocked out of her. "But we have to do something. Why did that guy call Dad 'Mr. Boulanger'? They must know his real name. And why are the Fallen doing this? Alec said that drugs *inhibit* a Grigori's gifts. If they want to use Dad for his visions, that makes no sense."

"Drugs do not eliminate one's gifts entirely," Helena replied. "He could still be useful to them, even in a drugged state."

Claire heaved a deep sigh. "That is so screwed up."

Helena looked equally solemn. "Quite."

Claire ran her fingers through her long brown hair. "Wait. What *power* was Dad using, which gave him an aura? He was just asking for a glass of water. But the man got all weird about it. What was it he said? 'I know what you're trying to do. And it's not going to work.' What did he mean?"

Helena shrugged. "I don't know."

Claire studied her grandmother, puzzled. She sensed that Helena was lying.

A memory bubbled up in Claire's mind. Something Vincent once told her. *You are closer to a Grigori in strength than anyone else on the planet,* he'd said. *The Fallen will go to any length to recruit you.*

And then the kicker:

Your genes may also be hiding the other half of your father's talents.

Her other power. The one she didn't know anything about but might develop someday. Claire's voice hardened. "Vincent said my dad has another ability, besides looking at the past and future. Do you know what it is?"

Helena glanced away, her lips compressed. "That is not important."

"How could it *not* be important? It could be the reason the Fallen are keeping him prisoner! Do you know, Mom?"

Lynn shook her head, her eyes wide.

"Vincent looked like he was *afraid* when he mentioned it," Claire continued. "What could the Grigori find so threatening?"

Still Helena remained silent.

"Please, Grandma. You *must* know what Dad's other power is. If there's a chance I might have that power, too, you need to tell me! I have a right to know."

Helena sighed. "All right, yes, I *do* know. And I suspect that is why the Fallen have taken Tom. But there is no point in discussing a mere speculation. *If* you have your father's other power, you will find out yourself in time. Trust me. I have good reasons for not telling you now."

"Name one."

"If you know about this power, you will start looking for it in yourself."

"No I won't! I swear I won't," Claire protested.

"You will," Helena insisted. "You will not be able to avoid doing so. You are tainted by your human blood, after all."

"Thanks for that," Lynn snorted.

"If you do possess this power," Helena went on, "the temptation to use it will be impossible to ignore. Trying it even once will only embolden you to make further attempts. The ramifications can prove extremely dangerous. Dear Lord, I see that the longer I talk, the more curious you are. This discussion is over."

Claire had never felt so frustrated in her life. A door had just been opened, then instantly slammed shut without a glimpse of what lay inside. "So. What? We're going to do *nothing* for my dad? Nothing at all?"

"We will, in time."

"Am I supposed to just forget about this, go about my day like everything's totally normal?"

"Child, nothing about your life has been normal for quite some time. Still, we all must soldier on."

"Cut the 'stiff upper lip' bullshit!" Claire exclaimed.

"Claire!" her mother admonished.

Claire marched for the door. "Let me know when enough 'time' has passed, Grandma, to look for Dad without pissing off the celestial guard or clueing in the bad guys. Meanwhile, this *child* will be in her room, avoiding her secret, evil power."

She slammed the door to her bedroom behind her, fresh tears threatening to fall.

nine

"I hate to say it, but I agree with your grandmother," Alec admitted as he unlocked the various deadbolts on his front door, clutching his cell phone in the crook of his neck, a bag of groceries in one hand and his apartment keys in the other.

"You're not supposed to be on her side," Claire complained over the phone, "you're *my* knight in shining armor."

Alec grinned as he closed the door, sparing a little mental focus to telekinetically flip on the lights. "I don't wear armor, love."

"That sexy leather jacket certainly looks like it protects you."

She sounded like she was cheering up a bit, albeit slowly. Alec was relieved his comment hadn't caused more of an issue. Dropping the grocery bag on the coffee table, he withdrew the knife from his boot and did his usual rounds. Kitchen clear. Weapons cabinet untouched. No one behind the curtains.

"All I meant," Alec explained as he confirmed that the closet and shower were empty, "is that you're safer if Helena doesn't draw too much attention to the search for your father. The less attention on you, the less Zachariah will come poking around."

"Mmmm, I guess." Claire's sigh echoed on the other end of the line. "Do you keep looking for Zachariah around every corner, like I do?"

"You should've seen me at the supermarket tonight." Alec couldn't help shaking his head in embarrassment at the memory.

"I'm sure I looked like a conspiracy nut, peering around the corner of every aisle before I went down it."

Claire's laugh helped to ease the tension that gripped his heart. For the past two days, since he learned that Zachariah was in town, it had been harder than ever to relax. But he knew he had to try. His former Grigori lifestyle had been all about the work, the protection of others above himself. The goal *now* was to find pleasure in providing another with comfort and affection and receive the same in return.

If only it were that easy.

A sharp noise outside brought his train of thought to an abrupt halt. It sounded as if a window had just been shattered. Not his, but somewhere nearby.

"Hold on a minute." Alec put down his phone, flipped off the lights, and peeked out between his blackout curtains.

Everything looked normal. The driveway that ran beside his building was empty. The street out front appeared vacant. But he'd *heard* breaking glass. Then something caught his eye: two figures were slipping inside a broken window of the house next door.

In an instant, Alec was at his weapons cabinet, phone in one hand, his other hand on the lock. The cabinet clicked open with a few additional bursts of mental energy. "I'm back, sorry," he told Claire.

"Where'd you go?"

"Looks like there's a B&E happening at the house next door." Alec scanned the various guns and edged weapons in the cabinet, debating which one to take with him.

"Oh no. Call the police!"

Claire's words caught Alec by surprise. "The police?"

"Yeah. Why do you sound all weird? Is there something wrong with calling the police?"

"No, I just ..." Alec felt foolish now. He hadn't glimpsed an aura. He had no reason to think the perpetrators were members of the Fallen. This was strictly a human-on-human crime, which wasn't, and never had been, part of his job description. "I was about to go *do something* about it."

"Alec, what the hell? I thought you said you wanted a break from action-hero crap?"

"Aye."

"We mere mortals have people trained to take care of that kind of thing."

"Sorry, you're right. Old instincts." Alec closed the cabinet. "I'll call it in, then call you back."

"You'd better." He sensed that Claire's nerves were back to where they had been at the start of the call. *So much for making her feel better*, Alec chastised himself as he disconnected the call, then reported what he'd seen to the local precinct.

Before calling Claire back, he paused, wondering what on earth he'd been thinking.

He'd felt a definite, nagging itch to go after those guys. Sticking his neck out like that might help ease the guilt he'd been feeling recently, for hiding out, living a normal, safe existence. But it also might expose him, bring Zachariah right to his doorstep. He'd be throwing away everything he held so dear.

He reminded himself that he had another reason for being here now, beyond himself. Claire. If he hadn't been here last fall, Claire would be dead. And if he didn't stay now, something else might happen to her.

Focus on that, he told himself. *You need to keep her safe.*

ten

"Why are you late? I could've looked at the callback sheet already and been halfway to precalc by now."

Claire had just climbed out of her car in the junior parking lot to find Erica waiting for her, visibly anxious. "I know. Sorry, sorry. My morning went way slower than usual. I had to carefully time when I crossed the common areas of the condo, so I wouldn't run into my grandma."

They hurried across the drop-off circle. The scaffolding from last fall was long gone, and the theater building sported a fresh, new, Spanish-style facade.

"So you two still aren't speaking?"

"Not if I have anything to say about it. Pun intended." Claire had spent most of the night before on the phone, telling first Alec, then Erica and Brian, everything that had happened, from the visions of her dad in captivity to her meltdown afterward. "I am *so* mad at her."

"Good luck keeping that up. The longest I ever succeeded giving my mom the silent treatment was a week. In return, she suspended my allowance and tightened my curfew to eight for a month."

"What happens to me doesn't matter. I'm worried about *my dad*. He could be in huge trouble and need our help. But

Grandma's putting the brakes on, and I can't do anything about it!" Claire groaned in frustration as they trudged up the south stairwell to the upper school.

"It'll be fine, Claire Bear. You don't want the Grigori or the Fallen breathing any further down your neck. Helena's not stupid. You just have to be patient."

"Being patient is hard."

They pushed through the heavy glass door into the newly renovated theater lobby. A few students were clustered around the bulletin board where the callback sheet was posted.

Erica took a deep breath. "Keep your shoulder ready for me to cry on if they didn't call me back. And don't feel bad, Claire, if your name's not on the list for a lead. With pipes like yours, you're guaranteed a part in the chorus."

"Right. The chorus is fine with me." She didn't have the experience to play a big part, anyway. She'd been so distracted by everything the past couple of days, she hadn't really been thinking about the play. But, she suddenly realized, she really wanted to be in it, just so she could share the experience with Alec and Erica.

The other students dashed off, gossiping, as Erica and Claire strode to the bulletin board and studied the sheet. It listed the main characters and the people called back for each one, starting with the boys.

"Neil was called back for King Arthur!" Erica cried. "That's so perfect."

"And Alec's called back for Lancelot. Sword-wielding do-gooder with a great voice. Sounds about right." Claire grinned as she scanned down the sheet.

There was only one girl's role listed: Guinevere. Four names were noted beneath it.

Claire sucked in an astonished breath. "Holy shit. Erica? I can't believe this!"

She and Erica had both been called back for the same part.

Erica hesitated, then said, "Way to go, Claire."

"You, too!" Claire high-fived Erica, and they shared a smile. "The part's yours for sure, but still, how cool is this?"

"Yeah, it's totally cool."

As they turned to leave the theater, though, Claire saw the smile leave Erica's face and sensed that her friend was annoyed and maybe a little … worried. Why? There wasn't a chance in hell that Claire would get the part.

Alec couldn't help but notice how much the dynamics of their formerly friendly group of four had changed over the past few days. It was bad enough that Erica and Brian were still in some weird, undefined place. But ever since the callbacks yesterday, Erica had been standoffish with Claire and him as well.

He couldn't blame her, really. Erica had been training and hoping to play the lead in a school musical for forever, and suddenly her best friend was serious competition.

It was now Friday morning, and the four of them were in snack bar line in the cafeteria, silent and moody.

Brian glanced at his watch and proclaimed, "Okay! That's the thirty-six-hour-and-five-minute mark. I'm officially weirded out. Why is nobody talking?"

"Nothing to say?" Erica shrugged, her eyes wandering.

"How is it that *you* haven't had anything to say for a *day and a half*?" Brian retorted.

"So I'm a chatterbox normally, then?"

"I'd say more like bubbly and cheerful," Brian countered in an obvious attempt to diffuse Erica's prickly mood. "Come on. Callbacks were yesterday. They were supposed to be the height of your entire theatrical career to date. Why haven't you said a thing about it?"

Erica remained silent. They'd reached the front of the line now. Alec bought two quesadillas, one for him and one for Claire. After Erica and Brian each grabbed chocolate-chip cookies, the foursome exited the cafeteria and headed for their table outside the library.

As they walked, Brian said to Alec and Claire, "What happened at callbacks, anyway? Care to fill me in?"

"It was weird," Claire offered. "Ms. Donnelly kept switching everyone around into different pairings. Erica and I and the two other girls who were called back read Guinevere with all the guys. And the guys had to trade off reading both Arthur and Lancelot. At the end, I had no clue what she was thinking."

"It *was* confusing," Alec agreed. "I half expected her to ask *me* to read Guinevere."

His attempt at a joke fell flat. After an awkward beat, Erica griped, "That would've been just what we needed. More competition."

Claire looked at her. "Are you seriously worried, Erica? I've heard that Ms. Donnelly likes to give everybody a chance at auditions. But you killed it. I'm sure she'll give it to you."

"There's no guarantee," Erica pointed out. "The year we did *Mack and Mabel*, she gave the lead to a ninth grader who'd never acted before."

"And that girl was *amazing!*" Brian enthused. "She came out of nowhere and totally rocked."

More awkward silence followed as they passed through the Science Quad. Claire gave Brian a death stare. He just looked confused. "What?"

"You're not helping, mate," Alec whispered in Brian's ear.

"Oh." Brian finally got it. "Sorry. When is the cast list going to be posted?"

"At the end of the day," Alec answered.

Brian looked desperate to catapult himself out of the gigantic hole he was in. Suddenly, his face lit up. "Hey! CB, couldn't you just, you know, *figure out* what's going to happen, ahead of time?"

"Huh?" Claire replied.

"You know." Brian mimed removing a glove and laying a hand on Alec's shoulder. "See what you can see?"

Claire looked appalled. "Are you crazy? Isn't that cheating?"

"Not unless you try to change the results," Brian said.

Erica turned to Claire, sudden interest in her eyes. "I wouldn't want you to change anything, Claire Bear. But all this waiting is killing me. I *have* to know. Please?"

"No," Claire whispered firmly. "You both asked me to never go spelunking inside your heads, and I promised I wouldn't. Plus, I'm not good enough to focus on a specific moment yet. Only Helena can do that."

"Oh. I forgot." Erica sighed. "I'm sure I can make it a few more hours." Erica gripped the straps of her backpack and trudged forward with them down the stairs.

When they reached the lower patio, Alec stopped in surprise. The weathered wooden table where they'd consumed half a year's worth of lunches and snacks was gone. The entire area was cordoned off by plastic and caution tape, and filled with construction materials.

"Great," Erica muttered, annoyed. "This is just *great*."

Claire sighed. "I am so sick of all the construction at this school."

"That's been *our* table for years! Where are we gonna—" Brian was interrupted as a pair of pale arms suddenly flung themselves around him.

"Hey, Bri! How's it goin'?" The cheerful speaker was a tall, pretty, blond girl, who was in the grade below them.

"Hey, Kayla." Brian smiled, awkwardly returning the hug.

Kayla shoved a book in Brian's face. "I found my copy of *City of Thieves* that we talked about the other night. You're going to love it!"

"Great!" Brian accepted the book. "Thanks."

Alec noticed Erica frowning at this interchange, her mouth twisting like she'd just eaten something sour.

"Oh no, isn't this where your table was?" Kayla asked, eyeing the nearby construction zone.

"Aye," Alec confirmed.

"Well, if you guys need a new place to hang," Kayla said brightly, "my friends and I totally own the shady spot in the North Quad. You should join us."

"Um. Thanks," Claire replied.

"Don't forget: North Quad. I hope they still have muffins left at the snack bar. Catch you guys later!" Kayla dashed up the stairs.

"She's … friendly," Alec commented, hoping to keep the mood light.

Erica, however, wasn't smiling. Her eyes locked on Brian. "What did she mean, 'the other night'?"

"Oh. Um. Well, Kayla and I went to a movie at the ArcLight. Her dad gets free passes."

Nobody said anything for a long moment as the news hung in the air. Claire and Erica both looked surprised. Alec waited, hoping for the expected disclaimer, "It's no big deal, we're just friends"—but it never came.

Without another word, Erica spun and darted up the stairs two at a time.

Claire shook her head. "Today's gonna be fun."

The minute the bell rang signaling the end of the school day, every student in class made a beeline for the door. Alec was a few steps behind Claire, aware that she was anxious to see the cast list, when their history teacher, Mr. Patterson, called out, "Miss Brennan? A moment, please."

Claire paused, eyeing Mr. Patterson warily. Alec hung by the door, concerned. Claire and Mr. Patterson hadn't started the year on the best of terms.

"What's up?" Claire looked uncomfortable as she approached the teacher's desk.

Alec had spent a lot of years observing people. He could tell that Mr. Patterson wasn't any more relaxed than Claire.

"I was just wondering," Mr. Patterson began. "Is everything all right at home?"

Claire stared at him. "Why? What do you mean? Did you hate my last paper again?"

"No, no, nothing like that. I was more trying to ask after your mother."

"My mom? Oh. Um. She's. Fine."

Oh, shite. Alec sensed where this was going, and from Claire's expression, it appeared that she did, too.

"I don't know if your mom told you this, but we went out a few times last fall."

"She did mention it," Claire returned awkwardly.

"Out of the blue, she stopped returning my calls and emails with no explanation. I just wanted to make sure that she—that you and she—are all right."

"We are. I promise. We moved last fall, and things got really busy for her after that. Selling houses takes a hundred hours a day, so she doesn't have time for much else."

Alec knew the real reason why Lynn had cut off communication. She was too freaked out by what had happened after Homecoming. Even though Mr. Patterson hadn't really been involved, Lynn said that the thought of seeing him again creeped her out.

"Claire," Mr. Patterson replied with a tentative smile. "Nobody should work that hard. Everyone needs to take time away for themselves. To that end …" He pulled a folded piece of paper from his pocket and offered it to her. "Would you do me a favor and give her this note?"

Claire paused. "Um. Well. It's really nice of you to think of her, but now is not the best time."

"There's never a perfect time for anything," he returned insistently. "Please, just give this to her. I have tickets to a play at the Music Center, and I'd love to take her."

Claire's eyes lifted to his, quiet sympathy behind them. "Sorry, but you need to stop, Mr. Patterson."

Mr. Patterson stared back at her, as if a bit confused. "What?"

"You need to just stop. I'm sorry, but trust me. This can't go anywhere with my mom. It's over."

A moment passed, a faraway look in the teacher's eyes. Then he blinked, nodded, and put the note back in his pocket. "Okay. I understand," he said firmly. "No problem. Have a good weekend." He turned away with a smile.

Wait, what? Alec's brow furrowed as Claire joined him at the door, and they exited outside into the North Quad. Something strange had just happened.

"Thank God *that's* over," Claire said, as they dashed up the stairs, then headed toward the theater building. "I thought Mr. Patterson would never let that go. But I know Mom's feelings on the subject, so I tried to let him down gently."

"Gently?" Alec glanced at her with narrowed eyes. "It was more like you slammed a door in his face."

"What do you mean?"

"I mean, it was clear that this thing with your mom was really important to him. But when you told him 'just stop,' he dropped the whole thing in two seconds flat. He didn't even look disappointed. Doesn't that seem odd to you?"

"Not at all. He saw my point. It was fantastic! Finally, an adult *listened* to me and understood what I was trying to say."

"Maybe. But from what I've observed, people don't usually give in so easily about things that matter to them. I still think the way that conversation ended was a bit *off*."

Before he could elaborate further, Brian exited the theater building and raced up to them, a serious look on his face.

"Alec! CB! The cast list is up." With a flourish of his arm, Brian bowed to Alec. "Your Majesty."

Alec barely had time to register the news, when Claire blurted: "What? Alec is King Arthur, not Lancelot?"

"He is." Brian turned to Claire and repeated the low bow. "And might I congratulate you, Your Highness?"

"What are you talking about?" Claire asked.

"You're Guinevere," Brian replied with a small smile. "It's official. You two are the happy royal couple."

Claire looked absolutely dumbfounded. "What about Erica?"

"She's Nimue."

"Who's that?" Alec asked.

"Exactly." Brian let out a sigh. "It's the fairy with barely half a song who puts Merlin into a coma."

"Oh my God," Claire cried, distressed. "Has she seen the list yet?"

"I don't know."

Just then, Alec caught sight of another figure coming up the stairs. It was Neil.

"And here's our knight errant," Brian commented, grinning broadly now.

"Neil is Lancelot?" Claire's eyes widened. "Awesome."

Every atom of Alec's being tensed up. He knew it was ridiculous. After all, Claire had chosen *him* over Neil, and ever since the Homecoming fight, her relationship with Neil had been practically nonexistent. But emotions and facts weren't always in sync. A chemistry still existed between those two, Alec could sense it.

Neil reached the landing and stopped, looking somewhat uncomfortable. "Hey." It was the first time in months that Neil had talked to them, outside of auditions. He extended a hand to Alec, his voice flat. "Congrats."

Alec automatically shook Neil's outstretched hand.

"Did you see Erica?" Claire asked.

Neil nodded stiffly. "Yeah. Not gonna lie, there were some tears."

"Crap." Claire sighed, a worried look on her face. "She's never going to speak to me again."

"I tried to convince her not to drive right now," Neil said, "but she wouldn't listen. Just insisted on getting the hell out of here." He managed a tight smile. "So. The drama will continue at the read-through Monday afternoon. Get excited." Neil continued past them up the hill toward the junior class lockers.

"Looks like it'll be a tense few months," Brian said, watching Neil walk away. "I'm so glad I don't have to be involved in any of that until tech week."

Unsure what to say, Alec remained silent. The only reason he'd agreed to try out was to spend more time with Claire. King Arthur was the leading role, so it was flattering that he'd been chosen to play it, and exciting to think that Claire would be playing his wife.

But at the same time, if Claire was Guinevere, the last person on earth Alec wanted to play Lancelot was Neil.

What had he gotten himself into?

eleven

"How much time do we have?" Claire asked.

Alec checked the digital clock in a novelty electronics store's window. "Ten minutes."

It was Saturday night, the day after the cast list had been posted. She and Alec were walking through the crowded night scene at Third Street Promenade, a pedestrian-only street in Santa Monica, after dining at a little Greek place.

Things had been quiet and awkward at dinner. Alec hadn't brought up the play, and neither had Claire, but she hadn't been able to think about anything else.

The play was practically all she *had* been thinking about for the past twenty-four hours. She could hardly believe that she'd scored the female lead. And opposite Alec! To think that Ms. Donnelly trusted Claire, an untried actress, to do such an important part was, well, flattering. And exciting. Her mom and Helena had been excited, too, when she'd told them.

At the same time, though, Claire felt really, really bad for Erica. Claire had texted Erica twice, saying *Call me*, and *I'm sorry*, but her friend hadn't responded. Claire understood why. She knew how much Erica had wanted that part and figured she just needed some space to deal with her disappointment.

Claire wasn't sure what she'd say to Erica when she did call, except to commiserate and say how sorry she was. But they definitely needed to talk.

She and Alec needed to talk, too—but for a different, related reason.

But now, as they rushed to catch a movie, they were still avoiding the topic. "You'd think our waiter would've *told* someone he was going on break for an hour," Alec added.

"It's okay, it's like we're back in New York." Claire grinned, extending her gloved hand to him. "Except I get to keep both eyes open."

Alec accepted her hand and pulled her along faster as they dodged other couples, strolling families, and a knot of people gathered around a group of street musicians. Claire glanced back, wishing they had time to listen, but the AMC theater was almost in sight.

Suddenly, three figures appeared directly in their path, forcing them to skid to an abrupt halt.

"Well," said the female of the group in a distinct, all-too-familiar British accent. "Fancy meeting you two here."

She'd hoped never to see Celeste again. The tall, raven-haired beauty wore a calf-length, red wool coat and high black leather boots. A red knitted beret perched at an angle on her head. Goth makeup accentuated her pale complexion and crimson lips.

Flanking Celeste on both sides were her usual cohorts. Javed was tall and broad-shouldered, his curly black hair tied back in a ponytail. Tattoos peeked above the collar of his black peacoat, snaking up and around his neck.

Rico, also dressed in darks, was shorter and stockier and sported a bushy goatee on a round, unfriendly face. A beanie with an LA Kings logo was tugged down over his head. "In a hurry?" he asked as he stared at Claire, legs spread wide and arms crossed over his chest like a bouncer outside a club.

"Just out for a jog." Alec's face went cold and he stepped in front of Claire as if to protect her. "How's your knee?"

Claire remembered that the last time Alec met up with these assholes, he'd left them both in a world of hurt. She could see on their faces that they remembered, too.

"It'll feel better," Rico began icily, "when it's jammed up your—"

"Rico, don't embarrass yourself again," Celeste interjected, patting him on the shoulder like he was the family dog. "They won't want to hang out with us if you act like a bitchy adolescent." She fixed Claire and Alec with a radiant smile.

"It's so great to see you," Claire lied, hoping to defuse the situation before it turned ugly. "But we're late to a movie, so we have to go."

She was about to move on, when Celeste gave her a sly glance.

"What a shame you're in such a rush, Claire. Here I thought you'd *want* to talk to us. I mean, considering how anxious you are to find your father."

Claire froze, her heart jumping into her throat. *Holy crap.* Alec was right; the Fallen *did* have a super spy network. Did Celeste really know something about Claire's father? Tamping down that thought, she struggled to sound nonchalant. "How's that any of your business?"

"We're making it our business," Celeste replied. "My boss wants to help you. Both of you, actually."

"Your boss?" Claire wondered who that was. But Alec was ten steps ahead of her.

"You can tell Mr. Malcolm *no thank you*," Alec said heatedly.

"You haven't even heard what we're offering." Celeste made a faux-offended face. "You, dear boy, have the local Watcher on your arse. We could keep him off the scent. And—"

"I've held my own so far," Alec interrupted. "I don't need your help."

"So *far*." Celeste's voice dripped with condescension. "*You* might be able to shrug this off, cowboy, but the *filly* might feel otherwise." Turning to Claire, she added in a more serious tone, "Claire Bear, my boss knows where your father is."

"He does?" Claire couldn't help blurting out, immediately wishing she hadn't sounded so obviously interested.

"Thata girl." Celeste smiled. "I know you're asking yourself, 'What's the catch? Nothing in life is free, blah, blah, blah.' But what we want in exchange is simply for you to embrace your true calling."

Claire was still so mesmerized by the words *knows where your father is*, she could hardly concentrate on what Celeste was saying.

"We're talking help for help," Celeste went on. "We keep Alec safe, and he goes back to policing rogue Fallen. For *us*."

"Policing rogue Fallen?" Alec repeated, incredulous.

"We do *try* to keep our own in line. The less visible we are, the better. And you are, after all, an expert in that area. As for Claire's gifts, I don't even need to tell you how helpful she could be at keeping our *innocent* brethren out of danger."

Alec narrowed his eyes. "And I suppose we'll strap on capes and leap off rooftops while we're at it?"

"I'm a fan of capes." Celeste shrugged. "Whatever floats your boat."

"Let's go," Alec told Claire, taking her hand again.

Celeste stood her ground, flanked by her flunkies. "I'd like to hear Claire's answer, tough guy."

Claire stood there, torn. She couldn't help being tempted. First off, with their power and resources, the Fallen probably *could* keep Zachariah off Alec's back. It would be such a relief to have him out of danger. Secondly, if the Fallen were holding her father captive, it *was* likely that Celeste or her boss would know where he was. And could maybe help rescue him.

On the other hand, did she dare enslave herself to these people, whom Alec had spent more than a hundred years fighting against?

Celeste cocked her head. "While you're considering, sweetheart, I should add: it's an all-or-nothing deal. Mr. Malcolm was very clear on that point. We need both of you fighting the good fight."

One look at Alec told Claire the answer. No matter how much *she* wanted what they were offering, it wasn't going to happen. He'd never give in to this. And he was right. How many times had he warned her that the Fallen's words were poison?

Claire shook her head. "Like I said before, we're running late."

"Of course. No pressure, you don't have to decide right this minute. Take the weekend to think it over, sweetie. We can pop by after school on Monday."

"No need," Claire insisted, tension boiling up in the pit of her stomach as she locked eyes with Celeste. "I've made up my mind. Back off. And *go*."

Celeste opened her mouth as if to reply, then paused. Her eyes seemed to glaze over slightly, as if she'd lost her train of thought.

At the same time, Claire felt the strangest sensation. Like the tension inside her core had exploded out in invisible rubber bands, stretching between her and Celeste. Claire took a small step back, slightly dizzy, and the tethers seemed to tighten.

Then, just as quickly, the feeling passed. Celeste blinked, and said hesitantly, with a hint of confusion, "Right. Let's roll, boys."

"You serious?" Javed fired back.

"Give me five minutes with this ex-Watcher in the alley," Rico told Celeste, fuming, "and he'll be saying yes with what's left of his teeth."

"I said we're bailing." Celeste spun and walked off purposefully.

"Enjoy your movie," Rico sputtered, the words sounding a lot more like *screw you*. Glaring at Claire and Alec, he and Javed moved after Celeste and disappeared into the crowd.

That was weird, Claire thought, her stomach still tight with anxiety. She'd never experienced anything quite like *that* before. Had Celeste tried some kind of new power on her? If so, what? And why?

Not wanting to worry Alec, she just said, "Thank God they're gone. Do you think we can still make the movie?"

Alec didn't reply. He stood frozen, with a bewildered expression, staring alternately at Claire and the spot in which Celeste had once stood.

"Hello? Earth to boyfriend?"

He still said nothing. The anxiety that had been building inside her reached a peak, and Claire couldn't hold back anymore.

"Alec, what's wrong? You've hardly said anything since yesterday! All through dinner and the car ride, not a single *word* about the play or the fact that my best friend may never speak to me again. And then we run into those three assholes, and it was like I had to defuse the whole situation myself! And now I'm yelling at you in public. Sorry."

"Claire," Alec said slowly, "do you want to get out of here? We need to talk."

As soon as Alec turned off the ignition, Claire turned to him impatiently. "So, talk."

They'd just arrived at the make-out spot favored by Emerson Academy students in the Palisades, high on a cliff overlooking the ocean. But they weren't making out. Alec wasn't even looking at her. Instead, he was sitting behind the wheel of his Mustang, brooding.

Finally, Alec said, "I'm sorry if you felt like I didn't protect you more, when Celeste and her idiots showed up. It was all I could do to restrain myself. I didn't want to make a scene."

"I get it. I shouldn't have said anything."

"As for the other stuff. I know I've been distracted since yesterday. And you're half-right. Part of it is about the play."

Claire felt the knots in her stomach seize up again. "I knew it. Ever since Brian told us about the casting, I saw your face, and I—"

Alec held up a hand to silence her. "I feel bad for Erica. Your friendship is so strong, I'm sure she'll get past it. But I've also got reservations about watching you play Guinevere every day for the next two months. Because although I'm excited about playing king to your queen, and I know we'll have fun doing it, there's this *thing* that keeps eating away at the back of my mind." He paused for a breath, still unable to meet her eyes. "I know it's stupid and adolescent for me to feel jealous, but the idea that *Neil* is going to be Lancelot, your *lover*, and you're going to have all these intimate scenes together ..."

He trailed off, searching for words. When he looked up, his eyes were filled with embarrassment, and his cheeks were red.

Claire felt the most delicious sensation wash over her, like she'd just been wrapped in a warm and fuzzy blanket. She leaned over the console, her face inches from his, and kissed him gently. "Have I ever told you that I love you?"

"You may have mentioned it once or twice."

She caressed his face with her gloved hand, pretending to mope. "That's your answer?"

His eyes twinkled now. He pressed his lips against hers and kissed her deeply. "You know I love you," he replied softly. "Better?"

"Infinitely. And thank you for sharing all that." She heaved a sigh. "What *I* haven't mentioned lately is that I've been freaking out about all this, too. I mean, the whole Neil/Camelot/love scene thing."

"You have?"

"Yes. That is, until I went online and found the script."

"And?"

"It turns out that Guinevere kisses *Arthur*. Which is *you*. But she never kisses Lancelot."

"Seriously?"

She nodded. "Lancelot and Guinevere have feelings for each other and sing this big romantic song and all, but the script just says they 'embrace passionately.' Which I'm assuming just means an overly dramatic *hug*."

It was Alec's turn to smile. "Okay then. I think I can handle that."

Claire felt a weight lift off her shoulders. "You gotta love the irony, though: *they're* the ones with the forbidden love in the play, not you and me."

"Well, where would the fun be in playing real life?"

"Exactly! Fun! That's what this is all about." She interlaced her fingers in his. "We're going to be okay. It's just a *play*. Right?"

Alec nodded mechanically.

As Claire leaned in to kiss him again, she paused, noting that his expression had darkened again. "You said I was half-right about your being distracted. Is there something else?"

"Aye."

Claire settled back in her seat, trying not to worry. "Speak."

Alec took a deep breath and plunged in. "Something strange is going on with you, and I don't think you even realize it."

"Strange?"

"It's the way people have been responding to you lately."

"You were responding to me just fine a minute ago," she said coyly.

"Not me. Other people. First Mr. Patterson, and now Celeste."

"I admit, something weird happened with Celeste, I don't know what. And Mr. Patterson always makes my blood pressure spike. But what does one have to do with the other?"

"In both cases, you were arguing with them, and they shut down and backed off when you told them to."

"I didn't *tell* them to. I—" She broke off uncertainly.

"You did," Alec insisted. "It's been bothering me. I knew I'd seen something like that before but couldn't put my finger on it. Tonight, I realized when it happened. It was on the subway platform, when Vincent was talking to your father. Vincent got this odd look in his eyes, then he apparently did what your dad told him to do. He jumped in front of the train."

"That wasn't really Vincent. It was an illusion he was projecting."

"I know. But Vincent wanted your father to *think* that what he was doing had worked."

"What do you mean, *worked?*"

"It was like your father was trying to hypnotize Vincent."

"Hypnotize him?"

"If I'm right, the same thing happened just now when you were talking to Celeste. And with Mr. Patterson. In both cases, you did something that changed their intention."

Claire stared at him. "But I didn't *do* anything."

"Maybe not *deliberately*. But were you doing anything deliberately the first time you got a vision?"

"No, but—" The hair on the back of Claire's neck started to prickle. Weirdo dizziness aside, she had to admit, Celeste *had* given in a little too easily. Claire had been too preoccupied with relief when the trio left to think about it. But now, something clicked. "*Holy crap.* Are you saying what I think you're saying? Do you think *that's* my dad's second gift? And—"

"And *your* second gift."

Every nerve in Claire's body was tingling. She could hardly breathe. "I can hypnotize people?"

"Maybe. Or something similar. It seems like some kind of brainwashing."

They were quiet for a long moment, Claire's heart racing as she tried to process this news. Was it really possible? Could she really get people to do whatever she wanted, just by *thinking* at them?

Why not test it right now?

She locked eyes with Alec, trying to restrict her mind to a single thought: *Scratch your head.*

Alec looked back at her, his brow furrowing. "Why are you staring me?"

"I'm trying to make you do something. Subliminally."

"I don't feel anything."

"Neither do I." Claire sighed. Then a thought hit her. "Maybe I'm not doing it right. What if I have to *say* what I'm thinking out loud? Both times this happened before, I was *telling* the person to do something."

"Hypnotists generally *do* make verbal suggestions."

"Right. Let me try again." Claire fixed her eyes on Alec once more, focusing her thoughts. "Scratch your head," she commanded.

"What?"

Claire smiled playfully. "You have an irresistible urge to scratch your head."

Alec crossed his arms. "Nice try."

"Boo." Claire stretched her legs out as far as they could go in the confines of the Mustang. "And here I thought I had this new, phenomenal cosmic power."

"You might. You just don't understand how to harness it yet."

"If this gift is actually legit, I wish it had shown up before. All my life, it's been such a fight to get my mom to listen to me. And my grandmother's even worse."

"So said every person ever born."

"How am I supposed to learn how this works without my dad to teach me?"

"Something tells me that even though the ability came from your father, his mother knows enough to get you started."

Claire thought about that. "You could be right. Helena's been so afraid to tell me anything about this. Now I know why. It would also explain why Vincent was afraid of me."

"A gift like this is dangerous and easy to abuse. Theoretically, you could convince a person to do almost anything."

Claire threw up her hands. "This is so backward! I've always felt like Celeste was the one trying to brainwash *me*. And she was *really* good this time. If you hadn't been there, I might have said yes."

"I know. That's why Malcolm uses her."

"Who *is* Malcolm, anyway?"

"Shane Malcolm is the head of all the Fallen cells in Los Angeles. If the Fallen are holding your father captive, he certainly would know where and why."

"Huh." *If I could just find this guy and touch him*, Claire mused, *I could probably get a vision of where my dad is.*

"No." Alec shook his head emphatically.

"What?"

"I don't have to be a psychic to know what you're thinking, Claire. And there's no way either of us can go to Malcolm to get that information. He's dangerous. Extremely so."

"But—" "I'm aware of how badly you want to find your father. But if you agreed to work with them in exchange for what you're dying to hear, the cost would be too great. You'd be aiding and abetting a group that places no value on human life."

"I know. But—"

"Worse yet, if we're right about your second gift, if the Fallen ever had you in their control, think of the damage they could do with it."

Claire heaved a frustrated sigh. "I wish I could brainwash them into telling me about my dad." She caught Alec's expression, and added, "Chill out! I don't even know how this thing works or if it works at all."

That evoked a slight smile, but his tone was still serious. "Just promise me you'll be careful with this and won't use it again until you've talked to Helena."

"Okay, but you know how cagey she's being."

Alec nodded. A slice of moonlight through the car window illuminated his handsome face and danced on his dark, golden hair. After a moment, he placed one hand gently on her arm. "The clock is ticking on your curfew. Do you want me to get you home now, so you can chat with Helena about this?"

"No way." She glanced at her watch. "We still have seventy-three minutes," she added, her voice lowering. "There must be something we can do to distract ourselves during that time." She leaned in and walked her fingers slowly up his arm. "Got any ideas?"

His grin widened. "I do." Then he drew her close, and his lips met hers.

twelve

Claire quietly unlocked the front door, her face still flushed and her entire body aglow from her backseat make-out session with Alec. The evening might have started badly, but it had sure gone better as the night went on. She still felt the echo of Alec's final steamy kiss before he dropped her off.

She shut the door carefully, trying to make as little noise as possible. Her curfew had ended an hour ago, but if she was lucky, her mom and Helena were already asleep and would never know. Slipping out of her shoes, Claire tiptoed through the living room and started past the kitchen, hoping to make it to her bedroom undetected.

"How was the movie?" Her mother's voice penetrated the stillness, making Claire jump.

Her mom was sitting at the kitchen table with a mug of tea and a book, the look on her face unreadable.

"It was okay," Claire lied. "The movie we wanted was sold out, so we had to go to a different one. It was a little longer, sorry."

"An hour longer, to be exact?" Her mom's tone was a little sharper now.

Claire's cheeks grew warm. "Yeah."

"If you knew you were going to be late, you could've texted or called."

"I guess I should have. Sorry."

"Or if you wanted to blow off the movie to make out with your boyfriend in the backseat of his car, you could have given me a heads-up about that, too."

Claire felt like her face was on fire. "Mom!" She wondered how on earth her mom knew about that. Or was she just fishing? "What makes you think I've been—"

"I don't think it, I *know* it. When you didn't come home on time, your grandmother and I were worried. So she did a little psychic searching and discovered what you were up to."

Claire gasped, both outraged and mortified. Her grandmother had *seen* her and Alec when they were … ? The very thought made her want to die of embarrassment. *Thank God they hadn't done anything too crazy or naked.* But still. "How dare you let Grandma check up on me like that? How long was she watching?"

"Does it matter?"

"Yes, it matters!" Claire was furious. "Grandma has no right to use her gifts to play Peeping Tom on me!"

"Yes she does. It's her job to look out for you, Claire, to protect you. We had no idea where you were. You could have been in danger."

"But I wasn't! This is embarrassing on so many levels, Mom. It's like having a parent read my diary, only ten thousand times worse!"

Lynn glanced at her with interest above her cup of tea. "You have a diary?"

"No! Mom, why can't you see that what she did is horrible? Aren't I allowed any privacy?"

"Not when you disrespect the rules you aren't. When you're going to be late, you tell me. That's the agreement we've always had. And you don't lie to me. Ever. That's two rules you've broken in one night. For that, you're grounded, and I'm confiscating your phone for a week."

"A week?" Claire was horrified. "What am I supposed to do without my phone for a week? And you can't ground me! Rehearsals for *Camelot* start on Monday after school."

"You can go to rehearsals, but you'll come straight home after that. No dates with Alec, no hanging out with friends, and no chatting on the phone or texting for the next seven days."

"Mom, I was only an hour late! That is so not a big deal!"

"It wouldn't have been if you hadn't lied about it."

Claire heaved a groan of frustration. "This is so hypocritical of you."

"Excuse me?"

"Have you totally forgotten what it's like to be young? You met my dad at the exact same age as me! Are you telling me you never got home just the teensiest bit late? That you never lied to your parents about anything?"

Lynn's expression turned stony. "What I did or didn't do is not relevant."

"Isn't it? Isn't that what this is *really* all about?" Claire was about to add, *You're worried that it's going to be 'like mother, like daughter,' aren't you? That I'm going to get pregnant like you did. That's why you're acting like a parole officer.* But she stopped herself. She'd said something similar to her mom once before, and the results hadn't been pretty. Instead, she insisted, "Mom, you don't have to worry about me and Alec. It's not like I don't know where babies come from. I won't do anything stupid."

"I'm glad to hear it. But this is about more than that, Claire. It's about trust between you and me. And you've broken that."

Claire was shaking. How could her mom punish her like this for something so small? "All my life I've done everything you wanted. Compared to some of the kids at school, I'm a saint."

Her mom hesitated, suddenly looking tired and deep in thought. "I don't compare you to other kids, Claire. They don't have the same risks and concerns that you do. But ..." She trailed off as if confused about something.

Claire was about to continue defending herself when she noticed something odd and familiar about her mother's expression. It reminded her of the same, vacant look on Celeste's face when Claire had talked to her earlier that night. That weird *binding* feeling was present again, too, like Claire was attached to her mom by a set of invisible strings.

Holy crap. Am I doing it again?

Claire almost gasped aloud as an idea took hold. Maybe Alec was right. Maybe she *did* have a second gift, the ability to persuade people to her way of thinking. It hadn't worked when she'd tried it on Alec. She wondered what she was doing differently this time. The only thing she could think of was that she was really pissed off. The anger ball in the pit of her stomach was threatening to choke her. Did intense emotion have something to do with this?

Another thought quickly followed. *What do I have to lose?*

Invisible strings. All they needed was a tug. Taking a deep breath, Claire stared hard at her mother, letting her anger fuel her focus while removing any trace of it from her voice, as she said, "Mom, I get it. I was late. I'm really, really sorry, especially for lying about the reason. I promise I won't do it again. Would you give me a break and let it go, just this once? Please? *Just let it go.*" She repeated the last phrase in her mind, *Let it go. Let it go.*

The weird look in her mom's eyes deepened. "All right," Lynn replied matter-of-factly. "I suppose we can let it go. Just this once."

It's working! Claire felt excited and a little bit guilty at the same time.

"Stop that this instant!" an angry voice called out.

The mental connection with her mother snapped. Claire whirled to find Helena standing in the kitchen doorway, her eyes smoldering.

"Stop what?" Claire tried to look and sound innocent.

"I know what you are doing," Helena hissed, striding forward and stopping just inches away from Claire.

"Really? Is that 'cause you're spying on me again?"

Without hesitation, Helena slapped Claire across the face.

Claire gasped in pain and surprise, one hand going to her cheek as she blinked away tears.

"Don't you dare try that again, on your mother, on me, or on anyone else," Helena told Claire furiously, "or so help me, I will do worse than that."

"Helena!" The faraway look had vanished from Lynn's eyes, replaced by shock and dismay as she wrapped her arms protectively around Claire. "What are you doing?"

"She deserved that." Turning her glare back to Claire, Helena added, "It seems my suspicions were correct. You have discovered your second gift, haven't you?"

A flush enveloped Claire's face, but she didn't reply.

"What second gift?" Lynn asked.

"Persuasion," Helena explained. "*Mind control.* Just like her father."

"*What?*" Lynn stepped out of the embrace and studied Claire, baffled.

"It happens when they concentrate their thoughts and speech together in a certain way. She just played you like a puppet, to get out of trouble."

"Wait, no." Lynn shook her head. "Everything was fine, we talked it out."

"No, you did not. You were terribly upset, then you let her off the hook without any punishment for what she did tonight."

Lynn turned to Claire. "Is that what happened?"

Claire couldn't help the blush that still stained her face, an admission of her guilt.

"How could you do that to me?" Lynn's expression radiated hurt and disappointment. When Claire didn't respond, Lynn turned to Helena instead. "Dear God. Tom never said anything about that kind of ability."

"Because it is very dangerous, and even he refused to use it unless he was in mortal danger. Claire, you must promise to *never do that again.*"

"Why?" Claire heaved a sigh. "I don't understand. You've been helping me to develop my visions. Why is this different?"

"You know the answer to that," Helena replied. "One should never deliberately change someone else's mind or bend them to one's will. It is not right."

"That's not always true. I accidentally used it to get three Fallen off my back tonight! If you teach me what you know about it, I could protect myself, so I don't always have to depend on you or Alec."

"There are other, better ways to protect yourself." Helena's expression hardened. "It can be more difficult to control a Grigori or a strong-blooded Nephilim, so relying on it is risky for only a Halfblood. More importantly, this power is too tempting to use. Being a Halfblood means you'll become highly skilled very quickly. How will anyone ever trust you again if they know you can toy with their minds? Ask your mother how she feels about what just happened."

Lynn's eyes had grown steely. "I don't even know where to begin, Claire."

Claire felt small. It took a huge effort to will herself to meet her mother's eyes. "I'm sor-"

"Don't say another word," Lynn interrupted. "You are officially grounded, and not just for a week. For as long as I see fit." She held out her hand, palm facing up. "Give me your phone."

With a deep sigh, Claire silently surrendered her phone to her mom.

"Now go to your room. I can't even look at you right now."

As Claire turned away, Helena's voice followed her down the hall. "And do not forget, I will be watching."

thirteen

Alec stood outside his favorite Vietnamese takeout place, waiting for his order. It was a chilly Sunday evening, and the pavement was still damp from the afternoon's rain.

He stared at his phone, rereading for the umpteenth time the messages Claire had sent from her laptop the night before:

> Heads up: Grounded. No phone/email.
> Not your fault. Lied abt why I was late.
> Love you.

Alec felt terrible. He hadn't meant to get her home late, they just got … carried away. Her mom must have been really upset to ground Claire for lying. He wondered if she'd had a chance to ask Helena about her newfound powers, and if so, how that went.

Being out of touch with Claire—not having any real idea what was going on—was frustrating. He felt disconnected. Like he was a Watcher again, waiting for his next shred of information, totally alone but expected to be at the ready at all times.

In the past six months, he'd become accustomed to the rhythms of normal human existence. He'd come to enjoy having actual relationships with people, kept alive by fairly constant communication. The emotions that went with it were … satisfying. More than satisfying. They filled the need deep inside that he'd always had in his old life. All the songs he'd heard about loneliness over the years made a lot more sense to him, now that he'd experienced a real connection firsthand.

A young man appeared at the window with a plastic bag of fragrant food. Alec paid in cash, as always, his stomach rumbling as he carried the container of cilantro-pork noodles out to his Mustang.

The sharp sound of a slap caught his attention. In the parking lot of the sleazy bar next door, a blonde in a tight, purple dress was being pressed against a silver Lexus by a tall, good-looking man wearing dark slacks and a pin-striped shirt. The man held his hand to his cheek as he tried to convince the woman to enter the car.

"Lemme go, Lance!" the blonde cried out. They both appeared to be intoxicated.

Alec hesitated. He'd seen this kind of drunken nonsense too many times to count over the past century. Was the blonde in any danger? The man bullying her was definitely bigger and stronger. Once again, the instinct to *do something* stuck in Alec's craw.

But then Claire's voice echoed in his mind: *We mere mortals have people trained to take care of that kind of thing.*

She was right, of course. This wasn't his business. It was risky to get involved. He could, however, alert the authorities and keep an eye out in case things escalated.

Opening the Mustang's door, Alec sank into the driver's seat, plopped his bagged dinner beside him, and made the call.

"Nine-one-one emergency," intoned the voice over his phone.

"I'd like to report a public disturbance," Alec began. Just then, as he watched the battling duo, something caught his eye. As the blonde pushed the man away, his face *flickered* for an instant. The way Vincent's illusions had sometimes flickered when his focus wavered.

Alec trained his secondary sight on the man. Sure enough, the guy had a bright blue aura—the color radiated by a Fallen who was using his abilities.

He's one of them.

The woman had no aura at all, meaning she was human.

Alec had seen Fallen with this "glamour" ability before. They could project different images of themselves to make themselves appear beautiful, when in reality they were disfigured fiends. They could also project images into their targets' heads to frighten or ensnare them. Similar to Vincent's abilities but less grand in scope.

It was a bad idea to insert himself in the situation, Alec told himself. He'd gone AWOL for a reason.

But the woman had no chance against this guy, and neither would anyone else. How could he just drive away and do nothing?

"Hello? Sir?" asked the voice over the phone. "What kind of public disturbance?"

"Never mind." *Not your jurisdiction.* Alec hung up without another word.

Alec stepped out of his car, moved to the trunk, and opened his guitar case, to reveal his portable arsenal of weaponry. His hands brushed over the various blades and firearms, settling on a heavy tonfa stick. He'd spent his entire life killing members of the Fallen and had no wish to kill again, so a blunt weapon like this—basically a police officer's baton—would still allow him to defend himself without lethal action.

Alec slammed his trunk with enough force to get the Fallen's attention. What had the blonde called him? Lance? As he'd hoped, Lance's head snapped in Alec's direction.

"I don't think she wants to go with you, Lance," Alec commented as he strode calmly up to the couple, hiding his tonfa from view.

"Mind your own business, asshole," Lance hissed. He had both of the woman's arms in his grip now. She leaned against the car, apparently too drunk or under his spell to fight back anymore.

"Wish I could." Alec gripped his weapon tightly as he closed the distance, waiting for his new adversary to strike.

And strike he did. Lance dropped his hold on the blonde, lashing out at Alec with a backhand. Alec brought the tonfa upward to block the Fallen's attack, bone colliding with steel.

"Motherf—!" The guy yelped in pain and staggered backward, cradling his forearm.

The blonde was so drunk, she slowly sank down to the pavement. Alec needed to end this quickly, so she wouldn't sustain further injury from a stray blow.

Without missing a beat, Alec spun the tonfa in his grip to club Lance over the back of the head. But this time he wasn't fast enough. His adversary ducked out of the way, channeling the momentum into a spin kick straight to Alec's chest.

Alec flew through the air, hitting the ground several feet away in the alley alongside the bar, his weapon clattering to the pavement outside his reach. He coughed, trying to catch his breath. Why was this guy so strong? His power was glamour-related, not superhuman strength.

"You people always underestimate us," Lance chuckled, removing a small vial from his pocket. Unscrewing the lid, he took a quick swig. A few drops of a deep red liquid landed on his striped shirt as he swallowed and licked his lips, his eyes suddenly growing glassy and bloodshot. He pocketed the vial and stalked toward Alec.

What was that? Alec wondered.

Although Alec was fairly certain he had superior strength and speed, Lance now seemed unafraid of tussling with him.

Scrambling to his feet, Alec moved for the tonfa. But as he reached for it, to his shock, the tonfa suddenly transformed into a rearing, leopard-spotted snake, snapping its ferocious fangs. Alec withdrew his hand instinctively, heart pounding in alarm.

Damn it, he's using glamours to mess with my head.

"Something wrong, Watcher?" Lance delivered a punch that made Alec see stars.

Alec smacked against the bar's sidewall. Suddenly, the dirty stucco swirled, and eerie, hand-like shapes seemed to reach out and grab him. The ground shimmered, then became a blazing-hot fire that filled the air with smoke and made his eyes water. Alec set his jaw, wishing Claire were here to dispel the illusions. *It's all in your head*, he tried to tell himself. *It's all in your head!*

Then the Fallen was on him, delivering a barrage of inexplicably superhuman punches to Alec's torso. He felt searing pain and a sharp, internal crack as a couple of ribs fractured. Alec's agonized yelp was stifled when one of Lance's hands closed around his throat.

Focus! Alec told himself, struggling against the iron grip around his neck. Every choking, haggard breath was a painful jab to his ribs. If he didn't act fast, this would be the end.

His eyes glaring through the smoke, Alec reached out with his mind, wrapping mental fingers around the only thing he could be certain was real: the Fallen himself. Coiling up the mental energy like a spring, Alec let loose a telekinetic burst that flung his opponent into the stacked wooden palettes on the other side of the alley, hitting them so hard they splintered on impact.

All at once, the fire, the smoke, and the restraining hands were gone. Alec grabbed his tonfa—no longer a snake—and raised it at the ready, just in case Lance wasn't out cold. But he just lay there, limp and still, his glamour gone and his true features revealed—an ugly, pockmarked face with pointed ears—proof that he was unconscious.

Alec turned his attention to the woman, hoisting her to her feet, wincing as agony lit up his rib cage. His injury didn't worry him. He healed so quickly, he'd be a hundred percent in a couple of weeks. But it hurt like hell all the same. Alec did thank the Fates that Lance had only tagged his face once, so he wouldn't have bruises to explain away.

The woman awakened from her stupor with a moan, looking up at Alec with confused, fearful eyes.

"Don't be afraid. I'm trying to help you," Alec said.

With a small shriek she pulled away, seized her purse from where it lay nearby, and ran off, heels clicking on the pavement as she disappeared into the darkness.

Alec heaved a frustrated sigh. Hopefully, she hadn't gotten a good look at his face and wouldn't report him to the cops. He glanced at Lance. He had to be moved, contained, so he couldn't follow Alec if he awoke.

Alec extracted the guy from the broken palettes, dragged him to the back of the Lexus, and unlocked the trunk with his mind. He yanked the lid open, intending to toss the Fallen inside—then stopped short. To Alec's surprise, the trunk was almost full.

It contained two large red coolers with the words BLOOD PRODUCTS IN TRANSIT and UCLA MEDICAL CENTER printed in white block letters on their lids.

What on earth is this guy up to? Alec had no time to figure it out. After that unfortunate display of powers, he couldn't risk another moment out in public.

Retrieving both of the coolers for further investigation, Alec hefted the unconscious man inside the cleared space. When Lance came to, he could bang on the lid or call for help on his cell.

Just before he closed the trunk, Alec remembered the mysterious vial—the one whose contents had apparently imbued its user with, well, superhuman strength. Alec fished the vial out of Lance's pocket. It had no label identifying what was inside.

Alec opened the vial. Its contents smelled like blood, and the splotches on Lance's shirt seemed to confirm that. Why was a Fallen transporting large quantities of blood? And why did drinking some of it cause him to go all Hercules?

The door to the bar suddenly banged opened as three average-looking guys staggered out.

"I'm telling you, it sounded like a fight," one of them slurred.

Alec slipped the vial in his own pocket, slammed the trunk shut, and ducked out of their sight.

"Looks like someone got their ass kicked," another guy stuttered with a laugh.

Somehow Alec needed to transfer the coolers to his own trunk without these guys' noticing. Peeking over the roof of Lance's car, he stretched out his mind and rattled one of the dumpsters at the far end of the alley.

The three men jumped in surprise. "Is someone in there?" one guy shouted curiously. The others followed him toward the dumpster to investigate further.

Alec grabbed the coolers, carried them to his car, and stowed them in his trunk. From the black lockbox he always kept there, he grabbed a GPS tracking device—a remnant from his former job. Head down, Alec scurried back to Lance's Lexus and attached the magnetic device to the inside of the bumper.

By the time the drunks were on their way back from the alley, Alec was behind the wheel of his Mustang and gunning his way out of the parking lot.

What the hell did I just stumble on? If what he'd just discovered was related to the Fallen as a whole—if blood was being stolen and transformed into some sort of enhancement drug—this could be huge.

Alec's jaw set with determination. Watcher or not, he couldn't—and wouldn't—just let this one lie.

fourteen

After her forty-eight-hour imprisonment, Claire's heart leapt when she saw Alec at their locker. They'd been sharing it ever since Alec had accidentally mangled her assigned one at the beginning of the school year.

"Hey," she said, wrapping her arms around him from behind.

Alec winced a little as he wiggled to loosen himself from her snare. "Hey."

"You okay?" she asked, releasing him.

"Fine." He turned to kiss her. "You just surprised me is all."

"The Master Assassin didn't sense I was coming? You're getting rusty."

"I'm not the psychic here." Alec smiled. "I guess I just have a lot on my mind. What happened this weekend? Did you get to talk to Helena?"

"Not the way I'd planned." Claire sighed. "Short version: We were right about my other power. I got desperate and tried to use it on my mom because she was pissed that I was late—"

"You're kidding."

"I know, I shouldn't have, but I had no idea it would actually work! Which it *did*, by the way. I mean, holy shit! Helena busted me for it. Hence, grounded for the foreseeable future."

"Shite, I'm sorry." He glanced at her with a worried look. "Although I have to admit, I don't actually know what grounding implies."

Claire grabbed some books from her locker and stuffed them in her backpack. "It means no friends, no fun outside of school hours, and worst of all, no *you*." Her heart caught at the thought. "Just straight home under lock and key. Mom took my phone and has stationed my laptop in the living room. Those messages I sent are the last ones I was able to sneak through."

Alec's expression was mixed. "I kind of get why she's so angry. I mean, even *I* am worried at the thought of you burdened with this gift."

His words almost took the wind out of her. "Burdened? By a *gift?*"

"It's a lot to deal with," Alec insisted, his tone serious. "But I trust you. And they should, too. A weekend of punishment would've been more than enough."

"I'll say. Instead, Helena's threatened to be a psychic security camera wherever I go."

"Bollocks." Alec looked way more sympathetic now. "Thank God she wasn't doing that the other night, when …"

"Actually, she was." Claire shot him an apologetic grimace.

"Oh God." Alec's cheeks turned red. "Well, so much for privacy."

"I wonder if she's watching us right now." Claire glanced skyward and pretended to look for a security camera, extending her middle finger. "Can you see this, Grandma?"

Alec's laughter was drowned out by the ringing of the first bell, signaling five minutes before classes began.

"To be continued at lunch?" Claire closed their locker.

"We could whisper about it in Spanish class," he joked, as they started walking toward the North Quad.

"Señora Gutierrez would give us EMD for not whispering *in Spanish*, and I'm not as fluent as you are in *everything*."

He laughed again. "I recall enjoying serving early morning detention with you. Since date nights are out, it might be the only way for some alone-time."

Claire sighed. "If I didn't think it would cause my mom to break my legs, I'd take you up on it."

It was all Claire could do to keep her mind on her bio quiz, even though she'd studied for it all weekend.

Being grounded was so frustrating. She needed quiet time with Alec, and that was not going to happen. And she desperately needed to talk to Erica about the whole *Camelot* thing.

Claire made her way to Concert Singers and took her seat in the music room. She called out to Erica, but either Erica didn't see Claire's wave, or she deliberately avoided looking in her direction, instead sitting on the far end of the soprano section and burying her nose in her music folder.

Claire couldn't help feeling hurt. She had tried to reach Erica after the cast list was posted. Claire suddenly wondered if Erica might have called or texted her since her phone was confiscated and was feeling let down that Claire hadn't replied. How was Claire supposed to let Erica know she'd been grounded if her friend wouldn't talk to her?

Across the room, in the bass section, she spotted Brian glancing her way. From his expression, it was clear he'd witnessed what was going on. The only reply she could give to his sympathetic look was a shrug.

"So now she's giving both of us the silent treatment," Brian said later, as he and Claire exited the theater building and started up the main stairs toward the cafeteria.

"This whole thing sucks. It's not like it's *my* fault that I was cast as Guinevere."

"Well, it kinda is," Brian countered.

Claire stiffened. "What?"

"You didn't have to try out."

"I tried out to spend more time with Alec," Claire replied defensively. "*And* with Erica."

"Still. You know how much she wanted that part. You didn't have to use your newfound singing power when you auditioned."

"I can't just turn it off, Brian. When I sing now, it just sort of … happens."

"Okay, so, you could've said no to the part."

Claire felt heat rise to her cheeks. "Say no?"

"Yeah. You could've told Ms. Donnelly that you don't feel comfortable with such a big part first time out and let Erica have it."

"But—" Claire began.

Brian held up a silencing hand and looked at her. "No one expects you to do that, CB. I'm just saying: Own up that you *want* the part. You're excited to go from zero to hero."

Claire heaved a sigh, embarrassed now. "Okay. You're right. But it's mostly that I'm excited about being up there with Alec."

"And Neil?" Brian reminded her.

Claire shrugged. "That less so."

"Either way, all of that's cool. You aren't *entirely* blameless, is all. Meanwhile, she's mad at me for something that's totally *not* my fault. I can't help if I'm not into her like she wants."

"True," Claire acknowledged. "But you are kind of rubbing it in her face, going off and dating Kayla so soon after you turned her down."

"I know, but I didn't plan for it," Brian cringed. "We'd chat about nerd stuff here and there and then … something just clicked."

"Shitty timing." Claire wanted to say more in defense of her best friend, but it was hard. Brian really was in a lose-lose situation here.

"When Erica doesn't get her way," Brian offered, "she gets dark and stormy for a while. We just have to weather this together. It'll pass. Eventually."

"Will it? In my case, I'm not so sure. I can't make up with someone who won't even look at me or talk to me."

"So call her. A bitch session over morning coffee is her favorite thing."

"You don't understand. I tried calling and texting her on Friday. She ignored me. And that was my only chance. I got grounded on Saturday, and Mom has my phone."

"Grounded? Why? What'd you do?"

By the time they reached the cafeteria, Claire had given Brian a brief summary of the date-night debacle and the fallout from using her newfound gift, leaving out the part about her grandmother's warning to never use the power. *That* rule stung. She might need that power someday, like her dad had in the subway. She'd never learn how to use it if she didn't test it once in a while, and she didn't want any more people judging her about it.

"Mind control?" Brian stopped outside the cafeteria door, keeping his voice low so they wouldn't be overheard. "Jeez Louise, you've gone all Emma Frost on us now."

"Huh?"

"X-Men. Most of them have one power, but for some reason, she and Wolverine have two."

"It's not a surprise," Claire whispered back. "Vincent predicted that because I'm a Halfblood, I'd have two abilities, just like other Grigori."

"Right, 'cause you're closer to the source than other Fallen, not hundredth or millionth generation."

Claire nodded. "I've been wondering what my second gift would be, and now that I know, it's kind of … overwhelming."

"I think mind control is *way* more badass—and useful—than your other psychic thing."

"Yeah, but it got me busted."

"Only 'cause your grandma's mojo is better than yours."

"Whose mojo are we talking about?" Alec said as he joined them at the door.

"Claire just told me about her new *gift*," Brian answered in a low voice.

"Ah."

Shooting Claire a grin, Brian added, "Warning, CB: If you ever try it on *me*, I will annihilate you."

"You'll have to go through me," interjected Alec.

"You'd have to find out I did it, first," Claire responded devilishly. "If I did it *right*, you wouldn't be able to tell."

Alec and Brian exchanged a worried look at that. Claire held up her hands as if to say *kidding!* and pushed open the door to the cafeteria with a smile.

Ten minutes later, the three of them exited the cafeteria, their lunch trays loaded with barbecued chicken, slaw, and corn on the cob.

"Where should we go?" Alec asked.

"That's right," Claire teased. "'The Table' is the only home you've ever known here."

"The best spots are all taken." Brian's eyes suddenly lit up. "Oh! Got an idea. Follow me."

Brian led the way through an adjoining hallway, then outside along a paved path around the administration building.

Before she could question Brian about where they were going, Alec glanced at her, lowering his voice as they walked. "Hey, I never got to ask you this morning. How'd you get your new *gift* to work on your mom when it didn't work on me?"

"Well for one thing, Helena said it might be a bit harder to mind trick a Grigori," she responded quietly.

"Oh?" "I guess it takes practice."

"Practice?" Alec's green eyes were wary. "Claire, you can't—"

"Yeah, yeah." She hurried on, "Grandma also said that because I'm a Halfblood, I'll probably figure it out pretty fast. And I have a theory. I think I have to be really upset or tense or something for it to have an effect."

"What makes you think that?" Alec asked.

"When I tried to use it on you, I was just being playful. When I used it on my mom, I was superangry. It felt like the power was coming from the knots in my stomach."

"So you need to get all emo to brainwash someone?" interjected Brian.

"Maybe. But I wasn't Hulking out; it was like it was all bottled up inside."

Alec nodded, deep in thought. "*That* must be why the Fallen want your dad."

"My dad?" Claire repeated as they arrived in the dappled sunlight of the North Quad.

"Yeah. Imagine what would happen if *he* used his gift to—" Alec cut off abruptly.

Claire understood why. Brian had led them to a lunch table beneath some shady trees where his new fling, Kayla, was sitting alone with her lunch tray. Spotting them, she rose with a huge smile on her face.

"Yay, you guys came!" Kayla leapt up and wrapped Brian in a warm hug. "I was so bummed—Mary is home sick, and Jess bailed to eat with her boyfriend in the theater lobby. I was afraid I was going to have to fly solo today."

Claire and Alec awkwardly sat down across from her and Brian, exchanging glances and wondering how much Kayla had heard.

They didn't have to wait long for their answer. Kayla's brow scrunched as she cut up her piece of chicken. "So, what's this about some guy using a gift?"

Crap. How was she going to explain this away? "Um, my mom has a … friend … who's really gifted," Claire stammered. "I mean, he's really, really good at … um—"

"Swing dancing," Alec interjected smoothly. "Claire's mom is taking swing-dance classes and asked the guy to be her partner, but he's too shy."

"Lame," said Kayla between chews. "My grandparents met at a dance. I'd love to learn how to swing! Maybe I could take the class with your mom?"

"I'll ask," Claire said hesitantly, desperate to change the subject.

The universe suddenly came through for her. At that moment, Erica walked by, part of the flock surrounding Gabrielle Miller. She looked a little awkward to be mingling with that crowd, but even more bothered when she glanced at Claire and the rest … all sitting with Kayla. Without a word, Erica continued on with her group to another table.

It was the second time Erica had snubbed her that day. Claire felt stung yet again.

Brian watched the gaggle pass by, then said quietly, "Hey CB, what would happen if you tried, you know … *swing dancing* … with *Erica?* Do you think she'd forgive you and start talking to you again?"

Claire shot him a *shut up!* look, horrified at both the implication of the euphemism, and the potential for Kayla to start asking more questions. "That's a terrible idea, Bri. You threatened to annihilate me if I ever tried 'dancing' with you, so why do you think she'd feel any differently?"

Kayla pouted. "Brian! Are you really so antidancing?"

Brian looked like a deer caught in the headlights. "Uh—well—"

Kayla cozied up to Brian. "I was hoping if I take the swing class, that you'd take it with me!"

Claire dug into her food, praying that this lunch would be over soon.

fifteen

"Welcome, everyone, to the start of our little play," said Ms. Donnelly.

Alec sat with the rest of the cast on the theater stage in a double ring of chairs. The drama teacher stood in the center, her auburn hair pulled into a ponytail and her eyes bright as she passed out scripts and rehearsal schedules.

"We've got the largest cast in Emerson's history," Ms. Donnelly continued, "and I'll tell you why. I've been very aware over the years that many students felt hurt or left out when I didn't cast them in a play or musical. This time, I decided to do something different and cast everyone who auditioned. Which gives us a big, wonderful chorus. I hope you'll all sing your hearts out. And that you're happy to be here."

Alec glanced around the circle of students, most of whom were smiling. Erica was an exception. He could tell that Claire, seated beside him, had also noticed Erica's bleak expression and was doing her best to mask her own feelings about the situation.

The other holdout was Neil, who sat directly across from them. He looked conflicted, like even he couldn't tell whether he was glad to be there or not.

"Here's how it's going to work," Ms. Donnelly went on. "Today, we'll read through the script start to finish. Mr. Lang will sing the songs to get you familiar with them. Then for the next eight weeks, you'll be dividing your time between choreography rehearsals with Mrs. Frank in the dance studio, learning the songs in the music room, and blocking out the play scene by scene in the theater with me, until we finally put it all together at the end. Take a look at the rehearsal schedules and plan your lives accordingly."

A quick perusal of the schedule showed Alec he would have very little time outside of school and rehearsal until the show was over. To his surprise, he found himself looking forward to it, partly because he'd be spending most of that time with Claire. But there was another reason, too. Whenever his duties had allowed him to attend theater in the past—in dozens of countries across the world—he'd enjoyed it, and often wondered what the experience of putting on a play was like. Now he was going to find out.

He wasn't worried about the acting part. As Claire had pointed out, for more than a hundred years, he'd been pretending to be something he wasn't. Hopefully, now he could use his skills for fun.

"For those of you who've never been in a play before," Ms. Donnelly continued, "no matter how big or small you think your role is, please know that if the rehearsal schedule calls for you to be here the entire time, that's not negotiable. If you have downtime, you're welcome to do your homework, but just be ready."

They soon segued into the reading of the play itself. Ms. Donnelly read the stage directions while Mr. Lang played the piano at the side of the stage whenever a song came up. He was a tenor with an exceptional range, enabling him to perform decent renditions of all the music. Those members of the cast who already knew the big production numbers were encouraged to sing along. Occasionally, Ms. Donnelly would halt the reading and mention lines she wanted to cut or change, which everyone marked on their scripts.

Although some of the students read through their parts casually, Alec did his best to act the words. Almost as if it were a competition, Neil gave his part an enthusiastic go as well. Alec was relieved to find, when it got to the romantic scenes between Guinevere and Lancelot, that he didn't feel as jealous or resentful as he'd expected. It still bothered him that Claire and Neil were playing lovers, but in this reading at least, it felt pretty tame and chaste. He had nothing to worry about, he told himself. He and Claire were solid. Their relationship was open and honest.

Well, that wasn't *quite* true. Alec felt a dash of guilt recalling the scuffle last night, which he still hadn't told Claire about. After his encounter outside the bar, he'd returned the coolers of blood to UCLA anonymously. According to the GPS tracking device he'd placed on the Fallen's car, the guy had escaped his trunk a half hour after their fight and driven off to a residential section of Silverlake. Alec had gone up there and checked out the house but saw nothing suspicious.

It was best not to bring up the incident, he decided. Claire hated it when he got involved in a fight, and she had plenty on her mind already. He had no idea what those bags of blood were for, but it was a safe bet that whatever the Fallen were up to, it wasn't good. Until he knew more, better not to add to her worries.

Glancing sideways at Claire, Alec noticed that she seemed more relaxed than she'd been in a long while, as if focusing on the script and the music allowed her to shove all the drama of school and home and her new gift aside. He suddenly realized that he was feeling more relaxed, too.

Maybe this play would be a good thing for both of them.

sixteen

Claire was walking past the library just as break ended Wednesday morning, gloveless and eating a blueberry muffin, when she noticed something strange.

Gabrielle Miller was staring into her locker with a frown.

More than a frown. Gabrielle's forehead was so furrowed that her perfectly plucked eyebrows were nearly touching. Her mouth was scrunched up into an almost-scowl, and Claire felt certain she detected a hint of moisture in the girl's eyes.

This was totally out of character for Gabrielle. She was the perpetual center of her own universe, with a sunny, confident personality. It was weird even to see her standing alone, since she was typically surrounded by a pack of admirers, both male and female (including Erica, nowadays).

Claire paused, popping the last bite of muffin into her mouth and wondering what was going on. Gabrielle took off her cardigan, tucking it around her backpack strap as she shrugged the pack onto her shoulders. Just then, her best friends darted up to her, Courtney shrieking "There you are!" while Ashley cried, "Omigod, you'll never guess who just asked me out!"

Gabrielle's dark expression vanished as though it had never existed, replaced by an instant smile. She slammed her locker shut, and the chattering threesome moved off, no one but Claire noticing the sweater slip out and fall to the ground.

Claire bent down and picked up the cardigan. The moment she touched it, Claire was struck by a jolt of heat and a slight twinge in her stomach. *Crap*, she thought, recognizing the signs of a vision about to start. She cursed herself for not putting her gloves back on. She didn't enjoy being temporarily tossed into someone else's mind and body, and was about to drop the sweater when some instinct told her to hang on and see where the vision took her.

As Claire straightened up, still holding the sweater, the world around her blurred and shifted.

She was standing in front of Gabrielle's locker. Manicured hands that weren't her own flipped the combination and opened the door. The locker interior was wallpapered with a collage of photos of members of the junior class, including Gabrielle's and Neil's portraits as Homecoming King and Queen, and team photos of the volleyball and tennis teams.

"Hey, Gabby," a male voice called out from the other side of the open locker door.

The hands tilted the door closed, revealing Jason Tate, who was at his locker down the row.

Butterflies danced in her stomach at the sight of Jason's self-conscious smile.

"What's up," she heard herself reply in Gabrielle's voice. "I've been looking for you."

"Oh, really?" One of Jason's dark eyebrows raised in surprise as he closed his locker.

"Yeah. The girls and I are breaking in my new Jacuzzi on Saturday night while my parents are in Palm Springs. Want to join us?"

Jason's other eyebrow lifted to join the first. "You want to hot tub in January? That's crazy."

"This isn't Minnesota! Anyway, we're gonna raid the bar. That should keep us warm."

"Wow …"

"Come on, I just got a new bikini. I need an excuse to show it off."

Something changed on Jason's face. His eyes flicked to the floor, as if he was trying hard to dig up the right words to respond. "Um. It sounds nice, but … not really my thing."

"Okay. So what is your thing?" Gabrielle responded quickly. "Movies? Roller coasters? Paintball? I'm free on Friday."

"Wish I could, but this Friday we're sort of doing family stuff." He looked genuinely sorry. "Thanks for asking, though. Catch you later." Shouldering his backpack, he gave her a small smile and walked off.

Claire felt a crushing sense of disappointment and confusion as she/Gabrielle turned back to her locker door, her focus zeroing in for a long moment on a photo of Jason in the posted collage. The image became fuzzy as her vision clouded with moisture. Blinking away tears, she took off her sweater, tucking it around her backpack. Then a female voice shrieked:

"There you are!"

Ashley's voice cried, "Omigod, you'll never guess who just asked me out!"

A bell was ringing somewhere.

The vision filled with static and abruptly ended. Claire blinked and found herself rooted to the spot where she'd picked up the cardigan. A bell was ringing, signaling five minutes 'til the end of break. Students darted past her, hurrying to class. Claire stared at the sweater in her hands, trembling as she struggled to make the adjustment back to reality.

A voice came from the end of the row. "What?" It was Neil, looking at her defensively.

Dear God, Claire thought. Brian once mentioned that she had a weird, thousand-yard stare whenever she got a vision. Had Neil noticed her doing that?

Claire cleared her throat. "Hmm?"

"You were staring at me."

Her cheeks flushed as she tugged on her gloves. "Uh, no, sorry, I was just thinking about … something. I didn't even know you were there."

Neil shook his head and tucked his thumbs into his backpack straps. "Figures."

As he turned and climbed up the nearby stairwell, Claire again called out, "Sorry!" but he didn't look back.

Still trembling slightly, she folded the sweater, stowed it in her backpack, and headed off to class, her mind whirling with what she'd just seen and heard between Gabrielle and Jason. It had obviously happened a few minutes ago and must be why Gabrielle had looked so upset.

Clearly, Gabrielle had a major crush on Jason. Based on the intense feelings she'd experienced while in the girl's point of view, Claire sensed that rejection was *not* a familiar emotion to someone as popular as Gabrielle Miller. Claire kind of felt sorry for her. The two of them weren't exactly best friends, but Gabrielle *had* been nice in the wake of the scaffolding incident, as well as during the whole Homecoming Queen/Princess thing.

She felt sorry for Jason, too. Everyone knew that Jason was so shy, he'd never dated anyone before—at least not at school. Did he really have some vague "family thing" on Friday night? Even if hot tubbing wasn't his thing, Claire sensed that Jason had wanted to say yes to Gabrielle's offers but didn't have the nerve. He seemed like such a nice, quiet guy.

Maybe he just needed a little push in the right direction. If Claire talked to Jason, said a few encouraging words, hopefully he'd grow a pair and ask Gabrielle out. Then he and Gabrielle could end up as happy as she and Alec were (without all the paranormal drama).

Jason was in AP bio with her that period. After class let out, Claire hurried up to him, pulling Gabrielle's sweater out of her backpack. "Hey, Jason!"

He paused and turned to her. Claire had never talked to Jason in her life, but Emerson Academy was so small, everyone knew each other's names.

"Hey, Claire," he answered, surprised.

"Gabby dropped this by her locker. I figure she'll want it ASAP. Would you mind giving it back to her?"

His eyes widened. "Me? Why?"

"I don't know if I'll see her again today, but you guys have ceramics next, right? I've seen you in there on my way to Spanish."

"Okay, sure." He took the sweater.

"By the way." Claire lowered her voice. "In case you didn't know: I overheard her talking to Ashley and Courtney. She's *into* you, Jason."

"Oh, yeah?" He looked down, like he had earlier when he was talking to Gabrielle. *Man, was this guy shy, or what?*

"She's dying to go out with you. All you have to do is ask." She saw hesitation on his face. He was clearly stalling, conflicted.

"Why do you even care?" he asked quietly.

"I care because I want to see you guys happy. I thought that knowing it was a sure thing would make taking a shot at it a little easier."

He shrugged a little awkwardly. "Okay. Well. I'll definitely give her the sweater."

Claire was frustrated. He obviously wasn't taking the bait. By the time he worked up the nerve to ask her out, they'd probably be leaving for college. *If only he'd get over his nerves and just … try.*

Then it hit Claire. She had the power of persuasion. Clearly, Jason needed more than a gentle push. And she could make this happen.

Helena and Alec kept telling her not to use her mind-control ability. But in this instance, she could really do some good. If it didn't work, who would even know? Just Helena, maybe, *if* she was watching Claire right now. But that was a chance she'd have to take. What was that phrase? Something about great power and great responsibility?

Jason was halfway down the stairs toward the art studio when Claire blurted, "Jason, wait!"

He turned to Claire with a quizzical expression. She hurried down to him.

"Listen to me." She drummed up all the emotions she was feeling into a tight ball inside her, training all her thoughts on her objective. "You and Gabby would be really good together. Just use the sweater as an excuse to talk to her, and ask her out."

She waited tensely for what seemed like an ice age, but he didn't reply, still appearing conflicted. Clearly, Claire needed to crank it up a notch. She focused more intently on the passion deep in her core. "You can do it," she went on, at the same time thinking at him over and over: *Ask her out. Ask her out. Ask her out.*

That did the trick. The now-familiar sense of connection between Claire and her target tugged at her like a fish caught on a line. She was thrilled to see Jason's eyes glaze over as he nodded, newfound confidence on his face. "Okay. Thanks." He turned, sweater in hand, and trotted off to class.

Score! Claire thought triumphantly.

She wished she could revel in her success with somebody—Alec especially. Claire fidgeted with the lapis-lazuli bracelet he'd given her, considering whether or not to tell him but then nixed the idea. He'd just lecture her again.

Better to wait on sharing until she had some positive results to gloat about. *Then* maybe he'd understand her point of view. After all, she just wanted to help people like he did.

seventeen

The clock on Alec's apartment wall read an ungodly 2:45.

It was Saturday morning, the start of a holiday weekend. Alec was itching for something to do. Play rehearsals took up a lot of his time now, and although enjoyable—the scenes with Claire and the singing part, in particular—it felt a bit frivolous. Homework took mere minutes for him to complete.

He wished he could fill his evenings with Claire, but she was still grounded.

The thought of occupying his time with any of the trappings of his former, spartan life—meditation, cooking, exercising, weapons cleaning—chafed at him. Even his apartment felt like a cage.

Frustrated, Alec gulped down some unsweetened iced tea and stared at his laptop.

A week had gone by since he'd attached the GPS tracking device to Lance's Lexus. Every night since, Alec had been waiting for the dot to move, indicating anything worth following. But it hadn't budged. After the beating Alec had dished out, it would be understandable if the guy kept still for a few days. But a week? Lance should be on the move by now.

People didn't randomly carry around trunks full of blood. Alec wondered if UCLA was the only place the guy was stealing from. Was he stealing anything else? Working alone, or part of a larger group? Alec had scanned the Internet for clinics reporting stolen blood but found nothing. Which didn't surprise him. The Fallen were good at covering their tracks.

If only he could tap the latest info on the Grigori Nexus. But connecting to that psychic network would alert his kind to his presence. In his old life, he could have roughed up a couple of Fallen lowlifes for information. But he'd promised himself not to go there anymore.

Something *wrong* was going on, Alec knew it. He needed to figure out what.

It was a risk to put himself out there. But surely he could do a little digging without drawing unwanted attention to himself? He *had* to get to the bottom of this thing. But that required help from his target.

A few minutes later, it happened. The dot on his screen finally started moving. Wherever Lance was going, Alec doubted it was a social call—it was 3 A.M. Alec leapt to his feet, grabbed his keys, and dashed to his car, setting the laptop on the passenger seat of his Mustang.

As he drove, Alec monitored the progress of the glowing mass of pixels as it slowly snaked across the satellite map of the city, hoping he could reach the target before it arrived at its destination. But Alec was still a good fifteen minutes away when the dot stopped at Cedars-Sinai Hospital in Beverly Hills.

To Alec's frustration, after only a brief stop, the GPS dot was already on the move again, continuing eastward on city streets. *Damn.* He'd missed whatever had happened at the hospital. At least he could find out where the guy was going now and what he'd taken, if anything.

By the time he caught up to the dot on his tracker, Alec found himself in a less-than-savory part of downtown. Amid a sea of old, abandoned warehouses, he spotted the silver Lexus turning down a small street. Alec followed the car until it pulled up to a sliding gate in front of a graffiti-covered concrete building, surrounded by a tall, chain-link fence. Watching from a discreet distance, Alec saw the gate open remotely. The Lexus drove inside, vanishing around the rear of the warehouse.

There wasn't a soul visible on the street or inside the fence. A security camera was mounted above a sliding gate. Alec made sure to park a good distance out of the camera's view.

Grabbing the tonfa from his trunk, Alec quickly made his way into a nearby alley. He followed the chain-link fence to a spot that was still out of sight of the camera. Holding his weapon tightly, Alec leapt into the air, using telekinesis to float the rest of the way over the fence and slow his drop.

When his feet met the pavement on the other side, they barely made a sound. Crouching low, Alec checked to see if anyone—or anything—had seen him. Thankfully, nothing stirred in the damp night air. However, some of the rusted warehouse windows glowed with light.

Alec moved around to the back of the warehouse, where he spotted a few parked vehicles, including the silver Lexus, which had its trunk open. From his vantage point, Alec couldn't see what was inside. A steel roll door large enough to fit an eighteen-wheeler was open nearby, greenish fluorescent light spilling out from the opening.

Moving closer to the light, Alec heard a sound from inside the building and ducked behind a dumpster. Peering around the edge, he saw Lance exiting the warehouse, accompanied by a heavyset man in a road-worker orange puffy jacket and a trucker-style baseball cap. From the trunk of the Lexus, the man hoisted out two coolers with the Cedars-Sinai logo.

The bags were labeled exactly like the ones Alec had seen before: HUMAN BLOOD.

So, this *was* all about blood. But why?

The heavyset man nodded, handed something small to Lance, and trudged back inside the warehouse. Lance stared at the thing in his hands as if it were a prize. Alec recognized it now: it was a small vial, identical to the one he'd confiscated outside the bar. Clutching it tightly, Lance hopped in his car and drove away.

Alec considered his next move. Should he could sneak inside the building to learn more? Just then, he spied a gaunt man with slicked-back gray hair, watching the scene from inside the roll door while balancing a pump-action shotgun on his shoulder.

Shite, Alec thought. He'd brought a stick to a gunfight.

Once the heavyset man was inside, the older guy dropped the door closed, leaving Alec alone to process what he'd seen. It seemed like the guys in the warehouse were using junkies like Lance to steal blood, which they turned into some sort of drug as payment.

From his pocket, Alec pulled the small vial he'd confiscated earlier. He had no way to analyze what it was. But—since it seemed to have enhanced Lance's strength and speed—Alec had an idea. The thought that members of the Fallen could be distributing something so potentially powerful was frightening. Going into the lion's den right now, though, so woefully unprepared, would be idiotic.

Not yet, he told himself, making his way back to the alley and over the fence. *Not tonight.*

It would take awhile to form a solid plan of entry. But he'd be back.

eighteen

A three-day weekend was absolute murder when you were grounded.

Claire spent the entire time barely speaking to her mom or Helena, just answering their questions with a simple "yes" or "no," and eating all meals in her room. Deep down, she felt guilty about what she'd done. She knew she'd screwed up. No one should try to brainwash their mom. But house arrest? For however long her mom felt like? That was harsh.

Claire sensed that her mother felt bad about the situation, too. Although she didn't ease up on Claire's punishment, her mom got up early on Tuesday morning and made Claire's favorite breakfast: French toast topped with melted cheddar and crispy bacon. It was too delicious to resist. Claire enjoyed every bite (actually eating in the kitchen!) and expanded her vocabulary of late to include a brief but neutral "thanks."

As Claire was leaving for school, Helena finally snapped, "Young lady, how long are you going to maintain this mono-syllabic routine?"

"How long until you get around to digging up 'intel' on your son?" Claire shot back.

"You're acting very adolescent about all this."

"I *am* an adolescent," Claire responded, hefting her back-pack and heading for the door.

"You do know that you're acting just like Erica, right?" Alec said bluntly on their way from AP English to Spanish class, after Claire told him about what had happened that morning.

"Meaning what, exactly?" Claire asked.

"You're ignoring their attempts at peacemaking."

"It's a totally different situation. If Mom and Grandma really want to make peace, they should unground me or actually bother to look for my dad."

Just then, Claire caught sight of Gabrielle Miller heading down the stairs, holding hands with Jason Tate, both of them with smiles on their faces. Claire couldn't prevent a gasp of delight. *It worked!* They looked so cozy together. *Guess he found time in his busy schedule to go out with her after all!*

Alec gave her a sidelong glance. "What's up?"

"Um … Nothing important," Claire said quickly. Now wasn't the time to tell Alec about her little experiment. It was just minutes before class, and he was already in a mood. Changing the subject, she added, "So, how was your weekend?"

Alec seemed to choose his words carefully. "Pretty boring without you around."

"Oh, I'll bet you say that to all the girls." Claire laughed.

The bell rang as they took their seats in Spanish. A couple of minutes later, Señora Gutierrez rushed in the door.

"So sorry I'm late. Office hours went long today." Pausing behind her desk to catch her breath, the teacher opened a folder, and added with a solemn expression, "Our first item of business today is one of my least favorite tasks: handing out warning notices."

Claire sat back in her seat, surprised. Warning notices were given out midsemester to anyone with a C- or less, reports that had to be shared with their parents.

Señora Gutierrez stepped forward with a single piece of paper, the size of a postcard. Claire felt bad for the unlucky student, whoever it was, and hoped it wouldn't be Neil. When the teacher passed by Neil, Claire blew out a sigh of relief. It seemed that her tutoring last fall was still paying off.

To Claire's complete astonishment, Señora Gutierrez stopped immediately before *her*, silently handing Claire the notice. Claire accepted the piece of paper mutely, her face growing hot with embarrassment. How could this be happening? She was doing just fine in Spanish. Wasn't she?

"Claire," the teacher intoned dramatically, "please do us the favor of reading your notice aloud."

The room had gone dead silent. Claire felt every pair of eyes trained on her and couldn't help but see the expression of pained surprise on Alec's face. Could her humiliation be any greater?

Her stomach churning, Claire quickly scanned the notice. Oh. *Oh!* A smile curved her lips, as she read aloud:

SPECIAL REPORT TO PARENTS
Class: *Spanish III*
Claire Brennan is not making satisfactory progress for the
following reason(s):
<u>*She refuses to dream in Spanish.*</u>
Grade to date: *A.*

The class erupted into laughter.

"Just an old Spanish teacher's attempt at humor," Señora Gutierrez announced with a little grin. "I hope you'll forgive me." She laid a hand on Claire's bare upper arm and gave her a friendly squeeze.

Claire started to join in the laughter, when all of a sudden she felt heat diffuse her body, and her visuals started to go wonky, signaling the onslaught of a vision. *Oh no oh no not now not now,* Claire thought. Then … *WHAM.*

Claire—as Mrs. Gutierrez—was reclining on a couch in an unfamiliar living room, her legs propped up on the coffee table, a red pen and a stack of papers in her hand.

"Mom," a female voice pleaded. "If you won't do it for yourself, do it for me."

Claire heard herself reply in Mrs. Gutierrez's voice: "I told you, I don't have time, Rachel. There aren't enough hours in the day."

A woman who looked to be in her early twenties sank down close by on the sofa. Her long, dark hair was twisted into a knot atop her head, and her brown eyes glistened with unshed tears as she clenched her hands in anguish. "You have to make the time, Mom. The doctor said exercise is really important for your heart."

"I get plenty of physical activity every day at school, just walking up and down those stairs."

"It's not enough! You heard the doctor. You have to raise your heart rate to a certain level, and you can only do that with sustained aerobic exercise for twenty to thirty minutes."

Claire/Mrs. Gutierrez laughed. "What? You want me to start jogging or dancing? At my age?"

"You have to do something, Mom." A tear trickled down the young woman's cheek. "I don't want to lose you."

"Stop worrying, honey. You won't lose me." Claire/ Mrs. Gutierrez turned back to the papers in her lap with a dismissive wave of her hand. "Now go home, it's late, and I have all these tests and papers to grade."

Claire's body shuddered slightly as the vision ended. Blinking, she found herself back in her Spanish classroom, her upper arm being jiggled by Señora Gutierrez, who was looking down at her with concern.

"Claire? Claire? *¡Dios Mío!* Are you all right?"

Claire caught Alec's eye. She could tell he knew what had just happened. If everyone in class had been glancing in her direction before, now they were positively staring. "Sorry. I'm fine. I was just ... so surprised by all this."

Señora Gutierrez let go of Claire's arm and stepped back, attempting a smile. "No, *I'm* sorry. It looks like that warning notice gave you a bigger shock than I'd intended."

A chuckle rippled through the classroom again as Señora Gutierrez went back to her desk. "*Ahora,*" she continued in Spanish, "Let's get started."

As class went on, Claire's mind kept drifting back to the vision she'd had. It worried her that her teacher had a medical condition—clearly, something to do with her heart—yet she wasn't following her doctor's orders. Señora Gutierrez's daughter was worried, too.

Claire's experiment with Jason had been so successful, she yearned to try again. What better way to practice her newfound talent, she thought, than to help someone in need? Maybe she could somehow ... *persuade* Señora Gutierrez to exercise.

She just had to figure out how and when to go about it.

Claire completed the daily written exercise as fast as she could and spent the remaining free time going through various scenarios in her head. By the time class was over, she had devised the perfect solution.

"So what did you see?" Alec asked quietly, as they left Spanish and headed for their next class with the hordes of other students.

Claire hesitated. If she told Alec about her vision, and he later got wind of a change in Señora Gutierrez's routine, he might suspect that Claire had had something to do with it. Making a face, she whispered, "Just some argument Señora

Gutierrez was having with her daughter. I had no business being there."

"Awkward."

"Yeah. Sometimes it sucks to have these visions."

During her break, Claire did some online research. When the final bell released her from AP bio, which she didn't share with Alec, she dashed to the upper level of the South Quad.

She only had fifteen minutes until she needed to be at the theater for rehearsal. Quickly, Claire found the small room that was shared by two of the Spanish teachers. She lucked out: Señora Gutierrez was just dropping into the chair at her desk for after-school office hours, and she was alone.

"*Hola*," Claire said.

The teacher smiled. "Claire? Is everything all right? I hope you didn't mind my little joke today."

"No, it was cute. I'm here about something else. Can I ask your advice about something? It's kind of a personal thing."

"Certainly. I don't know if I can be of help, but I'm happy to try."

Claire plunged ahead with the speech she'd prepared. "It's about my mom. Her doctor says she needs to exercise more, but no matter what I say, she won't listen. She says she doesn't have time. I'm so worried about her."

Señora Gutierrez's eyebrows lifted. "You sound exactly like my daughter."

"Do I? Somebody told me that you are obsessed with exercising, that you never miss a day at the gym."

"Oh, that's not—" Señora Gutierrez began with a short laugh.

"Which is why I came to you," Claire interrupted, focusing on her intense, inner emotions, and the subliminal message she was trying to send to Señora Gutierrez: *You need to exercise. You need to exercise.* "I found a gym not far from where we live, and I was wondering: do you know if it's a good place or not?" Claire handed the teacher a piece of paper with the gym's website and address.

"I have no idea," Señora Gutierrez replied hesitantly.

Her eyes, Claire noticed with growing satisfaction, were starting to look a bit glassy, and Claire felt lines of invisible energy growing taut between her heart and her teacher's.

"I hear they have great equipment and all sorts of classes," Claire went on. "I keep thinking my mom might be able to get some of her reading and busy work done while she's on the treadmill." As Claire spoke, she mentally pulled those lines like puppet strings, thinking at Señora Gutierrez: *Your life might be on the line. Schoolwork can wait. Join the gym! Join the gym!*

Gradually, Señora Gutierrez's face shifted to the silent, starry-eyed, complacent expression Claire had hoped for. "I have some money saved up," Claire finished, "and I was thinking of buying her a trial membership. What do you think? Should I do it?"

"I think that's a wonderful idea," Señora Gutierrez said, staring at the note Claire had given her. "I'm sure your mother will appreciate it. And you know what, I think I'll stop by this gym today myself and sign up for a membership."

"Great, Señora Gutierrez!" Claire cried. She'd gone for it—hook, line, and sinker!

As she sped down the hill to the theater complex, Claire couldn't stop smiling. What were Helena and Alec talking about, saying that this power of hers was dangerous? It was amazing! She was helping people!

"Hey, you look happy," Alec commented, as Claire raced into the theater auditorium, where the entire cast had assembled.

Should I tell him now? she wondered.

But this wasn't news you could just casually blurt out. Anyway, there was no time. Ms. Donnelly clapped her hands and invited everyone up to the stage to work on the first production number.

"I had a good day," Claire responded, kissing him. She'd tell him later, when they had time to talk about it.

The week was over before Claire knew it. Fridays were short at Emerson, letting out at one thirty, just in time for a late lunch.

Claire dropped Alec off in the village to pick up a pizza for the two of them, then took her car to gas up nearby. She'd just finished paying at the pump when she sensed someone behind her.

"Hey, Claire."

The familiar female voice sent panic rushing up Claire's spine. She whirled to find Celeste and Rico blocking access to the driver's side door.

What do they want now? And wait—they always traveled in a pack. Where was Javed?

Suddenly, Claire felt a rough hand on the back of her neck. There was a crackling sound, her whole body jolted—and to her horror, she was unable to move.

Claire was caught from behind and lifted off her feet. Every muscle in her body felt rigid, yet at the same time they were vibrating. Is this what it was like to be Tasered?

Rico opened the rear door of the car, and someone shoved her in the back seat.

It was Javed. Alec had told her that Javed's gifts were electrical, so he must have been the one who zapped her.

The trio piled into the car around her, the boys in the front and Celeste in back, with Claire's head on her lap. Rico gunned the car onto the street.

Claire lay there, paralyzed, unable to utter a word, her mind racing as she stared up in terror at Celeste. Why had there been no psychic warning from Helena that these three were about to abduct her?

"Don't worry," Celeste said softly, stroking Claire's hair, "this will all be over soon."

nineteen

Claire tried to speak. It was the only way her mind-control power seemed to work, and she needed to get herself free from the Fallen trio. But all she mustered was a hoarse moan. Desperately, she tried to grab ahold of Celeste's mind: *Let me go, Let me go.* But it didn't work.

Trying a new tactic, Claire focused on the touch of Celeste's bare fingers against her forehead, trying to get a vision from her as to why she was here and what they wanted. Nothing happened. Maybe getting her nerves fried by Javed had jumbled that ability, too.

She was stuck, powerless, on her way to who knows where. If her car had been left by the side of the road, Alec might have figured out she'd been kidnapped. But since they'd driven off in her own car, he'd have no idea what was going on. As they rumbled along, Claire prayed that Alec would worry when she didn't pick him up at the pizza place and would start looking for her.

That hope was dashed when Celeste reached into Claire's backpack and took out her phone. Using voice-recognition mode, Celeste dictated a message: "Hey, Handsome, so sorry, I gotta skip rehearsal. Family emergency. Don't worry, I'm okay." Celeste then shut off the phone, smiling.

As she stared up at Celeste's face, Claire caught a glimpse of a tiny, translucent plastic device just inside Celeste's ear canal.

They looked like the fanciest wireless earbuds Claire had ever seen. Was Celeste listening to music while she kidnapped her?

Claire was unable to see anything out the window except the tops of trees and telephone poles rushing by. Adrenaline pumped through her paralyzed body, only increasing the terror that seemed to infuse her every nerve. How long did a stun gun's effect usually last? Not that it mattered. Javed wasn't an ordinary Taser.

Finally, the car slowed to a stop just as she started to feel a tingling in her fingertips, a slow, painful awakening that gradually spread to the rest of her limbs. As the guys got out, Claire began to feel hot, and her skin started itching like crazy. She sat up, scratching her arms fiercely.

Celeste shook her head. "Don't scratch, sweetie. The feeling will pass, and in the meantime, you'll only hurt yourself."

Claire made fists, trying to get her bearings as Celeste guided her out of the vehicle. Javed and Rico shoved their hands under her armpits and yanked her upright. Claire violently yanked herself away from both of them.

"Easy, girl," Rico warned with a smug grin.

Finally, Claire felt steady enough to look around. They were parked on a circular driveway in front of one of the most beautiful houses she'd ever seen. It reminded her of one of her mom's travel posters of a fabulous hilltop estate in Tuscany. Three stories high, the sand-colored stonework and stucco building had countless arched windows and doorways and was topped by a red tile roof. The lush landscaping included tall palm and cypress trees, pale flagstone paths, and numerous flowerbeds.

"Can you walk?" Celeste asked.

"Let's find out." Claire was relieved to have her voice back even though it was a raspy crackle. She needed water, and her skin felt like needles were sticking into it. She took a step, then another.

"Wonderful. Follow me." Celeste walked off down a path that wound around the side of the house. Claire followed, with the boys close behind.

There has to be a way out of here, Claire thought. But a high fence surrounded the property, and there was no way she could just dash off, with Celeste's two meatheads marching behind her. Now that she had her voice back, though, she could try her new power again. This was exactly the type of situation she'd been arguing with Helena about—a time when her power was necessary to protect herself. She was thankful she'd been practicing.

Claire trained her thoughts on Rico and Javed. She'd never tried to influence two people's minds at once before, but it was worth a shot. "This is a bad move, guys," she said, knotting her stomach up with fury. "No way is Alec going to buy that B.S. text message." At the same time, she thought at them: *Let me go. Let me go. Let me go.* Waiting for her metaphysical fishing lines to catch hold, she silently repeated the mantra in her mind, continuing aloud, "Alec will be coming for me—and you—if you don't let me go right now."

"Great," sneered Javed.

"Let him come," Rico agreed.

Claire glanced back at them anxiously. No glassy eyes, no subliminal connection with her targets. Clearly, her efforts weren't working. Why? Helena had warned her that it would be more difficult to influence a Grigori or a Fallen. But she'd already done it successfully to Celeste two weeks ago. Claire tried again, saying, "Alec is probably on his way right now," while projecting: *Stop this. Let me go. Let me go.*

But all she got in response was another comment from Rico. "We'd look forward to it. Dipshit's been asking for it the past couple weeks."

Wait—what? That statement caught Claire off guard and disrupted her focus. *Asking for it?* What did Rico mean?

Before she could wonder any further, they emerged onto a stone terrace at the rear of the villa, which had an incredible view of the green treetops and scattered rooftops from downtown all the way to the beach. Yet all the windows on the house were shuttered by wooden blinds.

As Celeste opened a rear door, Claire had one last escape notion: what would happen if she leapt over the railing at the edge of the terrace? What was on the other side? A hill, or just empty space?

She never had a chance to find out because Rico and Javed grabbed her and forced her inside. The room they entered was shrouded in dim light, but Claire made out a long, mahogany table and numerous chairs beneath a crystal chandelier. She was then led down a darkened hallway, and finally through a brick-lined archway into a large living room.

Every single window in the room, as well as the French doors, was shuttered, letting in only narrow shafts of light. Through the dimness, Claire made out a high, open-beamed ceiling, a massive stone fireplace, and a bunch of comfortable-looking couches and chairs upholstered in tasteful colors. A glossy black grand piano stood in one corner. Everywhere she looked were antiques that rivaled Helena's in their beauty and uniqueness.

A low, central glass table held three pairs of silver candlesticks with tall, lit candles, illuminating platters of fruit and sandwiches, several crystal glasses, and a pitcher of some kind of dark beverage. To Claire's embarrassment, her stomach growled at the sight of the food. She hadn't realized how hungry she was.

There didn't seem to be anyone else there. Rico, Celeste, and Javed all just stood at her side, as if waiting for something.

"Well, this looks sufficiently dark and creepy," Claire commented.

"That's not precisely what I was going for," drawled a hushed male voice. The speaker appeared from the shadows of an adjoining doorway and strode into the room.

Claire stared at him, unable to prevent a little gasp.

He was the most handsome man Claire had ever seen. Well over six feet tall, he wore dark slacks, a purple button-down shirt, and a fitted, vintage tapestry vest that hugged his slender frame. He looked about thirty. His short, honey-colored hair and mustache were impeccably groomed, and spots of color bloomed in an otherwise pale face.

"I always hope," the man intoned, his ice-blue eyes sparkling with intelligence as he sipped red wine from a crystal goblet, "that my guests will find the decor rather pleasant."

Claire swallowed hard, searching for something to say. "Maybe you should try opening the blinds. And a window or two. And actually treat people like guests—instead of kidnapping them."

He nodded with regret. "Forgive me. But it was vital that I speak with you. We employed the most expedient method. Celeste assured me that you would refuse again if we asked nicely."

Again? Claire suddenly recalled what Alec had told her about this guy and how dangerous he was. "You're Shane Malcolm."

"Last I checked." The man smiled as he swirled his wine.

Claire bit her lip, glancing at Celeste. "*He's* your boss?"

"In the dreamy flesh." Celeste strolled to the table of food and plucked a sprig of grapes from a tray. Javed and Rico eyed the sandwiches hungrily.

"Please, help yourself, Claire," Malcolm said. "All this is here for you." He darted a glare at Celeste, who put back the grapes.

Although she was starving, Claire had no intention of touching anything on that table.

"Celeste," Malcolm added, "would you and the boys kindly leave us and keep an eye out for unexpected callers?"

Looking disappointed, the trio strode out of the room.

"Holler if you need a refill," Celeste said, nodding toward Malcolm's glass.

There must be some way out of this, Claire thought desperately. Her powers of persuasion hadn't worked on the others, and she had less confidence they'd sway someone as powerful as Malcolm—but there weren't many options left. Tightening her stomach into a ball, she forced her will into her words. "This is a bad idea. You should let me walk out of here."

Her mind kept hammering the thought: *Let me go, let me go* toward Malcolm's mind. But again, instead of the dazed look and tendrils of psychic connection she'd produced in others, Malcolm just cocked his head at her for a moment, his brow furrowing. Then his features relaxed, as if he'd suddenly realized something. "Ah, good, you *have* developed that talent after all. Well done."

Claire stifled a gasp. Had he just figured out what she was trying to do?

Tapping his ear, Malcolm shook his head almost apologetically and went on, "That's not going to work on any of us. We've learned to be prepared."

What was he talking about, Claire wondered. Why was he tapping his ear?

"You seem confused," Malcolm continued with a little smile. "Allow me to enlighten you. How do you prevent someone's vocal frequency from brainwashing you? You filter it out."

Then she saw it: Malcolm was wearing the same tiny, wireless earbuds as Celeste. Horror spiraled through her as she finally understood. *These people have figured out a way to block my power.* No wonder she hadn't been able to influence any of them. *The bodyguard in that hotel room who injected my father— was he wearing something similar?*

"Let's get down to business, shall we?" Malcolm gestured to one of the sofas.

This new development was so upsetting and distracting, Claire found it hard to process what he was saying. "What?"

"Won't you have a seat?"

"Why?" she said cautiously, struggling to stay calm. "How long is this going to take, Mr. Malcolm?"

"Just Malcolm will do, thank you. And that depends on you." He took another sip from his goblet. "I believe that we can help each other, and I hope that by the end of our conversation, you will agree."

"I doubt it." Claire sank reluctantly onto a couch and crossed her arms in front of her chest.

He laughed, a bold, infectious sound. "We're not off to a very promising start, I agree." He relaxed into a dark blue chair and set down his glass on a wooden end table that looked hundreds of years old. "Next time I see your father, I'll tell him his young lady is possessed of a fiery spirit."

"You know where my father is, I get it," Claire replied stonily. "You people keep dangling that like a carrot in front of me. How many times do Alec and I have to say it? We don't need your help."

"Is that so? From what I can tell, you aren't making much progress on your own. And Alec is no longer important in this regard. His late-night activities make it clear he isn't interested in working for my organization. Quite the opposite."

Late-night activities? That must be what Rico was talking about. "What do you mean?"

"He assaulted a member of my organization, stole crucial material, and has been poking his nose into matters that don't concern him. Specifically, he seems intent on screwing with my medicine supply, which *I* need to survive. In a way, he's trying to kill me, albeit slowly."

Claire was so shocked she didn't know how to reply. *What medicine supply?* Could it be true? Was Alec working nights, assaulting people, actually *stealing*? If so, it must be for a good reason. But she couldn't believe he'd hide something that big from her.

Malcolm took another sip of his wine, which left thick red streaks on his glass. "Are you telling me you didn't know?"

Claire shook her head, staring at the glass in his hand. *That's not wine*, she suddenly realized. *It's blood. Is that what he calls medicine?* Her stomach churned with horror and disgust.

"Interesting." Malcolm stared at her keenly. "I wonder what else you don't know. Are you aware, for example, of the primary reason the Grigori consider Halfbloods an abomination?"

Claire was momentarily caught off guard by this sudden switch of topics, but it was a subject she'd been intensely interested in ever since she'd learned what she was. She answered, "Yes. Alec's godfather said that a Halfblood's allegiances would always be questionable and their will is weak."

Malcolm shook his head. "I'm not talking about that ideological nonsense. It's not only their will that's weak. More importantly, it's their *tainted bodies*."

"Tainted? Tainted in what way?"

"As Halfbloods' abilities mature," Malcolm explained, "these rare, unfortunate creatures are generally torn between the two sides of their genes, resulting in debilitating physical weaknesses that accompany their great power. Genetic defects from inbreeding, if you will."

Oh my God, Claire thought. Was that why the visions sometimes made her sick? She wondered if she was doomed to something even worse down the line.

"Take me, for instance," Malcolm added casually. "I inherited near invulnerability and great strength from my Grigori mother, but my half-human body cannot bear the brunt of it."

That statement blindsided Claire. "Wait. You're a Halfblood?"

"Indeed," Malcolm nodded, setting down his glass. "It's why we needed to meet face-to-face. You and I are more alike than you know."

"That's impossible. Alec told me the last Halfblood was executed a millennium ago."

"That's the common *perception* of what happened, but it's untrue. I was very young at the time. The Grigori who slew my parents couldn't bring himself to kill *me*, so he lied to the Elders. I was cast out to fend for myself. A *Snow White* without any dwarfs."

"Nice story," Claire said, "but how can I believe anything you're saying?"

"I think you *know* how." Picking up a large, heavy, silver serving spoon from the nearby table, he pushed with one thumb and slowly, deliberately, began bending it in half. "Go ahead," he dared her. "Search for it."

All at once, Claire understood what he meant. He was using one of his powers—challenging her to look for an aura. Warily, she shifted her perception to stare hard at Malcolm, in aura mode. And then she saw it. Her jaw dropped. Malcolm's aura glowed a brilliant green. *Just like hers.*

"You're a lucky girl, Claire. It appears you haven't developed any *serious* side effects of your gifts. At least not yet. Whereas I'm crippled like a vampire. The heat of the sun or any flame burns my skin like paper, and I wither away to nothing without a fresh infusion of human blood."

Claire felt her eyes widen as she took that in. Alec had told her once that most mythological creatures were inspired in some way by encounters with Grigori or Fallen. "So," she replied, nodding, "even vampires are real."

"Not as some sort of species, no. But I imagine others with symptoms similar to mine helped inspire the myths."

Claire couldn't help asking, "Do you … bite people?"

"Wouldn't do me much good. I don't have fangs." Malcolm smiled, then touched his pearly-white teeth with his tongue. "I've had to resort to … less-than-pleasant methods in the past to obtain the sustenance I need. Now I just acquire my supply from blood banks. It's very neat and clean. Yet Alec's activities of late suggest he has a problem with that." He waved a hand and shook his head in annoyance. "Typical Grigori shortsightedness."

Claire knew there was no way this guy was telling the whole story. If Alec was against the operation, then Malcolm didn't *acquire* his blood supply legally. He must be stealing it. "Next you're going to tell me they're all against *us* or something, right? Like you and I are two peas in a pod on the same side?"

"But we are. Your Grigori protectors are holding you under their thumb. Alec lies to your face while Helena stalls the search for your father." The smile he gave her was dazzling. "*I* can find out where he is with a phone call."

Claire's heart jumped at those words. She shook off a shiver of temptation. There was nothing she'd ever be willing to give these people in exchange for their help. Still, she was curious. "How do I know you're telling the truth?"

Malcolm rose from his chair and crossed to her, extending his hand. "Go ahead, use your talent to see for yourself."

Claire hesitated, unsure whether she wanted to actually touch this man. On the other hand, here was a chance to get a vision of her father, with no strings attached. She could finally confirm for herself that he was still their captive, maybe even learn something useful in the process. Swallowing hard, she stood, removed her right glove, and took the hand he offered.

Instantly, she felt a charge of energy bolt through her—and she was no longer inside her own body, she *was* Malcolm.

He wore a black suit and thin leather gloves, and was seated in the backseat of a long, dark limousine. One of the rear doors opened, admitting a bright shaft of sunlight. S/he felt the force of it as it enveloped his body, a searing pain that weakened him and made him wince.

A tall man wearing a suit and tie, his dark hair neatly groomed, was forcibly ushered into the seat opposite.

Her father!

A broad-shouldered man climbed in and sat close beside her dad. He looked like a bodyguard. Claire noticed a glint inside the man's ears—he was wearing the same earbuds.

As the limousine pulled away from the curb, Malcolm's voice issued from her throat. "I would just like to say how much I appreciate your help in this delicate situation, and on such short notice."

Claire's father nodded, his face blank, his eyes expressionless, like a drone. "You're welcome. Sir."

Malcolm pulled his hand away from Claire, yanking her out of the vision. "Did you see?"

She nodded, disappointment spinning through her. She'd wanted to stay longer, to learn more. The dark living room spun for a second before coming back into focus. "You're drugging my father, aren't you, and holding him against his will! Why?"

"He is doing our organization a great service," Malcolm replied. "I'm not in charge of his situation, but I receive updates, and I assure you he's being made as comfortable as possible."

Claire straightened her spine in defiance. "A fancy suit and limo doesn't mean he's comfortable! What do you want with him?"

"If you agree to work with me, I will answer all your questions. Trust me, you will be far better off working with me. As a fellow Halfblood, I am the *only* being on earth who can truly understand you and what you suffer."

It was a deal with the Devil, Claire thought. Or was it? Malcolm had a point: on a basic level, he was more like her than Alec or Helena. And he seemed to know more about her mind-control gift than anyone else. Maybe he was the mentor she truly needed?

Or maybe he was the one doing the brainwashing, but without any fancy powers. Claire looked away from Malcolm, struggling to collect her thoughts. He was so attractive, and his gaze was so magnetic, Claire almost had to remind herself that she'd been brought here by force. Before she could work out an answer, she suddenly felt and heard a crackly sound on the edges of her mind. It was strangely familiar although she couldn't say why.

Claire, a female voice faintly intoned. *Don't listen … I've sent…*

The psychic message broke off. Claire recognized the voice: it was Helena, trying to contact her, the way she'd done in the past. But why had it come so late in the game? And why was the message so weak and full of static? She worried that Helena had been in another accident—or that Malcolm and his people had somehow gotten ahold of her.

At that moment, Claire heard a massive thud outside. Her heart leapt. Had Alec made it here to rescue her after all? Just then, one of the shuttered French doors burst open, emitting a blast of sunlight. But Alec wasn't there.

In fact, no one was standing in the entryway.

Malcolm recoiled into the shadows. "No one invited you, Watcher."

"Miss Brennan wasn't *invited* either," announced a male voice. Light bent and color flooded the empty space in front of them, giving form to the previously invisible intruder: Zachariah.

With a calm but unyielding strength, Zachariah added, "This ends now."

twenty

"Miss Brennan, please move to the door," Zachariah commanded.

Claire stood her ground, paralyzed with indecision. Although grateful that someone had come to her aid, Zachariah still posed a threat to her and Alec. She sensed the tension between the two men, who stood staring at each other, with Claire caught in the middle.

"Such bravado is unnecessary," Malcolm insisted. He picked up his wineglass. "We had a nice chat, but we're finished for now. Isn't that so, Claire?"

Claire nodded. "Definitely."

"Miss Brennan?" Zachariah eyed her expectantly.

She hesitated. Did she really want to leave with him? From Zachariah's expression, it didn't seem that she had any choice. She'd have to be very careful what she said around him. Hopefully, he'd just bring her home.

As she moved to join the Watcher, Malcolm called after her, "I do hope we'll be seeing each other again."

"Don't count on it," Claire replied though she wasn't so certain. Malcolm's offer was still stuck in her mind. It was unsettling to think that he might be the only person who could help her get the answers she wanted.

As she stepped out the door, Claire almost tripped over the unconscious body of Rico. She spotted Javed in a similar heap over by the pool. Celeste was nowhere to be seen.

"How'd you know where to find me?" Claire asked, as Zachariah led the way down the path toward the front of the house.

"Your grandmother sensed that you were in danger and alerted me."

"What took her so long?"

"I'll let her explain."

How cryptic, Claire thought in frustration. She yearned for a straight answer. "Is she okay?"

"She will recover."

Now Claire was genuinely worried. Despite all her recent frustrations with Helena, Claire loved her grandmother and didn't want anything bad to happen to her. Besides which, at times like this, it was *nice* having a guardian angel looking over her shoulder. Hoping Zachariah couldn't sense how uncomfortable she was in his presence, she added, "Thanks."

"It's all part of the job," he answered matter-of-factly, as they approached her car.

"You seem a bit shaken," he said. "So I'll drive."

As she got in, she couldn't help thinking that there was something anticlimactic about being rescued by a flying, invisible angel, then being chauffeured home in your own car.

Silence reigned during the drive back to the condo. Claire was too worried to speak, afraid she'd accidentally spill the beans about Alec, her search for her father, or her newfound talent.

There was a topic she was dying for updates on, though. "So," she said finally, "any news about Vincent?"

The pale Watcher shook his head. "His trial is in progress. Nothing has been decided yet."

Claire nodded. Well, apparently Vincent hadn't said anything about Alec. That was good.

As Zachariah pulled onto her street, another broken message from Helena suddenly infiltrated Claire's brain, accompanied by static: *Claire ... look up. Alec ... !*

What now? Claire's eyes snapped up to the windshield in alarm. Her worst fears were confirmed when she saw Alec getting out of his car in front of her condo complex, halfway down the block.

Panic surged inside her. A warning text would take too long and be too obvious. If only she could send Alec a mental signal, persuade him to drive off! But he was a Grigori and might not be as susceptible to suggestion. Plus, he was so far away. There was just one avenue left to her. Zachariah was also a Grigori, but at least he was sitting right next to her.

"Zachariah," she began, constricting her thoughts to a laser focus, "thank you for coming for me, and for driving me home. I'm so grateful." Simultaneously, she thought at him: *The young man climbing out of that Mustang may look like Alec, but he's not Alec. He's just another teenager.*

The Watcher glanced aside at her. "You're welcome."

Her mantra didn't seem to be taking. She had to try harder. Reaching out with every tendril her mind could muster, Claire tried again, her increasing dread fueling her subliminal message: *He's nobody. He's not Alec. You won't recognize him. You won't recognize him.* Aloud, she said, "I'm so fortunate to have you and my grandma watching over me."

Claire's heart pounded, waiting to see if her powers were having any effect. There was no thrum of tension signaling a connection. She couldn't tell if the buzzing she felt was a hint of contact or mere anxiety.

Zachariah said nothing as he steered the car into her condo's driveway, stopping just outside the entrance to the underground garage.

Continuing to mentally hammer away at Zachariah's mind, Claire said, "Thanks again. I can take it from here and park the car myself."

"As you wish." Zachariah shut off the engine.

Alec headed toward them, recognizing her vehicle. He was smiling and looked only mildly concerned. He must have believed the text Celeste sent him, had no idea she'd been in any danger.

Claire threw open her door and leapt out at the same time that Zachariah stepped out from the driver's side. Alec skidded to a halt a few feet away from her, his cheerful expression changing to horror when he caught sight of Zachariah.

Was this it? Were they both dead? Claire could hardly breathe, but she kept broadcasting her message to Zachariah while she addressed Alec neutrally, "Oh. Hi, I didn't know you were stopping by."

Claire could tell from Alec's body language that he felt as terrified as she did.

Zachariah stared at Alec with a wary expression. "Hey," he said slowly, as if in recognition. "You're—"

"He's a friend of mine from school," Claire interjected, focusing all her inner fear, tension, and emotion on Zachariah: *He's not Alec, you don't recognize him, you don't recognize him.*

Zachariah blinked several times, his eyes growing somewhat distant and unfocused. Squinting, he pressed one hand to his temple, as if he had a sudden headache. "A friend of yours?"

"Yes," Claire insisted with forced calm, keeping her mental projection on Zachariah while simultaneously struggling for an excuse to clue Alec in. To him, she added, "Sorry I missed rehearsal this afternoon. I ran into some ... *old friends* unexpectedly in the village, who insisted on *whisking me away.* I didn't want to go, so I was glad when my *cousin* here appeared out of the blue and brought me home."

Alec slowly nodded in comprehension but seemed afraid to speak.

Claire held her breath, waiting. Alec's life depended on what would happen in the next second.

Zachariah blinked again, still squinting as if pain, or maybe processing what she'd said. Finally, he gave Alec a tight smile. "Nice to meet you, young man." To Claire, he added, "I do hope you'll be more careful in future, Claire. Until next time. Good-bye." With that, he turned and walked off down the street.

Claire and Alec stood frozen in anxious silence, waiting until Zachariah turned a corner—where she presumed he'd find some quiet spot to disappear and fly away.

Once he was out of sight, Claire heaved a huge sigh. "Oh. My God. It worked. It worked! He didn't recognize you!"

Alec's eyes were filled with awe. "You used mind control on Zachariah?"

She nodded, falling instinctively into his arms and hugging him tightly.

"That was insane," gasped Alec. "I can't believe you got away with it. Are you okay?"

"Mostly."

Being in Alec's arms didn't totally have the comforting effect Claire had hoped for. Her relief, both at having deceived Zachariah and being back home, was tempered by confusion over what she'd learned today. Malcolm had insisted that Alec was messing with the Fallen. Malcolm had been so deadly earnest, she was inclined to believe him. So why hadn't Alec told her a thing about it? Since the day Alec had admitted what he truly was, she thought they'd both been entirely honest with each other.

Apparently, not anymore. She wondered if there was anything else he was hiding from her.

But, Claire reminded herself, *maybe he has a reason to?* She hadn't been entirely up front with Alec lately either, by trying out her mind-control powers despite his and Helena's strict insistence that it was dangerous. And lucky thing she had! Without practice, there was no way she could have saved Alec from Zachariah just now.

Claire stepped out of his embrace and gestured toward the passenger seat of her car. "Climb in."

After she pulled into the garage, parked, and shut off the engine, Alec asked, "What really happened today? I take it there was no family emergency?"

"Yeah. Celeste grabbed my phone after the boys threw me in the car." Claire turned to him, wishing she could ask *him* what had really been happening lately. But she didn't feel right bringing up his activities without admitting to her own.

"Did they hurt you?" Alec asked, anger burning in his green eyes.

She nodded. "A little." Taking a deep breath, she plunged in, relieved that she could talk to him about everything else that had happened today. "Then they took me to Shane Malcolm."

Claire's mom almost tackled her as she and Alec walked though the front door, clutching Claire in a python-like embrace.

"You're okay! You're really okay. Right?"

"I'm fine, Mom." Claire returned the fierce hug. After two weeks of awkwardness, suddenly all of the tension between them seemed to have melted away. Sometimes, Claire thought, it felt good to be in your mother's arms.

"I've been on pins and needles for hours." Lynn pulled back to look Claire over, as if desperate for visual reassurance that she was truly in one piece. To Alec, she added, "When Helena spotted Zachariah, then you arrived—I was so worried."

"So was I," Alec nodded grimly. "Claire averted a catastrophe."

Claire worried about the direction this conversation was heading. Was she going to get crap, now, for using her new ability on Zachariah? She knew, if any of them found out she'd been practicing it on others, it would spark an even lengthier debate. Not wanting to get into it, she quickly changed the subject. "Where's Grandma?"

"I'm right here," came a rather weak voice.

Claire darted into the living room to find Helena lying on the couch, dressed in yoga clothes, her forehead covered with a damp cloth.

"I made you some food," Lynn said, disappearing into the kitchen. "Helena said you'd be starving."

"Thanks, Mom. I am." Claire turned to her grandmother. "Are you all right?"

Helena raised an eyebrow. "So now you're talking to me?"

Did Helena always have to be so bitchy? Claire and Alec sat down across from her, his look of silent reproach reminding her that *she* was the one who'd been acting bitchy lately.

"Sorry," Claire said. "I guess I've been making everything harder than it needed to be. But you were right about one thing, Grandma. I'm glad you got inside my head today, after all."

"Well," Helena replied, "I appreciate your apology. To my chagrin, it seems you had a point, too. If *you* hadn't gotten *yourself* inside Zachariah's mind just now, we would all be in bigger trouble than you know."

So it's okay for me to use that power? Claire wanted to ask. But she could guess where that would go. "So you *did* see what just happened?"

"I saw everything."

"Then why didn't you warn me earlier? Why was every attempt to reach me so staticky?"

Helena took a deep breath. "I'd spent the morning deep in meditation, and it was enough to wring the life out of a tiger. When I came out of it, I was so exhausted I could barely move. By the time I foresaw what would happen to you, it had already begun, and I didn't have the energy to properly communicate with you."

"Why didn't one of you just call me?" Alec asked.

"I felt Zachariah could get there more quickly," Helena answered.

"True," Claire smirked, adding with her best *Back to the Future* impression, "He doesn't *need* roads."

Alec shook his head, visibly frustrated. "I would have dropped everything to find you. Instead, I spent all afternoon in rehearsal like a chump."

Claire eyed him with empathy. "It's not your fault. But for future reference: *Celeste* calls you Handsome, not me."

"Now I feel doubly stupid, thank you," Alec responded dryly.

Before Claire could reply, her mom appeared with a sandwich and chips. "I'm just glad you're safe, honey."

Claire grabbed the plate and tried not to inhale it all at once. While she was eating, Alec said, "Can we talk about the real problem here?"

Everyone looked at him.

"I hate to say it," he went on, "but for once, I agree with Vincent. What happened today makes it crystal clear that the Fallen want Claire and will never stop trying to pull her into their web, even if they have to abduct her in broad daylight to do it."

"Indeed," Helena commented.

"The worst part is, none of us had any way of preventing it, or reaching her after it happened," Lynn pointed out.

"We can't ever let them get to her again," Alec insisted.

"Hello?" Claire said through a mouthful of food. "Quit talking about me like I'm not here. And screw this 'we' stuff. If Celeste and her morons ever show up again, I don't want to be some little damsel in need of rescue. I need to be able to handle it myself."

"That's expecting a lot," Alec mused.

"Excuse me?" Claire bristled.

Alec put up his hands defensively. "When they come for you, it's in numbers. You can't physically take on a pack of them."

"What if I learn some fighting techniques?"

"Not a bad idea," Alec admitted.

"I could join my mom's self-defense class."

"When would you have time?" Lynn said. "You have rehearsals every day after school and need evenings and weekends to do homework."

"Then I'll drop the play." Claire was determined. "Erica wants my part anyway."

"No need for anything that drastic," Alec pointed out. "I can teach you a few things when and if you have a spare minute."

"Okay." Claire smiled. This would finally give her some alone time again with Alec, where she could try to figure out if what Malcolm had said about him was true. Suddenly remembering something, she added: "Wait. Mom. Is that okay? Or am I still grounded?"

Lynn shook her head. "Not anymore. In light of what happened today, I think we should all move forward. Alec, thank you for offering to step in and help."

Before Alec could reply, Helena sat up, removing the cloth from her forehead, and announced, "This is all very charming, and far be it from me to discourage anyone from improving their physical prowess. But we're neglecting one of the most critical matters at hand: Claire's ability to control minds."

Claire sighed. Despite her best efforts, the conversation was snowballing into criticism of her new power. But to Claire's surprise, Helena's next remarks were positive.

"I admit, your gift of persuasion did indeed prove crucial today," Helena continued. "In truth, it may be the greatest weapon you possess."

"What are you saying, Grandma?" Claire began, wanting so badly to tell everyone about the good she'd done so far with this new ability. "Are you giving me permission to—"

"No!" Helena held up a hand to silence Claire. "All my reservations still stand. As I said before, it is a dangerous talent and must *never* be used unnecessarily. Even the most innocent experimentation can have unforeseen and unfortunate consequences. Since this is not a skill *I* possess, I could not help you to hone it even if I wanted to. Therefore, I forbid you to use it except in a life-or-death emergency, such as what happened this afternoon."

Claire settled back in her chair with a sigh. "So the rest of the time, I'm just supposed to pretend I don't have this ability?"

"Yes," Helena insisted. "Let us focus our attention in another direction instead. Let's find a way to use your *other* clairvoyance talents together with mine, in a way that is both more effective and is acceptable to you. So that I can still look out for you, but you will not feel you are being watched all the time."

"How are you going to do that, Grandma?"

"Going forward," Helena suggested, "I can keep a little corner of my mind open and available for you. When you *want* me to look in on you, I can teach you how to send me a signal, similar to the way I contacted you months ago when I was bedridden."

"Like my own personal wormhole into your mind?" Claire asked, intrigued.

"An oversimplification, but yes."

"What if you're not available to receive the signal?" Alec asked. "What if you're meditating again, as you were today? It put you out of commission for a while."

"In future, I will not engage in deep meditation for such a lengthy period. Today's efforts, however, did pay off."

"How?" Lynn asked.

"Well. That is something I have been leading up to. I have interesting news to report." Helena's eyes glimmered as she sat forward, hands clasped. "I have been trying to locate traces of Tom's new aura for the past two weeks. And I finally found something."

Claire's heart quickened. "What?"

"I saw him leaving a courthouse in Cleveland surrounded by reporters. His hair was red, but it was he."

"Could you tell *when* it happened?" Alec asked.

"Not specifically. Based on peoples' clothing, I presume it was a summer day. And from the cell-phone models I saw, I would guess it was four or five years ago."

"What he was doing in Cleveland?" Lynn murmured.

"My guess is, he was with the Fallen," Claire answered. "Malcolm confirmed today that Dad's still in their custody."

"Damn," said Helena quietly.

"And they're taking him to courthouses?" said Alec, his eyes narrowing. "Why?"

"I do not know, but he had enough personal security to rival the Pope," Helena put in.

"To prove they have him, Malcolm had me take his hand for a moment. The two of them were somewhere in a limo, with a bodyguard next to my dad the whole time. Malcolm was thanking Dad for helping out with something, I don't know what."

"Since L.A. is Malcolm's territory, they were probably local," Alec mused. "It sounds like they're moving him around the country."

"But why?" Lynn asked. "If he has the power of persuasion, why doesn't Tom just brainwash his captors and escape?"

"He can't," Claire theorized. "I tried that on the people who kidnapped me today, but it didn't work. They were all wearing some kind of special earbuds, similar to what we saw Vincent wearing in the subway station. Looks like the Fallen *and* Grigori have devised a filtering technology to protect their minds from brainwashing."

There was a pause as everyone took this in. "That explains a lot," Helena nodded.

"That would work for the people keeping him captive," Alec commented. "But courtrooms are public. Helena, in your vision, did Tom ask anyone else for help?"

"No."

"Did he look too afraid to talk?" Lynn asked.

"He did not look afraid. If anything, he looked rather loopy."

"He was that way in *my* vision, too." Claire's heart hurt at the memory. "His eyes were blank. He looked like a zombie."

"Then he was *drugged*," Alec said.

Lynn looked horrified. "Do you think he's been drugged every day they've had him, for the past *sixteen years*?"

"It is possible," Helena acknowledged.

The chill of that thought filled the air.

"Whatever they're using him for," Claire said finally, "if they keep moving him around, he could be anywhere by now. How can we ever find him?"

No one volunteered an answer.

twenty-one

The clock ticked as they all stared at each other in silence. Alec cleared his throat.

"I don't know how we're going to do it, Claire, but I promise you, we will find Tom," he said. "In the meantime, why don't we focus on what we can do *now*? We can start your training tomorrow."

"Why wait?" Claire sounded driven, like she was charged up with adrenaline. "There's a gym in this complex, right? Let's go! After the day I've had, there's no way I can settle down or sleep until I know how to defend myself."

"It'll take awhile to become proficient, honey," Lynn interjected.

"Proper self-defense comes from muscle memory and reflexes, which take time to develop," Alec agreed.

"Well, what am I supposed to do if someone tries to grab me again tomorrow morning?"

"I have an idea," Lynn offered. "Something you can use to beat back any potential attackers in a pinch. Wait here, I'll be right back."

Two minutes later Lynn returned, carrying a small, black plastic handle, about nine inches long. Although Alec recognized it instantly, Claire looked confused—until Lynn whipped her hand downward, causing two feet of blackened, anodized steel to shoot out from the handle and lock in place with a snap.

"Good Lord." Helena shook her head.

"Whoa! What's that?" Claire asked.

"A collapsible baton," Lynn explained. "Personal protection in its simplest form, from a world teeming with paranormal crazies. I bought it months ago, after Vincent attacked us."

Claire took the weapon from her mother's outstretched hand, admiring it. "Cool."

"They're not strictly legal, but it made me feel better to have one in my purse. Now that I've had a few months to learn how to throw a punch, I think I can handle myself without it."

"Thanks, Mom. But how did you get this?"

Lynn smiled. "Your father taught me a thing or two about acquiring things under the table. For *safety*." Shifting her attention to Alec, she added in all seriousness, "As long as she keeps it out of sight, I know *I'll* sleep better if she's got that on her."

"See?" Claire turned to Alec. "My badass mom wants me combat-ready."

"Can you teach her?" Lynn asked.

"Of course," Alec said. "Let's get started."

"Again."

Alec held his tonfa along his arm, ready to block Claire's attack. She lunged with a combination of strikes he'd taught her. Effortlessly, Alec moved his own weapon to stop each attack.

"You're still telegraphing," he told her. "Remember, keep your shoulders relaxed."

Alec glanced at the clock on the gym wall. It was almost 1 A.M. The baton might seem like a simple weapon, but there were many techniques he'd been able to show her to use it for maximum effect. They'd covered some footwork, basic parries, and attacks to arms and legs, as well as a few disengages, so she could avoid getting the baton tangled up in a fight.

"It's so weird," Claire commented between hits. She looked tired but still determined. "If I'd been kidnapped a month ago, I'd be texting Brian and Erica all about it." She retreated a few steps, catching her breath. "But all Brian thinks about these days is Kayla. And Erica won't give me the time of day."

"Or me." Wanting to keep her on her toes, Alec moved in with a strike toward her body, which Claire evaded and blocked with only a slight stumble. "It's sad," Alec added as they sparred. "But I feel a little uncomfortable being around either of them now."

"Me, too."

"Speaking of Erica. At rehearsal today, Ms. Donnelly had Erica fill in as Guinevere."

"Oh?" Claire glanced at him.

"Sorry I didn't tell you earlier. With everything going on—"

"It's okay, I get it. How'd she do?"

"She was great, especially for being put on the spot like that."

"Of course she was." Claire sighed, guilt in her voice. "That must've been crappy for Erica, filling in for a part she didn't get."

"I wouldn't know. She didn't speak to me, except in character."

"Ms. Donnelly must be so pissed at me. I'll email her tomorrow with some kind of excuse, so she won't murder me on Monday."

"Too bad the 'cousin Zach' excuse won't fly."

Claire laughed briefly as she paused, lowering her baton. "Yeah. Maybe I should just come clean about all of it: that a mob boss had me abducted to try to recruit me to the dark side."

"Don't forget the part where one of his men Tasered you with his bare hands."

She laughed again, coming at Alec with what seemed like a basic maneuver. Then she surprised him by slipping her baton under his parry, slapping him lightly on his free arm.

"Nice," Alec complimented her. "But commit to your attack and don't hold back. That should've hurt me."

"Got it." She wiped her brow on her sleeve, resetting to the center of the room. Another thought seemed to occur to her. "By the way. I can't believe you never told me the head of the L.A. Fallen was a vampire."

"That's because there's no such thing as vampires," Alec quipped, readying himself for Claire's next volley.

"I'll give Malcolm this. I get why he's the one in charge. He's incredibly charming. Even though he was having an off day."

"An 'off' day?" Alec repeated, blocking Claire's blow.

Claire backed up, darting him a hooded glance. "Apparently, someone's been messing with his blood supply." Without missing a beat, she lunged at him.

What? The comment distracted Alec long enough for Claire to score a sharp blow to his thigh. He recoiled, winded.

"You okay?" she asked, her eyes wide.

"Fine. That was a good one." Alec held up a hand to signal that he needed to catch his breath as sudden worry knotted inside him. What did Claire mean by that remark? Did she suspect something about Alec's recent nocturnal activities? *No, no, that's impossible. If she did, she'd say so.* But the implication of her statement was illuminating. *Malcolm's blood supply.* Is that what the stolen blood was for? If so, why had it been delivered to that warehouse and not to Malcolm directly?

Claire padded over to her water bottle and took a gulp, her eyes on Alec, as if waiting to see what he'd say next.

He briefly considered whether or not to come clean about what he'd discovered. Originally, he'd kept quiet so as not to worry Claire. Now, he realized, an admission could prove even more of a problem. She'd almost certainly insist on coming with him whenever he investigated, which would put her in even greater danger. No, he decided. He wouldn't say anything yet. He hated lying to her, but it was better this way for now.

"So … what were you saying before?" Alec tried to sound conversational. "Someone's suicidal enough to interfere with Malcolm's blood supply? How did that come up?"

She stared at him for a long moment, her lips pursed. His response seemed to disappoint her. "I don't know. I think he was trying to make me feel sorry for him."

"Part of the propaganda, huh?"

With a look of annoyance, she closed the baton and slipped it into her waistband. "I think I'm done. Let's call it."

Alec wearily pulled his Mustang into the parking lot of his apartment complex. His body had finally healed from the sting of Claire's baton strike, but he still ached all over. When he reached his front door, he jerked to a halt.

His door was hanging wide open. All of the locks and deadbolts had—incredibly—been reduced to misshapen lumps of metal. Only a fricking arc welder could do this kind of damage.

Or, Alec realized, the paranormal ability to fry metal so hot, it melted.

Javed?

Quickly drawing his boot knife, Alec stepped inside and telekinetically flipped on the lights. What he discovered confirmed his worst fears.

His place had been trashed. The couch he slept on was a mess of stuffing. Every cabinet door and kitchen drawer stood open, their contents scattered.

Most upsetting of all: the big, metal storage locker where he'd kept his weapons was also standing open. Both doors had been completely bashed in—by the look of it, with bare hands.

Rico's?

The cabinet, which he'd used most of his remaining Grigori funds to stockpile, was completely empty. Not a lockbox, blade, or gun in sight.

Shite, Alec thought. If they came for Claire again, he would be defenseless.

twenty-two

Claire was so tired, she slept through the rest of Saturday. On Sunday, Alec called about coming over for an additional training session, but she told him she was too exhausted. Honestly, she wasn't sure she wanted to see him.

Sure, she hadn't told him or Helena that she'd tried out her mind-control power a couple of times at school. But that was harmless, and for a good cause. Was Alec, meanwhile, actually involved in something dangerous—like stealing from and provoking the Fallen—and lying to her about it?

Or was it *Malcolm* who was lying? He might have said all that stuff about Alec and stolen blood just to drive a wedge between her and Alec.

Alec had seemed so convincingly innocent during their training session. But he'd also spent a lifetime deceiving others as part of his former job. How could she trust that he was being straight with her? The idea that he might be deliberately hiding something sucked.

Things didn't get any better on Monday.

At rehearsal, after two weeks of learning song and dance numbers, they were scheduled to finally start blocking the scenes with dialogue. The scene where Guinevere first meets Arthur was up that afternoon. Despite all the paranormal crap going on in her life, and the fact that she wasn't too happy with

Alec at the moment, Claire had been looking forward to it. It was her first chance to share the stage with him, and it involved a cute case of mistaken identity.

When she arrived at the theater, however, she found Alec waiting for her, the director on stage moving a wooden box into place to act as a temporary set, and … Erica, sitting in the front row. Which was strange, since the scene only included Arthur and Guinevere.

"What's Erica doing here?" Claire whispered to Alec as she dropped into a fifth row seat beside him.

Before he could reply, Mrs. Donnelly said: "Claire, Alec, please join me on stage. Erica, thank you for coming."

Erica nodded. "Happy to be here."

As Claire and Alec darted on stage, the director explained, "I received your email, Claire. And though I understand that emergencies do happen, I don't want the production put in such an awkward position again. So I've cast Erica as your understudy. She'll be observing your rehearsals so she can learn the part, and—just to be clear—if there are any more unplanned absences, you'll be dropped from the play, and the part will be hers."

Claire felt like the wind had been knocked out of her. She darted a glance at Erica, who was busily studying her script. Claire's face felt red as she nodded mutely. Nobody else had an understudy. Clearly, Ms. Donnelly didn't trust Claire at all. Which was so unfair. None of this was her fault. She had been kidnapped! If only there were some way to explain that!

It was hard for Claire to concentrate at first. There was so much bullshit clouding her mind: a possibly lying boyfriend, a missing Grigori father, an invisible Watcher and a pseudo-Vampire both breathing down her neck, and on top if it all, a grueling need to turn herself into a lethal weapon. Not to mention that Erica was sitting in the audience watching Claire's every move. And taking notes.

After a while, though, she found herself caught up in the script, and she began to let all of that slip away and enjoy the moment. No longer was she a half angel with this host of problems, but instead a royal bride whose only worry was whether or not she could love the man she was marrying. Alec, in turn, was a charming young king, and it was a treat to hear him speak with a flawless, cultured British accent, instead of his usual Scottish brogue.

When rehearsal was over, while Alec stayed behind to help Ms. Donnelly move the temporary set pieces back into the wings, Claire caught up to Erica in the theater lobby.

"Hey! I just wanted to say—I know it blows to be an understudy—all work and no glory. And I'm so sorry I've put you in that position."

Erica paused near the lobby doors, seemingly considering her response. "Yeah, well. I won't put a voodoo curse on you."

"Thanks. I appreciate it." Claire smiled, relieved that Erica didn't seem angry. "Alec told me that you were really good on Friday."

Erica shrugged. "Where were you, anyway?"

Claire checked to make sure that the lobby was empty of other people. "Do you want the version I gave Ms. Donnelly, or the truth?"

"The truth, obviously."

Lowering her voice, Claire admitted, "I was abducted."

"Abducted? What? By who?" Erica looked shocked.

The memory of that tense afternoon was so vivid, it made Claire feel sick to her stomach every time she thought of it. "Celeste, Javed, and Rico," she replied quietly. "They grabbed me when I was up in the village—"

"Oh my God. Are you okay?"

"Sort of. They took me to their boss, who tried to recruit me way harder than Celeste ever has. In exchange for doing some sort of favor for them, he said he would tell me where my father is. Which was so tempting! I said no, of course, but—"

"What could you possibly do for them?" Erica asked.

"I don't know. Help them win the lottery? One thing's for sure, no matter what they ask, I'm not brainwashing anyone."

Erica stared at her. "Wait, *what*? Brainwashing?"

"Oh, crap, I haven't gotten a chance to tell you any of this." Claire sighed, then continued softly, "Remember when Vincent said I probably got a second power from my dad? And he was really afraid of it? Well, I've figured it out. If I concentrate, I can persuade people to do stuff just by *thinking it* while I talk to them."

Erica's eyes widened in stunned disbelief. "Are you serious?"

"Yeah. I've tested it a couple of times. I had to use it to trick Zachariah so he wouldn't arrest Alec. But the whole thing's become a total nightmare"—Claire glanced over her shoulder to ensure that Alec hadn't emerged yet from the auditorium, and continued—"because I haven't told Alec I've been practicing, and meanwhile, I'm pretty sure he's lying to *me*. I think he's somehow messing with the Fallen boss who had me kidnapped—who's like a freaking vampire! So now I'm trying to learn martial arts to—"

"Whoa whoa, slow down," Erica interrupted. "I mean, wow." Her eyes seemed to have glazed over, and not because of Claire's mind-control power. Abruptly, Erica reached into her pocket and glanced at her cell phone, then said, "Shit, Gabby's sent me like five messages. We have a study date, and I'm late."

"You two have a study date?" Claire asked.

"Yeah, who would have thought? But she's not as bad as her friends. She actually asks how I'm doing once in a while instead of just talking *at* me."

That put a lump in Claire's throat. *Like I've been doing to you now*, she thought. Aloud, all she could manage was, "Sorry."

Erica shrugged. Without another word, she turned and sped out of the lobby.

Sudden tears stung Claire's eyes as she stood there, watching her friend disappear. Once, Erica would have been there for her, every step of the way. Claire had tried so hard to recapture that, but instead she'd made things even worse.

"You killed it in there today," Alec said, suddenly appearing beside her.

Claire quickly wiped her eyes. "Not out here I didn't."

School, homework, and rehearsals took every minute of the following week, giving Claire little time to worry about the Erica situation.

Claire and Alec trained again that weekend, focusing on throws and tackles. She left the sessions a little more confident that she could defend herself (at least against a human attacker), but less comfortable with Alec. They hardly talked about anything except the training the entire time. Claire didn't know if it was because he was just focusing or if he felt the *need* to focus hard so he wouldn't inadvertently blurt out something he'd prefer not to share.

All this tension was driving Claire crazy. At the same time, she feared that if the truth came out, it would be even more disastrous. She and Alec had never had a fight before, and Claire didn't want to tempt fate by starting one. Once their trust was broken, she worried that it could never be fixed.

February started with a roar. A weather front brought heavy rain for a few days, which really sucked at a school whose corridors, lockers, and eating areas were almost all outdoors. Students scurried to class beneath umbrellas that threatened to blow inside out in the wind, and either crowded inside the steamy cafeteria during lunch and breaks, or huddled in areas underneath dripping overhangs.

That Wednesday evening, Claire finished her homework early and, miraculously, had a free moment to herself. She instinctively picked up the phone to call Alec, then stopped herself.

She couldn't remember the last time she'd had a couple of hours with nothing scheduled or planned. The mystery about her father was never far from her mind, but she hadn't had a chance to do anything about it in ages. Helena, despite all the new tidbits Claire had fed her, hadn't turned up any further information.

Maybe it was time to try something more conventional.

Malcolm hadn't given Claire anything concrete to go on. But her grandmother had: her dad had been outside a Cleveland courtroom on a summer day about four or five years ago.

Claire started by browsing the Cleveland Public Courthouse website. She found the Public Case Access System, where you could search for cases and actually view information regarding case participants and events. The problem was, she didn't have a name or case number, and the closest thing she had to a date was the season (summer) and a possible year.

She tried Googling everything she could think of.

Nothing came up.

Claire drummed her fingers on the desktop in frustration. Then she thought, why bang her head against a wall when she could enlist an expert?

She saw that Brian was online and opened a video chat. Brian's face instantly appeared on screen. "What up, CB?"

He was lying on his stomach on his bed, a bag of snack crackers in his hands.

"Hey, Bri. I need a favor."

"Can it wait? There are all these PC games on an awesome flash sale—"

"It's important," Claire interrupted. "Can I steal you away for a little while? I've hit a dead end in the search for my dad, and you are so much better at this than I am."

"Flattery will get you everywhere. Go on."

She told him what she knew.

"Huh," Brian commented when she'd finished. "Sounds like it was a high-profile case, so there *should* be info out there. Did you say your dad was surrounded by a bunch of reporters?"

"Yeah, that's what Helena saw."

"Let's try that angle, then, and hope we can narrow it down. Maybe a newspaper or a blog posted something. If we're lucky, they'll have snapped his photo on the way out the door."

For the next hour or so, she and Brian trolled the web, focusing on noteworthy cases in Cleveland from that time period. Whenever Brian found an interesting lead, he'd send Claire the link, and vice versa.

Finally, Brian said: "Hey, take a look at this URL. Is it him?"

She opened the link he sent. It was an article from a Cleveland newspaper with a photo of a red-haired man leaving the courthouse, security guards (or bodyguards?) holding his arms on both sides. A bunch of reporters were shoving microphones in the man's face. The caption under the photo read: "Frank Churchill leaving the courthouse after surprise testimony."

Claire's heart leapt with excitement. "That's totally him! But with a different name, and red hair like Helena said."

The news report was entitled "Deputy Mayor Arnstein Acquitted of Embezzlement Charges." Brian read from the article: "It should have been an open-and-shut case, complained Prosecutor Giletti. David Arnstein is personally responsible for embezzling millions from school system funds."

The article explained how a star witness, Frank Churchill, had been brought in at the last minute with testimony that convinced the jury of the defendant's innocence.

"Holy crap," Claire said. "So *that's* what the Fallen are using my dad for?"

"Well, if I were a criminal network with access to a guy who could brainwash an entire jury, he'd be the best witness ever."

"Wow." Claire sat back in her chair. "This explains so much. Now we know why they're drugging my dad. There's no way he'd help the Fallen like that otherwise."

"I enlarged the picture, but I can't tell if the security guards are wearing those earbuds you talked about."

"You can bet they are." She sighed. "This is so awful. This case was five years ago, but it's probably been happening on a regular basis for sixteen years! What do we do?"

Brian thought for a moment. "Well, we could—" His phone rang. "Hold on." He scrambled away from the computer. "Hey foxy," Claire heard him say. Then he added, "Wait up a sec." Leaning back into view, Brian whispered, "To be continued?"

Claire gave him a thumbs-up and ended the video chat, trying to hide her disappointment. She and Brian had just been getting somewhere, but now he'd switched to thinking with his *other* brain.

Even though they'd discovered what the Fallen had been doing with her dad all this time, it still felt like a dead end. How would it help her find out where he was *today*?

She decided to try one last thing: a search using the name "Frank Churchill." All it turned up, though, were zillions of references to a character in a Jane Austen novel. Claire shook her head. The Fallen had picked a great way to bury any reference to the alias they'd used for her dad. And she suspected they'd give him a new name every time he took the witness stand.

Checking the time, Claire confirmed it was too late to tell Helena and her mom about what she and Brian had just discovered. That would have to wait until morning. Which was just as well, since her eyes were growing droopy. Settling on her pillow, Claire's attention was caught by the blue-and-silver bracelet on her nightstand. A reminder of when things had been so open and honest between her and Alec.

She considered texting Alec so she could at least tell *someone* the good news.

But strangely, she didn't feel like it. As Claire drifted off, she pondered why. Was it just the fatigue talking? Or something worse?

A sudden, cold question snapped Claire awake again. Were her suspicions making her fall out of love with Alec?

twenty-three

C laire sat on the floor, tucked into a corner of the theater lobby before rehearsal, trying to squeeze in a few minutes of calculus homework. It was Friday after school, and Alec had insisted on heading up to the village solo to grab food for them, since her last trip there had been such a fiasco.

She hadn't voiced her late-night fears to Alec, hoping it could be chalked up to temporary insanity. But her head was still swimming with worries about their relationship. Struggling to concentrate, Claire was just finishing a set of problems when Ms. Donnelly walked in with Mrs. Travers, the theater-tech teacher in charge of building sets.

"I'm so frustrated," Ms. Donnelly commented as they strolled across the lobby toward their shared office. "I just found the most incredible costumes at Sony's wardrobe department. They're even willing to rent out their collection of *armor* from an Arthurian movie they made."

"Armor? That would be fabulous," Mrs. Travers replied.

"But it's expensive. With our budget, we're stuck with West Coast Costumes again."

"The stuff they had for *Sound of Music* was great."

"Yes, but West Coast's medieval collection is old and ugly, and they don't have enough stock for the entire chorus. We'll have to schlep up to the valley and scrounge for whatever else we can find. Meanwhile, Sony Studios has *stunning* gowns for Guinevere, velvet tunics for Arthur and the knights, and two dozen white gowns for *The Merry Month of May* number. It would be perfect."

"Have you asked Dr. Grant? Maybe he'll give us additional funding."

"I tried. No dice. He says they need the money for the basketball team."

Mrs. Travers sighed. "It's always about sports with him. You need to cast him in a role someday, then you'll get all the money you could ever wish for."

"It'll have to be *Damn Yankees*. I can't think of another sports musical," Ms. Donnelly replied.

"Great! He can play the Devil!" The two teachers laughed as they disappeared down the hall.

Claire chewed on the end of her pencil, mulling over what she'd just heard, a thought brewing in her mind. Something that would be an excellent distraction from all the worries weighing her down. The Performing Arts department at Emerson was always getting shortchanged in the budget. She'd heard Mr. Lang complain about it in Concert Singers, too.

How amazing would it be to rent movie-studio-quality costumes and armor for their production of *Camelot*? Ms. Donnelly had sounded so disappointed that she couldn't make it happen. But, Claire realized, *she* might be able to. All she had to do was try to *persuade* Dr. Grant to give them the money.

Doing so, though, would mean defying Helena's direct order never to use that power, except in a life-or-death emergency.

This wasn't exactly life-or-death. Or an emergency. It was just costumes.

But it would make such a difference for the play! The thought of wearing stunning gowns onstage, of seeing Alec in a velvet tunic and all the knights in armor, was too appealing to resist. Where was the harm, really, if she used her power just one more time? Helena had promised, after all, not to watch Claire's every move anymore. So she'd never find out.

Leaving her backpack in the lobby, Claire raced out of the theater building and up to the administration offices, hoping that Dr. Grant hadn't left for the day. She charged into the reception area and approached Mrs. Shapiro, the efficient, perfectly coiffed woman behind the front desk.

"Hi," Claire said breathlessly. "Is Dr. Grant still here?"

"Yes he is," Mrs. Shapiro replied, "but he's just leaving. Is there any way I can help you?"

"Has he forgotten about my appointment?" Claire said in dismay.

Mrs. Shapiro checked her computer. "I don't see any—"

Go right in, Claire thought at her, concentrating on all the tension in her gut. *He's expecting you. Go right in.* Aloud, she uttered, "Are you sure?"

Invisible energy thrummed between them, and Mrs. Shapiro's eyes glazed over slightly. "Oh, um—he's expecting you. Go right in."

"Thank you." Claire grinned and hurried past her into the inner office.

A lanky man with thinning gray hair and a neatly trimmed mustache was standing behind the huge mahogany desk, slipping papers into his leather laptop bag. He glanced up in surprise as she entered.

"Dr. Grant! I'm so glad I caught you."

He gave her a half smile, as if trying to place her. "I'm sorry, I was just leaving, Miss … ?"

"Claire Brennan."

"Oh right, from the scaffolding incident."

What a weird thing to be remembered for. Though his comment about the accident last fall did give her the perfect opening.

"Yes," she nodded. "Speaking of which, I wanted to say how grateful everyone in the theater department is for the lobby renovations you did. But now, the *dramatic arts* need your help. I'm here on behalf of the entire cast of *Camelot*, to request an increase in the costume budget."

Dr. Grant shook his head. "I already told Ms. Donnelly—"

"… that the basketball team needs the money. I know. But Sony Studios has *amazing* costumes from the *movies*." As she spoke, fueled by a ball of energy and emotion, Claire thought at him, *Give us the money. Give us the money.*

Dr. Grant's eyes seemed to glaze over a bit. "So I heard. But—"

"I'm so excited to be in the play this year," she continued, repeating the suggestion to him with her mind. "It's going to be a great show, but with those costumes, it'll be unforgettable."

It was almost as though Claire could feel something clicking into place in his mind, a sensation she hadn't experienced before. This time, it wasn't just flailing fishing lines, but *fingers* reaching from her mind. And they dug in like grappling hooks. In that brief second, she felt *in control* of Dr. Grant's consciousness, almost as if it were an extension of her own.

"I can probably find the money somewhere," he said, nodding. "Yes. I'll do that. I'll make sure that you have it."

"Thank you! Thank you so much!" She wanted to hug him, but restrained herself, flashing a huge grin as she backed out of the room. "Ms. Donnelly and the whole cast will be so grateful!"

Woo-hoo! Claire thought as she raced down the stairs back to the theater building. She was getting good at this! A flicker of guilt rose in her chest as she thought about what Helena and Alec would say if they knew, but she pushed it away. She'd helped with an important cause. She felt proud and excited. The extra practice seemed to have unlocked something new inside her. If she could trust in that signal between her and the person she was persuading, there wouldn't be the agonizing suspense wondering if it was working. She'd just *know* they were listening. That she was the one pulling the strings. Everything would go her way.

And no one would be the wiser.

When she popped back into the theater, out of breath, Alec was seated on a bench with a couple of cardboard food containers, finishing off a calzone.

"Where were you?" Alec asked, as she sat down beside him.

"I had to drop something off in our locker," she lied smoothly.

Alec glanced at her, as if sensing that something was off. But all he said was, "Why didn't you wait 'til after rehearsal? You've only got two minutes to eat now."

"I'll eat fast. Thanks for this." She ripped open the container and scarfed down the Penne Arrabiata he'd brought her, glad that chewing prevented further conversation.

They were rehearsing a scene from the end of Act One, where Guinevere realizes that she has feelings for Lancelot. Lancelot confesses that he's in love with her, too, just before Arthur walks in and asks Lancelot to join the Knights of the Round Table.

As they blocked the scene, focusing on who moved where and when, Erica sat on the sidelines watching, and everyone made notes in their scripts.

When they ran the scene again from the beginning, Claire felt the mood change. As she and Neil said their lines, now giving their performance the required emotion, it was almost as if the wall that had existed between them temporarily vanished. They were Guinevere and Lancelot, finally being honest with one another. She wished it could be like this in real life, so the horrible tension she felt around Neil would go away.

Neil seemed to feel it, too, because as their eyes met, she saw a vulnerability in his that had been missing for a long time.

It was like he was remembering what they'd once shared and missed it as much as she did.

Glancing offstage, Claire noticed Alec watching them intently. His whole posture radiated discomfort.

Another stab of guilt echoed through Claire's veins. The last thing she wanted to do was to make Alec angry. She wasn't in love with Neil. But she *did* miss his friendship.

But fixing these messed-up relationships required honest conversations that would be awkward at best. With Neil, it would mean telling him *everything*. All the paranormal crap that existed in the world around them, and had been happening to her specifically. She doubted he was ready to hear all that, let alone believe it.

As for Alec, today was the first time she'd ever deliberately lied to his face. She felt guilty about it. But then again, was she obligated to tell Alec everything? If he ever decided to come clean about his alleged late-night heroics, *then* she'd be honest with him.

Assuming they were still a couple when he got around to it.

God, Claire hated thinking like that. But she hated all of this pressure even more.

When rehearsal was over, Claire returned to her backpack in the lobby and checked her email on her phone. She was surprised to find an Evite to Erica's seventeenth birthday party. It was a week after Valentine's Day, and everyone was required to wear some form of necktie. Claire scanned the invite list and saw that it included the entire cast of *Camelot*, as well as all of Erica's new friends from the popular crowd.

Claire sighed. Erica used to be her best friend. There had been a time when Claire had known *everything* that was going on with her. It felt weird (and a little sad) to find out about an event this big via email. And sadder still to think that Erica didn't necessarily love the company of some of the people she'd invited but probably did it to keep up appearances.

Alec appeared beside her, his scowl from earlier now thankfully gone. "What's wrong?"

"Nothing really." She showed him the invitation. "I guess Erica doesn't hate us after all?"

twenty-four

The next day, as Alec worked with Claire on some new joint-lock and throwing techniques, he could tell she was distracted. He understood why. She was juggling a lot, from the residual stress of the Malcolm kidnapping, to the play, to the search for her father.

Alec was equally distracted. The only reason he even had a tonfa to spar with was because he'd kept a few weapons in his car. He hadn't told Claire about the break-in, or his weapons cabinet being demolished and emptied. He wondered if Javed and Rico had done the deed. Or some new player he hadn't met yet. Either way, Alec suspected it had been done in retribution for the blood he'd stolen. Blood that had apparently belonged to Shane Malcolm.

It meant they knew where he lived, so he was constantly in danger—and putting anyone around him in jeopardy as well. But he wanted to figure out what was actually going on, resolve the issue, and keep Claire safe, before having a drawn-out conversation about it.

By the end of the training session, they were both sticky with sweat and barely had anything to say to each other. Alec left Claire's apartment building determined to return to that downtown warehouse again and find out the truth behind this whole mess.

Over the past two weeks, he'd staked out the warehouse five times. On two of those nights, a new car and driver had shown up, dropped off bags of blood from a hospital or clinic, and left with a small vial—presumably as payment. Every time, the guy with the shotgun had watched over the transaction, pulling the metal roll door shut when it was completed. The lights inside the warehouse had stayed on for several hours, until its two occupants left.

If the Fallen were indeed stealing this blood to feed Malcolm, then why bring it here?

During the day, the warehouse appeared to be empty. Which meant daylight was the best time for Alec to investigate.

At dawn on Sunday morning, Alec arrived to find the parking lot empty. He leapt over the same fence he'd jumped before, armed with his tonfa. Dashing to the garage door, Alec placed his hand on the padlock, telekinetically turning the internal mechanism until it clicked open.

Pushing the heavy door up just enough to scoot himself under, Alec lowered it and slid the bolt, locking it from the inside. The room was dimly lit by light streaming in from the filthy windows high above. No security cameras were visible.

Alec took a quick look around. There was a makeshift kitchen, its cabinets stocked with dishware and glasses, plus a variety of snacks and beverages, alcoholic and otherwise.

A pair of large fridges hummed along the wall. One contained the remnants of takeout food. The other—no surprise—was stuffed with bags of medical-grade blood. Two large drums in one corner were marked HAZARDOUS / FLAMMABLE.

Alec darted to the far end of the space, where several long tables were set up like a medical assembly line. He spotted boxes of empty vials, a jar of white crystals labeled ANTICO-AGULANT, and an I.V. infusion pole holding an empty bag, the residue of blood visible inside it, a long plastic tube dangling down.

Nearby, a table held crates stuffed with vials full of red liquid, similar to the one Alec had confiscated.

It looked like they were mixing blood with something else, to create—what? And if those vials contained blood, he wondered, why weren't they being refrigerated?

His attention darted to a memo lying atop one of the workstations that read:

TURBO: 1mL CPDA-1 + 1mL Mal + 8mL Civ

What did it mean? A formula for something called Turbo?

The stolen civilian blood could account for the "Civ." Alec wasn't sure what "CPDA-1" was. Maybe the anticoagulant? And what was Mal, the third ingredient?

The sound of a car pulling up outside and car doors slamming made Alec's ears perk up in alarm. *Damn.*

He had to get out of here.

Spotting a side door, Alec ran for it. He heard a loud curse and the rattling of the garage door, as if someone were trying to yank it open.

Before he could make it to the side door, however, it was flung open. A broad-shouldered man burst inside. In the dim light, Alec couldn't make out the guy's face. Alec raised his tonfa, but it was knocked from his hand. The attacker spun Alec around, clamped down on his arms, and pressed something sharp against his throat.

Alec tried to arch his neck away from the bony spikes that had erupted from his captor's knuckles—a vivid clue to the man's identity. "Easy, Rico."

Rico tightened his iron grip in response. "Can't seem to mind your own business, can you, Watcher?"

Damn, Alec thought again. How was this guy so strong? Alec had bested Rico in a fight before, so why couldn't he release himself from the asshole's grip?

Alec felt a blast of heat, and noticed that the bottom of the roll door was glowing. The interior lock suddenly snapped, and someone on the outside yanked the door upward.

Javed silently strode in, muscles rippling beneath his black T-shirt as he flipped on the overhead fluorescent lights before dropping the roll door closed. "Didn't get the message when we ransacked your place, huh?" He smirked. "Nice arsenal you'd stockpiled there. We appreciate the donation."

Screw you guys, Alec wanted to say aloud, but didn't dare with a blade pressed to his throat.

Stopping at the table nearby, Javed grabbed a vial of red liquid from a crate, unstoppered it, took a hit, and handed the vial to Rico, who—while still holding tight to Alec—took a swig of his own.

Javed's eyes, Alec noticed, suddenly grew glassy and blood-shot, just like Lance's had that night in the parking lot.

"That stuff … taste good?" Alec choked out.

"It gets the job done." Javed cracked his knuckles.

Heels clicked across the concrete floor from the direction of the side door as a female voice intoned with a sigh, "Malcolm figured we might find you here."

Alec grimaced. He should have known that these assholes never went anywhere without Celeste.

She sauntered over, wearing a corseted outfit that left her shoulders bare. "I hoped he would be wrong. But it seems you never disappoint, Alec."

Alec strained to stay calm as his eyes darted around, search-ing for a way out. "What the hell … are you making here?" he managed to croak.

Celeste laughed. "You have to ask? This is Malcolm's oper-ation, after all. I thought you would have figured it out by now."

Alec fought to piece it all together. All at once, the answer became clear. He'd heard that Malcolm possessed great strength and near invulnerability. *That* must be what "Mal" stood for—*the third ingredient was Malcolm's blood*. They were making a power-enhancing drug for his lieutenants. "You're bottling … Malcolm's gifts."

"A little slow on the uptake, aren't you?" Celeste chuckled again. "Malcolm's been experimenting with this for years. It seems his abilities can be shared temporarily, in tiny doses, but only if mixed with a similar substance."

"So … you steal … human blood. Blood donated to … help people."

Celeste shrugged. "Blood can be replaced. But you can't. You do know that it's in your best interest to say and do nothing about this, right?"

"Otherwise … ?" Alec managed, the knife digging in sharp.

"Otherwise, you'll just start a war with Malcolm. And you don't want that. Malcolm's been known to take out his anger very definitively on the loved ones of those who've dared to cross him."

Alec's heart pounded. He didn't want to do anything that would endanger Claire. But how could he do nothing? Assuming he even got away from here alive?

"You seem conflicted," Celeste commented. "Let's drink to a compromise." She crossed to one of the kitchen cabinets, from which she pulled a bottle of high-proof whiskey and some glasses. Setting them on a wooden table, she opened the whiskey bottle and poured out four shots. "Here's the agreement: you promise to forget about what you saw here, and we won't kill you."

"No way can we trust this prick, no matter what he says," Rico snarled, his breath hot and fetid in Alec's ear.

"I say we just get rid of him," Javed agreed, flexing his fingers.

Alec's blood froze. How was he going to get out of this?

As he struggled to formulate a plan, he noticed arcs of electricity starting to crackle between Javed's clenched hands.

That's it! That was his way out.

Drawing on his inner strength, Alec reached out with his mind, telekinetically grabbed Javed's wrists, and yanked them wide apart. Bolts of electricity sprang from Javed's fingers like lightning and arced wildly in all directions, bouncing back and forth off the walls.

Javed recoiled, struggling futilely to control his hands, while Alec kept his mind trained on the source, continuing the electrical onslaught. Glowing spheres of energy pinged around the room like balls in a pinball machine.

The room quickly grew as hot as an oven. Vials of Turbo suddenly started bursting into smithereens.

Overhead, the fluorescent lights exploded, raining down a shower of glass. As shards painfully embedded themselves in Alec's skin, all three Fallen cried out.

Alec hadn't expected such an extreme result, but it had the effect he'd hoped for: Rico's grip on Alec loosened.

Alec took advantage and pried himself away, just as a bolt of unleashed electricity hit and exploded the whiskey bottle in Celeste's hand. Celeste screamed as flames erupted from the raw alcohol and spread like wildfire across the table and along the floor.

The room began to fill with flames and smoke. Alec grabbed his tonfa and sprinted for the side door. Pounding footsteps followed. Rico was after him, and the breakneck speed of his charge might overtake Alec before he made his escape. Alec dropped and ducked under the charging Fallen, who skidded and smashed into the door itself, breaking it clean off its hinges and toppling to the ground outside.

Alec jumped over Rico and out of the building without looking back, running as fast as he could for the fence, then over it. He dove into his Mustang and fired up the engine. As he peeled out of the parking lot, Alec glanced in the rearview mirror.

Smoke was pouring out of the open door to the warehouse, and the lick of flames was visible through the windows. Alec suddenly remembered the drums he'd spotted marked FLAMMABLE, and he slammed on the brakes.

Holy shite. What had he done? If those drums caught fire, that whole place could go up in minutes ...

To his relief, he saw Celeste and Javed dashing out, pausing to haul an unconscious Rico to safety away from the building. Alec called the fire department, then sped away.

Dear God. He hadn't meant to set the place on fire. He felt certain the Fallen trio would survive, but all of that Turbo—and Malcolm's entire operation—would go up in smoke.

Alec heaved a sigh, picking shards of glass out of his scalp, forehead, and hands as he drove. Well, so be it. If he hadn't acted as he did, they would have killed him back there. That operation was twisted. They were stealing blood that patients badly needed to make a dangerous drug to empower their own. If that building burned down, it was all to the good.

Even so, Alec's stomach clenched with nerves. Malcolm would be furious about this. Had Alec accidentally started something he would come to regret?

A sudden thought occurred to him. As he drove, he leaned over and popped open his glove box, staring at the vial of Turbo he'd confiscated a while back. He knew he should throw it away. Instead, he shoved the glove box closed. And drove on.

twenty-five

When Claire walked into Concert Singers class first thing on Tuesday morning, Ms. Donnelly was chatting with Mr. Lang by the piano.

"I don't know what happened," Ms. Donnelly was saying. "It's like a miracle."

Mr. Lang nodded. "Real-life knights in shining armor, huh?"

"What's a miracle?" Claire asked.

"Dr. Grant approved additional funding for the show's costumes," Ms. Donnelly answered, beaming. "We're going to get them from Sony Studios, and all of you will look fabulous."

"Awesome." Claire's heart soared. It was all she could do not to do a little happy dance. It had worked!

Later, as Claire headed to biology, Señora Gutierrez called out to her. "Claire! I wanted to thank you for that gym you mentioned. I signed up, I've been going three evenings a week, and I'm really enjoying it." Her cheeks bloomed pink as she added with a twinkle in her dark eyes, "It helps that the trainer is also *really* cute."

Claire laughed. "That's great, Señora."

The whole rest of the morning, Claire floated on a cloud, excited about her achievements. It was like the time she'd saved Neil from getting a D in Spanish. She felt like a superhero, righting wrongs and doing good in the world. If only she could tell someone about it, it'd be even more satisfying. But whom could she tell? Erica kept ignoring her. Brian was distracted by his new crush. If Helena found out, Claire would be in big trouble. She might even be grounded again.

The person she wanted to tell was Alec.

Well, Claire thought, at this point, why *couldn't* she share her news with Alec? She'd finally proven that she'd made things better with her newfound gift. It was time to come clean and stand by her choices.

At break, when she found Alec at their locker, she thought he looked distracted and worried. "Hey," she said.

"Hey." He gave her a brief smile.

"Are you okay?"

"Aye." He didn't offer more.

Okay, then. Claire took a breath, wondering where to begin. "I tried to call you last night. You didn't answer."

"Sorry. I, uh … left my phone on silent by mistake."

Bullshit, Claire thought. She wondered what he'd been up to. If she asked, would he tell her? If she went first, and divulged what she'd been doing, would he respond then? God, every-thing was so awkward lately. It was so long since they'd had a minute to themselves.

Maybe what they needed was some alone time. If they had a nice, romantic date, maybe it would set the proper mood. Maybe *then* Alec would open up to her about what he was doing. And afterward, she could fill him in on her own recent activities in a more private space.

"So. Valentine's Day is coming up," she commented.

"Aye, I'm familiar with the custom."

"I have a sneaking suspicion that's on your *Never Done That* list?"

He nodded. "I guess I should be asking … which do you prefer, chocolate or flowers?"

"Both?"

Alec's small smile at her joke made Claire feel worse. She shifted her weight, struggling to look at him.

"Or, neither. I don't know, Alec, we haven't exactly been all that … romantic lately. It's been ages since we had an actual date."

"Over a month, in fact."

It made her feel a little better to know that he'd been counting, too.

"Rehearsals seem to be getting in the way," he added, but his eyes were somewhere else, like he knew it was a lame excuse.

"It's more than that, and I think you know it."

Silence. She wished she could read what he was thinking or touch him to get a vision of what was going on. Or even brainwash him into telling her everything. But the first was impossible, the second might not even show her what she was looking for, and the third was … well, just a really, really bad idea.

"Why don't we do something about it?" Claire suggested finally. "Valentine's Day is on a Saturday this year, which is really rare. You want to do something special? Just the two of us?"

He lifted his eyes to hers at last, and in that instant she got a brief reminder of the sweet connection they used to share.

"Sure, let's do it. What do you have in mind?"

Since the weather was unseasonably warm, even for Los Angeles, Claire decided to take advantage of it. She'd thought of something special for her Valentine's celebration with Alec and had insisted on putting the whole thing together herself. She would surprise him; all he had to do was show up.

It was almost five o'clock now on the day itself, and Claire was rushing around like a maniac trying to get everything in order. She'd set up a table and two chairs on the rooftop of her building. The night before, her mom had helped her string twinkle lights from every available pole and post, and it made the simple garden area feel movie-grade romantic.

She'd spent hours in the kitchen preparing the perfect meal. She'd settled on prosciutto-wrapped asparagus and stuffed mushrooms for appetizers, and a *caprese* salad with fresh basil, tomatoes, and buffalo mozzarella as the second course. A slow cooker filled with braised short ribs was plugged into the electrical outlet in the rooftop's barbecue area, and it smelled delicious.

Now, with less than half an hour before Alec arrived, Claire focused on setting the table with the embroidered Parisian tablecloth, fine bone china, and sterling silverware that Helena had lent her. She adjusted two tall, slender red candles in silver candlesticks and set a crystal vase in the center of the table, waiting for the flowers that Alec had offered to bring.

She wondered what kind of flowers he had in mind. She couldn't remember if she'd ever told him what her favorite flower was, but peonies—such bright, elegant, intricately petaled flowers—always brought a smile to her face.

Claire had just finished filling the water glasses from a pitcher she'd brought upstairs when she realized she'd forgotten the other drink for the evening. She was about to run for the stairwell door when her mom walked through it, carrying just what she needed.

"Since we don't have an ice bucket," her mom said, holding a stainless-steel bowl filled with ice, in which were propped two wineglasses and a bottle of sparkling cider, "I hope this will do."

"Thanks, Mom! It'll knock one star off our review, but I think we can manage." Claire smiled as she positioned the wineglasses just so beside each place setting.

"The table looks beautiful. That's at least three stars right there."

"Ten minutes to go, and fresh out of the oven," came another voice. Helena appeared, carrying a tray covered in foil.

Claire's smile widened as Helena set the tray on the tile counter next to the slow cooker. "Thanks, guys. Well, I guess everything's ready. How do I look?"

The beaming, affectionate looks on her mom's and grandma's faces told her that they approved. Claire was excited. Her mom had actually sprung for a new dress for the occasion, something she hadn't done since Homecoming. Remembering what had happened *that* night made Claire cringe, and she quickly pushed the memory away. Tonight would be different. She'd found the perfect Valentine's Day dress. It was red (of course) and sleeveless, with a fitted bodice, a scoop neck, a flared skirt that showed off just the right amount of thigh, and a heart-shaped cutout at the back.

She'd somehow managed to squeeze in time, between all the cooking, to straighten her hair and put on a dash of makeup. The bracelet from Alec had been the final, finishing touch.

"I've never seen anyone more radiant," Helena conceded, "except perhaps for me, on several particularly memorable occasions in my youth."

Claire laughed.

"We'll give you two some space tonight," her mother added. "You deserve it. Just don't take advantage of it, okay?"

"An unnecessary warning," Helena commented dryly, looking at Lynn. "I seriously doubt that Alec would take your daughter on a rooftop lawn chair."

"Grandma!" Claire flushed the shade of her dress.

"And now we exit, stage right." Her mom ushered Helena into the stairwell. "The moment he arrives, we'll buzz him into the building so he can come straight up." The two women disappeared.

Claire lit the candles on the table. For some extra romance, she started the playlist on her laptop that she'd put together for the evening. It was an eclectic mix of slow jazz, soft bluegrass, and even some elegant flamenco guitar in honor of the first time Alec had played guitar for her.

The music added to the festive mood. Claire glanced about the rooftop. It looked and smelled awesome. Her plan was to watch the sunset when Alec arrived (it was supposed to set at 5:38 P.M.), then sit down, toast each other, and enjoy the food she'd prepared. Surely, all her efforts would put Alec in a relaxed and conversational mood. And while they ate, they'd be able to open up and talk to each other at last.

She wondered whether she should be sitting or standing when he arrived. Which would show off her new dress to its best advantage? Then she decided that was stupid. Instead, she peered over the waist-high wall at the edge of the roof, watching for Alec's Mustang. He should be here any second. Alec was never late; in fact, he prided himself on promptness. It was one of the things she loved about him.

A few minutes ticked by, though, without any sign of his car. Finally, she heard the sound of an engine approaching. Her heart leapt with excitement.

But it was a black Volvo station wagon that drove right by.

Claire sighed, waiting. She watched the sun sink beneath the horizon in a pinkish-golden glow, sad that she hadn't been able to share the moment with Alec.

A few more cars passed by. Claire looked up each time, but none of them were Alec. Antsy and frustrated, she went back to the table to her check her phone. It was five-fifty! Alec was twenty minutes late. Where was he? Claire checked for missed messages, but there weren't any.

She was about to text him, then stopped herself. She didn't want to be the needy girlfriend. It was too soon to worry. He was just late, that's all. Maybe traffic was bad. Maybe his phone had died. He'd be here soon, and everything would be fine.

The candles were burning down. Claire's stomach growled. She remembered that she hadn't eaten since breakfast. She'd been too busy decorating, prepping, and cooking. The aroma from the short ribs was tantalizing, but she didn't want to lift the lid until Alec got here. He wouldn't notice, though, if one of the mushrooms was missing, would he?

At six-fifteen, with still no sign of Alec, she peeled back a corner of the foil covering the tray of appetizers, snagged a stuffed mushroom, and popped it into her mouth. It was luke-warm, but it was flavorful. So good in fact that she couldn't resist taking a second one.

Her phone rang. Claire raced back to the table, slightly less starving now, and grabbed the phone. Finally, Alec was calling!

It was Erica.

Disappointment cut through her like a knife. Claire answered. "Hello?"

"Happy V-Day." There was a heavy note of sarcasm in Erica's voice.

"You, too," Claire replied. Why was Erica calling her *now*?

"Sorry to call in the middle of stuff," Erica said, the apology sounding more genuine than her previous statement. "You and Alec *are* in the middle of stuff, right? Like dinner or something?"

Claire detected another layer in Erica's voice, which sounded like sadness mixed with loneliness. "No, actually. Alec … hasn't arrived yet."

"Well, perfect timing, then. Everybody I know is off on some big romantic date tonight except me. I'm just sitting here at home alone, and I made the mistake of looking online. Gabby and her posse are tweeting the play-by-play of their evenings. And Brian just posted photos of himself and Kayla looking all snuggly. So, now I'm pissed off! It's like he's doing this just to taunt me."

Claire felt bad for her but really didn't want to talk to Erica about this right now. Her chest already felt so tight with stress about her *own* relationship problems, Claire didn't know if she could take someone else's. Especially someone who'd been blowing her off for weeks. Now suddenly Erica was in the mood to chitchat, because her new friends weren't around, and she was lonely and jealous of Brian's girlfriend?

"I'm sure Brian didn't mean to hurt you, Erica."

"He couldn't have waited until tomorrow to post pictures? This day sucks. What are you guys doing to celebrate?"

"I made dinner." Claire didn't feel like adding that Alec was more than half an hour late.

"I wish I had someone to make dinner for." Erica sighed. "Sorry I'm being such a whiny ass." After an awkward silence, Erica added: "So did you get my Evite? Are you guys coming to my birthday party?"

The change of subject caught Claire off guard. "Oh. I—"

"Almost everyone else has responded by now. When I didn't hear from you, I was worried that it got lost in junk mail."

"No, I got it, I just … to be honest, I wasn't sure if you really wanted me and Alec there, or if it was just a courtesy invite."

"What? Are you kidding? I definitely want you there."

That was the last thing Claire had expected her to say. "Really?"

"Totally! I know I've been in my own world lately, but I'm pretty over it at this point. My party's going to be awesome. I have like fifty people coming, there's going to be great food and music, and the necktie theme is going to be so fun."

"Sounds great, Erica." Claire hadn't expected to *ever* get an olive branch from her former best friend, let alone tonight of all nights. She was trying to refocus her attention on this turn of events, when she heard a car approaching below that sounded like it could be Alec's. Her pulse jumped. "Of course we'll be there," she added hastily. "Hey, Alec just got here, so I have to go."

"Oh. Right. Say hi to him for me. Bye." Erica hung up.

Claire stared for a second at her phone, feeling guilty about the abrupt way she'd ended the conversation. But it *was* Valentine's Day, after all. Phone in hand, Claire raced to the front wall and looked down at the guest parking area. It was getting dark now, but she could make out an SUV pulling into the lot. A man and woman she didn't recognize got out. Her heart sank.

Blowing out a sigh of disappointment, Claire realized she couldn't wait any longer. She *had* to know if Alec was okay. She made the phone call. It went straight to voice mail. She left a brief message, trying to keep her voice light. "Hey, dinner's been ready for a while, and I'm waiting for you on the rooftop. Hope to see you soon!"

She started to worry now. Had Alec been in an accident? In her mind, she saw his mangled Mustang wrapped around a telephone pole, an image that made her shudder. Then, with a gasp, she wondered: Was that an actual vision? Had it really happened? *No, no, stop it*, she told herself. It wasn't a vision, just the product of an anxious mind. There was a reasonable explanation for his lateness. There had to be.

The candles were halfway gone, wax dripping down the candlesticks and threatening to spill onto the tablecloth. Claire gently blew them out, cursing herself for not waiting to light them until after Alec arrived.

It was getting cool, and a breeze picked up, fluttering the tablecloth. Claire wrapped herself in the red shawl she'd borrowed from her mother and wandered around the rooftop, phone in hand, not wanting to miss Alec's call or text. She eventually tried checking Instagram, just to pass the time, but it didn't hold her attention.

The silence was deafening. The twinkle lights, which had looked so festive before, just looked sad and pathetic now.

Another hour passed.

Worry ate at her like a cancer. At the same time, Claire started to feel light-headed from hunger. She tried a prosciutto-wrapped asparagus, but it was cold and limp. She wiped her hands, too upset to eat anything else.

At eight o'clock, she unplugged the slow cooker. A glance through the clear glass lid told her that the short ribs she'd labored over so intently were now sludge.

Claire was about to retrieve the box she'd stashed in a corner and start packing up all the china and glassware, when she heard a car stop outside, the sound of a car door slamming, and hurried footsteps. She recognized Alec's voice as he muttered something into the intercom downstairs, followed by the buzz that let him in.

She sat down at the table. *So. Not in an accident after all. Just two and a half hours late.* A few choice comments she'd like to hurl at him, fueled by hurt and growing anger, bubbled up in her mind.

The stairwell door burst open so hard and fast it actually broke off its hinges, smashing into the stucco wall behind it and leaving an indentation. Claire leapt to her feet, startled, as Alec dashed through the opening.

"Claire, I'm—" He began.

He stopped short, taking in the lights and the festive setup, and whatever he was going to say died on his lips.

Whatever Claire had planned to say died, too, as she stared at him in shock.

Alec looked like he'd just been to war. His clothes were absolutely filthy and ripped, the knees of his khaki pants gone, one sleeve of his white-and-blue-striped button-down shirt pulled away at the shoulder. His face was flushed and streaked with grime and blood, there was an ugly scrape on his forehead, and the skin showing through the gaps in his clothing was red and raw.

Incongruously, he carried the remnants of what used to be a bunch of flowers, now just a bundle of wilted stalks wrapped in tattered cellophane and red paper.

As Alec glanced around, his eyes looked weird—bloodshot and kind of glazed and unfocused. He paused, seemingly flustered as he noticed the door and wall he'd damaged. In an apparent attempt to fix his blunder, Alec reached for the door handle, which crumpled in his grip like aluminum foil.

What on earth was happening? Claire had never seen him this strong.

She leapt to her feet and ran to him. "Oh my God, Alec! *What happened?*" She stopped a couple of feet away, afraid to touch him.

"I—" Alec hesitated, clenching and unclenching the fist that wasn't holding the flowers. One of his eyelids started to twitch. His voice sounded a little off as he said, "I'm really sorry I'm late, Claire. But I can't tell you about it. Not right now. So please don't ask."

"*Don't ask?*" Claire stared at the battered and bloodied man before her, dumbfounded and more hurt than she'd ever felt in her life. "How can you even *think* I'd be okay with that? Something horrible obviously just happened to you. I deserve to know about it!"

He shook his head, staring at the ground, as if unable to look her in the eye. A bit unsteady now, he reached out and braced himself with one hand against what remained of the frame of the stairwell doorway.

Claire suddenly recognized the odd look in his eyes. "Alec, are you *high?*"

His silence was an admission of guilt. He continued to stare anywhere but at her.

All the tension, suspicion, doubt, and worry that Claire had been bottling up for so long came to a head, her entire body vibrating with renewed fury and the need to speak out. "Alec! What the hell is going on with you?" she snapped.

"I can't—" he began.

"Did someone attack you, because you messed with Malcolm's blood supply?"

Alec's head snapped up in shock. But his expression told her she was right.

"Yeah, I've known about that for a while. Why have you been lying to me? Either you come clean with me right now or we're *done*."

Claire couldn't believe those words had just come out of her mouth, but at the same time, she wasn't sorry she'd said them. It felt like a relief to finally have it out in the open.

For a tortuously long minute, Alec just stood there, his face awash with conflicting emotions: surprise, guilt, pain, and regret, all overlaid with a deep uncertainty. At last, he took a long, deep breath, and said:

"All right, Claire. I'll tell you."

twenty-six

Three hours earlier, Alec loosened his button-down collar in frustration as he pulled his car out of the Los Angeles Flower Market parking lot. It had been hectic and crowded because it was Valentine's Day. Traffic getting downtown had been horrendous. He'd barely made it to the market before they closed for the afternoon, but it was the only place Alec could find Claire's favorite flower in this season.

Now the westbound traffic threatened to make him late. Drumming his fingers on the wheel impatiently, Alec decided to improvise. He yanked the wheel and veered off the freeway, deciding to take city streets instead. Maybe, using Waze, he'd get lucky and make it to Claire's on time. After how uncomfortable things had been lately, the last thing he wanted was to show up late on their first date in over a month.

Alec followed the suggested route on his phone, which would get him there with five minutes to spare. After a few sharp turns, the road dipped beneath a concrete-walled under-pass. He stopped behind a few other cars at a red light, then started to call Claire with an update.

Before he could make the call, the light turned green. Just then, Alec spotted a bright yellow HumVee speeding his way in the opposite lane.

Shite, I've seen that car before. Suddenly, with a loud roar, it veered into his lane and came straight at him. He gasped in horror as the oncoming vehicle deliberately rammed into the left front end of his Mustang, sending Alec veering off the road and up the curb in an explosion of metal and glass.

There was a sickening crunch, then everything went silent. Pain stabbed at Alec's chest, head, and spine. Warm wind blew across his face. Alec opened his eyes. As they slowly focused, he saw that his Mustang was smashed up against a traffic signal pole. The windshield was a spiderweb of cracks, and the side windows were blown out. Two people exited the HumVee and were heading toward him, hatred in their eyes. Rico and Javed.

They must have been following me, he thought groggily. How had he missed that? He'd figured Malcolm and his crew would be itching for payback after the warehouse debacle, and he'd spent the past week looking over his shoulder. He never thought that they'd try to kill him in broad daylight, though, with witnesses.

There were civilians all over the place. People who could get hurt if Rico and Javed started using their abilities.

Alec needed to draw the meatheads away from the road, and fast. But there was no way to extract the weapons from his trunk in time. He'd have to fight them hand-to-hand. Which would've been fine if the playing field were even. But his head pounded, his vision was still blurry, his hands were shaking, and sharp pain screamed in his back and ribs.

Alec could see spikes protruding again from Rico's knuckles and a rhino-like horn splitting through the skin of his forehead as he angrily shoved a minivan out of his way. Strength like that wasn't in Rico's deck of powers. That meant both Fallen boys were likely hopped up on Turbo again—an old stash, or one rescued from the warehouse fire—and Alec didn't have a chance at all.

Unless.

Painfully, Alec pulled himself over the gearshift toward his glove box, yanked it open, grabbed the vial of Turbo he'd confiscated, then clawed his way out of the car. Although injured, his powers came to his aid, helping him limp quickly up the nearby hill toward the top of the overpass, which was fenced in by concrete and chain link.

Slipping through a gap between the fence and the wall, Alec rounded the corner to discover what the overpass was hiding from the road: two sets of train tracks running across a wide, endless sea of small, sharp, gray stones. High, graffiti-covered walls towered above the area on both sides, preventing anyone from seeing what was happening by the tracks.

Alec hunched over, in so much pain he could hardly breathe. He could hear Rico's footsteps as he stomped up the hillside behind him and squeezed through the fence. Alec had no choice: without the drug, he'd be dead in minutes.

Unscrewing the cap, Alec swallowed the vial's contents. It tasted like blood, not surprisingly, but was more palatable than he'd expected it to be. Almost instantly, his heart started pounding, even faster than it had when he'd once injected himself full of adrenaline. Seconds later, his head stopped hurting and began to clear. Then the throbbing in his back and ribs began to ebb, and he could stand up straight again.

Before he could assess his condition further, Alec saw Javed burst into view. Javed stretched out his hands, sending blinding arcs of electricity through the air that knocked Alec straight to the ground, his clothes singed and smoking.

Suddenly, Rico's bone-clawed hands grabbed Alec and hurled him into the air. Alec landed with a thud, faceup on top of the rails, the breath knocked out of him as sharp stones cut into his back. Before Alec could move, Rico was there again, planting one heavy foot on Alec's chest, pinning him against the train tracks.

"No more running, asshole," Rico barked.

Alec tried to get up but couldn't. What good was the Turbo if he was stuck here like a pinned insect? A distant squeal signaled the approach of a train. Rico grinned.

Alec heard Javed chuckle behind him. Then he felt hands clamp onto his face before electricity jolted through his body again.

Alec's teeth rattled in his jaw. Strangely, though, as the assault continued, the pain began fading away. Soon, he didn't hurt anymore. *Anywhere.* Nor was he afraid. A warm current seemed to be building inside his body like a gathering storm, seeping into every muscle and vein. His strength and energy were returning—he could feel it—a sensation unlike anything he'd ever experienced before. Was the Turbo finally kicking in?

In their prior encounters, Alec had been playing nice with these guys, only hurting them just enough for that particular conflict to be over, everyone living to fight another day. But those days were over. He was angry, infuriated, that these two assholes had smashed his vintage car and destroyed his plans with Claire.

With a strength and speed that surprised even Alec himself, he brought both arms up sharply toward Rico's knee, knocking his leg out of joint with sickening crack. Rico doubled over with pain as Javed raced toward them.

Alec jumped to his feet, grabbed the horn protruding from Rico's forehead, and snapped it off with a jerk, causing Rico to howl in agony, then turned and stabbed the horn into Javed's side. Javed roared in anguish and fell onto the tracks, writhing.

The train was coming closer. With a flick of his wrists, Alec telekinetically hurled Rico toward a nearby metal power pole, mangling it, then lifted a cloud of stones with his mind and pelted them like hail at Rico, until the man finally fell limp and unconscious.

The train was only a hundred yards away now, blowing its horn for Javed to get clear. Kneeling down, Alec grabbed Javed by the collar. "The fire was an *accident*," Alec hissed. "I've told no one. But you can't just let it lie, can you?" Forcefully, he held Javed's head on the tracks. "Well, this is how it ends," Alec snarled.

"No," Javed pleaded, his hands shaking as he tried to pull out of Alec's grip. "Don't …"

The train was almost on them. The horn blared louder, a sound mingled with the squeal of brakes. It was so close, Alec could smell diesel. He'd killed countless times before, it was part of his job. But it had never before felt so necessary. Or so *righteous*.

Then something in him clicked. *What the hell am I doing?*

At the last possible second, Alec pulled Javed out of the path of the oncoming train. They both fell onto the ground, breathing hard.

Alec pushed hair out of his eyes with a shaking hand. *What did the Turbo do to me?* It was more than a physical enhancement, he realized. It had messed with his mind. Made him downright feral.

He had to get out of here before he broke his vow to himself—to never kill again. "If either of you comes at me again, I'll call in the full force of the Grigori on you and your boss," he snapped in Javed's ear.

"You … wouldn't," Javed croaked. "You're … a wanted man."

"I'd give myself up to send you all to hell." It might have been an idle threat, but the edge in his voice sounded real enough. Javed's bloodshot eyes were wide with fear, something Alec had never seen before.

Dropping Javed to the ground, Alec ran like hell for the road below. His car wasn't going anywhere. He could see his shattered phone inside—unusable. Along with the ravaged flowers he'd gone to such lengths to acquire. He spent the next few minutes trying to find an open store with a phone. When he succeeded, he tried to call Claire, but discovered he couldn't recall her number. He could usually remember *everything*. Had he actually forgotten? Had he suffered a concussion? Or was it because of the Turbo?

He arranged for a tow truck to haul his battered Mustang to a repair shop, then grabbed what was left of the bouquet he'd bought and rode westward in a cab, his head spinning, his blood so hot it felt like it was boiling.

What had the Turbo truly done to him? Alec was horrified by the sensation of rage that had accompanied all that power, how it had almost led him to murder. Staring at his tattered clothes and bloodied hands, he didn't even recognize himself.

twenty-seven

Claire stared at Alec, hardly knowing what to say. They'd been sitting at the table for nearly an hour, all the food untouched, while Alec filled her in on everything that had happened over the past three weeks, up through the accident and fight downtown that had ruined their evening. The whole time he was talking, Alec stared at his clasped hands, or at some distant point across the rooftop, never raising his eyes to meet hers.

Claire felt terrible after hearing what Alec had gone through. She was horrified that he'd been attacked, worried about his injuries, and it broke her heart to learn that his beloved car had been so badly damaged. But even as she struggled to process all he'd revealed, she still couldn't help feeling deeply hurt that he'd been lying to her for weeks over something this serious.

"So," Claire said quietly, "all this time that you've been doing all this dangerous stuff ... did you ever think to tell me about it?"

"Of course I did. Keeping this from you has been eating me up inside. I debated about telling you so many times. At first, I didn't want to worry you. As time went on, I worried that if you knew, you might try to stop me. Or even worse, you'd insist on coming with me, and I couldn't risk *that*."

"Why not?"

He finally raised his eyes to hers. "Claire, I didn't even know what I was dealing with until I got well into it. It's been hard enough defending myself. I couldn't have protected you as well."

"What have all these self-defense lessons been for if I can't even be trusted to hold my own?" Claire shot back at him.

"That's so you can handle yourself in an emergency. You've had such a … how should I put it? A *gung-ho* attitude lately—"

"A what?" she bristled.

"I was concerned that our training sessions had given you a false sense of security. You're doing well, but you're still very new at this. It wasn't my intention, but I ended up in life-or-death situations, Claire. I will *never* willingly put you in that kind of danger. You must know that."

"Okay, but you still should have told me. If you'd explained that you'd be safer without me along, I would have understood."

"Would you?"

"Yes!" Claire heaved a frustrated sigh. "You are such an idiot. If you'd given me a chance, I might have even been useful. I might have been able to *foresee* some of the dangers that lay ahead of you."

"That power isn't very reliable, though, is it? You never know what you're going to see, past or future." He folded his hands on the tabletop. "On the other hand, I can't help wondering why you didn't just brainwash me into telling you."

"*What?*" Claire was offended that he'd even think such a thing. "I would never do that!"

His eyebrows rose. "How can I be sure? I'm not the only one who's been withholding information the past few weeks."

Claire hesitated. "What do you mean?"

"You brainwashed Zachariah. I doubt you could go from having no idea how your power works to successfully using mind control on a Grigori unless you've been practicing."

Claire's face reddened, but she didn't reply.

"I noticed a few suspicious things before you messed with Zachariah's mind, and since. Like the sudden about-face with Dr. Grant and the costumes. You played a part in that, didn't you?"

"Okay," Claire admitted, guilt and embarrassment raising her defenses, "so maybe I *have* used my powers a few times, but it was always to help somebody else."

"And yet—to quote you—did you ever think to tell me about it?"

She bit her lip. "I wanted to, but things were so strained between us lately, I figured you'd be mad at me if you found out, and for no good reason."

"No good reason? Claire—"

"Look, it's not like I was doing it for my own personal benefit! What's wrong with Jason finally asking Gabby out? What's wrong with Señora Gutierrez exercising for the first time in her life?"

He paused. "If that's what you've been up to ... what's *wrong* is that they didn't do so of their own volition. You mentally manipulated them into it."

"But if the outcome was positive—"

"It may *seem* positive at the moment, Claire, but you have no idea what the final outcome will be. Time will tell, but trust me: it may not be at all what you wished or intended."

Claire sighed, frustrated. "What about Helena using her powers to see the future? Without her help, I would have been cougar chow months ago."

"You can't compare Helena's abilities to yours."

"Why not?"

"First off, Helena doesn't violate people's free will. She's just relaying information that people can act on or not. Second, she's a seasoned Grigori. You're completely new at this. You don't have the experience yet to judge when it's necessary and appropriate to use your powers. Helena and I both warned you. Using a gift like mind control at all is *dangerous*—not just regarding the fate of others but for *you* as well."

"*Why* is it dangerous for me? I don't understand."

"Think about it, Claire. It's what Vincent was talking about months ago. The more of an expert you become, the more tempted the Fallen will be to abduct you, like they did your father, and force you to use that ability for their benefit. Either by drugging you, or by threatening to harm the people you love."

"Oh." Claire felt her arguments deflate, like the air going out of a balloon. No one had put it that way before. She swallowed, and reluctantly said, "Okay. I get it. I'll stop experimenting. But if there's ever another emergency, like the time Zachariah almost recognized you, I'll use whatever ability seems necessary."

"Understood. And the same goes for me. In an emergency situation, I have to act."

"The stuff at the warehouse wasn't an emergency," Claire argued. "That was you *willingly* putting yourself in danger."

"Someone had to do *something*. The Fallen are making a powerful and dangerous drug. What if it slips into human hands? The destructive possibilities are mind-boggling."

"I thought the whole point of going AWOL was to leave that kind of stuff behind."

"That *is* what I wanted, what I'd been dreaming about for decades. And I really thought if I could just live like a human, it would be a relief, and all that I needed ..." He sighed. "But I can't ignore all this bad stuff happening around us. I just can't."

Claire stared at him, worry brewing in her gut. "What does that mean? You can't go back to the Grigori. They might execute you."

"Maybe, aye. But I can keep my ear to the ground and help out where I can. I think I did something important. Hopefully, Rico and Javed will be out of commission for a while and will leave us both alone. And by interrupting their production of Turbo, I've made the city safer for *everyone*, at least for a while."

Claire shook her head. "You can't have it both ways, Alec. You can't be a nice, normal high-school student by day and play Batman by night. And all this stuff you're doing, you might have just pissed off Javed, Rico, and Malcolm even more."

Alec sighed, his expression grim. "I *am* worried about that. But no matter how many times I go over it, I can't just ignore a major threat."

"You can't, or you won't?"

"If something of this magnitude happens again, I don't think I can let it go down any differently."

Claire stood up so fast, her chair clattered to the ground. "Well at least you're honest about *that*," she retorted angrily. "It's nice to know where I stand. Where *we* stand. You expect *me* not to use my new gift unless it's a matter of life or death. But you can jump into danger anytime *you* see fit."

Alec rose, heaving a deep sigh. "We're talking about two very different things, Claire. Can't you see that?"

"No, what I see is you saying you can do what you think is right, but I can't. And that's just bullshit." Tears spilled from her eyes. Wiping them away, she added, "Do you have any idea how much effort I went to, to make this a perfect evening?"

"I do. I'm so sorry, Claire. This is the last thing I wanted to happen." He started toward her as if he wanted to comfort her, but she backed away.

"Sorry for what? That my dinner was a disaster? Or that we've been sitting here arguing for half the night?"

"Both."

She studied him, noticing that his eyes weren't bloodshot anymore, and the visible cuts on his forehead, arms, and knees had almost healed. "Well, I'm done talking. I think you should just go."

Alec looked at her with a wounded expression, a pain deeper than Claire had ever seen before. He stood up wordlessly, arranging the remains of the bedraggled flowers in the vase with an unnecessary amount of care, before heading for the door. Pausing at the threshold, he turned back, his voice merely a whisper:

"Happy Valentine's Day."

And then he was gone.

Claire's heart felt like it had dropped out of her chest. She sank down at the table again, dabbing at her tears with a napkin, her attention falling on the flowers in the vase. Even though only a smattering of pink petals remained, she realized what they were.

Peonies.

twenty-eight

The next week was rough. Alec's Mustang was repairable, but it would be out of commission for at least a month. In the meantime he bought a second-hand bike to get around, since using a ride-hailing service would easily allow the Fallen to track his movements.

It seemed to work. No one else had come after him following the fight. Yet. Were Javed and Rico nursing their wounds? Had Malcolm decided to back off for the moment? Alec had no idea, but it was a relief to have a reprieve.

Life at school, on the other hand, was not as rosy.

Things were so strained between Alec and Claire, they barely spoke. They didn't train, they didn't talk in class, they didn't even meet for lunch. Most of Claire's books were missing from their locker. It appeared that she was living out of her backpack. An obvious attempt to avoid him.

Rehearsals were a misery. Claire made a point of sitting on the opposite side of the theater from him when she wasn't onstage. During their scenes together, she remained in character the entire time, with none of the fun asides they used to share. But far worse, Alec had to sit and watch while Claire and Neil practiced their romantic scenes together. Claire was doing a pretty convincing job, staring into Neil's pretty eyes with pining devotion.

On Thursday, they were rehearsing the scene that included the song "I Loved You Once in Silence." Claire, as Guinevere, was sitting in the partially completed set for the queen's bedchamber, brushing her hair. Neil, as Lancelot, entered quietly and paused a few feet away from her. In a hushed, tremulous voice, he said, "Jenny … ?"

Claire/Guinevere rose and looked at him in astonishment. He crossed to her, softly explaining that he'd seen her light in the window. He knew she was alone. He had tried to stay away, but he couldn't. And then, in a moment Alec bore with gritted teeth, Neil swept Claire into his arms and held her tight.

"Wait, wait, hold on a second," interrupted Ms. Donnelly.

Neil and Claire separated almost immediately, glancing at the director, who stood on the edge of the stage.

"Up to now, we've been treating this more or less as a chaste moment, but it's not working," Ms. Donnelly went on. "Lancelot and Guinevere have built up all these secret, passionate feelings for each other. They're deeply in love. They're about to admit it in song, and he's going to start a war over her. This is our only opportunity to see that passion. So I'd like to try adding a kiss."

Alec froze. He'd been so certain this wasn't going to be required. Even though he was sitting several yards away, Alec caught Claire blushing.

Neil's expression was definitely awkward. "Doesn't that violate Lancelot's code of honor?"

"So does their whole forbidden-love thing," replied Ms. Donnelly. "I think this is important. Let's try it."

"Do you want me to kiss him, or him to kiss me?" Claire asked uncertainly.

"How about if you both just go for it?" Ms. Donnelly suggested. "Let's back up a few lines to ramp into it."

Alec watched, his stomach knotting, as Claire and Neil each took a breath, went back to their former positions, and repeated the earlier dialogue. This time, their embrace became visibly more desperate. They pulled apart slightly, looking at each other hesitantly, as if trying to figure out how to arrange their faces. Then, in unison, their lips met in a firm but brief kiss.

When they separated again, the expression in their eyes held so much feeling and emotion, Alec felt like he'd been kicked in the balls.

"Okay, that'll do for now." Ms. Donnelly smiled. "I think it's going to work. And we have almost three weeks to get it right."

The rest of the scene, where Guinevere and Lancelot plaintively sang about their love for each other, was equally torturous to watch. Alec felt hot waves of anger racing through him. Or was it jealousy? He hated to think that he would stoop to such a low feeling. All he knew was that he wanted to strangle Neil. He had to grip the armrests on his seat to keep himself from leaping onto the stage. Why was he feeling this so strongly? It was just a school play, after all. They were just acting. Weren't they?

A sudden thought occurred to Alec. He'd been irritable all week, unusually so. He'd attributed it to the situation with Claire. However, he couldn't help wondering if the strength of his irritation was partly due to the residual effects of—or withdrawal from—the Turbo he'd taken.

What a mess he'd gotten himself into.

twenty-nine

The beat of the music throbbed in Claire's ears as she folded up her wet umbrella and stuck it in the bucket in Erica's marble-floored foyer. A clothes rack held tons of raincoats and parkas. Claire shrugged out of her own coat, hung it up with the others, and moved past the grand, sweeping staircase into Erica's living room.

The room was crowded with partygoers, there to celebrate Erica's birthday, the February rain forcing everyone to stay indoors. Erica's parents stood to one side, looking fairly vigilant in their role as chaperones. Claire hadn't been to many parties since she'd started high school, but from what she could glean, this was going to be a relatively tame affair.

Claire recognized people from the cast of *Camelot*, along with kids from the popular clique at school. They were all wearing something in tribute to Erica's obligatory necktie theme: everything from simple ties, suits, and tuxedos, to sexy maid and cat outfits with collars.

Happy Birthday banners (each letter printed on a colorful cardboard necktie) were strung from beams overhead, along with black-and-white balloons imprinted with tuxedos. A guy in a clown tie behind the bar was dispensing soft drinks. In the adjoining dining room, Claire caught a glimpse of Brian and Kayla standing cozily together beside a long table laden with finger foods.

Claire straightened the red satin bow tie she'd bought to wear with her white top and jeans, hoping it looked all right. It was so weird to be here without Alec. Every time she thought about him, though, her chest got tight with anger. They'd spent all week avoiding each other. She'd kept hoping he would change his mind, call her and admit that she was right, that he would give up his dangerous obsession. But that hadn't happened. Maybe it never would.

He'd said he loved her. Despite everything that was happening, she still loved *him*, so much. So shouldn't he put *them* first? No, he was sticking to some stupid ideal, some need to be a hero. Not only that, but now, he seemed to be just as mad at her as she was at him. Was it just because she'd practiced her new power a few times? Or was it because of what happened at rehearsals last week?

When Ms. Donnelly added that kiss, it was one of the most awkward moments of Claire's life. It had gotten easier every time after that, but they were just stage kisses. They didn't mean anything. Whenever they rehearsed that scene, though, Alec looked like he was ready to start World War III.

It was so ridiculous. She and Alec had all but broken up, so he had no right to be jealous. She and Neil weren't even friends anymore. Although deep down, Claire had to admit, she wished that she and Neil *could* be friends again. It would make things so much easier—and not just at rehearsals. As she looked around the room, she wished she had *any* friends right now.

"Claire!" Gabrielle Miller emerged from the crowd and pranced up to Claire. She was dressed in a sexy schoolgirl uniform, with the world's shortest plaid skirt, a matching necktie, a midriff-baring white blouse, knee-high stockings, and high-heeled shoes. "I love your bow tie!"

"Thanks. Your outfit is … really something." Claire managed a small smile.

"I found it online. The top is way smaller than advertised, I'm lucky I could get into it. Hey! I've been meaning to ask: aren't you the one who found my sweater and gave it to Jason Tate?"

"Yeah."

"It must have been fate that you asked *him* to deliver it. He ended up asking me out. We've been dating ever since, and it's been totally awesome."

"I'm so glad." This time, the smile Claire gave Gabrielle was genuine.

"Speak of the devil!" Gabrielle glowed as she turned toward the foyer, which Jason had just entered. "Have fun, Claire." She darted off and threw her arms around Jason, kissing him soundly.

Claire sighed. Even though she no longer had a love life, she was happy things were working out for *someone*.

She spied Erica a few yards away, laughing with two girls Claire had never met. Erica's outfit was *so* Erica: a 1920s-era black-and-white-striped gangster's pantsuit, matching necktie, and platform heels. A black fedora was perched atop her sleek red hair, and she wore bright red lipstick.

Gazing at Erica, Claire felt a stab of sadness. More than anything, Claire realized, she longed to win back Erica's friendship. But how? Shouldn't a relationship as close as theirs had been be able to rise above the thing that had happened with the play? She'd tried to mend fences by apologizing and baring her soul, but that had only made things worse.

Then again, when Erica was lonely on Valentine's Day, she'd called and shared *her* problems. Maybe Erica *did* still care, deep down. Maybe their timing had just been off.

Claire's eyes connected with Erica's, and Erica briefly smiled, excused herself from the other girls, and came over.

"Hey, Claire! You look cute." Her tone was a little flat.

"So do you," Claire responded. "Great outfit. And happy birthday."

"Thanks."

They exchanged a brief hug that Claire felt was more compulsory than heartfelt on Erica's part.

"Where's Alec?" Erica asked.

"We … came separately."

"Oh. Well, I'm glad you're here. It's nice to see you."

"Ditto." Claire figured she'd better grab this opportunity while she could. "Hey, can we talk for a minute? Alone?"

"Alone? Are you kidding? This is *my* party."

"I know. But ever since you called me, I've needed to say something. It's important."

Erica sighed. "Everything with you is *important*. I guess we can go to the gym. But I shouldn't be gone for more than five minutes, okay?"

"Okay."

Erica waved and smiled at people as she led the way out of the living room and down a hall into a room filled with exercise equipment. Erica stopped beside a treadmill and crossed her arms. "So, what's up?"

Claire took a deep breath. "Well. I feel bad because it's been so long since we really talked. And we used to be such good friends. Something happened to change that, I don't really understand what, but … if it's because of the play, or something else I did or said, I'm sorry. Really sorry. And I'm hoping we can fix it. Because I miss you."

Erica chewed on her lip, drawing an imaginary circle on the polished hardwood floor with her toe. Finally, she blew out a long breath. "I miss you too, but … things are different for me now. I have these new friends who don't mesh with you guys. They don't totally get me, but it's still easier to be around them, even if things never get too deep. I mean, I loved hanging out with you and Brian and Alec. But that kinda changed when you and Alec started dating. And now that Brian is dating Kayla,

I can barely look him in the face anymore. Then the play happened. It's hard for me to be around you because it just makes me remember that I lost out on something so big, something I dreamed of for so long … I know that sounds lame and super-selfish. But I can't help it."

"I get it." Claire kept her comment short so Erica could vent. It was the most she'd heard her friend say to her in months.

"Plus. It got to the point where I just couldn't take all your paranormal, life-and-death angel stuff anymore. I just want to be a normal teenager while I can, and being around you … to be honest, it's kind of exhausting."

Claire nodded. "I get that, too."

"And that time after rehearsal, when you dropped all that stuff on me out of the blue about being kidnapped by the Fallen and a new mind-control power—I'm sorry, but it was too much, I needed to tune out." Erica looked at her. "Is that really true? You can *brainwash* people now?"

"I shouldn't have said brainwash. That makes it sound really sinister. It's more like … *suggesting*." Claire felt her cheeks grow warm as she added, almost apologetically, "But if I focus, I *can* sometimes get people to do what I want."

"Good God. That *is* brainwashing, Claire."

"No, it's not. Really. Think of it like … like a Jedi mind trick, that I only use for *good*. Like I gave Jason the guts to ask Gabby out! I convinced Señora Gutierrez to make time to start exercising. I even got Dr. Grant to up the funding for our new costumes!"

Erica's jaw dropped. "*That's* why we got the costume funding? It was *you*?"

Claire shrugged, her blush deepening. "Yeah. Isn't it awesome? The knights get to wear real armor! And the girls' costumes are so …" She stopped, noticing that Erica wasn't thrilled like she'd hoped.

"That's really creepy, Claire."

"What do you mean?"

"Are you even listening to yourself?" Erica's eyes crinkled with disgust. "You can get people to do what you *want*? That is unethical on *so* many levels."

Claire sighed. "Now you sound just like Alec."

"Well, maybe you should listen to him." Erica paused. "Wait, is that why you came separately tonight? Something's been off between you two at rehearsal."

"We haven't exactly been speaking since Valentine's Day."

"Why not? Is he mad about this brainwashing thing?"

"It's not just that. Alec's been playing superhero again lately against the Fallen, and he refuses to back off, even though it almost got him killed. We had this big argument, and—it didn't go well."

"Shit." Erica's face softened into an expression of concern that Claire hadn't seen in a long time. It was like having a best friend again, if only for the briefest of seconds.

Before she could elaborate further, though, Courtney dashed into the room, screeching, "Erica! I've been looking everywhere for you. You promised to be my partner in pool, come on!"

As she was tugged out of the room by the arm, Erica shot back at Claire, "To be continued?"

Claire nodded, struggling to hold back another sigh. Just as she was getting somewhere with Erica, Courtney had to come in and ruin it all. Would she ever get another chance to make things right?

Just then, there was the sound of a toilet flushing. Claire started in surprise as a door inside the room opened ... and Neil walked out.

The look on Neil's face made it clear that he had overheard everything.

thirty

Alec stared at the kids around him.

It was the first time he'd been at a bash like this as a legitimate participant. In his past life, he'd always been in disguise, searching for his latest mark. Of course, he could argue, he was in disguise now as well, doing his best to pose as a human teen.

Certainly a good excuse for why he was feeling so awkward and angsty. The taxi ride he'd taken there—with arguably the worst driver in the world—hadn't helped him arrive in a calm state of mind, either.

As he wandered from the living room into the dining room, he didn't spot Claire and wondered where she was. The thrift-store paisley tie he wore over his T-shirt chafed at his neck. Trying to blend in, he picked up a plate and helped himself to a slice of necktie-shaped minipizza and some bowtie pasta salad. He chewed, searching for a friendly face among the crowd. Sure, he knew almost everyone by name, but he didn't have any relationships beyond Claire's small circle. And that had pretty much disintegrated.

He found Brian in the den, playing air hockey with Kayla. "Hey," Alec said, his spirits rising a fraction as he walked over.

Brian returned a "Hey, man," his attention fully focused on the game.

"Have you seen Claire?"

"Nope, busy dominating the ice. Ha! Take that!" Brian cried as he sent a puck flying into Kayla's goal.

"Don't gloat," Kayla retorted. "It won't happen again." Smiling at Alec, she withdrew the puck and placed it on the table. "He actually thinks he has a chance. He forgets I'm half-Canadian. Hockey runs in my veins."

"That's why he usually sticks to Ping-Pong," Alec commented with a grin.

Brian didn't notice the joke at all, but Kayla laughed, then directed her attention back to the table. In a blink, she scored a lightning-fast bank shot on Brian.

"Damn it!" Brian waved Alec away melodramatically. "Begone, Alec, you're bad luck."

Alec turned away, muttering a brief, "Sorry." Brian might have been kidding, but it didn't do anything to help Alec's mood. Or to make him feel a part of the festivities. Dumping his paper plate in the trash, he moved on to the family room, which was crowded with kids talking and laughing. He spotted two guys spiking their drinks behind Erica's parents' built-in bar. Alec continued on, seeking a quiet place where he could fester in silence. Maybe he could find a book to read.

At the far end of the hall, a doorway opened onto what looked like a home gym, where two people were staring at each other intently.

Claire and Neil.

As Alec watched, Claire grabbed Neil by the hand and pulled him outside, shutting the sliding glass doors behind them.

Alec stopped dead in his tracks, his fist tightening on a nearby doorjamb. What were Claire and Neil doing here, away from everyone else?

Through the glass doors, he could see them standing on the covered patio, silhouetted against the darkness by the landscape lighting. Looking far more intimate than he'd expect, based on their current status.

But what did he really know? It had been over a week since he and Claire had spoken. Had she taken refuge from their fight in the arms of her longtime crush? Neil looked damn smart, after all, in a gray blazer with a folded handkerchief peeking above his breast pocket, and one of those fancy ascots he seemed to love.

Alec heard a snap and realized that he'd splintered the doorjamb in his grip.

"What the hell, Brennan?" Neil yanked his hand from Claire's and stepped back. "Why'd you drag me out here?"

Rain beat down hard on the patio roof overhead and bounced off the flagstones beyond. "I didn't want anyone else interrupting us, or eavesdropping," Claire explained, wrapping her arms around herself against the cold night air.

"Well, excuse the shit out of me. I'm minding my own business, when suddenly I hear two voices blabbing about 'paranormal, life-and-death-angel stuff' right outside the bathroom door? And then—"

"Right, well—"

"Then you and Fisher are going on and on about—what was it? Mind-control powers? Brainwashing? MacKenzie being a superhero? The 'Fallen'?" Neil shook his head.

Claire took a deep breath. "Okay. Neil. If I tell you, you have to promise not to tell anyone else."

"What? Or you'll have to kill me?"

She sighed. "Do you promise?"

He threw up his hands, scowling. "Sure. Fine. Hit me."

Where to start? Claire knew he'd suspected something about her and Alec back at the Homecoming Dance fiasco, but for any of it to make sense, she had to go back to the beginning.

Well, almost the beginning. "Do you remember, last fall, when I offered to tutor you in Spanish?"

Neil's eyes narrowed. "What about it?"

"Well …" Claire felt sick to her stomach at the thought of what she was about to tell him. Knowing about this stuff had already damaged her friendship with Erica. But her relationship with Neil was already broken. This might be the only way to win back his trust. *If* she could get him to believe her. "*That* happened because I got a vision of a possible future where you were going to fail that test. Because I'm only half-human. And that's one of my powers."

Neil's scowl was replaced by an insulting smirk. "Half-human? Okay. Sure. So what's your other half?"

"Angel."

Now he rolled his eyes and shook his head. "I knew some kids were raiding the liquor cabinet, but I didn't think you were one of them."

Claire felt tears threatening the edge of her vision. "Neil, I'm being real here."

Neil backed away from her. "What does that even mean? When I asked you to be straight with me at Homecoming, you blew me off. And now your solution is to feed me this bullshit?"

Tears ran down Claire's cheeks now, warm against her skin. "Please. I've been holding on to this for so long because I knew you wouldn't believe me."

Neil's body language softened. But he said nothing.

"I need you to just listen to me right now, Neil. No interruptions until I'm finished. It'll probably be the weirdest thing you've ever heard, but I swear it's true."

Alec stood by the bar in the den. Another set of sliding glass doors overlooked the rear patio, giving him a silent view of Neil and Claire's pseudo-repeat performance of the Lancelot/

Guinevere scene. Claire was crying now. What was going on out there? What was she telling Neil?

Alec's heart lurched with frustration and pain. Usually, he was highly skilled at reading people, yet he had no idea how to interpret the look on Neil's face. All Alec knew was that his possibly ex-girlfriend was pouring out her heart to someone else, instead of him.

Alec tore his glance away. On the other side of the bar, two boys were adding vanilla-flavored vodka to their plastic cups of punch. Alec felt a weird twinge in his gut. Every time he'd observed people drinking alcohol over the decades, he'd looked down on them as if they were "lesser" somehow, for needing chemical alteration to relieve stress or have fun. He'd always believed that if he were ever lucky enough to pass for human, he wouldn't need that kind of thing.

Right now, though, a stress-relieving beverage sounded tempting. A voice in the back of his head warned him that it was a bad idea. He'd already experienced the effects of a stimulant when he drank the Turbo. Did he really want to alter his body chemistry again, this time with a depressant?

Yes, he did.

If I try it, Alec thought, *I'll finally know what it's all about.* Over the past six months, he'd indulged in a host of foods that had formerly been forbidden due to his strict training regimen. And the only side effect had been bliss. So why not this? *It's not like Claire will care, anyway*, his mind growled further, while that other, quieter voice countered, *Don't. There are good reasons you've avoided this one.*

"Screw it," muttered Alec to himself, swiping the vodka bottle. He looked around for a cup, but didn't see any. All he could find were a collection of shot glasses from the Fishers' world travels. Alec chose one from his native Edinburgh, and, with a bitter smile at the irony, poured himself a shot and gulped it down.

He couldn't taste anything at first. Just an intense burning sensation as he swallowed. He struggled not to gag, mostly from surprise, wishing he'd brought a Coke or bottle of water to sip from afterward. A "chaser," he'd heard it called. Yeah, there *was* a taste after all—a pungent, synthetic vanilla flavor trying its best to cover the mild, rubbing-alcohol odor behind it.

After a moment, all the unpleasantness passed, and he felt a warm sensation in the center of his chest. Alec took another shot. Although he was a newbie at this, and his Grigori healing abilities were surely combating the effects of the alcohol, something was definitely happening. There was a slight numbing sensation in his fingertips and his brain, and a weird distortion to his vision where everything seemed to be occurring a little slower. The new feelings were a welcome distraction. Numbness was just what he needed right now.

But the pain returned the second he glanced out the window at Neil and Claire. They were huddled together now, seated on side-by-side patio chairs. It looked like Claire was doing all the talking, wiping away tears as she spoke.

All at once, Alec understood what was happening. *Claire was telling Neil everything.*

Everything they had agreed to keep secret. Everything that could compromise Alec's existence here.

Once Neil knew what they both were—even if he didn't tell anyone—where would it lead? Neil could finally forgive Claire for lying to him back at Homecoming. Claire could finally have a partner who was a hundred percent human. Neil didn't come with any baggage. He was a far safer match for Claire. In the wake of Valentine's Day, would she choose Neil over him? Had she already done so?

Alec poured himself another shot and drank it down. Just then, Erica's father breezed into the room. Alec quickly slipped away from the bar, stealthily depositing the glass on a bookshelf at the far end of the room so as to not draw attention to himself.

His mind kept replaying the image of Claire and Neil in rehearsal, in their "passionate embrace." If he didn't get involved right now, he knew what would happen. Neil would take Claire's hand in understanding. Claire would look into Neil's eyes. And there'd be a repeat performance of their stage kiss, except this time it would be the real thing.

The thought of standing by and doing nothing while Neil stole his girlfriend was like an ice pick to the heart.

Claire dried her eyes and nose with the back of her hand and dared a glance at Neil, desperate to know what he was thinking.

He wasn't looking at her, just staring out into the rain.

She'd told him everything. About the first time she got a vision, the pain they used to cause her, the unexpected revelation that Alec had powers, too, the truth behind the scaffolding incident, her mysteriously missing Grigori father, her newly discovered grandmother, and all the drama behind her Halfblood relationship with Alec, the AWOL avenging angel. Even though she'd kept it as brief as possible, Claire felt like she'd been talking for hours before finally getting to the Fallen and the deadly fights on Homecoming. So much more had happened since then, but other than mentioning her abduction, she figured that was enough for now. She'd better stop and let everything sink in.

Neil had done as she'd asked, listening while saying nothing. Now, he still seemed to be sticking to her request, and the suspense was killing her.

Still not looking at her, he withdrew the handkerchief from the breast pocket of his blazer and thrust it in her direction. Claire choked back a laugh/sob. It was such a nice gesture, that despite whatever dark thoughts might be swirling in his head, he would notice—and care—how much she needed it. She unfolded the handkerchief and gratefully used it to blow her nose.

"So …" Neil began finally, staring at his shoes, "you're half angel, have two psychic powers, and supposedly no right to exist."

"Yes," she answered quietly, grateful that his tone wasn't mocking.

"Alec is an angel assassin," Neil went on. "He's over a hundred years old, but pretending to be a junior in high school. Your grandmother's on the board of directors of some angel society who are involved in a secret war with the part-angel-mafia-spies, who also recently kidnapped you. And last year, you were almost killed by a werewolf—"

"Were-cougar," she corrected, then instantly regretted it, because his eyes darted up to hers with detached disbelief and a hint of disgust.

"Claire, you just recapped the plots of every bad movie I've ever seen, all rolled into one."

Claire's shoulders drooped, fresh tears stinging her eyes. "I knew it was a long shot that you'd believe any of this. But I had to try."

Neil shook his head. "I'm sorry, but how do you expect—"

At that moment, a sliding glass door roared open. Alec staggered out and, without a word, grabbed Neil by the lapels of his blazer and hauled him to his feet.

"Alec!" Claire leapt up, appalled.

Alec's green eyes were cold as he yanked Neil's face close to his. "*Leave.*"

Neil put up his hands. "Calm down, MacKenzie."

"Let him go!" Claire cried. "We were just talking."

"I noticed," Alec spat out, his voice slightly slurred. "And I could tell where it was all leading."

"It was *leading* to me leaving anyway," Neil countered. Without warning, he brought one knee up hard into Alec's crotch. Alec grunted, dropping to one knee.

As if he thought things were settled, Neil turned to walk away. But Alec instantly rallied and lunged, landing a fist in Neil's kidneys. The blow sent Neil staggering forward.

Claire gasped. She knew how strong Alec was. A punch like that might have easily broken Neil's back, or worse. Thankfully, as Neil turned back to face them in fury, he seemed only winded.

Before Neil could retaliate, Claire darted between them. "Stop it, Alec!"

Alec's eyes burned with frustration, as if he were considering whether or not to shove her aside but decided against it. Instead, he telekinetically threw Neil into the air. Neil slammed against the nearby wall, where he remained, hovering a couple of feet above the ground, in Alec's mental grip.

"Alec, *please*," Claire cried, new tears starting to flow. But Alec wasn't listening, his focus was all on Neil.

Neil, his face alive with terror and confusion, still hovered in the air not far from Alec's splayed hand. "Holy shit," he murmured.

Claire had to stop this, somehow. Bracing one leg next to Alec's, she twisted her body, yanking him to the ground with one of the takedowns he'd taught her. As Alec's focus broke, Neil dropped to the flagstones, knocking over a potted plant with a loud crash.

Claire hauled herself to her feet, staring down at Alec, who looked glassy-eyed and disoriented in a way she'd never seen before. "What's wrong with you?" she hissed.

"He's been drinking," croaked Neil as he struggled to stand, stunned, his blazer and jeans streaked with potting soil. "You can smell it on his breath."

"Drinking?" Claire stared at Alec in shock and disappointment. First he was high on Valentine's Day, and now this?

"I. I'm …" Alec began.

But he never got to finish. A cluster of people suddenly appeared at the open patio door. Erica shoved through them and strode outside, flanked by Gabrielle, Ashley, and Courtney. Neil, dazed and dirty, was leaning against the far wall, while Alec fumbled a bit unsteadily to his feet.

"What in the bejeesus is going on out here?" Erica asked.

"I have no idea," Neil answered. Alec didn't say a thing.

"Have you morons been fighting?" Erica prodded.

"It was just a misunderstanding," Claire replied apologetically. "I think Alec got the wrong idea about.… Anyway, it's over."

"God, Claire, can't the world turn for five minutes without being all about your drama?" Erica cried.

"I didn't do anything," Claire countered.

"Really?" Erica laughed bitterly. "First, you drag me away from my friends and unload all this bullshit on me. Then your little love triangle starts dueling at my house?"

"Hold on a second—" began Neil, but Erica was on a roll.

"You ruined the play for me, and now, when I'm trying to have just one night that's for me, you're ruining that, too."

Claire swallowed hard. "I didn't mean to take the part from you, Erica."

"I don't believe that anymore." Erica strode forward, and said under her breath, "I used to think you got Guinevere based on your … *talent* for singing. But that thing you told me earlier? Now I know how *you stole my part*."

Claire was stunned. Did Erica just accuse her of brainwashing her way into the play? "Wait," Claire started, knowing she had to be careful what she said, with all these people listening.

Gabrielle inserted herself into the scene. "Don't." She pointed toward the door. "We're here to celebrate Erica, okay? Just go home. All three of you."

The *I can handle this myself* look on Erica's face showed she was a little peeved that Gabrielle was getting involved but letting it slide.

Everyone was silent in collective embarrassment, until Neil—after glancing at Claire and Alec—turned to Gabrielle and Erica, and said, "Whatever. Happy birthday, Fisher." He pushed through the crowd and left.

Alec followed. Erica stalked into the house, the crowd at her heels.

Claire stood there on the patio, the sound of rainfall echoing around her, feeling more alone than she'd ever felt in her life.

thirty-one

To say Claire was miserable would be the understatement of the year.

Alec couldn't look her in the eye, not that she wanted him to. Neil was more standoffish than ever, treating both her and Alec like they were freaks. Which they were. Claire could only hope he wouldn't tell anyone.

Erica, meanwhile, was acting more like Claire didn't exist than ever. At times, Ms. Donnelly would ask Claire to sit out a scene, so Erica could have a chance to run through it as Guinevere. Erica was excellent in the part, which only increased Claire's inner turmoil. She had to admit, Erica was partially right. Although brainwashing had nothing to do with it, Claire *had* gotten the role because of her Halfblood singing abilities. Before she'd awakened, Claire hadn't been able to sing to save her life.

Claire kept hoping Helena would turn up some exciting discovery about her father, to give her something positive to focus on, but that hadn't happened. So it was just schoolwork and rehearsal, barely speaking to anyone.

Ms. Donnelly was clearly frustrated with their current dynamic. At Tuesday's rehearsal, she complained, "Kids, this isn't my *hobby*. I believe in what we're doing here, and I need you to as well. When you're in this theater, the play is all that matters. Not your homework, not friend problems or your dating lives, none of it. Focus on your performance and honor the audience, or when we open two weeks from now, there won't be anything worth watching."

When rehearsal ended, Claire briefly caught a glimpse of Alec. He looked totally miserable. Quickly averting his eyes, he took off down the aisle, heading for the lobby.

Claire watched him go, her heart catching. She was equally miserable. Yes, she was upset by his macho Watcher attitude and his behavior at Erica's party. But she missed what they'd once had. Was it really over? If she went after him this second and said something, was there a chance they could fix their relationship?

Just then Erica appeared at her side. "If you're going to say anything to Alec," Erica said quietly, "make sure it's that you were wrong."

Claire paused, surprised that Erica was even speaking to her. "What?"

"You said he was upset about the brainwashing thing? Well, he was right. I just heard that Dr. Grant is getting endless flak for diverting funds for the basketball team's new uniforms into our play. One of the team dads just bailed on a ten-thousand-dollar donation he'd promised, and Ms. Donnelly has to write a letter to placate all the parents of the kids on the team."

"Oh crap."

"I mean, it's great that we've got the costumes and all, but what gave *you* the right to interfere?" Erica gave Claire a pointed look, then climbed up onstage toward a side exit.

Claire hurried up the aisle, her stomach churning. When she'd persuaded Dr. Grant, it had never occurred to her that anything could go wrong. She'd been so sick of the sports teams always getting all the money and wanted the arts to get a piece of the pie. But, just as everyone warned her, it had gone wrong. She'd put Ms. Donnelly in a difficult position. Damn it.

Claire pushed through the door into the lobby, looking for Alec. But he was already gone.

At lunch that day in the North Quad, Claire distractedly picked at her enchiladas. Brian and Kayla were chatting about an episode of some anime that Claire had never seen.

"I just feel bad that the werewolf led her on like that," Kayla was saying. "It's almost as bad as what Jason Tate did to Gabby Miller."

That caught Claire's attention. She looked up sharply. "What's up with Jason and Gabby?"

"Didn't you hear?" Brian said between bites. "They broke up."

"Not just broke up," Kayla corrected. "He came out to her."

The news hit Claire like a punch to the gut. "Came out?" *Jason was gay?* "Oh. God."

Kayla nodded somberly. "Gabby was crying so hard yesterday, she left school early. Today, she's still a total mess."

"I heard that Jason feels really bad," added Brian. "He's always known he was gay, but a few weeks ago he got this feeling he could try 'living a lie' with Gabby 'cause he really likes her. But finally … he just couldn't."

Claire felt like she wanted to throw up. *What have I done?* This was the second time that her new power had backfired.

Brian glanced her way, and his eyebrows rose. "What's wrong, CB?"

"Nothing," she said quickly. Tears stung her eyes. Brian had no idea what she'd been up to lately. She was suddenly desperate to have a friendly shoulder to cry on, but how could she fill him in, with Kayla sitting there? Then she remembered the euphemism they'd once used for her new power. "It's just that … a few weeks ago, I was … *swing dancing* with Jason, and I … convinced him to ask Gabby out."

Brian stared at Claire, confused at first. "You what?" Then his expression changed to comprehension. "Oh. *Oh!*"

"I swear, I didn't know."

"Wait, you and Jason were swing dancing?" Kayla asked, oblivious. "Were you both in that class your mom takes?"

Claire just nodded silently, staring at the pavement.

"You still haven't told me where I can sign up for it," Kayla complained, glancing at her watch. "Crap, I need to get to the art room early today." She stood, shouldering her backpack and kissing Brian on the cheek. "Ciao for now."

"Yeah." Brian pasted on a smile until Kayla left. When he returned his attention to Claire, he looked serious again. "CB. Did you really try to turn Jason *straight?*"

"No!" Claire lowered her voice, taking a shaky breath. "I had no idea he was gay. I thought he was just too shy to ask Gabby out, so I gave him a little … psychic nudge."

"Wow. Well, at least you didn't convince them to get married or something. It sucks now, but it'll blow over eventually."

No wonder Alec and Helena were so insistent that I not use that power, Claire thought. At least nothing bad had happened to Señora Gutierrez. Yet. "I'm a ruiner of all things," she muttered.

Suddenly, Brian's eyes lit up. "Hey, I've got something I know will cheer you up! I had a moment of pure *inspirato* during my free track this morning. Look at this." From his backpack, he grabbed his laptop and powered it up. "Remember that photo we found of your dad outside the Cleveland courthouse? I did a reverse-image search on it, and here's what I got."

"A what?"

"Reverse-image search. You give a search engine a picture, and it'll mine the web for anything similar."

Various pictures of men with different hair colors and hairstyles filled the screen. Some were clean-shaven, others had beards or mustaches, but almost all were wearing a suit and tie.

When Claire looked closer, she realized they were all the same man. "That's him! My father! That's amazing!"

"Check this one out." Brian clicked on an image of Tom with long blond hair and wire-rimmed glasses. Two bodyguards flanked him as they exited a white building. It was tied to a news article in German.

"When's this from?" Claire asked.

"May of last year." Brian autotranslated the page, resulting in an article in somewhat broken English. The title was clear enough, though: "Eyewitness Give an Important Testimony to Heinz Trial." The caption below the photo said it was taken at the Palace of Justice in Vienna.

"Vienna? Why was my dad giving testimony in some trial in *Vienna*?"

"Well, with his Grigori language skills, he'd be able to speak German like a native."

"So we were right about what the Fallen are using my dad for. But it's not just in the U.S."

Brian nodded. "They've taken that show global."

"Which means he could be anywhere in the world that has trials by jury."

"You've just got to get ahead of it, CB. Predict where they'll be next."

"How?"

"Maybe you and Helena could take a closer look at this moment in Vienna, the way you did in the New York apartment and subway? You might be able to see a pattern to how they move him around or find some other clue."

Claire looked at him, a smile spreading across her face. This was exactly what she needed: a mission. Something to take her mind off the other woes and fiascos in her life. "Thanks, Bri. You're brilliant."

"Tell me something I don't know," he replied with a grin.

Claire had learned her lesson. Although she was one for three in her mind-control experiments, her success with Señora Gutierrez didn't make up for the epic failures. She promised herself she'd never use that power again.

Alec, Neil, and Erica still weren't talking to her. Which hurt and made rehearsals awkward.

But at the same time, she was excited to have had a breakthrough about her father.

"Grandma?" Claire called Helena from the car on her way home. "I just learned something about Dad. Get ready to do some psychic shenanigans."

"If you refer to our mental sojourns in such a way again," Helena replied dryly over the phone, "I will ensure that you only accompany me in the projected form of a dog."

"I prefer a unicorn?" Claire bartered.

"That could be arranged."

Over dinner, Claire told Helena and her mother what Brian had discovered. Soon after, the three women were sitting in the living room, looking at the photo of Tom in Vienna on Claire's phone.

"This may not be as seamless as our jaunt through the apartment or the subway station in New York," Helena told them. "There, we occupied the same physical space, just at a different time. All I have to go on here is this image, the pictures we've seen online of the Vienna courthouse, and my experience there decades ago as a tourist."

They joined hands. Claire felt the expected jolt as she melded with Helena's mind. Closing her eyes, she found herself envisioning the picture of her father that Brian had found. The image rippled and faded into whiteness. The smell of car exhaust and the sounds of nearby traffic infiltrated Claire's senses, along with the hum of conversation in German. A breeze drifted through Claire's hair.

Suddenly, she was standing on a sidewalk in front of a massive, white marble building, with Helena and Lynn beside her. White marble columns and two statues of lions flanked a wide staircase leading up to three ornate doors. It was just like the picture online: the Palace of Justice in Vienna. Helena's projection of the building and its surroundings was so accurate, every last detail seemed real.

They were in Vienna! But when?

Half a second later, Claire had her answer. A few steps ahead of them, her father, wearing a long blond wig, was being led up the stairs by the two Fallen bodyguards from the photo. Press photographers and reporters clustered around them, snapping photos and calling out questions in German.

"Oh my God, it's Tom," Lynn cried, excited.

A couple of reporters walked straight through Claire, Lynn, and Helena, charging after her dad and his guards as they walked up the stairs, falling back only after the trio entered the building.

Lynn and Helena darted after Tom. Claire hurried to keep up, pausing briefly in confusion when her mom and grandma passed through the outer walls of the building and disappeared inside.

No matter how many times Claire had done this, it still felt weird to walk through a wall. She took a breath and dashed ahead, emerging inside a cavernous entry hall with an incredibly high ceiling. Claire had never seen anything like it. The entire place was made of carved marble, like something out of a fairy tale. Another wide staircase led up to a second-floor gallery.

Unlike the accuracy of the building's exterior, however, the projection of the inside wasn't entirely formed. As Claire glanced around, many areas—a side corridor, a section of the upper gallery, portions of the lobby where men and women in suits were walking to and fro—were blocked out by blobby, black shapes.

"I can't see everything," Lynn worried.

"It's my fault," Helena explained. "I have limited visual information, but we have enough to go on."

She was right. Her father and his bodyguards were clear as day. They followed their quarry into a courtroom. Everything about it felt old world, from the high, carved, wooden ceiling, to the paneled, carved backdrop behind the judge's bench. All the people in the room, from the judge and lawyers to the dozen or so people sitting in the audience, were vague, incomplete shapes.

Her father was in the witness box. Over the course of several minutes, her dad answered questions and gave some kind of speech. Since everyone spoke in German, Claire had no idea what they were saying. Stepping close to the two seated bodyguards, Claire confirmed that they were wearing the same type of earbuds Malcolm and his cronies had worn to cancel out her own persuasion powers.

As he spoke, her father's expression was blank, but he maintained an air of competency. Claire looked for signs of an aura. Sure enough, a muddy gold light shimmered around him. Her dad was definitely drugged and using his powers as he spoke.

Evidently, his testimony was effective, because as he was escorted out, a murmur of approval rippled through the audience. Claire knew she'd just observed something underhanded and criminal. At the same time, she couldn't help but be impressed. Her dad had just influenced an entire roomful of people. She could barely control one mind at a time.

"What happened?" Lynn asked, as they followed the trio from the courtroom.

"It's just as we thought," Helena replied. "Tom claimed to be an eyewitness in a murder case, and the defendant will no doubt get off. Not just because of his testimony, but because he used his power of persuasion on everyone in that courtroom."

"What a clever system," Claire added bitterly, "to keep the Fallen out of prison, whether they're guilty or not."

Moments later, they were outside, watching as Tom was guided into a limousine.

"What now?" Lynn asked.

"We take a ride," Helena replied. Without missing a beat, she stepped into the back of the limo, beckoning for Claire and Lynn to join her.

Claire couldn't believe this … she was going to ride in a limo with her father! As she climbed into the vehicle, the image was still incomplete, but Claire could see her dad sitting between the bodyguards. Helena and Lynn sat on the rear-facing bench, and Claire plunked down between them.

As the car took off, Tom kept his head in his hands, as if he were struggling to stay awake. "Where are we?" he mumbled in English. "What day is this?"

"It's Thursday," the first bodyguard answered with a trace of a German accent.

"Where are we going? I can't remember …" Tom's voice drifted off.

"We're taking you back to your hotel, Herr Wolff," the second bodyguard said. "You've had a big day, you need to rest."

"Oh," Tom replied. "All right." He settled back against the headrest behind him and closed his eyes.

Claire's heart ached. He looked so lost, so confused. It was infuriating that she couldn't do a thing to help him. Not only was she not really *there*, all this had happened almost a year ago.

After a short drive, the limousine pulled up to a hotel and stopped. Even more sections of the image were blacked out now, but Claire could make out a pair of men who stood waiting for Tom. Both were bald, and Claire recognized one from her vision—he was the same guy who'd injected her father in that hotel room.

Claire, Lynn, and Helena leapt out of the car, following Tom's captors as they guided him through the lobby, into a glass elevator, and down a series of vague corridors on the seventh floor. They unlocked the door to a hotel room and ushered Tom inside.

The door slammed shut in Claire's face.

"I'm losing the connection," Helena announced with a sigh. "We can't go any farther."

With that, all the sights, sounds, and smells around Claire zipped away, and she was back to sitting on her living-room floor in Brentwood. After a moment, Lynn went to the kitchen, returning with a glass of ice water for Helena, who was dripping with sweat and looking exhausted.

"I'm sorry," Helena said as she sipped the water gratefully.

"Don't be. That was great, Grandma. We confirmed everything."

"They seem very methodical," Helena commented. "I suspect this is a pattern. Wherever he's giving testimony, they take him directly from court to a hotel room."

"Did you recognize that bald guy who met the limo?" Claire asked. "He's the one who called Dad Mr. Boulanger. Maybe he's part of a more permanent detail guarding his room."

"That would make sense," agreed Helena. "The people carting him around to courthouses probably change with each international location."

"We have to rescue him," Lynn insisted.

Helena sighed wearily. "Believe me, I know. But to accomplish that, we'd have to know where and when his next court appearance is going to be."

"Is there any way to know that in advance?" Lynn asked.

Helena shrugged. "It's possible that I might foresee it. But I'd have to be really, really lucky."

Claire fell silent, the grim reality of the odds weighing on her mind. It could be years before her grandmother hit upon that information, if it happened at all. How would she stand the waiting, knowing that her father was in captivity, being manipulated and drugged out of his mind?

Suddenly, Shane Malcolm's offer rang in her ears:

I can find out where he is with a phone call.

Claire's stomach twisted. All she had to do was go to Shane Malcolm. She could strike a deal with him for the information, and …

No. It was a really bad idea. A deal that would have consequences. She put the thought out of her mind, hoping that another solution would soon present itself.

Because otherwise, her dad was doomed.

thirty-two

Alec and the rest of the cast had spent all weekend in final costume fittings and walking through the entire play while the lighting, stagehand, and sound crews made sure everything was ready for opening night.

Now it was Monday, three days until opening night, and nearing 10 P.M. They'd crawled through the first half of the play, with only a few screwups during set changes. The focus had been more on the technical aspects of the production the past few days rather than the acting. Which was a good thing, since Alec's mind was decidedly elsewhere, Neil was aloof as ever, and Claire seemed to be distracted, just going through the motions. She still hadn't said a word to Alec outside of the play itself, although once or twice he'd caught her glancing at him in a way that suggested she felt bad about the tension between them.

Thankfully, Ms. Donnelly had been consumed enough by technical problems not to call them out for their detachment.

Ever since the debacle at Erica's party, Alec had felt like an asshole. He should never have lost it like that, attacking Neil on the patio. Thankfully, the drinking had prevented Alec from hurting him more permanently. He'd like to blame his outburst on the alcohol but knew it was more than that.

Turbo had made him a walking ball of testosterone, and over the past two weeks he had only slowly been growing less irritable. Finally, he felt like himself again—more balanced, clearheaded. And therefore, hopefully, more worthy of asking Claire's forgiveness for what had happened at the party and for originally betraying her trust. Although could he even trust *her* again after what she'd done?

"Alec, I think your mic got switched off by accident." It was Brian, calling down from the sound and light booth at the back of the theater. "Can you take care of it?"

Alec reached under his green velvet tunic, felt for the switch on the wireless microphone pack he wore, and clicked it. A loud *pop* resonated in the speakers along the auditorium walls.

"Thanks, we're good, Your Highness," Brian said.

At the moment, the stage was set for the final scenes of the play. Alec stood alone in front of a backdrop of a hilltop overlooking a battlefield. Neil and Claire entered, somber as Lancelot and Guinevere, come to beg King Arthur to put an end to the war they'd inadvertently sparked. In the scene, Arthur refuses, explaining that it's too late. The Round Table—and his dream of peace—was dead.

Claire/Guinevere stepped forward to make the plea Alec had heard so many times before: begging Arthur to forgive her and Lancelot for their affair. But this time, her line seemed different, which caught his attention.

"So often in the past, Arthur, I would look up in your eyes, and there I would find forgiveness. Perhaps one day in the future it shall be there again."

As Claire spoke, the deep emotion on her face and in her voice made him wonder if she was speaking as Guinevere or as herself.

It struck a chord within him, but he still didn't know how to feel or what to do about it.

"But I won't be with you. I won't know it," she continued tearfully.

That was Alec's cue to hold out his arms, to silently show Guinevere that he still loved her and forgave her in spite of everything. Alec poured himself into the act.

But the rift between him and Claire was still very real. They had a long way to go if they were ever to make up. When Claire's face lit with joy and relief as she moved into his embrace, Alec could tell that she was feeling similarly conflicted. He wrapped his arms around her, holding her tight to his chest, wishing it would feel like home—but at the moment, everything was too broken.

As her brow pressed against his cheek, Alec felt Claire freeze, then her entire body tensed. He felt sweat break out on her forehead, and heard her give a small gasp, holding him even tighter as the hug extended a few seconds longer than usual. When she drew back, Claire was supposed to utter another line, but instead she just stared at him, her eyes wide with fear.

Something strange had just happened, Alec was sure of it. It wasn't like Claire to forget a line.

Then it hit him: *she'd just had a vision.*

Alec tried to catch her eye, but she was backing away now and looking at the ground. To cover, Alec moved on to *his* next line, saying softly, "Good-bye, my love ..." while Neil led Claire offstage. "My dearest love."

As he moved on to the last part of the scene, Alec's mind was working overtime, wondering what Claire had just seen.

He was certain she'd gotten a vision off of him. And it had terrified her. Was it about his past or his future?

After rehearsal, Alec raced across the junior parking lot toward Claire, who was almost to her car.

"Wait up!" He'd put this off far too long. He *had* to talk to her. "Claire!"

Claire paused, keys in gloved hand, her eyes fixed on the ground.

Confirming that they were alone, Alec asked: "What did you see?"

"What do you mean?"

"In your vision."

Claire hesitated, pressing her lips together. She appeared to be anxious about something. Yet when she spoke, her eyes flashed a little defensively. "What, no, 'Hello. How've you been?' That's usually how people start talking, especially after—what, a whole week?"

"I … sorry, you know I've never been good at saying the right thing. It just looked like you saw something back there, and I'm guessing it was bad."

"I don't want to talk about it, okay?"

"I wish you would talk about it. You seem worried. What you saw—has it happened yet? Is there any way I can help?"

That made her pause, as if she were turning the thing over in her mind. "I don't know. Right now I think it's better if—"

"Hey!" Neil walked up out of the shadows and stopped a few feet away from them.

Alec froze, cursing inwardly. *No, not now! We were finally starting to talk!*

"Guys, I'm glad I caught you."

"What is it, Neil?" Alec struggled to keep his frustration buried.

"It's been so tense all semester, and this past week has been the worst yet. I can't stand it anymore. I just had to say something." Neil took a deep breath, lowering his voice as he went on: "You got the wrong idea about us the other night at the party, man. Claire, she was telling me … stuff. *All* the stuff, about superpowers and angels and psychic shit and God, I can't believe I'm saying any of this like it's real, and …" He paused, as if trying to figure out what to say next.

Shite, Alec thought. His suspicions had been right. Now yet another person knew all the secrets that could condemn him to death. Alec looked wildly around, hoping against all hope that Zachariah wasn't watching and listening, invisible and insidious.

"And … ?" Claire prompted Neil.

"It's taken me a while to process it all," Neil continued. "I didn't want to believe it at first, I mean, who would? It's nuts. But if it wasn't real, how could you have tossed me up against a wall and held me there in midair by looking at me, Alec? It was like something out of a Stephen King novel! Which was scary shit, by the way, but since I'm still in one piece, I'm willing to let it go."

The memory of that altercation sparked a bundle of barbed emotions in Alec's gut.

"Then I thought about everything that happened around Homecoming," Neil continued, "with the scaffolding and that dead mountain lion and you all bloody and battered. It was the weirdest two months in all my years at this school. And I see it now. I get it. Look, I know that things have been heavy," Neil said, "and we're gonna have to take some time to sort it all out, but I just want you to know, I've got your back. You guys are awesome together, and trust me, MacKenzie, I wouldn't do anything to get in the way of that."

Awesome together. The words were painful. Even if Claire hadn't admitted to Neil how broken things were between her and Alec, Neil *must* have sensed it. Yet he seemed sincere. As if he thought they should be together.

Neil looked at them both as he continued. "I'm glad you told me, Claire. Glad to not feel like I'm being lied to and laughed at behind my back anymore. So, I'm hoping … can we just move on now and be done with all the secrets and weirdness?"

Alec heard Claire blow out a sigh of what sounded like relief, but she didn't reply. And when he glanced her way, she appeared conflicted. So Alec filled the silence.

"Uh—well," Alec heard himself say, "I'm not a fan of weirdness, but I have good reasons for keeping my … situation … a secret. So does Claire."

Neil patted his temple. "I get that, and all of it will stay right here."

"Great, thanks," Alec replied. "But … one day at a time?"

"Yeah," Claire agreed finally. "Just because I told you all that, Neil, it doesn't mean I can tell you everything going forward."

Neil nodded. "I'll take what I can get, Brennan."

She returned his nod. Neil turned to Alec now. "Like you said, one day at a time." He extended his hand. Alec shook it. "Ow, dude, go light. Go light."

Alec almost cracked a smile. "I was." Then he added, "And I'm sorry. For the fight."

"Not as sorry as I am," Neil said, massaging his hand with a wince. "I'll catch you guys tomorrow, then."

As Neil walked off toward his car, Alec looked back to Claire, hoping they could resume their conversation. But she was already slamming her car door and gunning the engine. She drove off with a quick wave.

thirty-three

As she drove home, Claire struggled to keep her mind on the road.

The conversation in the parking lot was a blur. She couldn't stop thinking about the terrifying vision that had hit when she'd hugged Alec.

But who could she tell about it? Certainly not Alec. At least, not yet.

Erica was out. Brian had been helpful in his own way, but he'd had a limited attention span lately. Neil? It was great that he didn't hate her anymore, but it's not like Neil could help with any of this.

Her mother would just tell Claire not to get involved.

Damn it, there was only one option.

"Grandma?"

It was nearly midnight by the time Claire got home. Helena wasn't in her bedroom, but the muted gleam of light on the living room's balcony gave her away. Quietly, Claire stepped outside and closed the sliding glass door, shivering in the cold night air as she wrapped her jacket more tightly around her.

Helena was seated at the far end of the balcony, sipping from a teacup. But Claire didn't spot a teapot on the small chair-side table. Just a whiskey bottle.

"I thought Grigori didn't drink," Claire commented as she dropped into the chair beside her grandmother.

Helena set the cup down, not even slightly embarrassed to have been caught. "After hundreds of years, everyone figures out their own way of coping with stress." Turning to study Claire, she added, "This business with your father has been *most* vexing."

"Yeah," Claire agreed. *But that's not all*, she wanted to add.

"Something *else* is bothering you at the moment, isn't it?" Helena asked softly.

Claire sighed. "I thought you weren't going to read my mind anymore."

"I didn't have to. It's written all over your face."

"I had a vision."

Helena nodded, as if she'd expected that answer. "Keep your voice down."

"It's freezing. Nobody's out here at this hour," Claire pointed out. "They're all asleep with their windows shut."

"Nevertheless."

Claire continued in a whisper. "It was about Alec."

"He does have a dark past. Who was killed in this one?"

Claire's heart pounded as she replied: "*Alec.*"

Helena's back straightened. "Oh, dear."

"It wasn't the *past* I was seeing. It was the future. I was looking through Alec's eyes. He was onstage. I think our play was over, because everyone was in street clothes and the set was being dismantled. Our director asked Alec to take a table out to the stairwell for storage." Sudden tears stung Claire's eyes. "He used to play guitar for me sometimes in that stairwell."

Helena reached over and took Claire's gloved hand in hers. The affectionate squeeze, although meant to convey empathy, only heightened Claire's sense of fear and pain. Her tears came fast and furious now as she spoke.

"So he/I took the table out to the stairwell. I sensed some-one's presence, but before I could react, something scraped across my throat. The pain! It was horrible! Blood gushed from my neck. I fell to the floor as Javed and Rico strolled past. Rico was pocketing a knife. I just lay helplessly on the ground as they disappeared up the stairs. And then, slowly … everything started to fade away." Claire could barely breathe as she finished, wiping her eyes.

"Dear Lord." Helena shook her head, deeply troubled.

"What am I going to do? *I just experienced my boyfriend's being murdered.*"

"Did you tell him?"

"No. We're not exactly on the best of terms at the moment, and—if I told him, would it even do any good? I mean, I wasn't able to stop the cougar attack even though I knew about it in advance."

"But Alec appeared and changed the outcome. You have to warn him about this."

"If I tell him, I know what he'll do. He'll try to find those guys, try to take them out ahead of time, and he might get killed anyway. Except then, I wouldn't have this advance warning. I wouldn't know the time and place."

"Why do Rico and Javed want Alec dead? Do you know?"

Claire hesitated. She didn't want to betray Alec's trust, but the only way her grandmother could truly help was if she understood the situation fully. "Alec's been doing some extra-curricular stuff lately, monitoring the Fallen. Shane Malcolm is bottling his own blood with stolen human blood, to make a supersteroid for his lieutenants. Alec discovered where it's being manufactured, and he … accidentally … burned the place down."

"Bloody hell! The damn fool."

"Javed and Rico attacked Alec on Valentine's Day and almost killed him. That's when Alec told me what was going on."

"Well. I'm glad you finally told *me* about it."

"Is there anything you can do, Grandma? To stop them from getting to Alec on closing night of the play? I mean, if Zachariah and the Elders knew about this blood-trafficking madness, would they go after Malcolm and take out Rico and Javed?"

"I don't know. I could go to them, keeping Alec's involvement out of the whole thing, but it would have to be handled delicately. And I can tell you right now, a Grigori investigation will take a long time. By the time they made a decision, Alec could already be dead."

Fresh tears welled in Claire's eyes. "So what do we do?" she whispered brokenly.

"I'm not sure yet."

"That's all you ever say lately," Claire griped, rubbing her eyes.

"I beg your pardon?"

"I'm sorry. But all we do is *talk* about this stuff. We never *do* anything. If we could just …" An image suddenly appeared in Claire's mind: of her standing in front of Malcolm's house. Malcolm, in the doorway. Looking at her with that charismatic smile of his.

That was it, she realized. Helena might not like the idea, but what choice did they have? Claire took a breath, and continued, "We could just negotiate."

"Negotiate? With whom?"

"With Malcolm. I could beg him to back off. Offer something in exchange, to get him to call off Rico and Javed."

Helena's eyes narrowed as she stared at Claire. "Offer *what* in exchange?"

"Me. Myself. He's been begging me to work for him. That's all I have to do. Say yes. And while I'm at it—"

"Claire," Helena interrupted fiercely.

"—while I'm negotiating to save Alec's life," Claire went on, "I could throw in one more request. I could ask where my dad is."

Her words hung in the air. Claire was determined to keep her face a blank as she stared back at Helena, whose hazel eyes were as cold as ice.

"Absolutely. Not."

"It's not just for me, or even for my dad," Claire shot back defensively. "This is to save Alec's life!"

Helena continued to glower. "Do you understand how dangerous it would be, to put yourself into Malcolm's debt? Do you have any clue what the Fallen would do with someone of your abilities?"

"I can guess," Claire responded, recalling the disturbing image of her father, drugged and bound. *But I'm going to do it anyway. To protect Alec, I'd do practically anything. Just as he's done for me.*

And I don't need your permission.

"I know I promised to stay out of your head," Helena snapped, "but if I have even the faintest inkling that you're attempting something so foolhardy as this, all bets are off."

Claire's jaw set. Alec's life was in her hands. She had no choice. She had to fix this. But there was only one way to do it, without her grandmother's hanging over her every thought.

She'd have to erase this conversation from Helena's memory.

Claire's stomach clenched at the notion. She'd promised herself never to use her mind-control power again. Twice, the outcome had sucked, big-time. *But not every time*, Claire reminded herself. It had worked on a Grigori before, kept Zachariah from recognizing Alec. Would it work on a psychic as powerful as Helena?

There was no way to know without trying. And if she was ever going to have a shot at it, she'd have to strike now, when her grandmother's senses were, hopefully, diluted from the whiskey in her teacup.

"Okay," Claire said, firing up the worry and fear and tension inside her. "You're right. I know you're right." As she spoke, she concentrated on this thought: *I'm not here. We never had this conversation. You've been out here alone all evening.*

Helena blinked. "Of course I'm right …"

Claire repeated the phrase over and over, both in her mind now and aloud. "*I'm not here. We never had this conversation. You've been out here alone all evening.*"

Her grandmother hesitated, shaking her head, as if struggling to concentrate. "Stop that," she said hoarsely.

Rising to her feet, Claire increased her focus, drawing on her emotions as she continued her mental and verbal onslaught.

"Damn it," Helena muttered, glancing at her cup on the table, seeming to grasp what was happening. "Damn, damn, damn …" She clutched her forehead.

Claire swallowed hard, a wave of guilt washing over her. She channeled it into the mental cables she cast out, an onslaught that took so much effort, she had to cling to the balcony railing to remain standing. "I'm not here," she persisted. "We've never had this conversation."

Helena took several long, deep breaths, holding up her hands and shrinking back, as if trying to avoid some ominous, unseen, oncoming force. "No … no … no … Don't …"

One strand of energy hit home, and coursed bitterly from Helena's heart straight into Claire's. "You've been out here alone all evening," Claire repeated emphatically, squeezing the rail until her knuckles were white.

With a slight shudder, Helena's eyes closed, and her entire body relaxed back against the chair, her head nodding forward, her chest gently rising and falling. A few seconds passed.

Instead of feeling victorious, Claire felt truly horrible. Moisture welled in her eyes as she whispered softly, "I'm so sorry, Grandma."

Claire almost collapsed against the railing, tears streaking her cheeks as she pulled out her cell phone. She scrolled through her contacts until she found the one Rico had added last fall and she'd somehow never been able to get herself to delete. Quickly, Claire typed out a text to Celeste:

> Ready to make a deal.
> Need to meet with Malcolm tomorrow.

A cold feeling infiltrated Claire's stomach as she pushed SEND. It was done. No turning back now.

Behind her, Claire heard a small intake of breath. She whirled to see Helena's eyes blink open. She glanced at Claire in surprise.

"Claire! Bollocks, I must have dozed off." Letting out a small yawn, she added, "How was rehearsal, dear?"

Claire's first challenge was to skip school without getting in trouble. While her mother was in the shower, Claire used her mom's phone to dash off an email to the school administration, saying that Claire wasn't feeling well but would hopefully be in after lunch. Then she deleted the email from the outbox.

Half an hour later, Claire was at the gas station in Brentwood village. As she sat in her car waiting for Celeste, Claire couldn't help feeling a little sick to her stomach. Not because of what had happened at this very spot over a month ago. Because of what was *about* to happen.

Once she met with Malcolm, and traded her services (whatever that might mean) for the help she so badly needed, there was no turning back.

But she *had* to protect Alec. And she had to know where her father was.

A charcoal-gray Tesla pulled up alongside her, windows rolling down. Celeste sat behind the wheel, glancing at Claire over a pair of sunglasses with heart-shaped lenses.

"Hey, doll," she purred as she unlocked the passenger-side door. "Hop in."

Claire locked her own car and warily approached. She noticed Celeste tug down the sleeves of her top, as if trying to hide a pinkish welt on her forearm. Had she been burned in the warehouse fire? Claire climbed into Celeste's car, checking the backseat.

"No Rico or Javed?"

"They're recovering from some injuries," Celeste said matter-of-factly. "But they'll be back soon."

Yeah. Just in time to murder Alec next week.

Celeste dangled a fancy blindfold, complete with faux-zebra-fur lining, in front of Claire. "Sorry, but until you talk to the boss, this is part of the deal."

Claire shrugged, leaning forward as Celeste put the blindfold on her. In an attempt to ease her tension, she said: "At least there are no matching handcuffs."

"Those only come when we know each other *much* better," Celeste replied.

All through the car ride, Claire tried to keep her mind occupied to make up for the lack of visuals. She tried to ignore Celeste's strong perfume and block out whatever music was playing on the car stereo. Instead, she kept running her fingers over the bracelet Alec had given her, reminding herself of why she was doing this.

After what felt like an hour, the car stopped, and Claire's blindfold was yanked off. Her eyes adjusted to the light as she exited the Tesla, once again on the steps of Malcolm's estate. Just inside the open front door, out of any direct sunlight, stood the man himself, crisp and coiffed, the smile in his eyes filling Claire with equal parts fear and loathing.

"Claire," Malcolm said, clapping his hands together. "How can I help you?"

thirty-four

All morning, Alec wondered where Claire was. She wasn't in any of their classes, she never visited their locker, or even the snack bar at break.

Was she sick? What if Celeste and her boys—assuming they were capable of walking again—had nabbed her again? If Claire was in trouble, he wasn't even certain anymore that she would call him.

Leaning on the balcony railing outside the library at lunchtime, Alec stared down at the parking lot, deep in thought. There was a time when he would have always known where Claire was. When she would have called or texted him just to say "hi" or "what's up" or "I love you." When she would have contacted him for even the slightest problem, and he would have been there for her in an instant.

Now there was just … silence.

This discord between them was driving him nuts. He couldn't stand it anymore. He had to do something. All he wanted was to get back to the way things used to be between them. They still had issues, but nothing would ever get resolved unless one of them made a move. Maybe he should take a cue from Neil and just talk to her.

Assuming … praying … that she was all right.

Alec made a deal with himself. If the next car that arrived in the parking lot was Claire's, it meant he had to step out of his comfort zone and open the door to a conversation with her *today*.

He waited tensely. A slight breeze ruffled the leaves of the eucalyptus trees on the hillside, stretching from the football field up to the old brick of the North Quad. Students sat in small groups in every direction, laughing and talking. He heard the first bell, signaling the end of lunch. He was about to turn away, when he saw it.

Claire's garnet Acura hybrid was snaking down the long driveway onto campus. Alec's heart pounded double time. As he watched Claire park and get out of the car, he let out a long, relieved breath. She was alive and safe. Thank God. Now it was time to get off his ass and fix this thing between them.

Unfortunately, there wasn't a second that day to talk to her. The dress rehearsal began minutes after school ended and lasted until after eleven.

Finally, when rehearsal was over and he'd changed out of his costume, Alec knocked on the door to the girls' dressing room. It was opened part way by a blonde named Flynn, one of the girls in the chorus. "Yes, Your Highness?" she joked.

"Is everyone dressed?" Alec asked.

"No! We're naked, avert your eyes!" With a laugh, Flynn flung the door wide, then forged past him along with three other girls, all wearing street clothes. "See you tomorrow."

"Later," Alec replied. From the doorway, his eyes took in the lone figure inside.

Claire had changed into jeans and a hoodie and was seated by one of the mirrors, removing her makeup. She turned, pausing at the sight of Alec.

"Hello. How've you been?" Alec began as he entered the small room.

"Someone's been taking notes," Claire replied, relaxing a bit. "I've been better. How are you?"

Alec thought it best not to answer that. He managed to keep his voice steady, despite his nerves. "You have a minute?"

"I have at least two." Using a square cotton swab, she wiped cream from her face.

Alec sat on the stool next to her. "I have to ask. You were gone all morning. And you were freaked out last night. I know something's not right."

She said nothing.

"And I know that whatever you saw yesterday," Alec continued, "you don't want to talk about it. But if you don't tell me what's going on, how can I help you?"

"What makes you think I need your help?"

"Maybe you don't. But I could just listen. If we're going to get past what happened, or even have a chance of fixing whatever's gone wrong between us, and stay together—"

"Is that what you want?" Claire interjected as she finished wiping off the last of the cream with a towel, then looked at his reflection in the mirror. "To stay together?"

"More than anything." He hadn't intended to be so blunt about it. But there it was.

Something in her expression crumpled.

"I screwed up," he said quietly, emotionally. "I shouldn't have kept secrets from you. It was wrong, and I'm sorry."

"Alec—" she began.

"And the party," he interrupted. "I was so stupid, but it had been so long since you and I actually had any … sparks, I guess. I couldn't help imagining things between you and Neil. All I want is to get back to what we had."

"So do I," she admitted softly.

His heart wrenched when she said that, with relief and hope and an overwhelming urge to sweep her into his arms. But it didn't feel right. Not yet.

"I didn't like keeping things from you, either," she went on. "And I don't want to. I was just so scared about … about being able to fend for myself. I felt like I needed to try out my new ability, but knew you'd get mad at me if I did. I wanted to prove that I knew what I was doing before I said anything. In the end, it kinda blew up in my face."

"Not everything went wrong," he offered, with an attempt at a smile. "Señora Gutierrez looks like she's lost ten pounds. And Zachariah would have arrested me by now if you hadn't gotten in his head."

She nodded, staring at her hands.

"Last night, I know you saw something that scared you. Can you tell me about it?"

She hesitated.

"Claire, we have to talk if there's going to be any chance of this working. We need to be honest with each other."

She stood up and slowly turned around to face him. "I agree. We do have to be honest."

Thank God. He rose from the stool where he'd been sitting. "Can we make that promise, going forward? No more lies or evasions?"

She nodded again. "No more lies or evasions. You're right. It *was* a vision. And when it hit me, I was so scared about what it meant. About whether or not I could … or should … do anything about it."

"What did you see?"

She took a breath, then said: "I saw … my father."

"Your father?" He hadn't expected her to say that.

"Remember awhile back, when I saw my dad in a courtroom, surrounded by reporters?"

"Aye."

She went on quickly and deliberately, as if anxious to get this out. "It's been so long since you and I have talked about any of this. But a few days ago, Helena and I got another vision of my dad in Vienna, giving evidence in a trial."

"Vienna? When?"

"Last year. Alec, he's definitely being held captive and drugged by the Fallen. Just like we thought, they're using his mind-control power to influence juries around the world, to keep members in their network out of prison."

"And you got another vision of him? By touching *my* forehead? That doesn't make sense."

"Yes it does. Because you were there."

"How do you know?"

"Because *I was you.*"

Alec sensed something a bit off in her voice. Was she skirting around the truth for some reason after she'd promised him no more lies or evasions? "Okay, go on. Where was this?"

"I/you were sitting on a couch in the lobby of the L Hotel in Taipei. Outside, in the distance, I saw a really tall, green skyscraper—"

"The Taipei 101 building," Alec interjected.

"Yeah, I found it on Google images."

"And? What was happening in the vision?"

"My dad was being escorted by a couple of Fallen from a limousine into the hotel lobby."

"When? Could you tell?"

"Yes! A TV monitor was on, playing the news. I could read the date in English along with the Chinese characters. It was March twenty-third."

"That's *two weeks* from now."

"Exactly." Excitement rose in her voice. "That's the greatest thing about this. Now we know where my dad's going to be, at a specific day and time in the future."

"Were you there, too?"

"I don't know. I was so busy taking it all in."

"Claire, this is great." The information and details in her story were so precise and clear. There's no way she was making this up. "It's the most we've ever had to go on. What I don't understand is, why were you afraid to tell me?"

She blew out a long breath, looking at her hands again as she answered. "Everything's been so awkward, Alec, especially since the party. I didn't know where we stood anymore. In this vision, all I saw was you, in the future, on yet another stakeout. I worried that you were going to run off and play superhero again without me, this time putting both yourself *and* my dad in danger."

"How could you think I'd ever do that?"

"After the past couple months, I didn't know what to think."

She looked so vulnerable, standing there, it tore at his heart. No wonder she'd been hesitant to reveal this. He blamed himself.

Without hesitation, he pulled her into his arms. "I'm so glad you told me. I actually think you *had to tell me*. Otherwise, how would I even know this was coming? Now, we can do something about it. Together." As he embraced her, he felt and heard the long sigh of relief that escaped her lungs. Her arms wrapped around him in response, her warmth enveloping him.

"I just want everything to be okay again," she whispered.

"It will be," he promised.

Claire pulled back a little and looked into his eyes. He saw in her gaze a reflection of his own repressed longing and all the buried emotions of the past couple of months. Their lips met in a kiss that began tentatively, then progressed into something fiercer.

When the kiss ended, Claire smiled up at him and said, "Yeah, it will be." She planted another soft kiss on his mouth. Then she paused suddenly, her eyes flashing as if some new idea had just occurred to her. "Oh!"

Alec looked at her quizzically, wondering what could have interrupted their moment. But he was pleased at seeing a smile on Claire's face, something he hadn't witnessed in what seemed like ages.

"How did I not think of this before?" she went on brightly.

"Think of what?"

"If *everything's* going to be okay, there's one more thing I have to do."

At break the next morning, Alec and Claire found Erica seated on a low wall near the library, taking notes from her history textbook.

"Hey," Claire said, as she and Alec came over. "Can we talk for a sec?"

"Okay." Erica shut her book. Her face was as expressionless as her tone.

Alec cleared his throat. "I messed up, Erica. Big-time. And I'm really sorry it happened at your party."

"So am I," Erica agreed. "You're just lucky nobody else saw what went down that night. You were using your powers on Neil, weren't you?"

Alec grimaced, nodding. "Aye. Again, I'm sorry. I'm hoping you can begin to forgive me."

"Well. It was really embarrassing, Alec. But I'll try." Erica looked at Claire, waiting.

Claire bit her lip. "I'm sorry about that night, too. Alec and I have been having issues, and I never meant to drag you into it."

Erica nodded silently.

"But aside from the party," Claire went on. "I've been feeling really bad for months now about the whole Guinevere thing. I know how much you wanted that part. So I just made a deal with Ms. Donnelly."

"What kind of deal?"

"She's agreed to let you play Guinevere for two performances: this Saturday's matinee, and next Friday night. And I'll play Nimue."

Erica stared at Claire. "Are you serious?"

"I believe her exact words were, 'If that's what you want, I'd be delighted to give her the opportunity,'" Claire replied.

Erica didn't leap for joy, the way Alec and Claire had been expecting. Instead, she sat quietly for a couple of seconds, a guilty, regretful expression creeping up her face. "Oh, Claire. That's so … I don't know what to say."

Claire's smile fled. "You could say, 'Awesome!' I mean, I thought this would make you happy."

Erica shook her head. "You shouldn't have to give up your part for me."

"I'm not giving it up. I'm sharing the glory."

"But you're great as Guinevere. And you've worked so hard."

"So have you. Look, we both know if I didn't have my particular lineage, the part would have been yours to begin with."

"My singing talent comes from my genes, too," Erica insisted. "Have you ever heard my dad belt out *That's Amore*? You won the part fair and square. And now I'm just embarrassed. Because I've been a total bitch, all whiny and jealous."

"No, you—"

"Yes I have. And I hid behind Gabby and her minions like an a-hole. I'm the one who should be saying I'm sorry." Erica stood and gave Claire a small smile. "You have way better chemistry with Alec and Neil, and you're better rehearsed. Let's give the audience what they're paying for."

"Are you sure?"

Erica nodded. "Absolutely. It means a lot, though, that you were *willing* to share the part. Thanks for that." She hesitated a beat, then opened her arms, inviting Claire into a hug.

The two girls hugged each other tightly. Alec noticed tears studding Claire's eyes. "Does this means we're friends again?" Claire asked.

Erica pulled back to look at Claire, her own eyes now glistening. "We never stopped. Just took a little … commercial break. But now, let's go back to our regular scheduled programming."

They both laughed. Alec was relieved that the tension between all of them was finally dissolving.

thirty-five

B ackstage in the wings on opening night, Claire was all jitters as she paced back and forth, decked out in her Guinevere costume, hair, and makeup. On the other side of the curtain, she could hear the three-piece band that served as their orchestra warming up, and the buzz of the audience as they took their seats.

She wasn't nervous just because of the play. Ever since her meeting with Malcolm, she'd been wracked with guilt. Malcolm had been only too happy to meet her terms, giving her the date and location of her father's upcoming appearance in Taipei as well as agreeing to keep Rico and Javed (and any of the Fallen) from hurting or interfering with Alec.

If only Claire could be honest with everyone about where she'd gotten her information. She'd had to brainwash her own grandmother, for God's sake. It had been so hard to lie to Alec's face, making up all that bullshit about a "vision" of Taipei. But she'd needed to tell him *something*. The lie was the easiest way to explain how she knew where her father was.

Of course, making the deal with Malcolm had come with a price. A price she didn't want to think about.

Her heart pounding, Claire peeked out from the side of the curtain to survey the audience. She spotted her mother and grandmother sitting front row center. In the light booth high above the back of the theater, she saw Brian among the crew, wearing his headset and busy at the console.

Drawing back out of sight, Claire felt a lump in her throat. She tried to swallow but started coughing.

"I warned you not to eat pizza for dinner," Erica declared, gliding up with a steaming styrofoam cup in her hands. She was ready to go on, dressed as Nimue and sporting sparkles in her hair. "Drink this: it's hot tea with lemon and honey. It'll help."

Gratefully, Claire accepted the cup and took a gulp. "Thanks."

Erica whispered, "But I'm sure your angel DNA will take over when you start singing, and you'll sound amazing as always." With that, she disappeared into the wings, her long chiffon gown fluttering behind her.

Claire took another sip of tea, trying to relax, when she spied Alec, dressed and made up as King Arthur, in the wings on the opposite side of the stage. Alec turned to a stagehand, borrowed his headset, and motioned to Claire to copy him. Stifling a laugh, Claire convinced the prop master to loan her his headphones, and held them to her ears, trying not to mess up her hair.

Alec's voice purred quietly over the headset, "I forgot to say this earlier: break a leg."

Claire felt all warm inside. "Same to you, my future husband."

"Okay, okay, lovebirds," Brian's voice complained in her ears, "this channel is for official business only. Please buzz off. And have a great show."

Minutes later, Claire watched Alec climb the ladder into the makeshift tree from which he would make his entrance. Just then, the overture began to play. Claire's heart raced as she shrank farther back into the wings, awaiting her cue. All thoughts and worries of the real world vanished from her mind as she concentrated on the performance that was about to begin.

"You were fantastic!" Claire's mom beamed as she thrust a floral bouquet into Claire's arms in the crowded lobby after the show.

"Thanks, Mom." Claire accepted the flowers and warmly returned her mother's embrace.

"It truly was a lovely performance," Helena decreed. "You were almost as good as I was four centuries ago, when I played Beatrice in *Much Ado* at the Old Globe."

As Claire accepted accolades from friends and strangers in the lobby, she couldn't stop smiling. The play couldn't have gone more perfectly.

Neil appeared at her side. "Good job, everyone."

"We did it!" Claire hugged Neil. Just then, Alec walked up. Claire stiffened, worried about what Alec might think. But Alec wrapped his arms around both of them and turned it into a group hug.

"One down, seven to go," Alec said, chuckling.

Claire suddenly caught sight of a man standing a few feet away, watching them through the crowd. She froze in horror.

Zachariah.

Why was *he* here? Was he spying on them? It had been over a month since Claire had brainwashed Zachariah. Had it lasted? Or would he recognize Alec and throw hand-cuffs on him?

Claire pulled out of the group hug, darting an anxious, meaningful glance at Alec, who saw the problem and shrank back slightly, his eyes panicked.

"Zachariah. What brings you here tonight?" asked Helena, her tone guarded.

"I came to support Claire." Zachariah stepped closer. "You were wonderful, my dear. You were very good, too," he added, glancing at Neil.

"Thanks," Neil said.

Claire's heart was in her throat. Her insides coiled in a knot as she got ready to throw a mental projection at the Watcher, hoping it wasn't too late to protect Alec.

But Zachariah held out his hand to Alec with a smile. "You were exceptional, young man. Your British accent was refreshingly perfect." He gave no indication that he recognized Alec.

"Thank you." Alec shook Zachariah's hand. "We've met before, I think? You're Claire's cousin?"

"That's right," Zachariah nodded.

"Well, MacKenzie was cheating," Neil teased, "since he's kind of a native."

"Oh?" Zachariah glanced down at his theater program now, apparently searching for Alec's name. "MacKenzie?"

Claire had another panicked moment as she shot Neil a reproachful glare. Would Zachariah recognize the name if not Alec himself? Neil seemed to catch her drift, and his face went red.

"I see: Alec MacKenzie." Zachariah looked back at Alec with a smile. "So you're English, are you?"

"Scottish," Alec replied calmly in his usual brogue.

The Watcher folded up the program and slipped it into his inner pocket. "Well, you were a wonderful Arthur, and it was a great production. Congratulations to you all."

"Thanks for coming, Zachariah," Claire replied, struggling to keep her voice even.

The Watcher gave a final nod and departed. When he was out the door, Claire grabbed Alec by the arm and whispered, "Thank God he still doesn't know you! I didn't realize I could do anything so long-lasting."

"See?" Alec whispered back. "Sometimes you and your powers *do* get it right."

"Sorry if I said the wrong thing," Neil said, "but why didn't he recognize your name?"

"I'm guessing because Grigori don't have last names?" suggested Lynn quietly.

Claire looked at her mom in surprise.

"She's right. MacKenzie is just a name I made up," Alec confided in a low voice.

Claire breathed a sigh of relief.

"Yeah, your father was the same way," her mother added. "He took my maiden name when we were living in New York."

When Claire returned to the dressing room later, all the joy of her achievements that evening began to fade as she thought about the terrible thing awaiting them on closing night: Alec's *murder*.

Thank God she'd taken steps to prevent it. It felt strange to be beholden to their enemies, to know that she'd have to use her gifts at some future date to repay her debt. Malcolm had been vague about what Claire would be expected to do in return.

Which wasn't very reassuring.

And it filled her with guilt that she had to lie to her friends and family about it. Still, she'd do it all again in a heartbeat. She had her boyfriend and best friend back. Alec would be safe. And when the play was over, they could go rescue her dad.

"Taipei? The land of my people?" Brian said, his eyes widening.

It was Sunday evening, their one day off after four successful performances. Explaining that she had something of great importance to talk about, Claire had managed to gather everyone who knew her secret in her living room: her mom, Helena, Alec, Erica, Brian, and Neil.

Her grandmother had ordered in delicious platters of Middle Eastern appetizers and sweet mint tea. After everyone had eaten, Claire had told them about her "vision," revealing her father's upcoming stay in Taipei. For Neil's and Erica's benefit, she'd also explained what the Fallen were using her father for.

Lynn's voice cracked as she said, "After all this time, you've finally pinpointed *where and when* he'll be."

"I know, it's so exciting, I can hardly believe it," Claire agreed, thankful that Helena had promised not to peek inside her head anymore and praying no one would ever guess where that information had come from.

"So, are we here to help plan a rescue?" Brian said eagerly.

Claire nodded. "Yeah, but just the planning part. Plus, after all the insanity recently, I didn't want to be keeping any more secrets."

"Got it," Brian nodded.

Helena leaned forward, clasping her hands. "To get the ball rolling, Claire and I had a powwow this morning."

"Grandma did her neat trick of projecting us into that time and space, and we mind-walked through it."

"Mind-walked?" Neil repeated, confused.

"Her term, not mine," complained Helena.

"It's kind of like virtual reality," Claire explained. "We can visit a specific place, or a past or future event, in our minds. Grandma can even rewind and fast-forward, it's awesome."

"Oh, like you did in New York," said Erica.

Claire nodded. "Exactly. The mind-walk gave us a lot of important info." Although the mind-walk was sketchy in parts, it confirmed everything Malcolm had told Claire and came close to matching the "vision" she'd invented for Alec. "We saw Dad deliver testimony in a Taipei courthouse, after which he's escorted back to the L Hotel."

"That will be the most reasonable place to rescue him," Alec interjected. "The courtroom is out of the question, and it would be too tricky to try to nab him in transit."

Helena nodded. "I was thinking the same thing."

"Four Fallen will be guarding him," Claire explained. "Two of them—a man and a woman—stay in the hotel lobby, on watch. The other pair, who seem to be his usual detail no matter where he's staying, take him upstairs to his room. All four guards are armed and wearing earbuds."

"There's also a security guard monitoring a bank of video cameras that cover the entire hotel, including the elevators," Helena added.

"Grandma and I were able to follow Dad as far as the elevator up to his floor, but no matter how many times we replayed it, the connection always broke right there. We think that's the time to grab him. Before they lock him in his hotel room."

Claire paused to let all that sink in. Everyone in the room appeared to be riveted.

"Wow," Erica exclaimed, setting down her glass of tea.

Neil's forehead furrowed. "So is this, like … a typical situation for you guys?"

Brian shook his head. "No way. This is definitely a red alert. We normally exist at yellow or orange."

Claire held back a smile. "Like I said, all this happens on March twenty-third, which is the first Monday of spring break, after the play and midterm week are over. We can't get the Grigori involved because Dad's still *persona non grata* to them. So it's up to us. And this may be our only chance." Claire turned to her mother. "So, Mom. Obviously, what I *want* to do, with your permission, is get to Taipei and snatch Dad. I'm hoping … praying, actually … that you're on board?"

"Of course I am," Lynn replied forcefully. "There's no way in hell I'm letting those sons of bitches keep Tom captive a day longer than necessary."

"My sentiments exactly," Helena chimed in. "Minus the profanity."

"Great," Claire said, relieved. "As for the rest of you—"

"Hey," Neil interjected. "I know I'm the new guy here, Brennan. And I can only speak for myself. But this is serious shit. If there's any way I can be of use, I'm in your corner."

"Same here." Brian nodded. "No way am I going to miss out on *this*. All I need is a plane ticket."

"I think I'm in," began Erica, "I'll just have to check with Gabby first."

Claire's jaw started to drop, until Erica held up her hand.

"Kidding! *So* kidding. But we'll need to come up with a plausible story for my parents."

"Whoa, whoa, whoa." Lynn stood up. "No one said anything about hauling a gaggle of teenagers halfway across the world on some amateur covert ops mission."

"It sounds more like a heist to me," Brian said excitedly, glancing around. "I only have one other condition: I may be the smallest in this group, but I'm not crawling through any air-conditioning ducts."

"This isn't a joke," Claire's mother insisted.

"Trust me, I'm not joking," Brian deadpanned. "It never ends well for the people who crawl through the ducts."

Helena set down her teacup. "They're not wrong about coming, Lynn. This is a complicated situation involving tight security. We're going to need every body we can to throw at the problem."

Lynn shook her head. "You're talking about waltzing into a crowded hotel lobby in a foreign country in the middle of the day, to kidnap a man who's surrounded by armed guards twenty-four/seven, in full view of video surveillance! We can't risk putting Claire's friends in a situation like that."

"I *get* that it's dangerous," Neil insisted. "I'm still in."

"Me too," Brian and Erica agreed in unison.

"Claire's in danger every day," Alec pointed out.

"At least this time, there's a way we can help," Erica insisted. "And it's for a really good cause."

After feeling alone for so long, Claire was surprised at how deeply touched she felt, having people at her back again. "Thanks, guys."

Lynn turned worried eyes on Erica, Neil, and Brian. "If anything were to happen to any of you, how would I ever face your parents?"

"A successful rescue will take a great deal of planning and coordination," Helena responded, "but if we work together, I believe we can pull it off, with no one the wiser and without anybody getting hurt."

With a reluctant sigh and nod, Lynn sat back down.

"Okay, people, I've got this." Erica pulled a notebook and pen out of her bag. "Let's start brainstorming."

It was Alec's turn to stand. "First off, be aware that this won't be easy. The Fallen have agents everywhere. At the end of this, it's crucial they don't know anyone here was involved. Because if you cross them, they never forget."

Claire cringed inwardly, knowing that Alec was speaking from personal experience and weighed down by her own guilty conscience. Eager to keep things moving, she said, "So it goes without saying, nobody else can know where we're going or why, and we pay for everything in cash."

"Speaking of which. If everyone goes, this could get really expensive," Lynn worried.

"Cost is not an issue," Helena commented. "I'm happy to finance the operation."

"Thank you, Grandma!" Claire cried.

"Don't get too excited," Helena responded. "We won't be staying at the L Hotel, or anyplace like it. And you're all flying coach."

"Wait, can we really fly a commercial airline?" Alec asked. "When we grab Claire's dad, I'm guessing alarm bells will go off among the Fallen, not to mention the Taipei police. It may not be a simple matter to get through airport security."

"Good point," Brian commented.

Everyone fell silent for a moment.

"Well," Neil offered quietly, "my uncle's a pilot, and he has a private jet."

All eyes turned to Neil. "Really?" Claire asked.

"Yeah," Neil answered, a little self-consciously. "He's like a zillionaire. If we offer to pay for the fuel and pilot, I might be able to convince him to give us a ride. He's a cool guy, and we can trust him to keep a secret. I suggest, though, we leave out all the 'angel' stuff."

"That's a good first step," Helena intoned.

"The rest will be cake," Erica exclaimed, glancing at her scribbled notes. "We just have to ace our midterms, blow everyone away with our performances in the play, and plan and stage a rescue worthy of a Hollywood movie."

Claire mustered a smile. "So, no pressure."

Brian looked around, making a mental count of the people in the room. "This works out perfectly. We'll be *Ocean's Seven*."

thirty-six

The squeak of nails being ripped from wood and the buzz of power tools filled the air.

"It seems like a waste to take this apart." Alec wielded his power drill, removing screws from the platform that had served as a throne room set piece.

"I know. They just built it three weeks ago." Claire collected the loose screws into a bucket.

"It's the way of the theater, folks." Erica gave a dramatic sigh as she pried nails from a backdrop frame. "Nothing is permanent. But the *experience*, that lasts forever."

"Uh-huh," Alec agreed. He looked over to Claire with a grin but noticed she wasn't smiling. She seemed to be deep in thought and kept glancing over her shoulder, as if worried about something. "Claire? You okay?"

"Yeah, fine."

"Your mind seems to be elsewhere."

"I'm just thinking about the show," Claire said quickly. "I'm sad it's over."

"Me, too. It went better than I'd expected," Alec admitted. "I didn't think we'd get standing ovations."

"They stood because they're our parents and best friends," Erica pointed out. "They always stand."

"Wrong." Brian walked up, pushing a rack of costumes. "Nobody stood at the fall play two years ago because the show was lame. You guys were *great*. Accept it. Move on." Lowering his voice, he added: "PS: We've got a plane to catch in T-minus 144 hours. Put your mental energy into *that*."

"Couldn't you have just said six days?" Erica asked with a grin.

"It's always 'T-minus X hours.' Maintaining appropriate lingo is a crucial factor in any successful operation."

"Yes sir, Admiral General." Alec gave Brian a faux salute.

At that moment, Ms. Donnelly stopped by, pointing to an end table that had once furnished the Royal Bedroom. "Alec, would you please bring that table down to the storage area in the stairwell?"

"Sure," he replied.

Before he could set down the drill, Claire leapt up and cried, "No! Wait, I'll do it."

"Thanks, Claire." The director headed off to another part of the stage.

Claire dashed anxiously to the table in question. Why did she seem so edgy? "Claire. I know you've been training, but that's too heavy for you."

"I've got it," she insisted. "Just keep drilling."

The table bumped and groaned across the stage floor as Claire awkwardly dragged it away. "For God's sake, Claire. Give it to me." Alec tried to yank the thing out of her hands.

Claire wouldn't let go. "Seriously, I can do this."

"Do you really want to play tug-of-war with *me*?"

With a reluctant sigh, Claire released her grip.

Alec hoisted the table above his head, making it look difficult in case anyone was watching. "You can open the door for me, if you like."

Claire stalked ahead of him, her entire body radiating frustration. It was like the clock on their relationship had been turned back two weeks, to when they were barely speaking. *What've I done to piss her off now?*

She held the door open for him to pass through, then raced ahead of him. Several old set pieces were crammed under the stairs, which snaked their way up to the library above. The door closed behind them with a slam.

Alec set down the table in the corner. Claire's eyes darted in every direction, like she was expecting someone to leap out of the shadows.

"You're acting weird, Claire. What's going on?"

"Nothing. I just think I'm on a Red Vines sugar high. And I'm antsy about … *you know* … next week. I don't feel nearly ready."

Before he could comment, there was the sound of footsteps on the stairs above.

Two seconds later, a tall, pale, blonde man appeared, descending the steps until he stopped in front of them. He wore gray slacks and a black leather jacket that looked elegant on his slim frame.

Alec felt the hair rise on the back of his neck. *Who the hell was this?*

"Claire. Congratulations. I hear the show was a success."

"How do you know?" Claire shot back, an edge in her voice.

"Celeste caught last night's performance," he answered, his smile charming.

Alec tensed at that, angry with himself. Once again, a member of the Fallen had been here, watching them, yet he hadn't noticed. At the same time, his mind was buzzing. How did Claire and Celeste know this guy? Then he put two and two together.

"Malcolm." Alec tried to suppress the fury in his voice as he stepped in front of Claire protectively.

"You must be Alec. How nice, after all these years, to finally meet you in the flesh."

"What are you doing here?" Alec asked.

"I came to see *you*, actually." Malcolm brushed a speck of lint from his lapel, his voice as smooth as glass. "Our intel suggested this was the most secluded way to slip in backstage and find you. How convenient for us both that we can meet in such a private space."

"Yes, very convenient," Alec said suspiciously.

"Until recently," Malcolm continued, his ice-blue eyes meeting Alec's, "it wasn't me who was going to come this way for you. It was my associates."

"Tweedledumb and Tweedledee, you mean?" Alec's lips pressed together tightly.

Malcolm chuckled. "After what you did to them, you can't really blame them. You three have a history, it seems. They *planned* to kill you this evening. Or at least, to *try*."

"Oh my God," Claire said, her hand going to her mouth.

Malcolm briefly glanced her way, then trained his eyes on Alec again. "When I learned of their intention, I was tempted to allow them to proceed. After all, you destroyed my factory."

"That was an accident. It was self-defense."

"Be that as it may, you were trespassing on private property, looking into something that is not your concern. You are the thorn in my side, Alec. Were you to be eliminated, I would be better off in so many ways." Malcolm let out a sigh. "Every way but one, that is."

"Meaning … ?"

"Were we to succeed in taking you out, the Grigori would surely get wind of it. And, even though you are a runaway, they would not take kindly to it."

Alec wasn't sure he liked where this was going.

"Furthermore, eliminating you might call attention to the … operation I've been running lately," Malcolm went on, "of which I doubt they would approve. I don't want the Grigori looking over my shoulder. I have been at peace with your kind for a great many years, and I'd hate to see that end."

"I never thought of it as peace," Alec replied tightly. "More like a stalemate."

Claire let out a breath but said nothing, her eyes still anxious.

Malcolm pressed on. "You've proven to be a formidable opponent. But I think we've both done enough damage to each other's lives at this point. So let's make a deal, shall we?"

"What kind of deal?"

"You tell no one about my recent … activities, and I'll dismantle the operation you found so troubling. In exchange, I won't tell the Grigori where you are. And I'll ensure that Rico and Javed forgive and forget. Sound fair to you?"

Alec's eyes narrowed. Was he really going to get off so easy? "You'll put an end to the blood trafficking?"

"I will. It was just an experiment anyway, and it's becoming a problem—giving my lieutenants more power than they are equipped to handle. I've decided I'd rather keep my blood in my own veins."

Alec wasn't sure he believed Malcolm. It was possible that he'd start up another operation in a new location, and all this was just to throw Alec off the scent. On the other hand, it'd be a relief to get Malcolm's goons off his back. And he couldn't risk Malcolm's giving him up to the Elders. But he wanted more. "If I accept your offer, will you stop hounding Claire to join the Fallen?"

Claire looked down. Alec sensed that she wanted to say something but was censoring herself.

Malcolm's lips twitched. "If you and I can come to terms, I think I can agree to suspend any further such *hounding*," he answered smoothly.

"All right then, I agree," Alec said, "but I can't promise to look the other way forever. Depending on what bullshit you pull in future, there may come a time when our agreement has to come to an end."

From the smile that widened across his face, it seemed as if Malcolm had been expecting that answer. "Understood." After a moment, he added, "With how hard you've fought to get away from your duties, you really are a fascinating creature, Alec. Once a Watcher, always a Watcher, I suppose."

"Looks like. So, that's it?"

Malcolm extended his hand. "For now." They shook hands, then Malcolm gave a half bow. "Good night to the both of you." Turning, he disappeared up the stairs with a burst of superhuman speed.

Malcolm's absence appeared to pop a cork from Claire. "Thank God," she exhaled.

Alec drew her into his arms. "You sensed he was coming, didn't you? That's why you've been acting so weird all evening?"

She nodded silently against his chest.

They stood there for a long moment, embracing. Alec felt as if a great weight had been lifted. Rico and Javed were off his back. Zachariah still had no idea who Alec was. And Malcolm was going to leave him and Claire be.

"You know what's the strangest thing about all this?" Alec asked.

"What?"

"Even though I know better, I actually kind of like him."

Claire stifled a laugh and pressed her head to his chest. "I know what you mean."

thirty-seven

Claire twisted her gloved hands in her lap, willing herself to stay calm as she took in her surroundings.

The L Hotel in Taipei was even more eclectic in person than in the mind-walk she'd shared with Helena. Heels clacked on the polished-stone floor, echoing off the wood-paneled walls and ultramodern ceiling, which dazzled with recessed lighting and a suspended multicolored neon sculpture. Three huge, round, leather benches, the size of beds, were scattered across the expansive space. Claire and Alec were seated on one of them, in full view of the glass front doors and the wall of windows that looked out onto the street.

Behind them, a large television hung on the wall, silently playing a documentary about Taiwanese temples. When she'd described this moment in her supposed "vision" to Alec, Claire had claimed there'd been a TV showing the news. She was just grateful there *was* a TV and hoped he wouldn't notice the discrepancy.

"You're sure this is the bench you saw me sitting on in your vision?" Alec asked.

"Yeah." Claire was having a hard time keeping track of all the lies she'd had to tell lately to make sure her deal with Malcolm remained a secret. In fact, she'd never seen Alec sitting on this or any other bench. Her glimpse into this future moment when she'd communed with Helena hadn't depicted Claire, Alec, or any of their friends at all.

Claire's pulse beat a rapid staccato as her thoughts darted back to that *other* tense moment, over a week ago, when Malcolm had shown up in the theater stairwell. She'd almost had a heart attack, worried that Malcolm would say something to blow her cover or Alec would guess at the bargain she'd made. Thankfully, Malcolm didn't, Alec had no idea, and now they were finally in position to use the information Malcolm had given her to save her father.

Claire swallowed hard, trying not to think about what *she'd* had to give in exchange. There hadn't been any other way, she reminded herself. They were here. Their plan was in place. Everyone knew their parts. They'd been over it too many times to count. They were ready to go.

And in five minutes, her father was going to arrive.

"Oh, Neil, you're too good to me!" Erica's voice rang out.

Claire glanced across the lobby. Erica was sitting beside Neil on the round bench closest to the busy front desk, cradling a dozen red roses and making a big performance out of smelling each one. She and Neil were dressed in designer jeans and jackets and look liked a rich American couple.

"Aren't they starting a little early?" Alec whispered to Claire.

"Erica insisted she wanted time to get into character," Claire explained.

Their phones vibrated simultaneously. It was a text from Brian to everyone:

> In position, over

Alec typed back:

> Only say over if you're on a radio :-P

Brian's reply came with lightning speed:

Focus on the mission, not my lingo

Claire responded:

How's my mom?

Brian replied:

Amazingly flexible, willing to take one for the team

Another text followed, this time from Helena:

Texting is laborious.

We should have connected our minds as I suggested

There was no way Claire was letting her grandmother into her head at the moment. She couldn't risk Helena's seeing the secrets Claire was concealing. She fired back:

No way. You already have enough to do

Helena had two primary jobs. First: take out the security cameras along their intended route, which involved cutting the relevant wires at the electrical circuit box in a lower-level corridor. Second: wait in their getaway van in the hotel's parking garage, where she could use her abilities to try to track their futures, and (hopefully) warn them of potential problems or dangers.

Two minutes ticked by. Helena wrote back:

Phase 1 complete. Heading to van now.

"Let's hope it takes as long to get a security technician out here as it does back home," Alec commented under his breath.

"And that we don't have to use any areas of the hotel we didn't black out," Claire added.

"I have faith in the plan." Alec shot her a small smile.

Claire checked her watch. One minute to go. Her pulse pounded in earnest now as she and Alec focused their attention on the front driveway, visible through the lobby's plate-glass windows and doors.

A limousine pulled up to the curb, its doors swung open, and two people stepped out and marched into the lobby: a tan, athletic man, and a shorter, ebony-skinned woman. They both wore dark suits, and the woman wore gloves.

Claire grabbed Alec's hand and squeezed it. "Lobby guards," she whispered. She recognized them from her mind-walk with Helena. As anticipated, they cautiously scanned the area, then moved aside.

Claire's eyes were riveted to the limo outside.

The bald man from her earlier vision stepped out from the backseat. Next came a guy sporting a bushy beard. The same bodyguards she'd seen in Vienna.

"Here we go," Claire whispered.

The two men waited by the rear door to the vehicle, then helped out a third man.

Claire caught her breath. *There he is.*

My father.

Now it was Alec squeezing *her* hand in silent acknowledgment as they watched the threesome make its way into the lobby, the bodyguards flanking Tom. He wore a navy-blue suit and tie. His brown hair was longish and shaggy. She noted the salt-and-pepper scruffiness on his cheeks and dark circles under his eyes as he passed by, staring at the floor, his eyes distant and glassy.

Two very different feelings washed over Claire. Excitement that she was finally, actually, in the same physical space as her dad. And heartbreak. Because even though her dad been cleaned up for his court appearance, he still looked like a prisoner. She had to suppress a strong instinct to bolt up after him then and there. *Stick to the plan,* she reminded herself. *Pray that it works.*

Alec gave Claire's hand another reassuring squeeze. Then he quickly closed the text thread with:

They're here. Good luck, everyone

The bodyguards and her dad crossed the lobby and made directly for the wide bank of elevators beyond. The lobby guards sat down on the empty bench not far from where Erica and Neil were seated. *Bingo.* Everyone was in place.

Claire and Alec stood and strode toward the elevators. Claire, straining to appear casual, felt like every slap of her Chucks on the floor squeaked so loudly that everyone would turn and look. But no one was even glancing at her.

No one except Erica, that is. Claire caught Erica's eye, intercepting a silent look that said, *Go girl. We've got this.*

Claire and Alec paused a few feet behind her dad and the bodyguards, who were waiting for an elevator. It was so strange to be standing so close to her own father and not be able to touch or even talk to him. *Yet.*

Tapping his foot impatiently, the bald bodyguard watched the LED counter as it progressed downward from ten to one. Finally, the "up" light gleamed purple, mirror-polished doors slid open, and several people stepped out. The guards ushered Tom into the waiting, empty car. Claire and Alec immediately followed.

Claire could hardly believe it. Her dad was standing barely a foot away, his hands clasped in front him, staring straight ahead. The space-age-style mirrors and floor-to-ceiling lights on every wall gave her a glimpse of him from every angle imaginable. She wished she could pause the moment, take the time to drink in the sight of her father. In the flesh.

But there was no time. She turned to face forward.

The bearded guy pressed the button for the twelfth floor. The doors closed and they started going up.

Alec hit the button for the fourteenth floor, then turned back to face the group. With a quick glance at Claire, who gave him a nod, Alec parted his hands, telekinetically ejecting both men's earbuds from their ears.

"Hey!" shouted Baldy, reaching up to figure out what had just happened.

Claire turned to face the two men, and said quietly, "Calm down." She'd never successfully used her mind-control talent on more than one person at a time, but this was a risk they'd needed to take.

"There's been a change of plan," Claire continued, working hard to balance her focus between the two guys as she spoke. "This man is sick and needs medical attention. You've been relieved of your duties. Return to the room and await further instructions. We can take him from here."

Dead silence followed. Tom stood like a zombie, as if totally unaware of what she'd said or what was happening. Claire's chest was tight from trying to hold on to the bodyguards' minds as she repeated the phrases in her head: *Return to the room. Await further instructions. We can take him from here.*

The two bodyguards stared at her quizzically. Beardy scratched his chin. "Who are you exactly?"

Damn it. These guys were fighting her. "You're not cleared to know that," she replied firmly, silently repeating: *Do what I say and don't argue. Do what I say and don't argue.*

To her relief, she finally felt her mental tentacles grab hold of both men. Their eyes glazed over, and they nodded simultaneously. "Yes, ma'am."

Claire let out a breath, still maintaining her concentration. The counter on the digital display showed that they'd just passed the seventh floor. Almost there.

To her dismay, the elevator slowed. *No, no, no!* She exchanged a worried glance with Alec as the elevator stopped at the eighth floor and the doors slid open. A young Taiwanese man wearing a skinny-cut jacket was waiting to board.

Alec held up his hand and said something in Chinese, which Claire assumed was a polite request not to board. The man's reply in the same language had a "the hell you talking about?" tone as he shoved his way in and hit the button for the top floor.

Claire froze, struggling to ignore the distraction and to continue controlling the minds of the two Fallen, who had both taken a step away from her dad.

Nine.

As the elevator hummed upward, the newcomer bent down to pick up something at his feet. *It was one of the earbuds.* Claire's pulse began to beat double time. Would this screw everything up?

Ten.

The guy held up the earbud and was about to speak, when Alec reached out with a smile and scooped the tiny device into his own hand, muttering something in Chinese and half bowing graciously. Then Alec quickly snatched up the three remaining earbuds from the floor and hid them in his pocket.

Eleven.

Claire kept directing her thoughts along the tendrils into her dad's handlers' minds. *Return to the room. Do what I say and don't argue. We can take him from here.*

Twelve. The elevator finally arrived. The young guy stepped out of the way, leaning against the sidewall of the car and swiping on his phone while the bodyguards got off. Her father started to dutifully follow them.

Alec placed a hand on Tom's shoulder to gently restrain him. "You're staying with us, sir."

Tom's eyes narrowed in silent surprise and uncertainty.

"It's all right, sir," Alec added in a reassuring tone. "We've been instructed to accompany you to another location."

Tom stayed where he was but looked confused. The body-guards continued down the hall. As the elevator doors closed, Claire heaved a sigh of relief, confident that the effect would be as long-lasting as it had proven to be in the past.

As the elevator went up, however, her father kept glancing warily at her, Alec, and the Taiwanese guy.

He doesn't trust us. "It's okay," Claire told her dad, smiling up at him warmly as she projected her thoughts: *Don't worry, everything's fine. We're going to help you.*

It didn't make any impression. The tethers thrown from her mind just seemed to bounce off. Claire darted an anxious glance at Alec, who she could tell shared her concern.

When the chime sounded their arrival at the fourteenth floor, Claire and Alec each put a hand on one of Tom's shoulder blades and firmly nudged him out of the elevator. Just as firmly, they urged him down the bizarre plastic-and-wood-paneled corridors and to a door labeled BACK STAGE, where the service elevators were hidden. Alec unlocked it with his mind and soon they were out of sight of any potential guests. From here they could return Tom discreetly to the lobby below.

Tom glanced at them as they walked down the drab gray service hallway. "Who are you? What is this?" His voice— deep and eerily familiar, from her visions of him—signaled his rising alarm.

"We're here to help you." Alec kept his tone even. "You're perfectly safe, I promise you."

"No! I don't know you." Without warning, Tom backed away from them and bolted down the hall in the opposite direction.

Instantly, Alec thrust his hand forward, catching Tom in his telekinetic grip. Tom lurched to a stop, struggling against the unseen force. "Get the elevator!" Alec grunted.

As Claire raced down the hall, her phone rang. She answered without looking. "What?"

It was Helena. "I just got an image of Alec and your father. Things aren't going to go as planned."

"No kidding. Already happening."

"Get him to the elevator," Helena replied. "I will meditate on what to do."

Claire shut off the phone and shoved it in her pocket as she ran. She reached the service elevator, hit the call button.

Alec slowly and deliberately reeled her father back toward them as if he were gliding on ice.

"No. Let go! I can't—" Tom gasped, trying in vain to fight Alec's invisible power.

Just as Alec joined her with Tom in tow, the elevator arrived with a ding. Claire was relieved to see Brian inside, as expected, attired in the surprisingly informal black T-shirt and slacks worn by their bellhops. Beside him sat a push cart draped by a white linen cloth, holding a flower arrangement.

"Hey," Brian began cheerfully, his expression snapping to horror when Alec, abandoning any attempt at delicacy, telekinetically thrust Tom into the waiting elevator car, then jumped in after him.

Claire followed, quickly hitting the button that started their descent.

"Tom, you need to calm down," Alec insisted as he struggled to hold the flailing man against the elevator walls.

"Help! Help! I'm being kidnapped!" Tom yelled at the top of his lungs. He threw a weak punch at Alec that missed, then shouted something equally urgent in what Claire presumed was Chinese.

"Mom, we need you *now!*" Claire called out, whipping the cart's tablecloth upward, exposing its occupant who was folded like a gymnast into the compartment beneath.

Lynn crawled out, pausing to stare at her husband with anxiety and excitement. Her voice cracked as she said, "Tom! Tom, it's me, Lynn. Do you remember me, honey? I'm your wife."

They'd hoped that seeing Lynn would be comforting and encourage Tom to go along peacefully. Instead, his eyes widened in fear, glistening now as he violently shook his head. "No, no. It's another trick. You can't be real. Please, let me go. I have to get back to my friends!"

"What's wrong with him?" Lynn asked, frightened.

"It looks like Stockholm Syndrome," Alec grunted, straining to hold on to Tom. "They probably tortured him until he didn't know what end was up, then convinced him that they're on his side."

"Jesus," Claire gasped.

"What should I do?" Brian interjected, worried, holding his phone at the ready. "This is the part where I'm supposed to tell Erica and Neil to get started."

"Not yet," Alec insisted. "We have to get him under control first."

Claire glanced at the elevator countdown. Any minute now, they'd reach the lobby and be in full view of the security monitors. Quickly, she pulled the emergency lever. The elevator lurched to a stop.

"I'll try mind control again." Claire closed her eyes and focused every ounce of her energy on Tom, speaking the same words she projected, "Please calm down. We're your friends. You were kidnapped. We're here to help you, rescue you, bring you home."

The effort took intense focus, but only seemed to make things worse. Tom became increasingly agitated. She could *feel* him battling back with his own mental powers.

"Stop it," he grimaced. "Stop it. Get out of my head." Tom yanked one arm free of Alec's grip and swung at Claire, shoving her into the elevator wall.

Claire cried out as her head hit metal with a sharp bang. Pain reverberated through her skull. Sparks showered in the edges of her vision as she grabbed her temple, woozy, and slowly slumped to the floor.

"Claire!" her mother shouted.

Everything that followed swam past Claire's eyes in spurts. Her mind felt fragmented. Her head pounded. She could swear she heard Helena's voice in the back of her mind, but it was garbled.

"Helena just texted," she heard Brian say. "Alec, she says you need to reset Tom."

Everyone's voices were fuzzy, like she was deep underwater. Her mom: "Reset? What's that mean?"

Alec, upset: "It's like a psychic enema. She wants me to connect his mind to the Grigori Nexus."

"But you need to *meditate* to access the Nexus," her mom gasped.

The Nexus. Claire knew that word. All at once, she understood what was happening. Shock and fear speared through her. She opened her mouth, desperate to say something, but her head was pounding too hard.

Brian spoke. "You think you can get *him* to meditate right now?"

"I can try." Alec winced, still working hard to control Tom. "It could get him back to his core self."

No, no, anything but that, Claire wanted to shout.

"But ... once you're connected, the Grigori will know where you both are." Panic laced Lynn's every word.

Claire found Alec's eyes, which stared straight into hers.

His voice was grave. "Yeah. There is that."

thirty-eight

Should I do it?

Alec's mind whirred. If he connected to the Nexus, it might be the end of everything. Claire. His freedom. A normal life.

Claire was staring at him, holding her head, clearly in too much pain at the moment to speak. But her eyes conveyed terror.

Could he risk losing everything and never see Claire again? Just to save this one man?

This one man who was Claire's father …

No time to think, idiot. Just do it. For her.

With a burst of strength, Alec hurled Tom to the floor, smashing into the room-service cart, which crashed against the back wall of the elevator, scattering broken pottery, flowers, and water.

Pinning Tom with all his physical and telekinetic weight, Alec grabbed both of the man's hands, gripped them tightly, and opened a corner of his mind—a corner Alec had hoped would remain forever closed. He felt Tom's energy flowing into him, and his own coursing back out. And then … *poof.* The world around them was gone. No sights, no sounds. Just infinite white.

Their minds were connected. To each other, and to the Nexus.

In that blank expanse, Alec still knelt atop Tom, but the man's struggling ceased. Instead, Tom's eyes snapped open, now sharp and clear.

"What's happening?" Tom began, his voice echoing in the emptiness. "Am I dead?"

"Not yet." The clock was ticking. Every second they remained here would make it easier for the Grigori to trace them. "Do you recognize this place?"

Tom glanced around, inhaling a worried breath. "The Nexus. I can't be here. It's too dangerous."

"For me, too."

Cold realization dawned in Tom's eyes. "You're one of *us*?"

"Aye." Then: "Tom. I'm on your side." Alec heard a slight, faraway whine in his ears that was gradually increasing in volume.

There were eyes on them. He could feel it. He had to get Tom up to speed and get out of here, fast. "What's the last thing you remember?"

"The last thing? I was ... in New York. I'd escaped the Fallen a second time. I know I'd called my wife, warned her to run, but when I got to my apartment the next day, she was already gone."

Shite. Alec's heart sank. *He thinks it was only the next day.*

"What am I missing?" Tom said flatly.

"You've lost some time. Eleven years passed between your phone call to your wife and your visit to the apartment."

"*Eleven years*? And how long since I was first taken?"

"Sixteen years." The whine was getting quite loud now. Any second, and the Grigori would have their location.

"Dear God. So it's true." Tom looked positively broken.

"What?"

"When they found me the last time, they said my wife and daughter were in Fallen custody. That they'd hurt my family if I didn't comply."

"They were lying. Your family's right here." With that, Alec released his grip on Tom and his connection to the Nexus.

The real world surged back, filling in the nothingness around them with a blast of color and sound. Once more, they were in the tight confines of the elevator, with everyone hovering over them anxiously. Alec pulled himself upright, offered his hand, and hoisted Tom to his feet.

"Tom?"

Tom turned to his wife, this time with relief and deep-felt emotion. "Lynn. Oh my God."

"We thought we'd lost you." Lynn burst into tears and fell into her husband's arms.

Tom held her tight, then pulled back from the embrace to look at her, tracing the worry lines on her face. "Has it really been sixteen years?" He noticed Claire, who was slowly standing up, her hand on her temple, her eyes wide and fixed on her father.

"Dad?" she whispered.

"Claire … ?" Tom stared at his daughter, astonished.

Claire wrapped her arms around both of her parents. "Dad," she said again.

Alec didn't want to interrupt the moment but knew he had to. "Claire, are you all right?"

Claire nodded, smiling—one of the happiest smiles he'd ever seen on her face. "Yeah. Thank you."

Tom's eyes filled with tears as he looked at Claire and Lynn. "All this time, it felt like a dream," he said quietly.

"Unfortunately, it wasn't," Alec replied urgently. "We need to get moving."

Claire's expression turned upside down. "What happened in there? Did the Grigori see you?"

"I sensed … something," Alec answered honestly.

"Great," Brian muttered. "Before, it was just the Fallen. Now we'll have Grigori on our asses, too. We have to book it, double time." Pushing the lever to restart the elevator, he looked at Tom, and added, in a surprisingly adept Schwarzenegger impression: "*Come with us if you want to live.*"

"Who are *you*?" Tom asked, semiamused, as the elevator zoomed downward.

"Commander of this rescue op." Brian winked, clicking something on his phone. "Okay. Message sent. Our fake love-birds should start the fireworks any second."

"Just stay close," Alec directed Tom, "and do exactly what we tell you."

"Got it," Tom replied.

The elevator touched down. As the doors slid open, a young woman's shout could be heard from the lobby.

"You bastard! How could you?" It was Erica, playing up her part for all she was worth.

"Let's go," Alec commanded, leading the way out of the elevator at a fast clip.

Neil's voice echoed from the lobby. "But baby, it didn't mean anything."

Pausing at the entrance to the lobby, Alec put up a hand, signaling his group to wait as he peeked around the corner. Erica was standing atop the round bench where she'd formerly been cuddling with Neil, a bouquet of roses gripped in one hand and a murderous look in her eyes.

"She was my best friend!" Erica cried.

Neil looked up at her. "I said I'm sorry."

"You're *sorry*? You think that makes it all right?"

Damn it, thought Alec. The distraction wasn't working. His group needed to dash across the lobby to the far end, where the parking elevators were. But the two lobby guards, still seated on another bench a few feet away and staring at their smart-phones, weren't paying any attention to the squabbling lovers.

Erica raised her voice and gestured dramatically. "You drag me all the way to China, then humiliate me like this in public?"

Neil backed away, raising his arms defensively. "It's not China. It's Taiwan."

"Same difference!" Erica's frustration looked genuine. Although everyone else in the lobby was staring at them, the Fallen guards hadn't taken any interest.

Somehow, Alec had to make things escalate. Reaching out with his mind, he pushed Erica's hand, causing her floral bouquet to smack Neil in the face.

Neil sputtered in surprise. "Baby," he said loudly, "don't make a scene."

The look of confusion on Erica's face changed to comprehension when she spotted Alec. "Oh, I'll show you a *scene*!" She lunged at Neil, smacking him repeatedly with the bouquet.

Neil shielded himself and backed away, deliberately colliding with the bench where the two Fallen guards were seated—and then falling with a great shout across both of their laps. The ebony-skinned female guard cried out in alarm, while the man tried to shove Neil off. Suddenly, Erica was leaping onto the bench, swatting at all three of them with her thorny roses.

"Now!" Alec hissed. He grabbed Claire's hand and started running across the lobby, glancing back to confirm that Lynn, Brian, and Tom were following.

As they ran, Alec telekinetically pressed the button to summon the parking-garage elevator. Behind him, he could hear Erica and Neil's dramatic confrontation continuing, giving them the cover they needed.

Alec rejoiced silently. They were almost home free. All they had to do now was make it to the garage, where they'd join Helena in the van and speed off to the airport.

To his relief, the elevator doors opened just as they reached them. Alec gestured for everyone to board and jumped in last. Claire punched the button for the garage level.

The elevator didn't respond.

"Come on, come on!" Claire cried, frantically punching at the button.

Damn it, Alec thought. *Hurry. Hurry.*

The doors stubbornly remained open. When Alec glanced back toward the lobby, his heart almost stopped.

At the far end of the room, Erica and Neil were still rolling around on the bench, flowers flying. But the female guard had pried herself loose from the commotion. As she shook herself off, her eyes traveled across the lobby expanse and connected with Alec's, then noticed the man standing next to him. *Tom.*

The woman gave a shout of fury and recognition, struggling to alert her partner.

Alec's stomach seized as the elevator doors finally closed. "They spotted us."

"Shit," Brian hissed under his breath. "The op is blown."

thirty-nine

Claire's gut tensed with anxiety as the elevator sped down-ward. "They'll be after us in minutes."

"What's the plan?" Tom asked, his tone expressing far more calm than Claire felt.

"Your mother is waiting in a van on B-3," Alec answered.

Tom's eyes widened. "My mother?"

But no one had time to fill him in further. Instead Lynn asked, worried, "What about Neil and Erica? If we were seen, are they going to get hurt?"

"There's no way the guards could know Neil and Erica were in on this," Alec insisted.

"They'll stick to the plan," Brian reassured everyone. "We just need to reach the van before those assholes find us."

Everyone's phones vibrated simultaneously. Claire gasped anxiously at Helena's message:

They're taking the stairs. Quickly!

The second the elevator touched down, they all burst out and ran like hell toward the van, which was waiting with the engine running about twenty feet away. The minute Claire slid open the windowless side door, Helena looked back from her spot in the driver's seat, and said urgently, "Shots will be fired any second."

Claire ushered Lynn and Tom into the van, and saw her father clutch hands with his mother for the first time in sixteen years.

Unfortunately, that joy lasted only a second. Alec drew a concealed pistol from beneath his jacket. "I'm ready."

"No you aren't," Helena warned him.

As Brian was climbing into the van, Claire heard two loud barks from behind them. Alec staggered backward. At the same moment, the passenger-door window, just inches from Claire's head, shattered in a blast of glass. Claire screamed.

Then a third shot rang out.

Brian toppled forward, his shoes dangling over the edge of the seat.

"Brian!" Lynn exclaimed from inside the van.

Claire heard Brian moaning in pain. She saw a hole in the sleeve of Alec's jacket, and it looked wet with blood. More gunshots rang out. Where were they coming from? Helena said their pursuers had taken the stairs.

"Claire! Get in the van!" Alec cried, shoving Claire toward the waiting vehicle, then crouching.

Instead, she ducked down beside him. Her mind reeled in terror. The garage exit was at the opposite end of the building, seemingly miles away. They'd never make it with the Fallen at their heels. Somehow, they had to take them out.

Inside the van, Claire saw her mother putting pressure on Brian's bleeding shoulder while her father wrapped gauze from Alec's emergency kit on the wound. What kind of nightmare had she gotten everyone into?

The Fallen guards suddenly appeared between the parked cars. They were almost on them. Alec leapt to his feet and telekinetically yanked the guns out of the guards' hands. Their weapons flew off and over a railing, clattering to the concrete below.

Alec fired his pistol. The guards scattered, the man clutching his thigh before dropping behind a car. The female guard was nowhere to be seen.

Suddenly, the male Fallen rose up in a flash, an identical man beside him. Then another appeared. And another. To Claire's horror, the guard was splitting into multiple versions of himself right before her eyes, until there were at least a dozen of him. All exactly the same, except they were missing their creator's leg wound.

Duplicates, Claire thought in dismay. *Of all the powers in creation, why did they have to be battling this one right now?* She recognized the dull gleam of earbuds in all their ears. *And I can't brainwash them.*

In unison, the duplicates began charging toward the van. Alec emptied his pistol trying to fend them off, but he only took out four of them. Incredibly, the injured clones fell and melted away into puddles of what looked like water.

Before Alec could reload, Claire saw the female Fallen barrel out from behind a column and shove Alec to the ground. His gun flew from his hand and skittered across the pavement, disappearing beneath a row of parked cars.

"I said get in!" Alec yelled at Claire again, pulling himself back up. He drew the long knife she'd seen him regularly hide in his boot.

No way. Claire knew that Alec could handle two Fallen at a time, but she doubted he could juggle *this* many single-handedly. She couldn't just hide in the van and wait.

Jumping to her feet, Claire removed the collapsible baton she'd concealed in her own jacket and snapped it open.

She heard her mother cry out, "Claire, what are you—?"

Claire slammed the van door shut before Lynn could finish her sentence.

Alec heard the van door slam, meaning Claire was safely inside.

Now I can take care of these idiots without worrying about anyone else getting hurt.

The duplicates were heading for the van like a horde of zombies. He had to stop them. But first, he had to take out the female Fallen, who was in his way. Hopefully, the talent she possessed wouldn't be as much of a pain as Duplication Guy's. He'd only encountered *that* ability once before. It had proven extremely difficult to beat.

It would be even tougher now, given the searing pain from the bullet lodged in his left arm.

Alec moved in sync with the Fallen woman as they paced in a circle, sizing each other up. The woman snapped a kick at his hand, trying to disarm him. Alec swept his dagger under her foot, then slashed at his attacker's ankle.

As the woman cursed and backed off, Alec's attention was momentarily diverted by grunts across the way. He flicked a glance in that direction and, to his annoyance, saw Claire, baton in hand, attacking a pair of the duplicates. *Damn it.* She seemed to be holding her own, but that couldn't last long.

Wrap this up, Alec thought. *What's this lady's ability?* Seconds later, he found out. The woman ripped off her gloves and touched the hood of a nearby red sports car. The color and texture of the vehicle flowed up her fingertips and along her arm, until all her exposed flesh became the same red metal.

Shite. She's one of those. Substance Mimics could temporarily replicate any material they touched across their entire outer shell. The plus side: the heavier the material, the slower this lady would be. But the downside …

When the woman attacked again, Alec's blade clanged against her metallic arms, sending sparks flying.

A stray swing tagged Alec in the side and all but knocked the wind out of him. He staggered backward onto the hood of a BMW. As she slowly stalked toward Alec, the Material Girl took the time to actually speak.

"Shame," she chided in a Nigerian accent. "Old reports made you sound a lot tougher." She swung her heavy metallic arms down toward Alec.

Rolling sideways off the vehicle, Alec narrowly avoided the blow, which deeply dented the hood. He backed up into the gap between the BMW and the SUV beside it, only to find himself trapped, a wide concrete pillar behind him.

Material Girl took another lumbering step forward, scowling as if annoyed by the weight of her new form. Bending down, she placed her fingers against the SUV's tires. In seconds, her skin transformed into solid black rubber.

Without hesitation, Alec closed the distance between them and plunged his knife into her rubbery chest. She didn't blink an eye, just swung a free arm into Alec's stomach, doubling him over.

"Too bad the higher-ups won't let me kill you," Material Girl leered. "But they won't mind a few bruises."

Before Alec could react, she began pummeling him mercilessly.

It took every ounce of Claire's energy to fend off the clones. No sooner had she shoved one to the side with her baton than another took his place. One grabbed her so fiercely by the wrist, she cried out in agony before striking his hand away. She managed to kick and smash several fatally in the head, causing them to liquefy. But the remaining hoard still kept coming at her in an endless, exhausting succession.

Behind her, Claire heard a heavy cracking sound. To her horror, three clones were pounding on the windshield of the van. It was starting to break.

Suddenly, the van moved. Through the window, Claire saw Helena's face set with resolve as she rammed the trio of duplicates into the wall, where they splashed and vanished.

With a squeal of tires, the van now moved backward, aiming for a pair of duplicates who were charging at Claire. She jumped out of the way as the van rolled over them, leaving nothing but glistening tire tracks.

Claire paused to catch her breath, worried that she hadn't seen the last of the clones. She spotted the original Duplication Guy still positioned behind a car, soaked in sweat. He looked like he could barely stand, as if he'd personally taken every one of his copies' hits.

As she watched, he grabbed a glass vial out of his pocket and drank its contents. Even from this distance, Claire could see the guy's body respond with renewed energy, his posture straightening as his expression turned to rage.

Claire realized what the substance was. Alec had described it often enough. *Turbo*—the enhancement drug that had almost gotten him killed.

Seconds later, the guy split into another version of himself, equally beefed up and angry.

Claire's spirits plummeted. No way could she fend off an army of Turboed Fallen on her own. A few car lengths away, Claire saw Alec deep in a battle with the female. A knife handle sprouted from the woman's chest, and her skin looked like a rubber tire. *How the hell did that happen?* Alec seemed to be getting the shit beat out of him.

Ignoring the newly minted clone, Claire ran to Alec and swung her baton with a crack across the Fallen woman's shoulder, forcing her aside, where she collided with a car. Alec took advantage of the reprieve to tug Claire backward, just as the woman retaliated with a rubbery swing.

Alec extended his arm, fingers outstretched. The Fallen woman flew backward into a concrete pillar between two parked cars, bounced off, and landed atop the roof of a nearby SUV.

A few yards away, Claire saw that Duplication Guy had nearly finished making eight more copies of himself. They didn't have much time. "What's her deal?" she quickly gasped, gesturing to the woman they'd just bested.

"She can mimic any material she touches," Alec replied, equally winded.

"Great," Claire wheezed. "Did you pull their earbuds?"

"No." Alec squinted in the Fallen woman's direction, twitching in apparent frustration. "Damn it. I should have done Material Girl's earlier. Now she's too far away."

"Well, Duplication Guy's just gone Turbo."

Alec's expression was hard. "Get in the van."

"Not until you do!"

"They'll never let us just drive out of here."

Material Girl rose to her feet atop a car, yanking Alec's dagger from her torso. The duplicates were stalking their way. Claire could see Helena and her mom inside the van, watching with stricken looks on their faces. *Dear God, was Brian okay? Were they all going to die?*

At least, Claire thought, *I'm going to go down fighting.*

"We can do this," Claire said forcefully. "I'll take care of *her*. Just get Duplication Guy's earbuds."

"Aye aye." Alec kissed Claire's forehead roughly before turning and rushing the oncoming clones.

Heart in her throat, Claire readied her baton. Just as Material Girl landed in front of her with the knife, Claire struck the woman across one ear. The baton bounced back, but the woman clutched her ear in pain, plucking out a crushed earbud and throwing it to the ground.

Claire suppressed a grim smile. *One ear is better than nothing.* "Back off," she cried, anger and fear fueling her voice and thoughts. "End this fight *now*. Let me and my friends go."

She repeated the words out loud, focusing all her energy on Material Girl's brain. But her powers had no effect. *Oh no. I must not be strong enough to overcome the remaining earbud.*

"Nice try," the rubbery woman smirked as she closed in, twirling Alec's blade in one hand.

Do something, fast! Claire thought.

As the Fallen woman lunged at her, the blade aimed for Claire's throat, Claire pivoted and swung again with her baton, knocking the woman off balance. As Claire hoped, Material Girl stumbled and reached out to break her fall. The instant her hands came into contact with the concrete floor, her skin began to change. Into concrete.

Score! Claire thought. Now the woman would be too heavy to move. Wouldn't she?

Apparently not. Her opponent rose to her feet, moving more slowly than before, but now stone-faced and furious.

Claire gasped in horror. She'd only made things worse. One swipe from Material Girl's concrete hand hit Claire's baton full on, snapping the metal in half and wrenching it from her grasp. If the next hit connected with Claire's chest or head, she knew she'd be dead.

Out of options, she turned and ran toward the van.

I'm sorry, Alec, she thought, tears welling. *I'm so sorry.*

It was chaos. Eight duplicates were throwing punches, kicks, and grabs at Alec from all directions. So far, nothing had connected, but evading them was exhausting.

Alec ducked the next wave of attacks, trying to figure out how to get to the original guy, who still stood out of the line of fire. If Alec could take down the master, the slaves should all disappear.

One of the clones grabbed Alec's legs, toppling him to the ground. Alec spun before they could lock a grip on him, kicking upward with both his legs and his mind. The duplicates scattered backward like they'd been hit by a shock wave.

Jumping to his feet, Alec spied Claire in the distance, running for the van, with Material Girl—her skin now gray like concrete—in hot pursuit. *She's not going to make it*, he thought. Alec stretched out both arms, willing another burst of telekinetic force outward. It caught Material Girl in the knees, sending her sprawling to the pavement in a clatter of stone on stone.

Drained, Alec almost wished he had a vial of Turbo to even the odds. How else would he ever win this fight? He caught his breath and readied himself for the next move, when two arms, tight as steel, wrapped him in a choke hold.

"It's over," hissed Duplication Guy in Alec's ear. His voice dripped with a Slovakian accent, and his breath stank of cigarettes.

He might be right, Alec thought. Struggling to stay conscious, Alec reached up with both hands and felt for the guy's ears, dug his fingers in, and tore loose his earbuds.

Alec tried to call out to Claire, but he could barely breathe. And then he felt blackness closing in.

Claire made it to the van and slid open the side door. Her mom and dad sat cradling Brian, their hands and shirtsleeves laced with blood.

"Claire! Alec did it!" Helena called out urgently from the front seat.

Claire spun around to see Material Girl rising from the pavement, and Alec being choked, surrounded by clones. If Duplication Guy's earbuds were out, they had one last chance.

But this was it. If she couldn't persuade the asshole to let Alec go, he was going to die. They were all going to die.

Claire dug deep into her body to gather all the strength she had left and projected her thoughts and voice at their two main opponents: *"It's over. Back off. Leave us. Go!"*

Material Girl stood. Duplication Guy kept his hold on Alec. No thought-lances were hitting home. No glassy-eyed stares anywhere. Instead, the new band of duplicates started heading toward the van like another onslaught of zombies.

It wasn't working. It really was over. But not in the way she'd hoped. They were all lost.

Just then, a steady voice behind her declared: "*She said it's over.*"

Tom slipped from the van and stood beside Claire, a look of grim determination on his face. "Do you hear me, assholes?" he commanded quietly. "Everything stops. *Now.*"

Claire held her breath. She knew her dad's abilities were way stronger than hers, but he'd been strung out on drugs when they'd first found him. Had he recovered enough to actually control the Fallen?

It certainly looked like it.

All at once, the duplicates just … stopped. So did their master—although Alec was still in his grip.

"Let the boy go," Tom demanded. "And call off your dogs."

Duplication Guy complied. Alec fell to the ground, gasping and coughing. Instantly, all the clones melted, splashing into puddles on the concrete.

Tom strode up to Material Girl, who wasn't moving a muscle. "I think that's enough mimicry for one day." His eyes were like ice.

Immediately, the woman's flesh resumed its original appearance.

Tom took the knife from her hand, glaring at both body-guards, his tone authoritative. "We're leaving. Stay here until the authorities arrive. You will have no memory of this incident."

Material Girl and Duplication Guy nodded, their eyes glazed. Claire watched this exchange in awe. Would she ever be able to command others so easily?

Alec, massaging his throat, walked up to Tom. "Thanks. That was …"

"Better than they deserve," Tom finished, gesturing to Alec and Claire to get in the van. "Let's go."

Alec sank down wearily on the rear seat of the van beside Claire and Lynn, a bit stunned by the demonstration of power he'd just witnessed.

"That was *amazing*, Dad," Claire said.

"It was," Lynn agreed, eyes filled with relief. "You were all amazing."

As Helena sped out of the garage, they passed several uniformed security guards bursting out of a stairwell in confusion. Tom glanced back at the group from the front seat, as if he couldn't believe he was really here. "If we succeeded, it's due to all of you. I can't thank you enough for getting me out of there."

"You're welcome, son," Helena replied, darting an affectionate glance at Tom. It was the most emotion Alec had ever seen on her face.

Sometime during the fight, Claire had gotten a split lip and only now seemed aware of it. "You okay?" Alec asked.

She nodded, eyes wide. "I can't believe we just survived that. How you doing, Bri?"

"Okay," Brian mumbled from the middle bench, apparently on painkillers. The remains of his T-shirt sleeve had been cut away, replaced by a heavy bandage around his right shoulder. "Your dad's like a cross between Professor Xavier and a SWAT paramedic." He held up a brass bullet. "Look! A souvenir."

"Luckily, the bullet went straight through," Lynn explained.

"He'll need recovery time," Tom reassured her, "but not a hospital visit."

"Thank God." Claire looked relieved. "What are we going to tell his parents?"

"Tell 'em I went off on my own and got mugged," Brian interjected groggily. "That'll totally fly. And there's no way they can check on it."

The van barreled up by the front entrance of the hotel, where Neil and Erica were waiting, visibly anxious. They both leapt in, then froze, taking in the blood on the seat, Brian's bandaged shoulder, and the remnants of the first-aid triage littering the floor.

"What in the holy hell?" Neil said.

"Long story." Claire gestured to Tom in the front seat. "Guys, I'd like you to officially meet Tom. My dad."

Before any greetings could be exchanged, Helena called out, "Sit down and buckle up, kids. We have a plane to catch." Then she stepped on the gas.

epilogue

"Tea?" Helena held up her favorite bone-china pot. "It's my personal blend, Earl Grey and hazelnut."

"I'll stick with cocoa for now." Claire smiled, blowing steam from her mug.

She and her grandmother were sitting on the rooftop of their condo in Los Angeles, beneath a sunny afternoon sky. A couple of folding tables had been set up for an early dinner, and she'd hung the same twinkle lights she'd put up on Valentine's Day. This time, hopefully, with happier results.

"You're healing nicely, my dear," Helena commented.

Claire grazed her fingertips over her wrist and her lower lip, grateful that the bruises she'd sustained during their fight in Taipei were all but back to normal. "Poor Brian. It'll be weeks before he recovers."

"Thank goodness he didn't suffer permanent damage. And that Alec recovered so quickly."

Claire grimaced. "I may be half-Grigori, but I could never dig a bullet out of my own arm."

"I pray you'll never have to," Helena replied.

Claire had treasured every day of the past two weeks since they'd rescued her father, thrilled to get to know him at last. Her parents had gotten over their initial awkwardness and looked tremendously happy to be back together.

One lingering worry, however, was still eating away at Claire: did those few moments Alec and her father spent in the Nexus expose them to the Grigori? No one had voiced the worry aloud, but Claire knew that if they *had* been exposed, someone could be sent to arrest them at any moment.

A fluttering sound from overhead caught her attention. Claire looked up but didn't see anything. Until a male silhouette suddenly materialized in the air about six feet away, making her jump in surprise.

"Zachariah." Claire gripped her mug anxiously.

Why is he here?

The Watcher landed with quiet grace, adjusting his long tan coat as he strode toward them. "Good evening."

Helena shifted in her lounge chair uneasily. "What an unexpected pleasure, Zachariah."

Claire's pulse began an erratic dance, her eyes darting to the rooftop's stairwell door. Any second now, her mom and dad and Alec would be coming up the stairs. What if the "spell" she'd put on Zachariah no longer worked? If she didn't do something fast, Zachariah might recognize Alec and would *definitely* recognize Tom. But there was no way of warning them without drawing attention to herself.

"Apologies for not calling ahead," Zachariah stated formally with a half bow to her grandmother. "We've all been scrambling over some recent activity."

"Really? What activity?" Claire's heart continued to thud as she whipped mental fishing lines toward Zachariah's mind: *The man who resembles Tom is not Tom. You won't recognize Alec. It's not Alec.*

"I should preface this by saying that I am … I am … fully aware that my news might not be welcome." Zachariah's eyes grew a bit dazed as he spoke. "Even so, I felt that … you had the right to be looped in. And I—" He broke off.

"Looped in about what, Zachariah?" Helena gave Claire a knowing glance.

Zachariah cleared his throat, blinking rapidly as he turned to Helena. "It is … regarding your son."

"My son?" Helena repeated, sitting forward with deep interest.

Claire continued her silent mantra, her gut tensing with worry. "You've heard something about my father?"

"Yes, he—" Zachariah began.

The stairwell door opened. Lynn strode out first, carrying a bowl of salad. "Let the feast begin!" she cried with a smile. Directly behind her followed Tom and Alec, with platters of broiled salmon and a tray of side dishes.

Claire leapt to her feet. She hoped Zachariah couldn't sense her alarm.

Her father, however, didn't seem the least bit distressed. Setting his platter on the table, he strode directly up to the Watcher. Although his smile was cordial, Tom's eyes were as steely as the last time Claire had seen him use his powers. "Hi. I'm Gregory," he said, extending his hand.

Gregory. Claire remembered that Alec had invented a mythical "Uncle Gregory" during his first days at Emerson, a tribute to his Grigori origins. Still worried, she resumed her silent, mental onslaught toward Zachariah's mind.

Zachariah blinked a few more times, then calmly shook Tom's hand. "It's a pleasure to meet you, Gregory."

Alec stepped forward. "Nice to see you again, Zach."

"Yes, Mr. MacKenzie, I remember. You're Claire's friend from school. You were brilliant in the play."

"So I heard." Tom nodded. "I was sorry to have missed my nephew's theatrical debut."

Claire swallowed her relief. She wasn't sure if it was her powers or her father's that had done the trick—or maybe it was a combination of the two—but *it had worked*. Zachariah had no idea that he was standing right in front of the two Grigoris his entire organization was desperate to find.

Still, she couldn't relax. What was the news Zachariah had come to share?

Zachariah glanced at Helena. "Forgive me. I didn't realize you were entertaining. I can come back later."

"Don't leave us in suspense," Helena cut in quickly. "You said something about my son?"

"Yes, well. You understand, given your company, I cannot go into the particulars."

"Sure you can. Just go on as if we're not here." Tom's eyes were penetrating as he stared at the Watcher.

Zachariah paused, his own eyes glazing over briefly. Blinking rapidly, he turned back to Helena. "All right then. I came to tell you that, after all these years, it appears your son is still alive. He finally showed up on our radar again in Taipei."

Claire's spirits sank. Their worst fears had come true. That moment in the Nexus *had* exposed them.

"Have you spoken to him?" Helena snapped, eyebrows raised.

"No, but he seems to have been in the company of another agent who's also AWOL. It appears as though the two have gone rogue."

"Gone rogue?" Lynn repeated. "What have they done?" The tremor in her voice sounded genuine—and no wonder. Having Zachariah say these things right in front of his actual targets was stressing Claire out. Even with all the mind control in place, she felt like she was sitting on nails.

"It appears that they roughed up some Fallen in a hotel and escaped."

"You keep saying *appears*," Claire interjected. "Does that mean you don't have proof?"

"At this time, all we have to go on are second- and thirdhand reports. All the relevant security cameras had been disabled. But we have a very strong hunch that it was him."

Tom and Alec shifted but said nothing.

"If my son has gone rogue, that is most unfortunate." Helena shook her head.

Zachariah turned to Lynn now. "I understand, madam, that you were married to a man you knew as Tom Brennan?"

"Yes. We're still married."

"I beg to differ. A union between a human and Grigori is forbidden, and therefore was never legal. Have you heard from him over the past sixteen years?"

"No," Lynn lied.

"Then I think it's safe to presume," Zachariah said dispassionately, "that he no longer considers himself tied to you. If he ever did. Otherwise, he would have contacted you long ago."

"I see," Lynn replied, her face a mask of repressed emotion. "I'm sure you're right."

"The missing Watchers are being actively sought by the Elders," Zachariah continued, now addressing the group as a whole, "and are considered outlaws. I want to make it clear that should either of them attempt to contact you, it is your responsibility to contact *us* immediately."

Helena nodded, unsmiling. "Of course." She thanked Zachariah for sharing the news.

After exchanging matter-of-fact good-byes, the Watcher said, "I can see myself out the, ah, conventional way." Zachariah made for the stairwell door and closed it behind him.

When the sound of his footsteps finally died away, Claire dropped into a chair and breathed a heavy sigh. "Holy. Crap."

"You said it." Lynn looked from Claire to her husband. "Which one of you made that happen?"

"Both of us," Tom responded. "Claire got it started, and I finished the job with a few … tweaks, to make sure he won't ever be able to identify me or Alec in future."

"What do you mean by *tweaks*?" Claire asked.

"I'll teach you someday." Tom smiled. "In the meantime, you've made impressive progress, Claire, considering how new you are at this."

"Thanks, Dad."

Claire was trying not to think about the fact that she'd used her power a couple of times with *not*-so-impressive results, and once on her own grandmother, when the stairwell door banged open again and Brian, Erica, and Neil barreled through it.

"Sorry we're late!" Erica announced cheerfully, as she added a bowl of fresh salsa to the food table. "Prima Donna here had some issues with his sling."

"I took a bullet for the team, Erica. Literally." Brian handed a bag of chips to Alec's waiting hands. "I think that gives me a pass."

Everyone laughed as they greeted the new arrivals, exchanging hugs. "Hey, Brian, it just occurred to me," Neil commented, setting out the tray of brownies he'd brought, "didn't you end up in a sling last fall, too?"

"It seems to be my fate," Brian noted with a grin. "At least this time, it's my other arm."

"Which has to be a pain, since you're right-handed," Claire pointed out. "How do you type?"

"Yeah," Erica worried, "or play Ping-Pong?"

Brian puffed out his chest confidently. "Fear not. I'm a one-handed master on a keyboard, and I can play Ping-Pong southpaw. I challenge you to a game anytime."

"Done!" Erica answered. "Tomorrow? After school?"

"You're on."

Claire smiled. Though their relationship might never be the same, Claire was glad to see that their little adventure had helped reignite Erica and Brian's friendship.

"So. Did we miss anything?" Neil asked.

Claire glanced at Alec, wondering where to begin. But he just shrugged casually. "We'll tell you after dinner."

"Good. I'm starving," announced Erica, "and that salmon looks amazing."

As they unwrapped the food, and everyone lined up to help themselves to the feast, Claire's phone vibrated. She moved to the back of the line and glanced at it covertly.

Claire's heart went into overdrive and her hands grew clammy. It was a text.

From Celeste.

> Hey girlfriend, heard you got home safe.
> Boss man hopes you're healing nicely …

The message was creepy and disturbing. Further proof that the Fallen really *did* know everything she was up to. The *hopes you're healing nicely …* part felt particularly ominous. As if Celeste were about to add: *because we've got work to do.*

Claire quickly deleted the message and put away her phone, grateful that everyone was too busy serving themselves and finding seats at the tables to notice how distracted she was.

Everyone, that is, except Alec.

"You okay?" he asked quietly, concern marring his handsome features as he came up to her.

"Fine." Claire nodded. But he knew her so well. Did he suspect something?

"You don't look fine. You aren't still worried about what Zachariah said, are you?"

Claire swallowed hard and forced herself to nod again. "Yeah. How can I not be? The Grigori are looking for you now. For *both* of you."

Winding his arms around her waist, Alec drew her close and gently leaned his forehead against hers. "Claire," he said softly, "they *never stopped* looking for us. And after all this time, they still haven't found us. We'll be all right."

Alec pressed his lips against hers, a warm and affectionate kiss that she returned with all the love in her soul.

"You promise?" Claire whispered when the kiss ended.

"I promise."

"Break it up, lovebirds," Brian called out. "People are trying to eat here."

Laughter trickled across the rooftop as Alec kissed Claire again. Exchanging a smile, they crossed to the food table to heap their own plates.

Everyone was happily chatting as they sat down at the table. Claire tried hard to get in the spirit of the festivities. She knew she had so much to be grateful for. Her dad was finally free of the Fallen's control and off the horrible drugs they'd kept him on. And Zachariah would never recognize him or Alec. But …

Worry kept gnawing at her.

"Claire Bear?"

Erica's voice snapped Claire out of her reverie. "Hmm?"

Her friend raised a mug of hot apple cider. "I think our little gathering needs a speech from the mission commander."

"That was *my* job," Brian protested, eliciting chuckles.

"It all started with Claire," Erica insisted. "So. We're waiting!"

Claire cleared her throat awkwardly and stood. "Okay. Um," she began. "I think you all know what's in my heart. Thank you so much everyone, for all that you did."

Even though it didn't end as well as I'd hoped for, Claire left out. She'd presumed that her father's rescue might have unforeseen consequences, and now she understood that it had. Yes, they'd thrown Zachariah off the scent. But he was only one person. Sure, her father was free. But now he was back on the Grigori radar, a wanted felon. Equally frightening, the rescue operation had called attention to Alec.

Despite Alec's reassurances, Claire knew that they weren't safe.

Claire looked to Alec first, then at Erica, Brian, and Neil, managing a tight smile. "The past few months have been rough. I'm sorry that all my problems spilled over onto you guys. You all came through for me, above and beyond what I could have ever wished for from friends."

She put an arm around her father, gazing up at him with a smile filled with affection. "I have my dad back, and I couldn't have done it without any of you. Without *all* of you."

"And I'm very lucky to be here," Tom added, wrapping her in a hug. "Again, thank you all."

Applause followed. Mugs were raised and clinked. And everyone dug further into their food.

Claire picked at her own meal, barely tasting it. She was glad Alec seemed too absorbed in conversation with her father to notice her inner turmoil.

Overshadowing everything was the dilemma of her own creation. The secret she was still hiding from everybody.

The words of Celeste's text spun in her mind.

Boss man hopes you're healing nicely.

Boss man. Ugh. She had a *boss* now. Not a parent or a teacher, but someone who could control her because she owed him a debt. If she didn't let him collect, he would tell her whole family the ugly truth about why Alec was still alive and how she'd learned where to rescue Tom.

Worse, though, Malcolm could tell the rest of the Fallen, and/or the Grigori, where their freed hostage was hiding. And the names of everyone who'd rescued him.

Claire had zero leverage over that man. But if she hadn't gone to him, Alec's and her father's fates were unthinkable.

Claire looked around at her friends and family. Three angels, three teenagers, and her mom. All this joy. All the trust they had in her. It had been tested recently, but it had held.

But only because they didn't (and couldn't ever) know the truth.

That she was beholden to the Fallen.

ABOUT THE AUTHORS

SYRIE JAMES is the bestselling author of twelve critically acclaimed novels translated into eighteen languages. Syrie loves paranormal romance and all things 19th century. Her books have been Library Journal Editor's Picks and won numerous awards including the Audie for Romance, Women's National Book Association Great Group Read, B&N Romantic Read of the Week, Best Snowbound Romance (Bookbub), Best of the Year (Suspense Magazine and Romance Reviews), and Best First Novel (Library Journal). Syrie thoroughly enjoyed working with her son Ryan on *Forbidden* and *Embolden*, her only forays into novel co-writing. Syrie is a member of the Writers Guild of America and has addressed audiences as a keynote speaker across America and England. A theater enthusiast, she has also written, directed, and performed in numerous stage productions.

RYAN M. JAMES has enjoyed co-writing not only *Forbidden* and *Embolden* with his mother, Syrie, but also two screenplays. By day, he works as a performance director, lead editor, and co-writer for the video game industry, recently being honored by the Writer's Guild of America for his work on *Uncharted 4: A Thief's End*. By night, he conjures stories for print, screen, and web, including an independent feature, a handful of short films, and the machinima webseries *A Clone Apart*. He, his brilliant wife, and their vertically-challenged corgi live in Los Angeles within walking distance of Syrie.

Syrie and Ryan both welcome visitors to their websites syriejames.com and ryanmjames.com, and invite you to follow them on facebook, Instagram, and Twitter.

Don't miss the exciting first book in the Forbidden series:

FORBIDDEN

She should not exist.
He should not love her.

Claire Brennan has been attending Emerson Academy for two years now (the longest she and her mom have remained anywhere) and she's desperate to stay put for the rest of high school. So there's no way she's going to tell her mom about the strange psychic visions she's been getting or the creepy warnings that she's in danger.

Alec MacKenzie is fed up with his duties to watch and, when necessary, eliminate the descendants of his angelic forefathers. He chose Emerson as the ideal hiding place where he could be normal for once. He hadn't factored Claire into his plans….

Their love is forbidden, going against everything Alec has been taught to believe. But when the threat to Claire's life becomes clear, how far will Alec go to protect her?

**FORBIDDEN is available in print,
ebook, and audiobook versions.**

DRACULA, MY LOVE

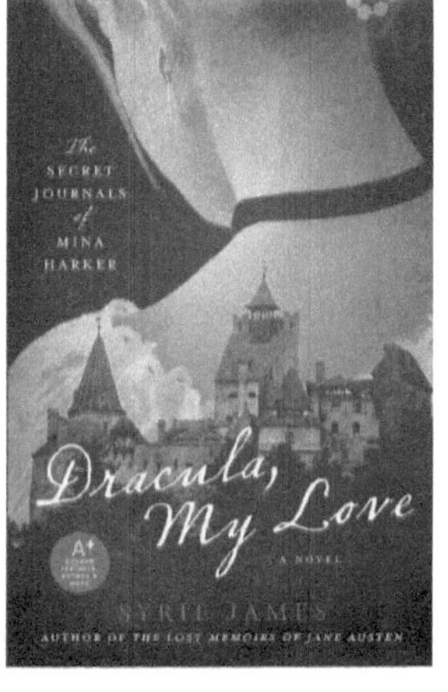

Struggling to hang on to the love she's found within her marriage to her husband, Jonathan, Mina Harker is drawn into a secret, dangerous affair with a charismatic but enigmatic man. Although everyone she knows fears him and is pledged to destroy him, Mina sees a side to him that others cannot: a tender, romantic side; a man who's taken advantage of his gift of immortality to expand his mind and talents; a man who is deeply in love, and who may not be so guilty of evil after all.

Yet to surrender is madness, for to be with him could end her life. To make her choice, Mina must learn everything she can about the remarkable origins and sensuous powers of this man, this exquisite monster, this … *Dracula.*

> "A spooky yet thoroughly romantic love story."
> —*Chicago Tribune*

> "I loved it! A gripping story, infused with passion, excitement, and emotional turmoil. This vampire can bite my neck any time!" —*American Book Center*

DRACULA, MY LOVE is available in print, ebook, and audiobook versions.

THE LOST MEMOIRS OF JANE AUSTEN

What if, hidden in an old attic chest, Jane Austen's memoirs were discovered after hundreds of years? That's the premise behind this "thoughtful, immensely touching" novel (*Regency World Magazine*), which gives us insight into Jane Austen's mind and heart.

When Jane Austen's father dies, Jane, her sister Cassandra, and their mother are left homeless and nearly penniless. On a fateful trip to Lyme, Jane meets the well-read and charming Mr. Ashford. Inspired by the people and places around her, and encouraged by Mr. Ashford's faith in her, Jane begins revising *Sense and Sensibility*, hoping to be published at last.

Written in a compelling and witty style that echoes Austen's own, *The Lost Memoirs of Jane Austen* reveals the untold story of Jane's impassioned, life-changing love affair, and offers a possible scenario for the inspiration behind some of her most beloved romantic tales.

"A love affair equal to anything Jane Austen wrote."
—*News Review*

"Deserves front-runner status in the field of Austen fan-fiction and film." —*Kirkus Reviews*

"Austen and Mr. Ashford seem a perfect match in matters of head and heart." —*Publisher's Weekly*

"Through humor, Jane comes alive ... the reader blindly pulls for the heroine and her dreams of love." —*Los Angeles Times*

"Tantalizing, tender, and true to the Austen mythos, James's book is highly recommended. —*Library Journal* Editor's Pick, starred review

THE LOST MEMOIRS OF JANE AUSTEN is available in print, ebook, and audiobook versions.

www.ingramcontent.com/pod-product-compliance
Lightning Source LLC
Chambersburg PA
CBHW030138310726

48970CB00005B/1479